"Don't think anyone can get past your defenses?"
Ethan asked.

Brenda was beginning to look wary, but she kept her voice firm when she answered, "Not if I don't want them to."

"Hmm." It must have been his reckless streak that compelled him to reach out and tug her into his arms and press his mouth to hers. Even though he knew it wasn't a good idea.

And maybe Brenda had a reckless, adventurous side of her own, because instead of pushing him away, she clutched his shirt and kissed him back. As though she had wanted this as badly as he did.

Almost as suddenly as the kiss had started, it was over. Staring at her from a safe distance, Ethan pushed a hand slowly through his hair. "Well. I guess that proved something."

She spoke a bit hoarsely. "What?"

"Your defenses aren't quite as good as you thought."

Dear Reader,

It's hard to believe that the Signature Select program is one year old—with seventy-two books already published by top Harlequin and Silhouette authors.

What an exciting and varied lineup we have in the year ahead! In the first quarter of the year, the Signature Spotlight program offers three very different reading experiences. Popular author Marie Ferrarella, well-known for her warm family-centered romances, has gone in quite a different direction to write a story that has been "haunting her" for years. Please check out *Sundays Are for Murder* in January. Hop aboard a Caribbean cruise with Joanne Rock in *The Pleasure Trip* in February, and don't miss a trademark romantic suspense from Debra Webb, *Vows of Silence,* in March.

Our collections in the first quarter of the year explore a variety of contemporary themes. Our Valentine's collection—*Write It Up!*—homes in on the trend of alternative dating in three stories by Elizabeth Bevarly, Tracy Kelleher and Mary Leo. February is awards season, and Barbara Bretton, Isabel Sharpe and Emilie Rose join the fun and glamour in *And the Envelope, Please....* And in March, Leslie Kelly, Heather MacAllister and Cindi Myers have penned novellas about women desperate enough to go to *Bootcamp* to learn how *not* to scare men away!

Three original sagas also come your way in the first quarter of this year. Silhouette author Gina Wilkins spins off her popular FAMILY FOUND miniseries in *Wealth Beyond Riches.* Janice Kay Johnson has written a powerful story of a tortured past in *Dead Wrong,* which is connected to her PATTON'S DAUGHTERS Superromance miniseries, and Kathleen O'Brien gives a haunting story of mysterious murder in *Quiet as the Grave.*

And don't forget there is original bonus material in every single Signature Select book to give you the inside scoop on the creative process of your favorite authors! We hope you enjoy all our new offerings!

Marsha Zinberg

Marsha Zinberg
Executive Editor
The Signature Select Program

SAGA

GINA WILKINS

WEALTH
BEYOND RICHES

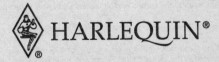

HARLEQUIN®

TORONTO • NEW YORK • LONDON
AMSTERDAM • PARIS • SYDNEY • HAMBURG
STOCKHOLM • ATHENS • TOKYO • MILAN • MADRID
PRAGUE • WARSAW • BUDAPEST • AUCKLAND

ISBN 0-373-83685-6

WEALTH BEYOND RICHES

Copyright © 2006 by Gina Wilkins.

www.eHarlequin.com

Printed in U.S.A.

Dear Reader,

Isn't is fascinating to read news stories about ordinary people who win big lotteries? Isn't if fun to imagine what it would be like to no longer have to worry about paying bills or counting pennies or eking by until the next paycheck?

Like everyone else who works hard for a living and sometimes frets about life's spiraling expenses, I've certainly fantasized about such things on occasion. Yet I can't help noticing that those real-life stories don't always have happy endings. Several studies I've read have shown that sudden wealth often creates more problems than it solves—causing rifts between family and friends, changing values and ethics, adding new stresses to the newly rich. Reading sobering accounts like that makes me stop and count the blessings I do have, and to realize that I have wealth beyond riches in the love and support of my family and friends.

So...while I might fantasize occasionally about becoming an instant millionaire and indulge in telling stories about people who find themselves in that situation, remind myself often of how lucky I am to have a loving husband, three amazing children, a wonderful extended family and some very special friends. I am also fortunate enough to pursue a career I dreamed about from the time I was very young. You won't find my name on a list of the most wealthy and powerful people— but if there were a list of people who felt the most blessed, my name would certainly be included.

I hope you enjoy my latest excursion into fantasy as we follow what happens to suddenly wealthy young schoolteacher Brenda Prentiss in *Wealth Beyond Riches*.

Gina Wilkins

For my son, David, with love.
Thanks for the word!

And to Courtney,
for the brainstorming session at the Red Lobster!

CHAPTER ONE

ETHAN BLACKLOCK straightened, leaned against the handle of his shovel and wiped his dripping brow with one deeply tanned forearm. A baseball cap shaded his face, and dark glasses protected his eyes from UV radiation, but he had no particular fear of the sun—even on a hot June afternoon in Dallas, Texas.

He much preferred this heat to the hell of his teenage years.

Looking around in satisfaction, he noted that he had made quite a bit of progress today. The gardeners employed by his family when he was growing up wouldn't have accomplished as much in twice the time.

Not that there was anyone to take pride in his achievements other than himself. His twice-widowed mother, Margaret Hanvey Blacklock Jacobs, would rather die than admit to her friends that the son she had groomed to become an attorney like her father, then both her husbands after him, had become a mere "gardener," instead.

He snorted at the errant thought and tightened his callused hands around the shovel grip. Maybe his mother was ashamed of him, but he took great pride in the success he'd had with his fledgling landscape design business. With a grunt of exertion, he plunged the blade into the hard-baked earth, savoring the clean smells of dirt and sweat.

By the time he walked into his kitchen on that Monday evening, he was tired, filthy—and satisfied that the small, but profitable job he had completed that day had been a big success. Well worth the fourteen hard hours he'd put into it. The clients were pleased, the check had already been deposited, and he was ready to move on to the next project.

Life was good.

Maybe he would never get rich with his small business, but no one owned him. No one controlled him. No one tried to change him. He couldn't ask for more than that.

After washing his hands in the sink and drying them on a paper towel, he opened the door to the stainless steel refrigerator and pulled out a beer. He needed a shower and some food, but a few minutes of crash time in front of the TV sounded good first. He'd missed the early evening news, but there was probably a baseball game going on somewhere.

He had just walked into the living room when someone knocked on the front door. With a regretful glance at the armchair in front of the TV, he crossed the room and opened the door without bothering to check who was on the other side.

His caller was dressed in a suit that might as well have been embroidered "hand tailored." A good-looking man in a squarely built way, Sean Jacobs was a year older than Ethan's thirty-one. His sandy-brown hair was thinning at the temples, but had been styled by an expert. His shoes were Italian leather, and his tie probably cost more than Ethan's entire outfit of denim shirt, jeans and steel-toed work boots.

There had been a time when Ethan had dressed like Sean, himself.

"Sean," he said by way of greeting, stepping aside to allow his stepbrother to enter. "What brings you here?"

Sean's divorced father, Ferrell Jacobs, had married Ethan's widowed mother almost twenty years earlier. Ferrell died eight years after that. A heart attack—the same thing that had killed Ethan's father, Howard Blacklock, when Ethan was still very young.

Both of Margaret's husbands had been high-powered, workaholic attorneys, which some people blamed for their untimely deaths. Ethan had always figured his mother nagged them both into early graves. If he hadn't broken away from her during his senior year of college, he'd probably be dead, himself, by now.

Rather than answering the question, Sean took a moment to study him as they stood in the middle of Ethan's small living room. From the grubby, inexpensive clothes to the dried mud caked on the tops of Ethan's boots, Sean seemed to miss no small detail. "Been working today?" he asked with an awkwardness that was uncharacteristic of the usually glib lawyer.

"Yeah." Ethan made an ironic gesture toward Sean's work "uniform." "You?"

Sean acknowledged the slight dig with a very faint smile. "Yes."

It had been several years since they'd seen each other. Their last meeting had been cool, though not acrimonious. The biggest obstacle between them was that they had absolutely nothing in common, other than having rather briefly been stepsiblings. Because he had nothing particularly against Sean, Ethan tried to inject a reasonable amount of warmth into his voice when he said, "Have a seat. Can I get you a beer? Soda? Or I could make some coffee, if you want."

"No, thanks." Sean chose a chair and looked around the room with open curiosity. He had never been to this house before, and it was obviously not what he had expected.

Ethan's tastes ran to 1950s retro styles. Tiered maple tables flanked a dark brown leather sofa with exposed maple frame. Throw pillows in olive, orange, gold and brown stripes were tossed haphazardly on the sofa. Two olive leather, cube-shaped ottomans sat side by side in place of a traditional coffee table. Two side chairs with maple arms, and seats and backs upholstered in the same stripes as the throw pillows were positioned so that they provided a view of the fireplace and the incongruously modern flat television screen mounted above it.

Ethan didn't often access the modest trust fund left to him by his paternal grandfather, but he'd done so to buy that state-of-the-art TV. After all, a guy had his needs, he had rationalized.

Framed 1950s posters and pop art covered the butter-yellow walls. Chrome lamps with bold, round shades sat on the end tables, along with art pieces crafted of brightly colored glass. Built-in maple bookcases crowded with novels, books on landscape design and die-cast metal hot rods flanked the fireplace. The retro style carried over into the kitchen, with its vintage chrome-and-orange vinyl dining set, stainless steel appliances and yellow porcelain sink.

The master bedroom was done in a similar retro style, in brown with avocado and persimmon accents. The second bedroom served as his home office, and was filled with more 1950s memorabilia in addition to his desk, drawing table, filing cabinets and other business necessities. The bungalow had only one bathroom, which was decorated with yellow porcelain and multicolored ceramic fish that matched the colorful fish printed on the vinyl shower curtain.

His mother would absolutely hate the place. Which, he supposed, was part of its appeal to him.

Ethan would bet Sean was comparing this rather quirky little house to the mansion filled with soaring ceilings, marble floors and European antiques in which Ethan had grown up. It was a different world— exactly what he had wanted.

As much as Ethan got a kick out of haunting flea markets and junktique sales, Sean had always shown a taste for the elegant antiques and designer decor favored by Margaret's high-profile social set. Ethan re-membered being dragged on an antiquing outing with Margaret and Ferrell when he and Sean were maybe thirteen and fourteen, respectively. He had been bored out of his mind, interested only in a collection of dusty old die-cast toys he'd found in one secluded corner.

Sean, on the other hand, had examined every piece of old furniture and china, looking for markings and dates, much to the pride of his rather pompous and pre-tentious father. Margaret had just been annoyed that her own son would rather be throwing a football or digging in the dirt than learning the fine details of antiques ap-preciation.

"I assume there's a reason for this visit? I doubt you

were just in the neighborhood and wanted to check out my decorating skills."

The smile faded from Sean's face, leaving him looking so grim that Ethan was now convinced beyond doubt that this was no social visit. "There is a reason, of course. First, I want to express my sincere condolences for your loss. I know you and your mother have been estranged for a number of years, but I'm sure her death has been difficult for you."

Very slowly, Ethan placed his half-empty beer can on a black granite coaster on the nearest end table. "My mother is dead?"

Looking stricken by Ethan's reaction, Sean groaned. "Surely your cousin called this morning to tell you Margaret passed away. He told me he would."

Ethan kept his face impassive. "No. But I haven't checked phone messages yet today. What happened?"

Sean answered quietly, "She fell down the stairs. The housekeeper had gone to her daughter's house in Tulsa for the weekend, and she found Margaret at the foot of the stairs when she returned early this morning—sometime around 6:00 a.m. The police were called, of course, but there was no reason to believe it was anything other than a tragic accident. The doors were all locked, the security system was set and there was no evidence to indicate that anyone else had been in the house. Apparently, your mother made a misstep at the top of the stairs—probably during the night, in the darkness—and broke her neck when she fell. She'd been having balance problems lately. Betty told the police it was the third time Margaret had fallen in the past few months, though she escaped with nothing more than bruises before. Betty was devastated, having been with Margaret so long. She felt guilty for taking the weekend off, though I assured her no one could possibly blame her. Margaret was always so stubbornly independent."

Ethan hadn't known about the earlier falls, but that was no surprise to either of them, since he hadn't been a part of his mother's life in a long time.

"I'm sorry you weren't notified sooner," Sean said, when Ethan remained silent. "As Margaret's attorney, I was the first one Betty called after the police, and then she called your cousin Leland. We tried dialing your number here, but there was no answer. Leland assured everyone he would track you down and let you know. But maybe we simply misunderstood. Maybe Leland assumed I called you, as I thought he had."

"I was at the job site by five-thirty this morning. But I had my cell phone with me, as I always do. It wouldn't have been that hard to dig up the number." Ethan wasn't particularly surprised that his cousin hadn't called, since they'd despised each other since childhood, but he would have thought someone would have bothered to pick up the phone.

"I'm sorry, Ethan," Sean said again, awkwardly.

"So, this is a sympathy call?"

"Partly, of course," Sean agreed too quickly. "I am sorry for your loss."

"Right." Since they both knew he hadn't talked to his mother in more than three years, and that conversation had been loud and angry, Ethan figured there had to be more to this visit than simple protocol. "When's the funeral?"

"There won't be one. Your mother left explicit instructions that she was to be cremated quickly, without ceremony. She had become quite reclusive in the past few years, so there weren't a lot of friends to notify."

Ethan shrugged. "I'm sure Leland will take care of everything quite competently. And if you think he just accidentally forgot to call me today, then you're more naive than I remember. Leland and I were never what you would call friends."

Sean grimaced. "I remember. You called him a brownnose and he usually referred to you as 'the Neanderthal.' Those were the more flattering of the nicknames you had for each other, I believe."

Being in no mood for stories about his less-than-idyllic past, Ethan abruptly changed the subject. "You said sympathy was 'partly' the reason for this visit. What's the other part?"

Sean cleared his throat. "You know, of course, that the firm handled all of Margaret's legal affairs."

Ethan resisted the urge to respond with the juvenile and rather dated, "Well, duh." After all, his mother's father had started the law firm in which both of her late husbands, and now her stepson, had all practiced. It had been her fondest, and vehemently expressed, desire that Ethan would follow in their footsteps, which had led to their most frequent and most heated arguments.

So this was about the settlement of Margaret's considerable estate. Made sense. Ethan was her only offspring. Other than her nephew and a couple of distant relatives, there were no other survivors.

Something about the way Sean drew a deep breath warned Ethan that his stepbrother did not consider himself to be the bearer of good news. Had Ethan been disinherited? No surprise there. Margaret had probably left everything to some foundation or charity...or to Leland. Though the very idea made his jaw clench, he supposed it was a very real possibility.

"I hate to be the one to break all the bad news to you, Ethan, but your mother left almost all of her estate in a testamentary trust. The primary beneficiary is a young woman named Brenda Prentiss."

Ethan wasn't able to hide his reaction to that news. His eyes widened in surprise. "Brenda Prentiss? Who the hell is she?"

"She's a local elementary schoolteacher. She works part-time as a bank teller during summer vacations to earn extra money, probably to pay off the student loans she accrued during college. Single, twenty-six years old, orphaned with two older siblings, no record of ever having been in trouble with the law."

"What was her connection to my mother?"

"I have no idea. And, apparently, neither does Ms. Prentiss."

"I don't understand."

"I spoke with her by telephone this afternoon. She was utterly shocked by her inheritance. She claims she never met your mother, and has no idea why she was named in Margaret's will."

Ethan shook his head slowly. "That's crazy."

Sean made a suitably confused gesture with one hand.

Ethan could almost feel his head swim as he tried to make sense of any of this. "Maybe Mother knew her parents?"

Sean shook his head. "Not as far as Brenda knows. She says she never even heard the name. Nor were either of her siblings named in the will. No one I've spoken to today has ever heard of Brenda Prentiss. Even Betty was thoroughly confused. She's certain Ms. Prentiss never visited your mother's home. And she would know, of course."

"Surely Mother left something for Betty. She always promised she would take care of her." Betty had been Margaret's housekeeper for thirty-two years, starting the year before Ethan's birth, when Betty, herself, had been a thirty-year-old widow with a twelve-year-old daughter.

At the time she had started, Betty had worked for Margaret five days a week, eight to ten hours a day, going home to her daughter on nights and weekends. After her daughter graduated high school and struck out on her own, Betty had moved into the cozy suite Margaret, then widowed for the second time, had commissioned off the kitchen. She had become indispensable to Margaret after that, serving as housekeeper, cook, secretary and companion.

Reaching into the inside pocket of his suit jacket, Sean pulled out a folded sheaf of papers. "I've brought you all the details of your mother's will. I thought you deserved to know. She left Betty a tidy annual sum from the trust to supplement her retirement, and she left a one-time cash bequest to your cousin, Leland. With the exception of a few charities, the bulk of the estate's proceeds will go to Ms. Prentiss."

"So, you're here to tell me I've been written off with nothing?" Ethan kept his tone light, almost bored, even though he was still reeling from the series of shocks Sean had just given him. "Trust me, that comes as no surprise."

"Actually, that isn't quite accurate. Your mother did leave you something."

"She figured out a way to leave me a headache?"

Sean's answering smile quickly faded. "Not quite."

"Don't tell me she's left me her damned cats." The only genuine affection Margaret had ever shown had been reserved for her succession of pampered cats. For as long as he could remember, she'd had at least two at a time, and they had received the hugs and coos she had never been capable of offering to her only child. There had been a period when he'd been rather jealous of the cats. It had been a long time since he'd cared enough for it to matter.

"No. The cats went to Ms. Prentiss, along with instructions that she's to care for them for the remainder of their lives."

"Lucky Ms. Prentiss. So, what did she leave me?"

"Everything inside the house that personally belonged to your father. That was the way she worded it, which is admittedly vague. The house and grounds, themselves…"

"…went to Ms. Prentiss," Ethan recited with him.

"Yes. For the duration of her lifetime, to be passed down to her children, should there be any. If she dies without progeny, the estate passes back to you, if you survive her, or your children, if you do not. If you have no surviving offspring, the remainder of the estate is to be divided between your cousin and several charities."

His throat suddenly, unexpectedly tight, Ethan nodded. There were several of his father's belongings that he wouldn't mind having for sentimental reasons. As for the rest of it—screw it. He wasn't going to fight over a penny of the inheritance he had willingly walked away from years ago. "Will my father's things be delivered to me?"

"See, here's the deal. Oddly enough, Margaret didn't list any of the items in question. No one else knows what belonged solely to your father. I'm sure it was another oversight, but there's no way for anyone else to make the decisions. You'll have to make arrangements for a supervised visit to collect what you want."

"Oh, sure. *That* won't be at all awkward."

"I'm sorry, Ethan. Someone should have realized earlier that Margaret didn't include an inventory of your father's belongings with her will. But I'm sure Ms. Prentiss will be accommodating."

"Didn't you just tell me you've never met her?"

"Um. No. I haven't."

"Then she could be the wicked witch of the west, for all you know."

Sean shrugged apologetically. "I suppose there's a possibility she could make things difficult for you, though I don't know why she would. After all, she's inherited a great deal from an apparent stranger to her."

"Mother must have changed since I saw her last. She was never what anyone would call impulsive. Or gullible, if this Prentiss woman pulled some sort of scam on her."

"I've seen your mother fairly regularly over the past few years, and I would have sworn she was as shrewd as ever, right up to the end."

"You always got along with her well enough."

Sean shrugged again. "There was never a reason for me to argue with her. She didn't try as hard to interfere in my life as she did...er..."

"As she did in mine. True. Of course, you're living

the life she wanted for me. On track for a partnership in her father's firm. She probably regretted that I was her biological son and not you."

"Oh, I doubt that." But the hollowness of Sean's reply made Ethan wonder if Margaret had said those very words to him at some point.

"So, what about you? Was the stepson remembered in the will?"

"Actually, no. But then, I received my share of Dad's estate when he died. I didn't expect anything more from Margaret. I've been named the trustee, to handle the trust as stated in your mother's will. I'll receive an annual fee for my administration and supervision of the estate, of course."

Ethan couldn't help being just a little skeptical. Surely Sean would rather have inherited the estate, himself, than see it go to a stranger. After all, Sean had always had a taste for the expensive life, and his father's estate hadn't been as large as Margaret's.

"Were you the one who drew up the will?"

"Irving Styles handled that. She changed it eighteen months ago. I knew there had been a revision, but I wasn't privy to the details until Margaret died."

"Irving Styles was my father's closest friend in the firm. Didn't he question Mother leaving her estate to a stranger?"

"I don't know. Irving died three months ago. I'm surprised you didn't know about it."

Irving had been Ethan's godfather. Yet another death no one had bothered to tell him about. "Guess I don't keep up with the news the way I should."

"I, er, suppose it isn't necessary for your, um, gardening business."

"Landscape design," Ethan murmured without offense. "And maybe I should start concentrating more on business news, if I want my company to grow. But frankly, I've done okay with my small-time business. Made enough off word-of-mouth referrals to support myself and a small crew. I just haven't been in any hurry to deal with the hassles of a larger operation."

"Well, as long as you're happy...." Making it clear that it took a lot more than this to keep Sean satisfied.

Ethan wouldn't describe himself as a "happy" guy, exactly, but he was close enough that he had no real complaints. Had he gone along with his mother's demands and followed Sean into the firm, he had no doubt he'd be ready to hang himself by now. Assuming he'd lasted this long, of course.

"Read over those pages, and if you have any questions, you know how to contact me. Let me know when you're ready to collect your father's things, and I'll contact Ms. Prentiss for you to make the arrangements. As trustee, I'll be there, too, of course, when the two of you meet."

"Thanks, Sean." Ethan looked pointedly toward the door.

To be honest, he needed some time alone now. He'd been so busy trying to hide his feelings about his mother's death that he hadn't had a chance to examine them, himself.

Sean hesitated before taking the hint. "You know, if you want to contest this will…"

"Contest it?" Ethan raised an eyebrow. "You're the one who said Mother seemed in possession of all her faculties up till the end. I assume she had enough sense to make sure the will was valid."

"Well, yes, but I also pointed out that no one knows who this Prentiss woman is, or why Margaret would have left her an inheritance that some would insist should rightfully be yours. Under any testamentary trust, the will must be probated, so if you want to try to make any changes, this would be your chance… even though I would have to testify, of course, that Margaret seemed to be in perfectly sound mind, in my judgment."

"I walked away from Mother and her money a long time ago," Ethan reminded him flatly. "I wouldn't let her manipulate me with it then, and I have no intention of fighting for it now."

"Even if you find reason to believe Brenda Prentiss somehow committed fraud to get hold of your mother's estate?"

"You said you've done some basic checking on her—have you found anything to suggest that Brenda Prentiss coerced my mother into drawing up that will eighteen months ago?"

"Well…no," Sean admitted. "And I find it hard to believe that Irving wouldn't ask questions…but, still…"

"Still, it's bizarre," Ethan conceded. "And totally unlike the Margaret either of us knew. But that doesn't mean she didn't know exactly what she was doing. For all we know, she picked a name at random out of the phone book—just to piss me off. She'd probably be pissed, herself, if she knew that once again, I just don't care. Her money was always a threat she used against me. No way I'm giving anyone else the opportunity to hold it over me. So, if the mysterious Ms. Prentiss wants to squabble about my dad's things, she's welcome to them. As far as I'm concerned, the war is over."

Even as Sean made his way to the door a few minutes later, he didn't seem quite convinced that Ethan was resigned to letting all that money go without at least a token resistance. He promised to contact the mystery heir about Ethan's inheritance, and to get back to him, but he was still shaking his head when he walked down the flagstone path to his expensive car.

Glad to be alone again, Ethan shut the door, then closed his eyes and rested his forehead against the wood.

BRENDA PRENTISS didn't know exactly what she expected to see when she entered the offices of D'Alessandro and Walker Investigations on Thursday afternoon, but it wasn't the efficient-looking operation she found inside the Dallas, Texas high-rise. She had never been to a private investigation agency before, and she was aware that her expectations had been influenced by movies and television.

Rather than a hard-bitten, shady character in a seedy, dark room, a fresh-faced redhead in a brightly lit, impeccably decorated waiting room greeted Brenda with a smile. "Good afternoon. May I help you?"

Now that she was here, she wasn't entirely sure how to proceed. She had come on an impulse, and she wished she had taken a little more time to think about what she would say. "Um…my name is Brenda Prentiss, and I don't have an appointment. Maybe I should come back to talk to an investigator another time?"

The receptionist made a reassuring gesture with her right hand, causing half a dozen thin silver bracelets to jingle cheerily. Her trendy, colorful clothing made Brenda feel almost dowdy in comparison, even though she was wearing the blue jersey T-shirt dress that she had been told made her eyes look bluer and flattered her figure, which she had always considered merely average. "I'm sure someone will be available to see you. If you'll have a seat, I'll let them know you're here."

Perched on the edge of a comfortable chair upholstered in a nubby, sage-green fabric, Brenda noted that the receptionist hadn't even asked the general nature of her reason for wanting to talk to an investigator. She supposed that sort of discretion was imperative in this type of business.

She doubted that she looked like the "usual" client of a private investigation agency—whatever that might entail. With her blond hair and fair skin, her oval face dominated by long-lashed, blue eyes, Brenda was usually mistaken for being younger than her twenty-six years. Her wardrobe and accessories reflected the less-than-substantial salary she earned at the elementary school where she'd taught for the past two years, even when supplemented with her summer banking job, so she knew she didn't look like the type who could afford to hire an expensive P.I.

Suddenly asking herself what she was doing here, and how she could possibly explain it without sounding like some sort of psycho, she glanced toward the door, wondering if she should make a break for it before it was too late.

"Ms. Prentiss?"

It was already too late.

Swallowing hard, she rose, clutching her bag in white-knuckled hands. The man who had spoken stood in the doorway of the reception area. He, too, was the direct opposite of the seedy P.I.s of film and TV. Wearing a dark suit and white shirt that nicely set off his athletic physique and dark coloring, he gave her a smile obviously intended to set her at ease.

Her first impression was that of a handsome man in his early forties. Upon closer inspection, she mentally adjusted his age upward by a good ten years, but he was still a remarkably good-looking man.

"I'm Tony D'Alessandro," he introduced himself. "May I help you?"

She recognized his name from the placard on the entrance door. When she had asked to see someone, she hadn't really envisioned meeting with the senior partner of the company. "I don't have an appointment," she said in case he had mistaken her for someone else. "I just need a consultation."

"I have a little time free now. Come on back to my office, and we'll see if there's anything I can do for you."

The receptionist didn't seem to find it at all odd that the big boss was making time for a meeting with a young woman who had simply wandered in off the street. Apparently, despite the elegance of the decor, the atmosphere around this place of business was habitually informal. Maybe Thursday afternoons were always slow in the investigation business.

Tony D'Alessandro led Brenda past a large room filled with computers and busy users, past several offices with closed doors bearing brass nameplates, and into another office at the end of the hallway. His name was on the door, but once again, she was a bit surprised upon entering.

Judging from what she'd seen thus far, she would have expected the senior partner of this thriving investigation and security consulting company to have an impressive, perhaps even luxurious office. Tony's office, while very nice, was obviously a work space, with a big, cluttered wooden desk, overflowing bookcases and a large credenza almost hidden beneath stacks of files and computer equipment.

And photographs. Framed photographs crowded almost every free space.

"Family," he explained, noticing the direction of her attention. "I've got a wife and four kids ranging from twenty-three to fourteen. Between us, my wife and I have seven siblings and over a dozen nieces and nephews, whose proud parents give us frequently updated family portraits."

"That's a lot of family." Unable to even imagine having that many people in her life, Brenda sank into the big leather visitor's chair Tony offered her, while he settled behind his desk.

"A *lot* of family," Tony agreed, sweeping a pile of papers out of the way so he could clasp his hands loosely on the desk in front of him. "So," he said then, seeming to sense that she was ready to talk, "what can I do for you?"

She tucked a strand of fine, collar-length blond hair behind her right ear in a characteristically nervous gesture. "Something very unnerving happened to me this morning, and I can't seem to come up with an explanation, even after worrying

about it for several hours now. I think I need professional help."

He nodded, and the movement caused the bright
overhead lights to glitter in the silver scattered liberally through thick hair that had probably been pure
ebony when he was younger. "Go on."

"I, um…" She reached into her bag and drew out a
folded sheaf of legal papers. Reaching across his desk,
she handed it to him, motioning for him to read the neatly
typed words on the pages. "First, you should probably
know about this. Maybe it's only my imagination—but
I can't help worrying that the situation described in this
letter is connected to what's been happening to me."

Frowning, Tony looked from her face to the letter
in his hand. His eyebrows shot up as he read, and he
pursed his mouth in a silent whistle. "If I understand
correctly, you've very recently been named the beneficiary of a testamentary trust currently valued at
several million dollars, not counting the value of a
sizeable estate on an acre of ground in an exclusive
suburban neighborhood. You will receive a substantial
amount of money monthly, in addition to the use of the
estate, for the rest of your life."

Her knuckles went white as she gripped her bag
even more tightly. "So I've been told."

"I'm sorry about your loss. Were you close to—"
he glanced at the letter again "—Margaret Jacobs?"

"You see, that's part of my problem." She leaned
slightly toward him. "I've never met Margaret Jacobs
in my life. I have no idea who she was, or why she left
me a fortune when she died. And now—well, maybe
I'm just crazy. I don't even know how to word this so
that you won't think I'm a lunatic or something."

"Ms. Prentiss." D'Alessandro leaned slightly across the desk and gave her an encouraging smile. "Trust me, okay? Just tell me why you're here."

Drawing a deep breath, Brenda said in a voice that came out little more than a whisper, "I think someone tried to kill me today."

CHAPTER TWO

"So, Carly, did ya notice the hot chick who just went into your pop's office? He closed the door pretty fast behind 'em, hmm?"

Carly D'Alessandro didn't look up from her keyboard—not that she expected Peck Verady to take the hint. The guy was a master of self-delusion, his favorite fantasy being that he was irresistible to women. "She's a client, Verady. You know—work? Now go away and let me get back to mine."

"Hey, c'mon, chica. Everyone gets a break sometimes, yo. Especially the boss's daughter—and niece, if you figure in the other two bosses."

She didn't need to be reminded of her relationships. Nor of the familial pressure responsible for her sitting at the keyboard being harassed by Peck the Prick when she could be lounging on a beach with some of her college friends, instead.

It wasn't as if she needed the money. Her mom was loaded, and Dad had done all right for himself with the agency. Her other friends with money weren't sitting in a boring office all summer. Several of them were in Cancun at that very moment. But, then, they didn't have fathers who were totally obsessed with instilling "old fashioned work ethics" in their offspring.

"So, anyway, Carly, how about if you and I go have some fun later? Have a few drinks, listen to some music—maybe dance a little."

She would rather pluck out her eyelashes. One by one. "Can't. Not old enough to drink."

Not for another five months and six days, anyway.

"Oh." That took him aback for a beat, but he recovered with his usual obliviousness. "I bet you've got fake ID. Rich college girl and all. Know your way around a computer and a laser printer, right?"

"No, I don't have a fake ID—and no, I don't want you to get me one. And, no, I don't want to go out with you," she added, figuring blunt honesty was the only way to get through to this guy. "Now would you *please* let me finish this?"

"Oh, I get it." He lowered his voice and glanced in the direction of her father's closed office door. "Papa wouldn't approve of you flirting with the help, right?"

She had heard that Peck was a genius with a computer. When it came to women, however, he seemed to be severely challenged. "Just go away."

"Carly."

Her father's voice had never been so welcome. Peck jumped like a bunny and hopped off to his own computer station. Carly spun in her chair. "Yes?"

"Bring a couple bottles of water in here, will you? I'm all out in my office fridge."

She nodded and stood. At least fetching water gave her a break from the name searches she had been conducting all freaking day, she thought wearily. Not to mention a break from the agency's pet computer geek.

BRENDA HAD WELCOMED the offer of water, even though it meant causing Tony to go to the extra trouble of having some brought in. It had given her a chance to organize her thoughts.

A young woman with glossy, shoulder-length black hair, beautiful dark eyes and a mouth that even another woman could acknowledge as blatantly sexy strode through the door carrying two bottles of water. Add to her other attributes a drop-dead figure in a white summer sweater and a short red skirt, and Brenda wondered how any male in this agency was able to function coherently.

"Brenda Prentiss, this is my daughter, Carly. Thanks, cara." Tony smiled at the young woman as he accepted the bottles of water and offered one to his potential client.

Tony's daughter. Noting the proud and protective gleam in his eyes, Brenda decided that her question had just been answered. None of the men in the agency would likely be brave enough to make a pass at Carly with her father watching her like a guard dog.

"Sure, Dad. Anything else?" Carly looked at Brenda with open curiosity.

"No, that's all, honey. Thanks."

"Okay. Guess I'll get back to the computer, then." Looking as though she would rather be going for extensive dental work, Carly turned and left the office, closing the door again behind her.

"Now," Tony said, having waited until Brenda had taken a sip of her water, "you said you've never heard of Margaret Jacobs…."

"Never," Brenda assured him. "Trust me, I've been trying for the past four days to figure out why a total stranger would have made me the beneficiary of her will. It simply doesn't make sense. I keep thinking they must have the wrong person—that maybe there's another Brenda Prentiss out there somewhere who should be notified, instead—but the trustee of the will says there's been no mistake."

"I agree that this is highly unusual," Tony said, and she could tell she had intrigued him. "Mrs. Jacobs left no explanation why she chose you as her heir?"

"No. The attorney who drew up her will died several months ago. The trustee—another attorney with the same firm—wasn't given any details of the will before her death. Apparently, no one who knew her ever heard her mention my name. It was almost as if she chose me at random from a telephone book or something, which is just crazy."

"She had no other heirs?"

Brenda swallowed hard. "I've been told that she has a son who's a few years older than I am, and a nephew. Apparently, she and her son were estranged. I was led to believe that she and her nephew got along well, but for some reason, she chose not to make him her primary beneficiary, though she did leave him a one-time cash bequest."

"So, presumably, both the son and the nephew could very much resent a stranger lucking into what might have been their inheritance."

She moistened her lips and nodded. "I suppose, even though Sean Jacobs, the trustee, told me that the son doesn't want the money. He said the nephew was infuriated by his aunt's will, and has been looking into ways to contest it."

Tony frowned, his pen hovering over the pad on

which he'd been making notes. "You said Sean Jacobs is the trustee, not the son?"

"No. It's a bit complicated, but apparently Sean's late father was married to Margaret, who had a son from a former marriage. So Sean and Margaret's son are step-brothers, but I didn't get the impression that they're close."

"Wonder how Sean Jacobs feels about his step-mother leaving her estate to a stranger," Tony murmured, making another note on his pad.

"I've only spoken to him on the phone so far, but he seems very nice," Brenda replied. "We're supposed to meet tomorrow, along with Ethan Blacklock, Margaret's biological son. Margaret's will stipulated that Mr. Blacklock was to receive all of his late father's possessions from the house, but she didn't leave an inventory of the items. So I'm supposed to be at the house tomorrow with Sean and Ethan while they remove the things that belonged to Ethan's father."

Tony frowned again. "Surely the will hasn't already been through probate?"

"No, but as trustee, Sean said he has power to allow Ethan to take his father's things before the probate is finalized—with my permission. I told him that I would certainly not try to interfere with Ethan taking the things that belonged to his father. I feel strangely enough about being the heir to his mother's estate."

"Everything you've told me so far is highly unorthodox."

"I'm aware of that. Which is why I still have trouble believing it's true. I've been so stunned by everything, so sure that it's all a mistake that will be corrected soon."

"Who have you told about your inheritance?"

"Not many people. It's been less than a week since I was notified. How do I explain this inheritance when I don't understand it, myself? I told my brother and sister, of course, and my best friend from the school where I teach, Diane O'Brien—who's a bit of a gossip, so she might have told some of our coworkers. I didn't think to ask her to keep it a secret. As for what happened this morning, I haven't told anyone. I don't want to scare them without first finding out if I'm just imagining things."

"Okay, I think we've set the scene enough now. Let's talk about why you really came here. What makes you think someone tried to kill you this morning?"

As a prelude to that incident, she told him about the disturbing telephone calls she had been getting since late Tuesday afternoon. Hang-up calls, about ten of them in all. She would answer the phone, hear someone breathing angrily on the other end of the line, and then the call would be abruptly disconnected, leaving her listening in bewilderment and growing apprehension to a dial tone. There was never an answer when she tried to return the calls with the * 69 feature.

"You said it sounded like 'angry' breathing," Tony interjected quietly. "What do you mean by that?"

Feeling a bit foolish, she shrugged. "I don't know how else to explain it. It's just a feeling I got—that someone was really furious on the other end of the line. As far as I know, I haven't done anything to make anyone mad at me lately, so I can't help wondering if the calls are connected to this trust."

"It's a reasonable assumption," Tony assured her, apparently sensing her self-doubts. "Two strange things happen to you in one week, so it's natural for you to try to connect them."

She nodded. "Anyway, every day at just after noon—when I'm home, for lunch, as I am several days a week during the summer months—I walk out to the mailboxes on the street in front of my duplex to check my mail. The mail carrier almost always comes at twelve-forty-five. You can practically set your watch by him, and it's become habit for me to go out and check at that time. I was standing in front of the mailbox today, looking through the bills and ads, and this big, black truck tried to run me down. If I hadn't dropped a bill onto the grass and moved after it at that moment, I'd have been hit hard."

She swallowed, reliving the panic she had felt when the big vehicle had sped past her so close that she could feel the heat radiating off of it. She had spun around, stared rather blankly at the tire ruts dug into the grass in front of the mailboxes only inches from where she'd stood, and only then thought to look after the vehicle. By that time, it had already been turning the corner, and she'd gotten only a glimpse of the back bumper.

She had gotten no other details, she explained to Tony. No one else had seen the incident, since it was the middle of a weekday and few of her neighbors in the small duplex complex were at home.

"People speed down that street all the time," she added conscientiously. "We're always complaining about it, because there are children in the complex and we worry about them going out into the road and being hit. But this truck swerved right at me, Mr. D'Alessandro. It went off the pavement and onto the grass where I had been standing only moments before. Had it not been for me dropping that bill…"

She shivered at the thought.

"That must have been horrifying for you," Tony said, and even though she tried, she couldn't hear any condescension in the remark. "On top of everything else that's happened to you this week, it's no wonder you were frightened."

"I thought about calling the police, but I didn't know what to tell them," she admitted. "I don't think they would take a few creepy hang-ups seriously, and I have no proof, of course, about the near hit-and-run. And well, to be honest, I'm not sure they would believe that I've been left a lot of money by a stranger. That sounds so far-fetched, even to me, that I'm just not sure they would buy anything I say."

"It is possible that it was only coincidence, you know," he reminded her gently. "A reckless driver who looked away from the road for a moment, then panicked and sped away when he or she realized what had almost happened."

"I'm aware of that possibility," she agreed without taking offense. "It's another reason why I didn't call the police. But the more I thought about it, the more it bothered me. That, combined with this inheritance that makes no sense to me, is what made me think someone should look into this whole situation and try to find an explanation. If I'm really the right Brenda Prentiss, then why did Margaret Jacobs leave me her estate? And is it really possible that someone wants to get rid of me because of that, or am I just being paranoid? I need some answers, Mr. D'Alessandro."

"Call me Tony," he said, turning to a new page in his notepad. "And that's what I do—I find answers."

Somewhat reassured, she allowed herself to relax in her seat as he continued to ask her questions to which she had pathetically few answers.

TONY ESCORTED BRENDA out of D'Alessandro and Walker Investigations with a promise to get back with her if he found any answers. It appeared that several of his employees had already left for the day. She glanced at her watch after parting from him, and was surprised to realize that it was just after five o'clock.

He had spent quite a bit of time with her, asking what had seemed like hundreds of questions, trying to jog her memories about her benefactor. That had been a waste of time, of course. There were no memories to jog. She simply didn't know the woman.

She wouldn't have blamed Tony if he didn't believe her. After all, who'd ever heard of anyone inheriting a sizable estate from a total stranger? Yet Tony had treated her with nothing but respect, accepting her answers with a grave consideration that made her feel increasingly better about having come to him. He assured her that he would assign someone to look into her situation immediately. As she'd left his office, he'd urged her to be careful, and to be on constant guard— which either proved that he believed her, or that he was simply humoring her until he decided for himself whether she was of sound mind.

Feeling suddenly drained of all the nervous energy that had kept her going that day, she followed the tantalizing scent of fresh-ground coffee into a coffee shop across a large, crowded lobby from Tony's offices.

She wasn't the only one who needed a bracing jolt of caffeine before heading into rush-hour traffic, she noted. She had to stand in line for several minutes before she was able to order.

Though many of the other customers had ordered "to go," there were enough people remaining in the small shop that she wasn't sure she was going to be able to find a place to sit. She was just about to give up and carry the beverage with her when she heard someone say her name. "Brenda? Here's an extra seat."

Glancing to her right, she recognized Tony D'Alessandro's beautiful daughter, Carly. The young woman was smiling and motioning toward an empty chair on the other side of the tiny round table where she sat with what appeared to be a steaming cappuccino. "You're welcome to sit here, if you like," she said.

With a smile of gratitude, Brenda slid into the empty chair. "Thanks. Is it always this crowded in here?"

"Depends on the time of day, but, yeah. It's a popular place."

After taking a sip of her latte, Brenda could understand the shop's appeal. The coffee was excellent. Just what she'd needed.

Carly leaned forward a little. "Do you mind if I ask a personal question?"

Expecting to be asked about her business with the investigation agency, Brenda responded guardedly, "What do you want to know?"

"Where did you buy that cute T-shirt dress? I've been looking for one just like that."

Brenda relaxed, though she was a bit bemused.

Carly was so polished and put-together, hardly the type who usually asked *her* for fashion advice.

With a little shrug, she named the discount department store where she'd bought the dress—and quite a few other items in her wardrobe. She would bet that Carly never shopped there.

Judging by Carly's expression, she'd have won the bet. Still, Carly looked more intrigued than put off. "Really? Maybe I'll look there when I get some free time. It's not like I have anything better to do this weekend," she added in a disgruntled mumble.

"Plans fall through?" Brenda asked sympathetically.

Carly wrinkled her perfect nose. "What plans? All my friends are out of town. I don't have anyone to make plans with, except for my family, and I see them every day as it is."

"*All* of your friends are out of town?"

"Well, most of them," Carly amended. "The ones I'd want to hang out with this weekend, anyway. They put together a two-week summer trip to Cancun, but I had to stay here and work. My dad's idea, needless to say."

Brenda set her coffee cup down and studied Carly in surprise. "Are you still in college?" she asked, which was her semitactful way of asking Carly's age. She would have thought Carly was closer to her own age.

"Just finished my sophomore year," Carly confirmed with a nod.

"Really? Where do you go?"

"Baylor."

It didn't surprise her at all that Carly attended a pricy, private school. "What's your major?"

"Art history." Carly took a sip of her cappuccino, then added with a mischievous grin that made her look more her true age, "It drives my dad crazy. He can't figure out how I'm going to make a living with an art history degree. And since I have to pretend I have no trust funds to fall back on, I'm supposed to worry about things like that."

They really were from different worlds, Brenda thought with a shake of her head. She had known from an early age that she'd have to work for her living— but then, she had never expected to inherit a tidy sum before her thirtieth birthday, either, she reminded herself. "I assume you have a plan?"

"I'll probably go into interior design. It's what I really enjoy doing. But in the meantime, it's fun to mess with Dad's mind, you know?"

Brenda couldn't help but be amused. "I'm sort of like that with my older brother. My father died when I was a junior in high school, and ever since then, Richard has tried to overcompensate for me in the paternal department. He got even worse when our mother died just over three years ago. He's backed off some during the past couple of years, but he still can't resist a few lectures when we get together. You know, how I should be planning for my future and trying to get a better job and saving more money…"

Which made her think again of the life-changing inheritance she had received that week. Neither Richard nor their sister, Linda, knew quite how to deal with their little sister's sudden wealth, which hadn't stopped Richard from starting all new lectures.

Carly didn't know about the inheritance, of course, but she seemed struck by Brenda's revelation. "You lost both your parents? I'm so sorry."

Brenda nodded somberly. "I had just obtained my master's degree in education from UT-Dallas when Mom died."

"You must be older than you look," Carly commented candidly.

"I'm twenty-six." Because Carly had spoken so frankly, Brenda did the same. "And you look older than your age, if you don't mind my saying so."

"I'm twenty. People always assume I'm older."

It was more a matter of carriage and attitude than appearance, Brenda decided, discreetly studying Carly's face. Carly carried herself with a confidence and composure that was advanced for her years. Brenda couldn't help but be a bit envious, since self-confidence was something she still struggled with on a fairly regular basis.

They chatted inconsequentially for another few minutes, and then Carly glanced at her watch and sighed. "I'd better go. My folks are expecting me for dinner." She tossed her curtain of glossy, black hair, and Brenda could almost hear a few men around them practically swallow their tongues along with their coffees, since several of them had been not-so-subtly eyeing Carly for the entire time Brenda had been sitting there with her.

Oddly enough, she thought with a faint smile, she liked Carly, anyway.

THERE WERE A FEW MESSAGES on Brenda's answering machine when she returned to her tidy duplex apartment. A couple of friends had called to say they wanted to talk to her soon, which made her wonder if Diane had been telling them about Brenda's inheritance. And Sean Jacobs's secretary had called to confirm that he would meet her at the estate at 6:00 p.m. the next day.

Tony had suggested she take someone along with her on that meeting. He had offered to be the one to accompany her, if she wanted, but he thought it might be even better if she took her brother or a friend.

Drawing a deep breath, she picked up the phone and dialed her brother's number. He answered on the second ring, having recognized her number from caller ID. "Hi, Brenda. I tried to call you earlier, actually, to see how you're doing. I wish you would get a cell phone. I still think everyone has to have one these days…what if you have an emergency?"

It was typical of him not to let her talk. And typical, as well, for him to express concern for her safety.

He had been nagging her for six months to get another wireless phone, ever since she had let her service drop in a cost-cutting move at the beginning of the year. Practically from childhood, she had been warned about the dangers of credit card debt and the necessity of living within her means—first by her parents, and then by her brother.

Thirty-four-year-old Richard was an insurance agent, good with money, and he spent a lot of time worrying about his youngest sister's finances. He was always trying to help her out, but she rarely accepted anything from him. It wasn't as if he had lots of extra money to give away, having recently opened an office of his own, with all the accompanying overhead and concerns of embarking on a new business venture.

Besides that, she had spent the past three years

trying to convince her brother that she was an independent, competent adult. As far as she was concerned, accepting money from him would completely negate that message. If her sister, Linda, married and the mother of two, had been too proud to ask for assistance during a rough financial period last year, Brenda certainly wouldn't be any less self-sufficient.

So, no wireless phone. She bought her clothes in discount stores, drove an inexpensive car, had basic cable TV, ate lots of brown-bagged lunches and she had no credit card charges that she couldn't pay off at the end of the month.

It was still difficult for her to mentally process the possibility that pinching pennies would no longer be a necessity of her life.

Richard now had all new worries about her. He was as confused by her inheritance as she was, and even more suspicious of it. He wanted her to get an attorney and an investment counselor, and he wanted her to talk to him before she signed anything. She wondered how he would react when she told him about her visit to the private investigator. She had no intention of telling him about the truck that had so narrowly missed her that day. Richard would go ballistic if he thought she was in danger. He would probably refuse to let her out of his sight from then on.

So, she would tell him she'd hired an investigator, but only to look into the connection between her and Margaret Jacobs. She figured that discretion was definitely called for in this situation.

"Brenda? You there?"

"I'm here," she said. "And, Richard, there's something I need to tell you."

"I REALLY APPRECIATE you coming with me today. I know you're busy at work this week." Brenda had already made several variations of that statement during the drive to Margaret Jacobs's estate, but since the atmosphere in her brother's car had turned tense again, she'd said the first thing that popped into her head just to fill the silence.

"The work stuff can wait," Richard replied firmly. "I want to know what the hell is going on here."

Tall and slender, thirty-four-year-old Richard was blond, blue-eyed, handsome in a buttoned-down, conservative way. Brenda had idolized him from childhood, though she'd been trying for almost that long to convince him that she didn't need him constantly watching over her. It hadn't been difficult to convince him to accompany her to this meeting with Sean Jacobs and Ethan Blacklock at the estate that would soon be available for her use. In fact, he would have insisted had she not invited him along.

Following the directions they had been given, they passed a couple of intimidatingly large houses—and then Richard braked at the end of the street, staring at the imposing structure in front of them. "You've got to be kidding me."

Gazing through the windshield, Brenda had to make an effort to reply. "This is the address he gave me."

Two massive brick posts topped with light globes flanked the wide, circular driveway that led off the dead-end street. There was no fence, as such, though a low stone wall marked the front of the property—a full acre, she would guess, of landscaped grounds. No gates blocked the entry to the driveway, which rather surprised her, since she'd thought people with this much money were security fanatics. Glancing at the other houses on the immaculately groomed street, she estimated that about half sat behind massive gates.

The house in which Margaret Jacobs had lived was a large, traditional red-brick with a double-door entry at the top of a short brick stairway flanked by curving wrought iron banisters. Large brass-and-glass light fixtures were installed on either side of the doors. An arched transom gleamed above, with a huge Palladian window on the second floor. She counted a dozen other gleaming, multipaned windows trimmed with black shutters. A garage opened on one end of the house; the other end sported a towering brick chimney. Though she was no expert, she estimated the house to be roughly five times the size of the entire duplex in which she now lived.

Brenda couldn't picture herself sprawled in a lawn chair here in her shorts and flip-flops with a can of diet soda. She often sat that way behind her duplex on sunny afternoons to watch the neighbor kids playing, occasionally even leaving her chair to join them in a game of soccer or tag football.

What did the children in this neighborhood play? Backyard polo?

Richard parked in the driveway in front of the house, and they opened their car doors simultaneously. He stayed close behind her as she walked up the steps and onto the porch, and for once she was almost grateful for his hovering.

"I can't believe this house is yours," Richard muttered as they stood in front of the huge double doors.

"Conditionally," she reminded him. "It's not like I can sell it or anything."

"But, still…"

Still. This estate was a huge leap from the duplex. Or from her sister's crowded little house that was barely big enough to hold Linda and her husband and their two small children. Or even from Richard's comfortable one-bedroom apartment close to his newly opened insurance office. This place was as close to a mansion as Brenda had ever visited.

The door opened before she found the nerve to press the doorbell. A nice-looking man in a beautifully cut gray suit and a power-red tie greeted them with an easy smile. "You must be Brenda."

"Yes. And this is my brother, Richard Prentiss."

"Sean Jacobs." He held out his hand to Richard, hiding any surprise he might have felt that she had brought her brother with her. "I'm the trustee of Margaret's estate, so I'll be working with your sister on a regular basis."

Though Richard shook the man's hand, his tone was very reserved when he said, "I have quite a few questions for you."

"I'm sure you do. Please, come in." And then he turned back to Brenda with a slightly sheepish laugh. "That sounds a bit presumptuous of me under the circumstances, doesn't it? After all, for all intents and purposes, this is your house—at least it will be after probate."

She gave him a weak smile in response and stepped into the house when he moved aside. Richard followed close behind her.

The two-story foyer was lit by the late-day sun

streaming through the fan-shaped transom over the doors and the Palladian window above, in addition to a spectacular crystal chandelier. A sweeping staircase with spindles and banisters of some dark wood led upstairs. Art hung on the walls and a rug that looked old and intricately woven covered the center of the polished marble floor. A formal living room opened off one side of the foyer, an even more formal dining room off the other side.

She'd been told that Margaret Jacobs had died from a fall down the stairs. These stairs? Was she even now standing near the spot where Margaret had drawn her last breath? She shivered a little at the thought.

Pushing the disturbing image out of her mind for now, she tried to envision herself coming into this house after work and throwing her jacket over the banister, kicking off her shoes and heading to the kitchen for a diet soda and a tuna sandwich. The image simply wouldn't form in her head.

"It's…beautiful," she said, sensing that Jacobs was waiting for her to say something.

"It's a bit stuffy," he said with a smile that was unexpectedly charming. "But then, so was Margaret. You will have quite a bit of leeway with redecorating to your taste once you move in."

Following him into the living room, Brenda wondered if she would ever have the nerve to even shift the position of a carefully placed candlestick, much less to consider redecorating.

Catching movement from the corner of her eyes, she turned to see three cats of various sizes and colors padding into the room through an open, arched doorway, all looking curious about their visitors. A smile spread immediately over her face, and she knelt to pat them, laughing when they fell all over each other to compete for her attention. Apparently, there wasn't a shy one in the bunch. One was solid black, one mostly white and the other a gray tiger-stripe. Each wore a collar with a small metal tag inscribed with a name.

"Hello, Fluffy," she greeted the purring white cat. "And Toby. And Missy," she added, acknowledging the gray and the black cats in turn. Margaret Jacobs hadn't exactly been creative when it came to cat names.

"My sister is crazy about cats," Richard commented in resignation.

"So was Margaret. Almost obsessively so." Sean shook his head. "She was a…complicated woman. Very cool and controlled, extremely reserved…except with her cats. They were treated like pampered children."

"These are the cats she asked me to care for," Brenda commented, looking up from the affectionate felines. "I wonder how she knew I love cats? I had one of my own until he—he died a few months ago of kidney disease." There was still a little catch in her voice when she spoke of Domino.

"Yes, that was a big stipulation of the will. You're to provide a home and loving care for all four cats for their lifetimes, which could be quite a while since two of them are under a year old."

"Four cats?" Brenda frowned in confusion at the three cats winding around her.

Sean followed her gaze, then frowned. "I'm sure there were four."

She looked around the room, then back toward the

arched doorway that led into the foyer. Two green eyes peered at her from behind the doorjamb. A pointed ear twitched nervously above the eyes, as if to hear everything they were saying. Here, she thought, was the shy one. "Come here, kitty," she coaxed, reaching out a hand. "Come on. I won't hurt you."

The little calico crept toward her. Gently pushing the others aside, Brenda offered the calico her fingers to sniff and then she scratched the cat's head, eliciting a tentative purr in response. This tag read "Angel."

"Hello, Angel," she cooed, and was rewarded with a sweet "meow" and a gentle head butt against her hand.

The cats were climbing all over her now, liberally shedding hair over her black slacks and black-and-pink top, but she merely smiled and lavished them with attention. They'd lost the owner who had loved them, she reminded herself. They were probably hungry for affection and attention.

She wasn't sure what suddenly changed in the room. Maybe it was something she heard, or sensed, or a sudden alertness in the cats that made her look toward the doorway through which she had entered the room.

Compared to Richard and Sean, the newcomer looked rough and dangerous. They wore jackets and ties; he wore denim and boots. They were coiffed and groomed; his dark brown hair was shaggy and he needed a shave. And he was glaring at her in a way that made a funny shiver run all the way down her spine.

Here, she thought, was Margaret Jacobs's disinherited son. And he was not at all happy to see her making herself comfortable in this room.

CHAPTER THREE

WHEN ETHAN WALKED IN, the woman was sitting on the floor playing with the damned cats, looking for all the world as if she felt right at home. Her hair was blond, her eyes blue. Though he knew her to be twenty-six, he would have guessed younger, especially when she laughed at the cats. The humor faded from her expression when she looked up at him.

She rose slowly, tumbling cats all around her. Average height, he noted. Slender figure. She looked nervous now, an impression reinforced when she ran her hands down her thighs, then clasped them in front of her.

Sean spotted him then, and moved toward him, putting himself between Ethan and Brenda Prentiss. "There you are, Ethan. I was beginning to think you'd changed your mind."

"I thought about it," Ethan drawled, flicking a glance at the stern-looking man standing just behind Sean's left shoulder. The resemblance to Brenda was unmistakable; he had to be her brother.

Sean confirmed that guess by making the introductions. "Ethan Blacklock, this is Brenda Prentiss and her brother, Richard."

No one offered to shake hands, though Ethan acknowledged Richard with a curt nod that was returned the same way. Brenda looked at him with anxiety evident in her eyes. "This is very awkward," she said in a low, slightly husky voice. "I'm so sorry about your loss."

Because he still didn't know how she had finagled her way into his mother's will, he didn't allow himself to be suckered by her apparent sincerity. "I'm sure you've figured out that my mother and I weren't exactly on the best of terms."

Now she looked distressed. Either she had the worst poker face he had ever seen, or she was one hell of an actress. "I really don't understand how I ended up in her will. As far as I remember, I never met your mother. I can't imagine why she chose me."

She had bewildered innocence down pat. Her brother, however, was scowling and looking as if someone had stuck a poker up his backside. Could he be involved in this somehow?

"I find it hard to believe Mother chose a name at random," he said coolly to Brenda. "I assume there's some connection you're not telling us about."

Her eyes widened. This expression, he decided in detachment, would probably be described as wounded outrage. And he wasn't any more convinced by it than any of her other performances.

It was her brother who spoke up then, his tone holding a note of warning as he moved closer to his sister. "Brenda told you she didn't have an explanation. She isn't hiding anything from you."

Ethan swept him with a cool look. "Then maybe *you* know something."

Richard's eyes narrowed, and anger darkened his

fair complexion. "I knew nothing about any of this until Brenda called me. Before that, I'd never heard of your mother. I have no more idea than my sister how she ended up in the will."

Sean cleared his throat rather forcefully. "This is an awkward situation for everyone here. It would make it much easier if we remain courteous."

The fact that he looked directly at Ethan as he spoke made it clear who he was talking to, primarily, but he had positioned himself close enough to Richard to include him in the caution.

Because he was aware that he was the one who had set the combative tone—and because, damn it, Brenda Prentiss suddenly looked so distressed that he was starting to feel almost guilty about it—Ethan nodded tersely. "Let's get on with it, then."

Satisfied that he'd made his point, Sean turned back to Brenda, his tone softening. "Maybe you'd like to sit down a minute?"

She lifted her chin in a sudden show of strength that had Ethan looking at her again. "Mr. Blacklock wants to 'get on with it.' I think that's a good idea."

She was good, he'd give her that. He'd gone from suspecting her, to feeling a little sorry for her, to almost respecting her—and back again. And he still didn't know who the hell she was.

"I can make this pretty quick," he said, turning abruptly to Sean. "Other than the few things that are already in my possession, my father had his grandfather's pocket watch, and his great-grandfather's shaving mug. I'd like to have those. And there was an old family Bible that belonged to Dad's mother. I want that, too, if it's still around here somewhere."

"Your mother wouldn't have gotten rid of a family Bible," Richard said.

Ethan flicked him a look. "It wasn't *her* family," he said with a shrug.

He happened to glance Brenda's way then. She was searching his face as if she'd heard something in his voice that intrigued her. Suddenly feeling as if she was seeing entirely too much, he turned back to Sean. "That's it. Shouldn't take that long to find them, and then I'll get out of here."

Sean looked puzzled. "That's all you want? Margaret arranged for you to take anything that personally belonged to your father. That could be interpreted rather generously, you know."

"Mother disposed of most of Dad's stuff after he died. She got rid of the rest in a big cleaning spree after *your* father died. I took some things with me when I left after college, but I've regretted not taking the items I just listed."

Sean glanced at his watch. "If you know where they are, we should go ahead and get them. And then I have a form for you and Brenda to sign, verifying what you've taken."

Switching from briskly professional to a more casual tone, he added, "I've got to admit that this is one of the more unusual legal situations I've encountered. The trust Margaret set up is as eccentric and complicated as she was. We may never know what she was trying to accomplish with all the twists and turns she incorporated into it, but she and Irving made sure it was all legally binding, so I'm going to do my best to stick to every detail."

Effectively reminded that he had been taking his annoyance out on the wrong people, since Margaret had been the one to create this mess, Ethan toned down the prickliness when he said, "I think I know where to find everything. I'll just go get them and take off and then you can—"

"Ethan." Looking uncomfortable, Sean shifted his weight. "Why don't we all go? Brenda and Richard haven't seen the house yet."

"You don't really expect me to give them a tour of—" Suddenly struck with the truth, Ethan narrowed his eyes, his anger returning sharply. "Hell. You don't trust me out of your sight in the house."

"I didn't say that," Sean reminded him quickly. "I'm just trying to keep everything open and unquestionable."

"Right. Wouldn't want anyone accusing me of pocketing the silver on my way to find Granny's Bible." He was half tempted to turn right then on one work-booted heel and leave this house for the last time, taking nothing with him but what was left of his pride. But, damn it, he hated the possibility of his great-grandfather's pocket watch ending up in Richard Prentiss's pocket, or the old Bible tossed into a Dumpster.

"All right, come on," he snarled. "We'll take a damned tour. Watch your steps, folks, the stairs are kind of steep."

"Ethan—"

Ignoring Sean, Ethan turned and stalked out of the room without waiting to see if the others were following. He knew full well that they were.

SO MUCH ANGER, Brenda thought, watching Ethan's back as he preceded them through the house. And yet…was it pain she had seen in his brown eyes before he'd turned away? Was he more hurt than angered by the deliberate insult of his mother's will? She couldn't tell.

He set such a fast pace that she didn't get a close look at anything they passed on the way up the stairs to the master bedroom. She got fleeting, rather dazed impressions of art and antiques, heavy fabrics and lots of dark woods. Everything she saw looked beautiful, but slightly untouchable. More like a museum or a historical tour house than a real home.

Ethan had grown up here, she realized suddenly. For all his facade of being a working-class, tough-guy laborer, his roots were white-collar and privileged. Though she knew almost nothing else about him, Sean had told her that Ethan had willingly walked away from all of this after earning a college degree, rather than having been turned out on the street by Margaret.

He must have had compelling reasons to turn his back on his family home and his own mother. And now, rather than fighting for expensive art and antiques or other estate treasures, he had asked for nothing more than a few sentimental family items.

Or was that simply the impression he wanted to give? She couldn't help remembering how close that dark truck had come to mowing her down yesterday. She didn't want to think Ethan might have been involved in that incident—she didn't want to believe that *anyone* had deliberately tried to hurt her—but she couldn't help remembering that if anything happened to her, everything reverted back to Margaret's son.

The master bedroom was as spacious as she would have predicted, and as stuffy and formal as she had come to expect in this house. The furniture was massive, the fabrics dark and heavy. Even the high tray ceiling and tall windows didn't lighten the feel of the room. Two marble columns divided the bedroom from an equally large sitting room with a fireplace and glass doors that led onto a private balcony overlooking the rather sterile and unused-looking back lawn. The sitting room should have looked inviting. Instead, it looked stiffly elegant.

A large, painted portrait dominated the wall behind the huge, four-poster bed. "That was Margaret," Sean said when he saw Brenda looking at it. And then he watched her more closely, as if waiting for her to have an "aha!" moment and suddenly announce why Margaret had named her in the will.

Trying to oblige, she studied the portrait carefully, but futilely. "She doesn't look familiar. Is this portrait a good representation of her?"

He nodded. "Yes. It looks exactly like her."

Much too aware of the three pairs of eyes focused on her, she examined the posed portrait. The woman was tall and angular, her salt-and-pepper hair impeccably styled, her face looking relaxed, but not exactly approachable. Her son didn't bear much resemblance to her, she noted. He must look like his late father. "How old was she?"

"She was sixty," Sean replied. "Her death was entirely unexpected."

"Was there any question that her death wasn't an accident?" Richard asked, speaking for the first time in a while.

"There was an investigation," Sean replied, glancing quickly at Ethan, as Brenda did. There was no expression at all on Ethan's face now. "A brief one, to be sure, but the police found nothing to indicate that she didn't simply fall in a tragic misstep."

Richard looked at the portrait with Brenda, and he, too, shook his head, saying he didn't remember ever seeing her before. He said aloud to Ethan what Brenda had thought just a few moments earlier. "You don't look like her. Totally different coloring and build."

Ethan shrugged. "She always was very thin and angular. I guess I take after my father more. From what I remember, he was a bit more sturdily built."

Brenda had noticed for herself, of course, that Ethan's solid-looking physique appeared to be carved from long hours of hard work, an impression further enhanced by his tan and the sun-lines etched around his eyes and mouth. Just casual observations, she assured herself.

"For just a moment, I thought she looked a little familiar," she said. "But I just can't place her. I honestly don't remember meeting her. I simply have no idea how I ended up in her will."

She met Ethan's eyes without flinching when he searched her expression, clearly trying to gauge her honesty. After what felt like a very long scrutiny, he nodded, though she couldn't tell from his expression whether he'd decided to believe her, or was still withholding judgment. She didn't know why she should be so anxious about that—it wasn't as if his opinion mattered that much to her, she assured herself.

"As Sean pointed out, my mother was a...difficult and complex woman," Ethan said. "I never understood what went on in her mind, and I'm not sure anyone else ever really knew her that well, either—including the two men she chose to marry for social and financial reasons."

Brenda noted that Sean didn't seem particularly offended by his stepbrother's assessment of their respective fathers' marriages to Margaret. Maybe he was already familiar with Ethan's opinions—or maybe he agreed with them.

"God only knows why she picked you," Ethan continued. "To be honest, I'm not sure she did you any favors. The money never made her happy—and it sure as hell didn't give me a cheerful childhood or a close family. It would have been just like her to choose a stranger just to more clearly illustrate her contempt for me and the choices I've made."

She saw the pain clearly this time, the old feelings of loneliness and rejection. It was odd, really—neither his voice nor his expression had changed, both remaining distant and guarded, clearly intended to reveal as little about himself as possible. She wondered for a moment if she was only imagining that she observed more. Projecting, as well as she could, how she herself would have felt in his position.

She turned impulsively to Sean. "What if I refuse the inheritance? What if I don't want it?"

All three men looked at her as though she had lost her mind.

"Brenda—" Richard murmured, placing a warning hand on her arm.

"You certainly have the prerogative to refuse," Sean answered her slowly. "Though I can't imagine why—"

"If I refuse," she insisted, "would everything go back to Ethan? Free and clear?"

Sean nodded. "In the event of your death without offspring or your refusal of the inheritance, the estate would revert to Ethan. Should he predecease you, also without children, everything is to be divided between Ethan's cousin, Leland Grassel, and a few select charities. Margaret made it impossible for you to leave the estate, itself, to your siblings, though should you accept it, the generous annual stipend is yours to bank, invest and pass on as you desire. All of this was explained to you already."

She made an impatient, dismissive gesture with one hand. "I didn't understand all the legalese. I still don't, for that matter."

"Just don't make any impulsive decisions, Brenda," Sean advised without looking at his stepbrother.

She moistened her lips nervously and spoke to Ethan, trying to gauge his reaction. "She was your mother. This was your home."

"And I walked away from it," he said roughly. "Hell, I *ran* away from it. The only memories left for me in this house are miserable ones."

"And that should make *me* want to live here?"

He shrugged. "Maybe it will be different for you."

"And if I refuse? Are you going to walk away from it all again? Let it go to your cousin?"

"I dislike my cousin only marginally more than I dislike my mother's petty, vindictive games," he replied evenly. "I wouldn't willingly give him anything."

"Then you *would* accept the inheritance," Richard charged, not sounding at all surprised.

"I would probably leave it in the trust for my kids, in the unlikely event that I ever have any," Ethan answered after only a moment's consideration. "At the very least, I'd make Leland wait around for me to die before he could enjoy the fruits of my grandfather's and my father's labors in that damned law firm."

"Not to mention *my* father's labors," Sean murmured. "And my own, for that matter. I'd like to believe I'm still contributing to keeping the firm financially solvent—as well as Margaret's many other investments, for that matter. But the point is, Brenda, this is what Margaret wanted. Ethan's already told me he has no intention of contesting the will."

She bit her lip, feeling terrible about this entire situation. Even having never known Margaret Jacobs, even having been treated quite generously by the woman, she still found herself actively—and perhaps unfairly—disliking her. How could any woman hurt her own son this way?

"Do you mind if I ask you one personal question?" She spoke softly to Ethan, looking up into his eyes to exclude the others from this conversation.

Ethan frowned, considered for a moment, then shrugged. "Might as well ask. Doesn't mean I'll answer."

"Fair enough. What drove you and your mother apart?"

He seemed oddly startled by that question. "I wouldn't go to law school," he said after another lengthy pause.

She waited for more. When it didn't come, she asked, "Surely that wasn't all of it. She wouldn't have disinherited you for that reason alone, would she?"

"That was the most important reason, as far as she was concerned. Law school symbolized her need to control me and my future—and I couldn't live with that."

"What *did* you want? Are you pursuing it?"

Looking even more surprised, he nodded slowly. "I own a landscape design business. Small-time right now, but I have plans for it. She said she had no intention of acknowledging a 'common gardener' as her son. That's a direct quote, by the way."

It was her turn, now, to decide if he could be believed—just as he was still making up his mind about her insistence that she had never met Margaret Jacobs. She turned to Richard, gazing up at him in an appeal for his guidance. "This isn't fair," she said. "I never asked for this. It isn't right for me to have what should be his."

Richard placed his hands on her shoulders. "You'll do what you think is right. But don't make up your mind too quickly, Bren. Take time to think about all the ramifications. As Sean pointed out, this is what Margaret wanted. She must have had her reasons."

Torn between her acknowledgement of the validity of his advice and her desire to walk away from this entire quagmire and go back to her life exactly as it had been before, she twisted her hands in front of her. A soft meow made her look down. The cats had followed them upstairs. The calico and the white one were winding themselves around her ankles, while the other two had jumped onto the bed, looking perfectly comfortable there.

"I don't—"

"Let me make this easy for you," Ethan said roughly, turning toward the huge triple dresser against one wall. He opened a small top drawer, plucked out a gold pocket watch, showed it to them all, then stuffed it in his pocket. "The shaving mug is in a cabinet in the master bathroom—at least, it was the last time I saw it. I'm not sure where the Bible is, but once I find it, I'm out of here. Sean's quite right, Brenda. I have no intention of fighting you for anything. You and the cats are welcome to all of it."

"But—"

"Listen to your brother, Brenda," Sean broke in. "Don't make any decisions now. Give yourself time to understand exactly what you'd be giving up. Maybe to try to figure out why Margaret chose you."

Picking up little Angel and holding the warm, purring body close against her, Brenda eyed Ethan from beneath her lashes as she nodded slowly. "All right. But I'm not committing to anything at this point."

"No one's asking you to," Sean assured her. "Well—except for taking care of the cats. The temporary care I arranged for them ends today. If you can't at least come feed them every day starting tomorrow, I'll have to have them boarded or something until we decide what to do with them."

"Don't look at me," Ethan muttered, glaring at the cats on the bed with what might have been animosity. "I don't do cats."

That made it easier for Brenda to nod and say, "I'll take care of them."

Looking relieved, Sean smiled. "Great. I'll get you the keys and security codes before you leave this evening."

"You're just going to give me the keys to this place?" she asked in disbelief.

"Why not? The whole estate is yours to use now. As trustee, I have the authority to turn it over to you at any time, even though there's still the formality of probate to seal the deal. We'll discuss the other arrangements after Ethan's collected his things."

Brenda looked at the portrait over the bed. Was it only her overactive imagination again, or did Margaret look smugly satisfied, as if everything was going exactly the way she had planned?

Feeling an eerie sense of being trapped in a web woven by a very clever and conniving spider, she tightened her grip on the timid calico and averted her eyes from the portrait.

SEVERAL HOURS LATER, Ethan paced restlessly through his own bungalow, trying to wind down enough to go to bed. He needed to be at a job site early the next morning, and he really should get some rest first. Still he paced, trying to draw his usual comfort from his casual decor and his collection of quirky and light-hearted curios. All so different from the house he'd left that evening, a reassuring reminder that his life was his own now.

Yet he couldn't stop pacing. Couldn't turn off the questions swirling around in his head.

Had Brenda seriously considered turning down the inheritance, or had she simply been putting on a show to allay his suspicions? If it had all been an act, she really should move to Hollywood, because there was a gold statuette there with her name on it.

What financially strapped young schoolteacher-slash-bank teller would walk away from a sizable, unexpected windfall? Then again, a lot of people had thought *he* was crazy when he'd turned his back on that same money at the age of twenty-one. And again three years ago, when he'd reiterated his determination not to claim a penny of it if it meant sacrificing the independence he had worked so hard to attain.

But he'd had a good reason to walk away. What was Brenda's reason? Guilt? Pity? He didn't want either of those emotions aimed at him. Could be the lady was just a little impulsive. A little too emotional.

He paused by his dresser, studying the gold watch and the gold-rimmed, white china mustache cup sitting there side by side. Both had been exactly where he'd expected to find them.

He hadn't found the Bible.

He couldn't believe his mother would have gotten rid of something she'd known had been that important to him. It was his history, a connection to the father he had known so briefly, to the grandmother who had died when he was still a toddler. Neither side of his family was particularly long-lived; his only connection to his ancestors had been the few things they had left behind, and that his parents had kept. The Bible had meant something to his father, and even Margaret had once treated it with some respect. So what had she done with it?

After searching for half an hour, he'd given up, trying to hide his disappointment. Once again, Brenda had seemed distressed on his behalf. If the emotions she had displayed that evening were genuine, she really needed to get control of that soft heart of hers. Or someone was going to stomp it flat.

He'd left her with a request that if she ever found his grandmother's Bible, she should have it delivered to him. She had promised earnestly to do so and had then added, "I still haven't made a decision about what to do."

Keeping his skepticism firmly in place, he had merely nodded and replied, "Might as well enjoy the money. Someone should."

He didn't really ever expect to hear from her again. Even if she had been serious about refusing the inheritance, he was sure someone—her brother, for example—would talk her out of it. She would settle into the house with the cats and a generous income, and it wouldn't be long before she developed a taste for the good life. And then, so much for Miss Wide-Eyed Innocence.

Throwing himself onto his bed, he lay on his back and stared at the ceiling, his mind filled for a time with uncomfortably vivid images of those big blue eyes.

CHAPTER FOUR

RICHARD ACCOMPANIED Brenda to the house again on Saturday to take care of the cats. She was rather nervous when she punched in the security codes and unlocked the doors—almost as if she expected the police to arrive at any moment and haul her away for breaking and entering.

Sean had spent quite a bit of time showing them around the place, telling her where to find everything she needed for the cats—food, treats, litter boxes and so on—even giving her the key to Margaret's late-model Mercedes. "Everything is here for your use," he'd reminded her when she expressed surprise. "You can move in at any time. Just let me know when you would like to do so, and we'll make arrangements to have Margaret's things boxed up and stored or sold—with the proceeds going back into the estate, of course—and your things brought in."

"First thing I would do to this place is to bring in some lighter colors," Richard said critically as he followed her and the four attention-hungry felines to the kitchen. "Everything's so dark and formal, not really your style."

"My style now is pretty much hand-me-downs and resale shops. I wouldn't know how to begin redecorating a place like this. If I were to decide to live here, that is."

"You might as well. I know you feel guilty about Ethan, but you shouldn't. This was his mother's choice. And his. You heard him say he didn't want the place."

She glanced around the large kitchen with its commercial-quality appliances and impressive array of modern conveniences. "Yes, but, really, Richard. Can you honestly see me living in a place like this?"

He gave her the smile she loved most—the one that was warm and sweet, natural and unguarded. A smile she hadn't seen very often since his painful and unpleasant divorce a couple of years earlier. "I can't imagine anyone who deserves it more," he said simply. "You'll be well set financially, but I can't imagine you letting it change you."

Brenda couldn't imagine anything staying the same if she moved in here. She wasn't sure how her friends were going to react to her new circumstances. She had talked to her sister for a long time by telephone that morning, and even Linda was still having trouble comprehending that her little sister had suddenly become a wealthy woman.

While Linda had said she was pleased by Brenda's good fortune, there had been some awkwardness in the conversation. After all, Brenda was well aware that Linda and James, her husband, had been through serious financial problems after the failure of a small business in which James had invested almost everything they had. The business failure had almost driven them into bankruptcy. They had been working very hard—James at two jobs—ever since to recover, accepting little help from anyone except for free baby-sitting by James's mother, who lived close to them.

At least Richard still acted the same around her—so far. He had been overprotective before, and that hadn't changed. She couldn't imagine how he would react if she told him about the creepy phone calls, another of which had awakened her at five o'clock that morning.

A loudly ringing telephone interrupted her thoughts, the unexpected and eerily coincidental sound making her jump. She looked at her brother for a moment, then found the telephone extension beneath a cherry cabinet. After hesitating only a moment longer, she picked up the receiver. "Hello?"

Nothing. Gripped by an all-too-familiar tension, she repeated, "Hello? Is anyone there?"

She heard the breathing. Rapid. Agitated. Angry. And then the crash of someone slamming the other phone into a cradle.

Her hand wasn't quite steady when she hung up the extension.

"Brenda?" Richard frowned as he studied her face, which she would bet had just lost several shades of color. "What's wrong? Who was that?"

To give herself a moment before answering, she walked to the cabinet in which the cat food was stored and pulled out the heavy plastic container filled with kibble. She poured portions of the food into four matching ceramic bowls arranged on a large mat in one corner of the spacious kitchen, then carried water dishes to the stainless steel sink to wash and refill. "This sink is huge," she said. "I could almost take a bath in it."

"You aren't answering me. What was that phone call? Why did you look so shaken when you hung up?"

"It was probably a wrong number. Or maybe someone who was expecting the housekeeper," Brenda prevaricated. "Whoever it was didn't say anything. He—or she—hung up after I spoke. I guess I'm still just feeling anxious about being in this house. Like I'm trespassing or something, and I'm going to get caught at any minute."

Richard seemed to accept her cowardly explanation as reason enough for her show of nerves. He patted her shoulder, then reached around her to assist with carrying the water bowls to the mat. "The interloper feeling will fade as you spend more time here. Especially when you have your own things around."

"Even if I do move in, I don't see my things fitting into this place."

"Then bring in some new things that do fit in. Sean said you have quite a bit of freedom, as long as you clear any major changes with him. It isn't as if you can't afford it. Your monthly household allowance is more than you've been making in salary up until now—and that doesn't even count your annual income. You can hire a decorator to help you change things more to your tastes."

For some reason, that made her think of Carly D'Alessandro, and her friendly, confident-looking smile.

Brenda could use a little of Carly's confidence, herself, just now.

"OKAY, ONE…TWO…THREE…*push.*" With a grunt of exertion, Ethan strained to shift a massive, flat boulder, assisted by the two young men who worked with him on most of his landscaping jobs. They were used to working Saturdays like this when a deadline loomed, and they worked hard and mostly without complaint, so he paid them as well as he could, keeping them all happy.

The boulder would be the centerpiece of a stylized cactus garden. It had been set into place by the small front-end loader Ethan used at most bigger job sites, but he'd decided it needed to be moved some six inches to the right. Once that was accomplished, he stepped back, mopped his forehead with his shirtsleeve and surveyed the results.

"Yeah, okay," he said. "That looks better."

Accustomed to his perfectionism on the job sites, Bud and Manuel nodded in relief and moved off to bring the buckets of white rocks that would be poured around the base of the boulder.

"So this is what you do."

Recognizing the voice immediately, Ethan turned reluctantly to eye the heavyset man who stood behind him. "What are you doing here, Leland?"

His cousin looked around the site for a moment before answering. The job was a sweeping lawn around a newly constructed house in a golf-course community just outside of Dallas. The houses were big, a bit cookie-cutter in style, designed to appeal to young, upwardly mobile couples out to impress their coworkers. Having a friend who was a contractor had led Ethan to several profitable assignments. His work had gotten quite a bit of positive attention and leads on several new contracts. As proud as he was of his accomplishments, he doubted that Leland would appreciate his efforts.

His cousin proved him right. "You should be buying a house like this, not doing the gardening for it."

"Sounds just like something Mother would have said. What did you do, promise you'd harass me in her place after her death?"

He wouldn't have been overly surprised if Leland agreed. Kissing up to his aunt had been forty-year-old Leland's primary job for the past few years, though officially he worked as an executive in a mortgage loan company—a position Margaret had secured for him when he'd disappointed the family by flunking out of law school. Leland made a good income, but not enough to support him in the style to which he would have liked to become accustomed. Margaret's estate would have supplemented his lifestyle quite nicely— a fact he'd surely been counting on since Margaret and Ethan's final split.

"Why are you here?" Ethan repeated when his cousin refused to respond to his sarcasm.

"You're never at home and you wouldn't return my calls." Leland's voice had just a slightly whiny edge that had always gotten on Ethan's nerves. But then, he had never liked the guy, so maybe he was predisposed to find fault with him. "I had to hunt you down just to talk to you."

"I didn't return your calls because I have nothing to say to you." Ethan motioned to his crew to keep working. "I notice you didn't bother to try to call me until after Mother's cremation. Thoughtful of you to notify me of her death."

"I thought Sean called you." This time the whine was unmistakable. "He handled everything else, didn't he?"

"Neither of you were overly concerned about letting me know."

"Well, why should we be? You hadn't even spoken to your mother in three years. Do you know how badly that hurt her?"

"No, as a matter of fact, I don't. She might have been furious, but I sincerely doubt that she shed any tears over me."

"Tears didn't come easily to Aunt Margaret. You know that. It didn't mean she didn't care."

"Uh-huh. She cared so much about both of us that she left her house and the proceeds of all her investments to a total stranger."

Leland flushed a mottled red that had the unfortunate effect of making his round face look rather like a tomato. "That's why I want to talk to you. The will hasn't been through probate yet. There's still a chance for us to fight it in court."

"I have no intention of fighting it."

Leland spoke more gruffly to hide the intimidation he'd often displayed around Ethan, despite being almost ten years older. "You can act as nonchalant as you want, but you know this isn't right. Who is this Prentiss woman? What kind of scam did she run to pull this off? She could very well be a professional con artist. Are you okay with having her get away with that? Profit from it?"

"Sean found no reason to believe Brenda Prentiss is anything other than what she appears to be—a young schoolteacher who doesn't remember ever meeting Mother."

"There's something fishy about that. Margaret wouldn't have just chosen a name at random."

"Mother did anything she wanted, however she wanted to do it," Ethan said flatly. "Of course, she thought she was the only one who had that right. Everyone else was supposed to march to her orders."

"Fine. Then fight *her.* Don't let her get away with screwing us out of the family estate."

"Us?"

"Well, you know. Family. Margaret was my mother's sister. Even if you walked away from it, the estate should have gone to me, damn it, rather than some stranger. Part of that money came from my grandfather, too."

"Your mother inherited as much as mine did when Grandpa died. Then your parents lost most of theirs through frivolous spending and bad investments while Mother made sure she held primary control of the law firm through a couple of shrewd marriages. I suppose if you really want to emulate Mother, you can divorce Patty Ann and marry a rich attorney. Or two."

From what he knew about Leland's spend-happy, younger wife, the divorce alone would boost his financial situation significantly. Margaret had detested Patty Ann, which could well be part of the reason Leland had been cut out of the will with nothing more than a token bequest his wife would run through in less than a year.

Ethan wouldn't have been particularly surprised if Leland would have dumped his wife had Margaret ordered him to do so. But he supposed even his mother hadn't sunk that low. Or had she simply not cared enough about Leland to try to control him? She had always spoken of him with a hint of contempt in her voice.

"Hey, Ethan, where's the border of this bed supposed to be?" Manuel called out, leaning against a rake. "How far do you want these rocks spread?"

"Hang on a minute, Manuel. Look, Leland, I've got to get back to work. If you want to take this on, it's your call, but frankly, I think your chances of success are slim. Sean told me the will is legal and binding, and that Mother was in full possession of her mental faculties when she had it drawn up. You're only her nephew, so I don't know how much weight the courts will give your petition."

"But you're her son—"

"And my statement would be that I willingly distanced myself from my mother several years ago, and that she had every right to do whatever she wanted with her money."

Leland was so irate by then that his eyelids were twitching. "You'd rather have the money go to some conniving bimbo than your own cousin, wouldn't you? You hate me that much."

"I don't hate you." Ethan was just bored by now, and he made no effort to hide it. "To be honest, I don't have any strong feelings about you at all. Now, if you'll excuse me, I've got to get back to my 'gardening.'"

"You're going to regret that you wouldn't help me with this," Leland warned as Ethan turned away. "You'll get tired of digging in the dirt eventually—especially now that your mother isn't around to punish with it. You'll think of all you could have had—even if you had shared part of it with me—and you'll wish you had a chance to get it back."

Ethan had nothing more to say. Without looking

back at his infuriated cousin, he rejoined his crew, who were watching him with open curiosity. "Bring the rocks out to here," he instructed, motioning toward a spray-paint line he had drawn earlier. "The border rocks go here. Just like I've marked in the plan."

He was aware that Leland lingered a moment longer, as if trying to decide whether to try again. He was relieved when Leland apparently decided he would be wasting his time and left with an irritated squeal of car tires.

His cousin had been right about one thing, Ethan thought wryly. He would much rather see the money go to Brenda Prentiss than to Leland.

BRENDA'S ROOMS looked smaller than usual when she walked in and tossed her purse onto a rather battered table that had once belonged to her aunt Hazel. Her hand-me-downs and bargain purchases looked a bit shabbier today.

So why was she still so much more comfortable here than she'd been in Margaret's elegant mansion? That was the way she still thought of it—as Margaret's house. She didn't know if she would ever think of it as her own.

The walls of her rented home were thin, and she could hear noises drifting in from outside. Cars going by on the busy street. Children playing in the scraggly grass area that lay between the three small brick duplexes that made up the rental complex.

Prior to the week before, she'd have been able to hear sounds coming from the other half of her duplex. Her latest neighbors had just moved out, leaving the building oddly quiet. Picturing the empty apartment next door made her think again of Margaret's empty house. Those poor cats, spending all that time alone there, missing the woman who had apparently loved them. And poor Margaret, in a way, because no one else seemed to miss her at all.

She hadn't eaten lunch, so she was hungry. She opened her refrigerator and wrinkled her nose at the skimpy selection stored inside. She took out some slightly limp salad ingredients and a leftover chicken breast from the night before, deciding to combine them with a little Italian dressing and some shredded cheese for a cold chicken salad. Had her budget allowed, she would have called for takeout, but she'd spent her food allowance for that month already.

Clutching a knife, her hand froze, suspended over the chicken. It had just that moment occurred to her that she could pretty much order anything she wanted. All she had to do was pack her bags and move into Margaret's house and she would start receiving part of the money. Sean had told her that it would be perfectly legitimate for him to okay that, since Margaret's will had stipulated specifically that she wanted Brenda to take care of the cats.

No one could argue that the best way for her to care for them would be to move in with them. And she could not live there without a sufficient allowance for food, cat supplies and other household necessities. Sean had suggested a figure that had made her jaw drop. That amount would be increased significantly after the will was probated, he had informed her.

It was more money than she had ever imagined having at her disposal. As Richard had pointed out, she would be receiving more per month than she made in almost a year of teaching. There was just something…something not right about that. She hadn't done anything to earn that money, as far as she knew.

There were things she could do with the money. She could repay her school loans. She could pay off some of her sister's debts. She could help Richard get his fledging insurance business more solidly established. She could do a few things at the little school where she taught. And yet…

For some really strange reason, she found herself suddenly wanting to talk to Ethan again. She didn't know why she seemed to have become so obsessed with him after only one meeting, but she hadn't stopped thinking about him for more than a few minutes at a time since he had given up his search for his grandmother's Bible and left his mother's house.

She sighed and shook her head. This whole situation was going to drive her crazy.

SHE WOKE IN THE MIDDLE of the night to total darkness and a cacophony of unsettling sounds. Groggy and confused, she lifted her head from the pillow. A piercing shriek made her wince, and someone seemed to be hammering nearby. Was someone shouting? She coughed, realizing only then that she was having to struggle to breathe.

The smoke alarm. Finally awake enough to realize what was happening, she sat up, coughing hard. Smoke filled the room, obscuring what little light came in through the closed blinds at her one small, high-placed window.

Her bare feet hit the carpeted floor and she crouched as she moved toward the open doorway, trying to stay below the smoke. She had just enough presence of mind to remember that was the proper procedure during a fire.

Fire. Even the thought of the word caused panic to rise in her throat, pushing out another hard cough. She made a deliberate effort to stay calm as she made her way blindly through the short, smoke-filled hallway.

The pounding grew louder as she neared the front door. Her eyes streaming now, she fumbled with the locks, trying to hold her breath in an effort to control the coughing. The door opened, and a pair of arms reached in to pull her outside. She drew in big gulps of fresh air, and was then wracked by spasms of renewed coughing. The wail of sirens sounded in the distance, getting louder as they drew closer. People were milling around in her yard, jabbering in excitement, lit by a strange, orange flickering glow.

The young man who had pulled her out of her house pounded on her back. "Are you okay?"

"She will be if you stop hitting her," someone else said.

"She's coughing! I'm just trying to help."

"You're about to knock her flat on her face. How's that helping?"

"I'm okay," Brenda gasped, quickly sidestepping any further "assistance." "Thank you."

She shivered, more from reaction than cold. Her purple T-shirt-and-shorts pj's set was both modest enough and warm enough for the summer night, but someone wrapped a blanket around her shoulders. Murmuring her appreciation, she huddled into it. Her eyes were focused on the duplex—and the smoke now billowing from the windows.

She could have died in there, she thought numbly. And she couldn't help wondering if someone had tried to ensure that very outcome.

ETHAN HAD NOT EXPECTED to return to his mother's house. He certainly hadn't predicted he would do so within days of leaving for what he had thought would be the last time. But then, he hadn't expected to be accused of attempted murder two days later, either.

He punched the doorbell, then barely gave it time to finish chiming before hitting it again. Richard Prentiss opened the door.

"So," Ethan snarled, eyeing Brenda's brother with animosity, "have you moved in, too?"

Prentiss scowled. "I'm just here for my sister. What do you want?"

"I want to talk to her."

"What about?"

His voice cold, he replied, "That would be my business, not yours."

"For heaven's sake, Richard, would you let him in?" Brenda sounded vaguely irritated when she spoke from behind her brother. "I'm sorry, Ethan. He's being way overprotective today."

"Yeah, well, it's a good thing I'm here now," Richard growled, still glaring at Ethan like a tough guy in a Hollywood bodyguard role. "You would just welcome him inside, I guess."

"Of course I would. Why wouldn't I?"

"Oh, I don't know. Maybe because someone tried to turn you into toast last night?"

Brenda planted both hands on her hips and glared at her brother. "He had a solid alibi. He was playing poker with friends until after the fire was set."

Ethan was unreasonably irked that she knew that.

"Yeah, well, he could have hired someone to do it."

Losing patience, Ethan slammed the door behind

him, causing the squabbling siblings to turn simultaneously to look at him. "He can speak for himself."

Brenda blinked, then nodded toward the living room where they'd first met. "Come in, Ethan."

She wavered a minute after they entered the room, looking uncertain about her role as de facto hostess in his former home. He settled that, himself, waving her to one of the two chintz-covered couches while he sat on the edge of a carved-wood-and-brocade chair. Richard stood behind the couch where his sister sat, still in his bodyguard role.

As if summoned by a signal inaudible to humans, the four cats appeared en masse from the doorway, swarming through the room, sniffing ankles, tumbling over each other and finally staying close to Brenda, the calico in her lap. Both Brenda and her brother were dressed very casually—jeans, sneakers and comfortable tops—as if settled in for a lazy Sunday afternoon at home. Unlike the last time they'd seen each other, Brenda wore no makeup, and her blond hair was pulled into a loose ponytail rather than neatly styled.

She still looked good, he thought reluctantly.

"I see you've chosen to move in here, after all," he said, making a quick decision to stay on the offensive.

"It wasn't as if she had much choice," Richard snapped. "Someone burned down the place where she lived before. When he heard about it, Sean suggested—and I agreed—that she would be safer here for now than in some temporary, rented place."

"Yes, I heard about the fire," Ethan shot back. "A P.I. came to my house today to ask me where I was last night. It was pretty clear he saw me as an arson suspect."

Brenda's fingers twisted in her lap. "We don't know for certain that it was arson," she said. "It's still under investigation."

"What happened?"

She shrugged. "It started in the kitchen. It was suggested that perhaps I left a burner on, and maybe a pot holder or a tea towel caught fire."

"Did you?"

"I don't think so. But I couldn't swear that I didn't, either. I was distracted last night. Talking on the phone with a friend, then stewing a while about all this inheritance stuff. I suppose it's possible that I left a burner on by accident."

He searched her face, noting that she was pale, a bit hollow eyed, but otherwise looked okay. "Were you hurt?"

"No. I inhaled some smoke, but nothing serious. I was checked out at the emergency room and then released to my brother."

"What about your things? Was your place a total loss?"

"Pretty much," she replied, her voice a bit huskier now and what might have been a quick sheen of tears in her eyes. She continued tonelessly, "I lost just about everything. Richard had to buy me a few clothes and necessities at a twenty-four-hour Wal-Mart on the way to his place from the hospital. I didn't have anything particularly valuable—some hand-me-down furniture and discount store items. A few things that belonged to my mother and my aunt."

And those were the possessions for which she grieved today, he thought, reading the emotions she was trying to hide.

He didn't know whether to tell her he was sorry for her loss or to remind her that she would never have to shop at a discount store again if she didn't want to. Because he still hadn't decided quite what to make of her, he did neither. Instead, he asked, "Did you cook dinner last night?"

She seemed surprised that he'd asked—as if no one else had thought to do so. "Um, no, I didn't, actually. I made a cold chicken salad from leftovers."

"And did you turn a burner on later? After dinner?"

She frowned in concentration. "I thought about putting the kettle on for tea—but then I changed my mind. I think. I honestly don't remember whether I turned a burner on or not."

"Are you trying to convince her that she caused the fire?" Richard demanded aggressively.

"Actually, I'm just trying to find out if it's *possible* she caused the fire. And then I want to know why she hired a private investigator, and why he felt it necessary to interrogate me about my whereabouts last night."

"Isn't it obvious?" Richard asked. "If anything happens to my sister, you're the one with the most to gain."

Ethan pushed down a surge of anger, since he had learned years ago that in any confrontation, cool and collected was much more effective than heated and emotional. It was one of the lessons he had learned from his late mother.

"I told you I won't fight for my mother's estate. I sure as hell wouldn't kill for it," he said evenly.

"As if you'd admit it."

"Look, I haven't come in here throwing around accusations, have I? What if I accused your sister of setting the fire herself?"

"Why the *hell* would she do that?"

"Oh, I don't know. Maybe to give her an excuse to move right in here without waiting for probate? To turn the sentiment her way in the will settlement? To claim needs that outweigh the trustee's natural discretion in giving her advances from the estate?"

"You son of—"

"Richard, would you mind making a pot of tea?" Brenda asked quickly, half turning on the couch to look up at him. "My throat's still pretty raspy from the smoke."

Furious with Ethan, Richard seemed almost stunned by her request. "You want me to leave you in here alone with him?"

"You don't really think he's going to set fire to the living room while you're gone, do you?"

Her dry question made the corners of Ethan's mouth twitch with a reluctant half smile.

Richard shook his head. "This isn't a joke, Brenda."

"I realize that. Please."

Her brother hesitated, glaring from her to Ethan and back again, then turned with a frustrated exhale and stalked out of the room, leaving Ethan and Brenda alone for the first time.

CHAPTER FIVE

BRENDA TURNED BACK to Ethan apologetically after Richard was gone. "He's several years older than I am," she explained. "Our parents are both dead. He thinks that makes him responsible for watching out for me. This…well, this unexpected development in my life has sort of thrown him off-kilter. He doesn't quite know what he should be doing."

"So he takes it out on me."

"I'm afraid so."

Ethan sat back in the chair and rested his right ankle on his left knee. "He did make a valid point, you know. I *am* the obvious suspect if something happens to you."

She held his gaze steadily. "I know."

"That's why you sent the P.I. to interrogate me?"

"I'm sure that's why he came to see you. It would be an obvious first stop for him."

"When did you hire him?"

"Thursday. After someone tried to run me down with a truck."

He dropped his foot to the floor, momentarily startled out of his nonchalant pose. Brenda would have bet anything that his surprise was genuine. "Someone tried to run you down?"

"Yes. I missed being hit by a matter of inches. I had

almost convinced myself it was merely a frightening near accident, a random act of recklessness, but after last night…well, I can't help wondering."

He searched her face. "You really think someone is trying to kill you?"

She couldn't quite suppress an instinctive shiver. "I don't want to believe that, obviously. But you must admit it looks suspicious. Within days after I received this inheritance, I was involved in two near tragedies. I lead a quiet life, Mr. Blacklock. Things like this don't happen to me."

"It's Ethan. And my life isn't exactly nonstop excitement, either. I'm a simple landscape designer."

She didn't smile. "I don't think you're a 'simple' anything."

"The question is, do you believe I'm a potential killer?"

She hid a ripple of nerves behind a lifted chin and a cool tone. "You're the one who pointed out that you're the obvious suspect. However, you did have a solid alibi last night. And Tony, the private investigator, said you had an equally strong alibi last Thursday morning, when the truck almost hit me. You were on a job site with a client and a crew."

"I don't like having someone check up on me without my knowledge," he said with a scowl. "It sounds like something my mother would have done. I hope you haven't inherited her arrogance along with her money, Miss Prentiss."

"It's Brenda," she replied, mimicking him from earlier. "And I didn't give the investigator specific instructions. I simply asked him to try to find out how I ended up in your mother's will, and whether there's anyone upset enough about it to try to hurt me because of it."

"And naturally he thought of me."

"Naturally," she agreed.

He leaned forward, his expression grave. "Look, Brenda. I understand you've been through a lot this past week, and I can see why you'd be searching for answers. Heck, I would be, too. But I've got to tell you, I doubt that anyone's targeting you because of my mother's will. For one thing, I really am the only one who would benefit if anything should happen to you. For some reason we'll never figure out, Mother set up the will so that your siblings would get nothing, so they're obviously not suspects. My cousin is a jerk who would have loved to get his hands on Mother's estate, but he wouldn't get it if anything happened to you, either—not unless something happened to me, too."

"So it keeps coming back to you."

"I guess it does. But if that's the case, then you're perfectly safe. I haven't tried to harm you—and I have no intention of doing so in the future. You can believe that or not, but it's the truth. This place, that money—it never made me happy, when I lived here before. It never made my father happy, and God knows my mother never was. I can't see where it's brought much luck to you so far, either."

"Trying to scare her into turning everything back over to you?" Richard asked as he came back into the room carrying a steaming cup of tea. Still glaring at Ethan, he handed the cup to Brenda.

She accepted it with a sigh. "You could have brought something for everyone. Would you like anything, Ethan?"

"No, thanks. I've got work to do." He stood, pretty much ignoring Richard as he focused on her. "I just wanted to know if I should expect to be hauled off to jail anytime soon."

"I shouldn't think so," she reassured him with a slight smile in response to his dry tone. "I didn't mention the incident with the speeding truck to the police, since I had no witnesses or evidence to verify that it happened. As for the fire, that's being investigated, but everyone in authority there seemed to think it was simply my negligence that caused it."

"Unless they find evidence to the contrary," Richard interjected. She'd had to tell him about the truck after the fire, of course, and he was still fuming that he hadn't been told before. At the moment, he was taking his fear and frustration out on Ethan. "Evidence that points to you."

"That's not going to happen," Ethan responded without looking away from Brenda.

She nodded. "I'll accept your word for it—unless I'm given any reason to change my mind."

"Fair enough."

"And, by the way, I didn't intentionally set that fire, either. You can accept my word for that."

"I will—unless I'm given any reason to change my mind."

"Fair enough."

He turned and headed for the doorway, apparently intent on leaving without another word. But then he paused and looked back over his shoulder, his gaze catching and holding hers. Awareness jolted through her in a way that startled her. The one thing she would not have expected today was to fight an inconveniently timed attraction to Ethan.

"You should keep the security systems turned on," he advised. "Mother didn't have much patience for such matters. She didn't think any common criminal would presume to touch her things. She wouldn't install a gate because she didn't want to block the view of her rose gardens from the neighbors she wanted to impress. But she did have a state-of-the-art security system installed throughout the house, and I know she kept it maintained."

Even though she told herself it was foolish to be touched by his show of concern—which could very well be nothing more than an act—she was, anyway. "Thanks. I will. Sean showed me how to work everything."

After hesitating only a heartbeat longer, he turned and left, not waiting for anyone to show him out.

"There's something about that guy that rubs me the wrong way," Richard muttered after Ethan was gone.

As if to more clearly illustrate how muddled her mind had become during the past few days, Brenda found herself wondering how it would feel to be rubbed the *right* way by Ethan Blacklock.

CARLY PARKED HER CAR in front of the house that had belonged to the late Margaret Jacobs and reached for the envelope on the passenger seat beside her. Though courier service wasn't high on her list of favorite pastimes, it certainly beat sitting at a computer being harassed by Peck the Prick. It was a pretty Monday afternoon and besides, she liked Brenda Prentiss, from what little she knew of her. Not to mention that she had been intrigued by Brenda's story.

Her father hadn't discussed the case with her. He

would have considered that unethical. He just didn't realize how skilled she was at figuring out what was going on around her. A bit of judicious eavesdropping, some surreptitious, upside-down file reading, a little putting two and two together—and she knew a lot more about the ongoing investigations than anyone suspected. Hey, it was more interesting than figuring accounts payable and accounts receivable, she told herself self-righteously.

So, anyway, Brenda Prentiss had apparently inherited money from a mysterious benefactor. And now it was possible that someone was trying to kill her because of it. Which was terrible, of course, because Brenda seemed like a really nice person—but Carly had to admit that it was the most interesting thing that had happened since school let out for the summer.

Carrying the envelope she had been asked to deliver, she ran lightly up the steps to the front door. Nice house. Almost as big as the one she'd grown up in, though there wasn't as much land surrounding this one. Carly was in the rather unusual position of having been raised by a mother who'd inherited a great deal of money from the parents who had adopted her as a toddler, and a father who hailed from a huge, proudly working-class Italian-American clan. As a result, she was comfortable in almost every situation, and not easily impressed by flashy material possessions.

She pressed the doorbell, hoping Brenda would invite her inside. It would be rude not to linger awhile if Brenda was in the mood for company. And if she just happened to stay for more than a few minutes, it would be too late for her to return to the office that afternoon.

It wasn't Brenda who opened the door, but a tall,

rather nice-looking man with dark blond hair thinning at the temples, narrowed blue eyes and a forbidding frown that faded a bit when he saw her. Perhaps he'd been expecting someone else?

"I'm Carly D'Alessandro," she said. "From D'Alessandro and Walker Investigations? I have a delivery for Brenda Prentiss."

"I'm her brother, Richard. I'll accept it for her."

Looking him straight in the eye, Carly lied, "I'm supposed to give it to Brenda personally. You understand, I'm sure."

He searched her face, then did a quick up-and-down sweep that was totally checking her out. Carly knew that look, and she was glad she had worn a flattering scoop-neck white top and a short khaki skirt that made the most of her legs. There was a fresh coat of glittery lavender polish on the toenails revealed by her heeled thongs, and his attention seemed to linger there for a moment before he stepped back with a slight jerk and a faint flush on his cheeks. "Come in. Brenda's in the—uh, the den."

Amused, Carly strolled inside, giving her glossy black hair an extra little swing on the way past him. She was aware that Brenda had just moved into the house the day before, and it was obvious that Richard was still trying to figure out how to refer to all the rooms.

As for the decor… She wrinkled her nose. "Stuffy," she pronounced. "Looks like it was decorated by someone's grandmother. Not mine, she's cool—but somebody's."

Richard seemed surprised by her frank assessment of the place. She realized she spoke without thinking sometimes—okay, lots of times—a trait that had gotten her into hot water on numerous occasions, but she couldn't imagine why he'd be offended by her comments. It wasn't as if he'd personally decorated this house.

And then he smiled. The transformation to his face made her stop and stare at him, her breath lodging hard in her throat. "You're right," he said. "That's exactly what this place feels like."

Wow, she thought, her head spinning a little. Mr. Buttoned-Down had just turned into Mr. Hottie. She checked his left hand. No ring. Promising. "So you're Brenda's brother. She and I had coffee last week. I like her."

"So do I." He waved a hand toward one of the doorways that led off the foyer. "She's back this way."

"Thank you." She made sure there was an extra little swish to her step when she preceeded him. A very practiced and subtle glance back assured her that he noticed. She stifled a smile.

The Brenda Prentiss case had just become even more interesting.

BRENDA HEARD HER BROTHER enter the den, but she wasn't aware, at first, that he wasn't alone. Her back to the doorway, she sat curled into a deep sectional sofa facing a large-screen television they had discovered hidden behind paneled cherry doors in an elegant entertainment unit. A rather impressive collection of classic films on videotape and DVD filled one cabinet, along with a selection of classical music CDs. A news program was playing on the TV now, but Brenda paid little attention to what was being reported.

This room had obviously been used frequently. Two other large, comfy chairs were grouped for conversation and viewing, and a cat play area filled one corner of the large room, including carpeted climbing towers and napping platforms. Three of the cats were busy there now, the calico sleeping on the couch next to Brenda. A desk and bookcase had been built into another corner. The desk held a small computer, a very basic printer and a telephone.

A wet bar with a small refrigerator, a sink and a glass-fronted cabinet filled with sparkling stemware was located in the back corner. The refrigerator had been stocked with several types of beverages and a wine rack had been built into the base of the bar. Brenda could picture Margaret sitting in here with her cats, watching old movies and reflecting on her life. The vision made her sad, as she was getting an increasingly clear vision of a bitter, unhappy woman.

Maybe she was wrong, she mused. Maybe Margaret had been perfectly satisfied alone in her big house with her money and her pets and her antiques. Maybe she hadn't missed her husbands or her son, or regretted the things she had done to drive Ethan away.

Which was still very sad, of course, for Ethan's sake. Behind all the anger and defensiveness Ethan had displayed around her, Brenda was sure she had seen a great deal of old pain banked in his dark brown eyes. And it made her heart ache for him.

She was trying to stay objective. Trying to keep in mind, as Richard reminded her practically every few minutes, that Ethan could well be her adversary—perhaps even a dangerous one. But everything inside her rebelled against the possibility that the man she had seen as wounded, guarded, maybe a bit too stub-bornly proud, would have resorted to violence just to get his hands on his late mother's money.

"Brenda, you have a visitor," Richard said from behind her.

She stood and spun around, her heart beating a bit more quickly. She hadn't expected to see Ethan today—and she didn't.

"Carly," she said with a smile, deciding to examine her disappointment later. In private. "It's nice to see you again."

"You, too. I brought you a packet from my dad. A report, I think. He said if you have any questions to call his cell phone."

"Thank you." She took the envelope and set it on the low coffee table, turned off the TV with the remote control, then waved toward a chair. "Can you stay for a minute? Would you like something to drink?"

"I'd take a diet soda, if it isn't too much trouble," Carly agreed with an alacrity that suggested she had been hoping for an invitation.

"I'll get it." Richard moved toward the refrigerator, bumping awkwardly into the bar on his way around.

A bit surprised by his uncharacteristic clumsiness, Brenda glanced at him, and noted that he seemed to be having trouble looking away from their guest. Her left eyebrow rose a fraction of an inch. It crept a bit higher when Carly smiled up at Richard through her lashes as he handed her a glass he had filled with ice and soda, and Richard flushed in response.

Carly definitely knew how to wield that look, Brenda thought in admiration. Richard seemed very close to swallowing his tonsils.

Turning to Brenda, Carly effectively dismissed Richard—and that, too, was a clever flirtation tool, since it left Richard standing there looking a bit foolish and even more intrigued by her.

Brenda felt almost as if she should be taking notes from this expert at getting a man's undivided attention.

"Brenda, I was so sorry to hear about the fire," Carly said, suddenly somber. "Dad said you lost nearly everything."

Her amusement faded instantly at the reminder. Brenda nodded, swallowing a hard lump in her throat. She had cried enough over her lost treasures, she told herself. She wouldn't do so again—not in front of anyone, anyway. "Thank you. And, yes, my things were pretty much ruined. Anything that didn't burn was ruined by smoke and water damage."

"What are you doing for clothes?"

Brenda glanced down at the inexpensive jeans and T-shirt that, along with the similar outfit she had worn the day before, made up her entire wardrobe at the moment. "This is pretty much it, I'm afraid. I'm going to have to buy some new things. Fortunately, I had renter's insurance, so I'll be compensated for most of what I lost."

Carly lifted her perfectly arched brows. "You don't really have to worry so much about that, do you? I mean, you can afford some new clothes now, right? Surely the trustee or whoever's in charge of this estate would see to that."

Brenda couldn't help thinking about Ethan's suggestion that she could have burned down her own apartment in order to get quicker access to his mother's money. That accusation still stung, even though she knew he'd flung it mainly as a defense against the allegations Richard had been making against him.

Sean *had* offered to release some emergency funds to her as soon as he'd heard about the fire. She still just felt odd about taking the money.

Fluffy, the white cat, leapt into Carly's lap and began to knead her thighs, making a comfy place to sit. Carly smiled and patted him with the ease of someone who was fond of animals. Richard shifted in his seat, doing a terrible job of trying not to stare at their stunning guest.

Give it up, Richard, Brenda thought in indulgent amusement. She doubted very much that young, restless, beautiful Carly D'Alessandro would be interested in a divorced insurance salesman fourteen years her senior.

Carly looked up from the cat. "If you want, I can go to the mall with you and we can pick out some things. I've got a few hours available this afternoon."

"You don't have to go back to work?"

"No, I can take some time off if you need me." Carly gave her a winning smile. "I'm sure my dad would understand, you being his client and all."

Brenda couldn't help grinning at Carly's transparency. Given a choice between going back to work and shopping with Brenda, it was obvious which she preferred. And she was pretty sure she could get away with it as long as she was "helping out a client."

Because she'd have felt like a real spoilsport if she ruined Carly's clever plan, Brenda nodded. "Thanks. That would be great. But my purse was lost in the fire. I don't have a checkbook or a credit card or anything. I've ordered new ones from my bank, but it will be a couple of days before everything's replaced."

Richard reached into his back pocket and took out his wallet. "Take my credit card. Get what you need."

Oh, man, he was so full of it, Brenda thought, barely resisting rolling her eyes. He'd already bought her two discount-store outfits and a pair of sneakers—and she suspected he'd had to dip into savings to pay for those. He was doing well to keep his business afloat in addition to his living expenses. He was totally putting on an act for Carly's benefit—which was so unlike her brother that she couldn't help eyeing him quizzically as she murmured, "Um, thanks. I'll pay you back, of course."

His face just a little red, he cleared his throat. "I guess I'll clear out of your way and leave you to your shopping. It was a pleasure to meet you, Carly."

Carly gave her ridiculously long, lush lashes a bat or two. "It was nice to meet you, too."

Richard bumped into the doorjamb on his way out of the room.

Brenda blinked as she looked in the direction in which Richard had disappeared. How very odd. And then she turned to look at Carly, who was looking back at her with a grin she couldn't help returning. And then they were both laughing.

"Your brother," Carly said after a moment, "is really cute."

Brenda blinked again. "You think so?"

"Totally. So is he, like, married or anything?"

"He's divorced."

"Recently?"

"Not really. His ex has been remarried for almost a year."

"Kids?"

"No."

"So what does he do?"

"He's an insurance agent. He just opened his own office."

"Oh." She seemed a bit daunted by the prosaic reply, as if some of her initial interest in him had faded—as Brenda had expected. "Well, he's still cute."

"I think so, too—but then, I'm his sister, so I probably mean it differently than you do."

"He's going to expect you to pay him back for the clothes, you know."

Brenda chuckled. "I would insist even if he didn't expect it, and he knows that, too. He was just trying to impress you with how generous and charming he can be."

"I know." Carly's dimples flashed. "I have an older brother, too."

"How old is he?"

"Twenty-three, but he's always been Mr. Responsibility. Jason thinks being the oldest brother puts him in charge of nearly every situation."

"That's Richard," Brenda said with a commiserative sigh.

Carly set the white cat on the floor. "Ready to shop?"

Sliding Richard's credit card into her pocket, Brenda stood. "Sure. Why not?"

This could be yet another very interesting experience in a week full of surprises, she mused as she followed Carly out of the room.

"...AND THAT WILL BE EVERYTHING I need this time," Ethan concluded Monday afternoon, then stuffed a scribbled list into his jeans pocket.

Raine Scott, manager of Camelot Nursery and Outdoor Decor, stuffed her pencil into her loosely bundled brown-and-gray hair and nodded. "Everything will be delivered to the site by one o'clock tomorrow afternoon."

"Good deal. Thanks."

The woman he had known for more than twenty years looked at him with grave brown eyes. In the past millennium, Raine would have been called a hippy. Long, slightly bushy gray-streaked hair, usually worn twisted into a bun or a long braid. A wardrobe that consisted of T-shirts, beaded vests, long cotton skirts and sandals. No makeup, and jewelry that looked handmade. He didn't know much about her background, except that she and his mother had formed an odd friendship years ago based on their mutual love of gardening.

Ethan thought of Raine almost like a surrogate aunt. He had seen her nearly every Saturday during spring and summer, when the nursery had been a regular stop on his mother's Saturday errands routine—he had been expected to accompany her until he was in his midteens. Raine had even visited their home regularly, making deliveries, tending the rose gardens, decorating the house with fresh greenery and winter blooms for Christmas. Having no children of her own, she had grown fond of Ethan, encouraging his interest in plants and landscaping, teaching him about fertilizers and mulches and natural pesticides, letting him help her around the nursery when his mother agreed.

Margaret hadn't interfered when Ethan had taken a summer job at the nursery at fifteen; she'd said it would encourage him to have a strong work ethic.

She'd seemed to believe that a hot summer of manual labor would make him all the more amenable to a cushy attorney's office later. She had become concerned when he continued to work at the nursery on weekends and holidays, and the following summer, but even then she'd taken for granted that he would eventually get the gardening business out of his system.

When he had finally acknowledged during his senior year of college—after he had applied for and had been accepted to law school—that he wasn't cut out to be an attorney, he'd told Raine first. She had tried to persuade him to change his mind, pointing out that his mother would be devastated, and that he would probably never make the kind of money in the landscaping business that he could have in the guaranteed partnership that would be waiting for him when he finished law school.

Raine had actually argued with him more heatedly than he'd expected, trying to convince him to get his law degree and then decide what he wanted to do with it. But when she'd finally realized that he had made his choice, and that nothing she could say would sway him, she had reluctantly accepted his decision and offered to help him in any way she could.

Because he knew her so well, he could see that something was troubling her now. "What's wrong, Raine?"

"We haven't had a chance to talk much since Margaret died. How are you, Ethan?"

"I'm okay. Really. But thanks for asking."

"Ethan." She reached out to lay a weathered, callused hand on his, which rested on the sales counter. "She was your mother. Don't pretend to me that you haven't grieved for her, despite your differences."

He hesitated—and then he released a long breath and admitted to her what he had told no one else. "Okay. It has been rough. I just never thought it would happen like this, you know?"

"I know, hon. Like me, you probably thought you and Margaret would settle your quarrel someday. That she would accept the life you've chosen, and maybe even be proud of the success you've had with it."

"I guess that would have been too much to expect. But I think I always secretly believed we'd make up someday. Have some sort of relationship again, even if it was never a warm and fuzzy one. Even if she hadn't accepted what I did, I thought maybe someday she would acknowledge my right to choose for myself. But she couldn't even grant me that."

"I haven't seen her much in the past three years. She never really forgave me for not trying harder to talk you into going along with her wishes, even though I assured her I tried to convince you to go to law school. It was only because she knew how hard I had tried that she continued to be my friend after you quit school. But our friendship finally fell apart when you started your own business three years ago. That was such a final blow for her, and I guess she blamed me for encouraging your interest in landscaping when you were a kid."

"That was unfair. But typical of her."

"She loved you, Ethan—in her way. She didn't want you to have to struggle to get by when all that wealth and influence was available to you."

"I'm not sure she cared about that as much as her own need to brag about her son, the attorney." He knew he sounded jaded, but then, he'd dealt with Margaret a great deal more than Raine had.

"Now, Ethan, give her some credit. It isn't as if she's still here to defend herself. And what I was going to say is that, even though I didn't see her often during the past three years, when I did, I could tell that she was unhappy with the situation between the two of you. I truly believe she was working up her nerve to call you and make amends. It wasn't easy for her because of her overdeveloped pride, you know, but I think she could have overcome it eventually. It was so unfair that she passed away before she could win that personal battle."

"I guess so." Ethan wasn't so sure his mother had wanted to reconcile as much as Raine suggested, but he supposed it wouldn't hurt to humor her.

"And what's even more unfair," she continued more heatedly, "is that she didn't have time to revise her will. You know she must have changed it in the heat of temper, and that she always intended to change it back. She never would have left everything to some stranger if she'd been thinking clearly."

Ethan shrugged. At least Raine seemed to understand that the will was less important than the fact that Margaret had died without settling anything with her son. "I don't really know about that. It isn't as if I didn't expect it. Mother told me the last time I saw her that she would write me out of her will, and I had no reason to think she wouldn't follow through on that threat."

"It's just something else I'm sure she would regret if she'd had any idea…" Raine's voice trailed away as she shook her head sadly. "Is there any chance that she *did* change her mind? Perhaps she left a revised will somewhere in her house that superseded the one she made in anger."

"She didn't, Raine. She left everything to Miss Prentiss, supposedly for a reason. She handled everything through the law firm, leaving Sean in charge of administering the estate. She knew what she was doing, and she had eighteen months to change her mind if she wanted to. But don't worry about it, okay? I'm doing fine. The business is paying its way, and I still have some of my trust fund to turn to in an emergency. I'm not going to starve."

She patted his hand. "I know that. I just hate that Margaret slighted you yet again when she died. You deserved better, Ethan. You're such a good man. She should have been proud to have you as a son."

He gave her a smile. "I, for one, am proud to have you as a friend."

She flushed, and what might have been an uncharacteristic glimmer of tears brightened her eyes for a moment before she pulled her hand away. "I guess we'd both better get back to work. Don't you worry, Ethan, I'll take care of you."

Glancing at the order in her hand, he nodded. "Thanks. I'll expect the delivery at one."

"It'll be there."

He made his way outside then, feeling a bit more cheerful than he had when he'd entered, thanks to Raine.

CHAPTER SIX

PILES OF SHOPPING BAGS surrounded them in the booth as Brenda and Carly munched on nachos and sipped fruit punch at a Mexican restaurant in the mall. They had shopped for almost two hours—as interesting an experience as Brenda had predicted.

She discovered Carly had excellent taste, and had been a valuable assistant in selecting a versatile mix-and-match wardrobe for Brenda. Finally declaring she'd shopped enough, Brenda had called a halt. Carly was the one who had said she was "starving" at that point. Somehow they had ended up here, with piles of food in front of them and piles of bagged clothing around them.

"This was fun, wasn't it?" Carly said, dipping a tortilla chip into a scoop of guacamole.

"It was, actually."

"You sound surprised."

"I don't usually enjoy shopping all that much," she admitted. She didn't add that she'd actually been a bit nervous about leaving the fortress of Margaret's house, and had been unusually jumpy when they'd first arrived at the mall. Carly's enthusiasm had soon distracted her from those feelings. "It's usually hard for me to find anything I like, or that looks good on me."

"Really? Because we found a lot of things that looked great on you today."

"You have a real talent for finding the right things."

"A talent for shopping. My dad would be so proud."

Brenda chuckled in response to Carly's ironic tone. "I'm sure you have many more talents."

"Oh, sure. Just none that Dad gets overly excited about."

Brenda thought of the friendly, considerate man who had set her so at ease in his office. "Is he really so demanding?"

Carly sighed. "He's a wonderful father," she admitted. "I'm crazy about him, really. Sure, he and Mom are a little strict, but it's only because they take their responsibilities as parents so darned seriously. They want us to 'live up to our potential,' and find productive careers. But mostly, they want us to be happy."

"That's not such a bad thing."

"No, it's not. I'm grateful to have them, I really am. I just don't want to disappoint them."

"Something tells me that isn't likely to happen. I watched your dad with you. He's so proud of you, he was practically glowing."

"Thanks." Carly munched the chip, then changed the subject. "So, how does it feel to be living in the house you inherited?"

"Strange," Brenda admitted. "I picked one of the guest bedrooms to sleep in last night because I can't imagine sleeping in Margaret's bed, but I still didn't rest very well. I kept hearing strange noises."

And wondering if someone had tried to burn her apartment down while she had slept inside, she added silently.

Perhaps Carly could add mind reading to her list of talents. "Did you ever hear if the fire in your apartment was deliberately set?"

"Not for certain, but everyone seems to think it was an accident. That I left a pan on a burner, or a pot holder or dish towel too close to the stove or something like that."

"Is that what *you* think happened?"

Brenda wished she could answer. As hard as she had tried, she could not remember turning on the stove Saturday evening. She was certain she'd changed her mind about putting the kettle on, and she didn't know why she would have turned on a burner for any other reason. But did she really believe someone had sneaked into her kitchen and deliberately set the fire?

"I just don't know."

"Brenda." Carly set her glass down and leaned forward over the table. "I know I'm not supposed to know very much about your case, and I promise my father hasn't told me much of anything, but I have another talent. Snooping. I know you've inherited a lot of money from someone you don't remember ever meeting, and I know you've had some disturbing things happen to you since you found out about it. This whole thing must be really weird for you."

Torn between bemusement at her frank admission of snooping and appreciation for the genuine concern in Carly's dark eyes, Brenda nodded. "It has been… bizarre. Two weeks ago, I was broke, living in a cheap duplex, saving pennies for a budget vacation. Now I'm living in a mansion, taking care of four cats and being told that I'll have access to more money than I can even imagine spending. Strange things have happened to

me, making me downright paranoid about my safety for
the first time in my life. I've met the son and stepson
of the woman who left me all of this—one has reason
to hate me, and the other is going to be in charge of everything I receive for the foreseeable future."

"Wow." Carly's eyes were huge now. "No wonder
you're feeling all freaked."

"That, is an understatement," Brenda said fervently.

"So, tell me about the stepbrothers. Is either one
cute?"

Brenda was startled into a laugh by Carly's question.
She thought of how young Carly was—but once again,
she suspected that Carly was more mature than the
average twenty-year-old. She would almost bet that unexpected question had been a deliberate ploy to distract
her from her anxiety, and maybe make her smile.

"Actually, they both are," she replied, picturing
Sean and Ethan. Especially Ethan. While Sean might
be the more polished and classically handsome,
Ethan's rather rough, and all-natural masculinity was
the more fascinating, as far as Brenda was concerned.

"Yeah? Tell me about the one who doesn't hate
you."

Brenda hoped neither of them did, but she knew
who Carly referred to. "Sean Jacobs. Margaret's
stepson, and trustee of the estate. He's been quite
helpful. He's one of the few—other than your father—
who seems to believe me when I say I have no idea
why Margaret made me her beneficiary."

"Is he married?"

Still smiling, Brenda used a tortilla chip to scoop
up a bite of meat, beans, cheese and sour cream. "I
don't know for certain, but I don't think so."

"Mmm." Carly tapped her chin for a moment, then shook her head. "Better be suspicious if he starts getting too flirty too soon. He might have figured that if he couldn't inherit the money, maybe he can marry it. Not that he wouldn't be genuinely attracted to you, of course," she added hastily. "You're so pretty and interesting, any guy would be nuts *not* to ask you out."

"Thanks," Brenda said dryly. Now, not only did she have to worry about someone trying to kill her for the money, she'd be concerned about someone wanting to romance her for it.

Looking a little flustered, Carly said quickly, "What about the other one? The son. What's he like?"

"Surly," Brenda replied without even hesitating. "A little bitter—not about the money, as far as I can tell, but about the way he and his mother parted. From what I've been able to piece together, she was a very demanding and controlling woman, and he seems to have a lot of emotional scars from his childhood."

"Uh-oh."

Brenda lifted an eyebrow. "What do you mean by that?"

"You're attracted to him. That could be a problem."

Feeling her face warm, Brenda asked, "What makes you think I'm attracted to him?"

"Take it from someone who's had a thing for 'bad boys' since I was fourteen. I know the look."

"It isn't like that. I just feel sort of sorry for him, that's all. His mother died and left his childhood home to a stranger, and now people are accusing him of all sorts of terrible things."

"With good reason," Carly reminded her. "According to what I, um, accidentally overheard at the office, the son is the only one who really stands to benefit if anything happens to you."

"He doesn't want the inheritance. He said he walked away from it ten years ago and he has no interest in it now."

"Sure, that's what he said, but be realistic. He probably assumed he was still in the will, no matter what his mother threatened. He certainly isn't going to admit it if finding out he wasn't drove him to desperate measures."

"Do you enjoy reading mystery novels, by any chance?"

Carly wrinkled her nose. "Well, yeah, but that doesn't mean real-life villains don't really exist. For all you know, this guy could be one."

"Carly, he's a landscape designer."

"Well, sure. By day. By night...who knows?"

Brenda laughed ruefully and shook her head. "And I thought *my* imagination was getting out of control."

"Okay, you're right," Carly conceded. "But even Dad agrees that something is strange about this entire situation. I just want you to be careful, Brenda. New friends are hard to find."

Brenda's smile felt a little strained. "Thank you for your concern. I promise that I am being careful. My brother would make sure of that even if I weren't concerned about it, myself."

"Oh, right. The cute insurance guy. Did you ever notice how blue his eyes are?"

Brenda reached for her punch, wishing just for a moment that it was something a bit stronger. Spending time with Carly D'Alessandro was oddly tiring, leaving her feeling as if she could use a little extra energy just to keep up.

Still, she wouldn't forget about Carly's warnings.

THERE WAS A MESSAGE from Sean on Ethan's answering machine when he arrived home Monday evening. Without pleasantries, Sean got straight to the point, letting Ethan know that Leland was causing trouble, making a nuisance of himself at the law firm, threatening lawsuits, blaming everyone around him that his aunt had cheated him out of what he felt should rightfully be his.

"I just thought you should know," Sean concluded. "Give me a call if you want to talk or if you've changed your mind about joining him in a lawsuit."

"I won't be joining Leland in a lawsuit or in anything else," Ethan growled to his empty kitchen, jerking open the door to his refrigerator.

He would be glad when this damned will had been through probate and Brenda had a clear claim to everything, he told himself. It would serve Leland right—and himself for that matter.

THE TELEPHONE RANG sometime after midnight, rousing Brenda from a restless sleep. Still painfully aware of the last time she had been abruptly awakened, she sat up with a jerk and gasped, her heart pounding in her chest. Only then did she realize that the sound she heard was a telephone, not a fire alarm.

She made a grab for the extension on the fussy little antique table beside the bed she had chosen to sleep in. "H'lo?"

The raspy breathing was as familiar to her by now as a distinctive voice.

"Damn it, who are you?" she all but shouted into the phone. "Why do you keep calling me?"

The breathing intensified, and then mutated into a harsh, genderless whisper. The call was disconnected before Brenda could make sense of the words. She didn't bother to try calling back, she knew no one would pick up the phone on the other end of the line.

Her palms damp, her hands trembling, she fumbled to replace the receiver.

SEAN PAID A VISIT on Tuesday afternoon. Brenda had almost not answered the phone when he'd called, out of fear that she would hear nothing but eerie breathing on the line. Only her concern that it could be Richard or her sister made her pick up the receiver. She was greatly relieved to recognize Sean's nicely modulated voice.

She was waiting to let him in when he arrived promptly at one o'clock, just as he said he would. Dressed in one of his neat, dark suits, he looked civilized and professional, a welcome sight after a near-sleepless night and a morning filled with anxiety.

After greeting her with a warm smile, he paused and searched her face with a frown. "Are you okay? Forgive me, but you look a bit…strained."

She debated telling him about the phone call, but she said only, "I'm just not sleeping very well."

"It's no wonder," he replied, his expression sympathetic. "After all you've been through lately, combined with your strange surroundings, it would be a miracle if you *were* able to sleep. Is there anything I can do to help you?"

Waving him to a chair in the front parlor, she shook her head. "I can't think of anything just now, but I'll let you know."

"You look very nice. New clothes?"

She glanced down at the brightly colored top and skirt Carly had selected for her. "Yes. I went shopping for a few things on Monday."

"Good for you. Get what you need, Brenda. I assure you, you can afford it."

She wasn't quite ready to talk about the money. "Can I get you anything to drink? I can make a pot of coffee."

"That sounds good. Thank you."

"I'll be right back." She hurried out of the room toward the kitchen, wondering if it would ever feel natural to her to play the hostess in this house.

The cats were in the kitchen, gathered around the food bowls she had filled just before Sean had arrived. They meowed when she entered, and two of them wound around her ankles while she brewed, then poured two cups of coffee. She had to place her feet carefully to keep from stepping on them, but she was getting accustomed to that. Angel, the calico, abandoned her food and followed Brenda when she left the kitchen to rejoin Sean.

She found him standing in front of an antique Chippendale table on which two silver-framed photographs were displayed, along with a couple of old-looking silver boxes. Brenda had studied those pictures, so she knew what Sean was seeing. Two stiffly posed family portraits. The older one depicted Margaret, a tall, somewhat self-conscious looking man who must have been her first husband and a little boy of four or five with tousled brown hair and a slightly anxious expression. Ethan, she had determined, looking as if he'd just been ordered to smile and was trying his best to comply.

The other portrait was of Margaret's second family. A balding, heavyset man in the husband's seat this time. Margaret sitting beside him looking a few years older than in the other photograph, but otherwise wearing the same composed, unrevealing expression. Two teenage boys stood behind them, Ethan and Sean, looking much as they did now. Ethan's expression suggested that he would rather be anywhere else on earth, wearing anything except the jacket and tie he had on. Sean was relaxed and comfortable in front of the camera, wearing his dark suit as easily as most teens wore jeans and T-shirts.

"Sorry," he said when he realized he was no longer alone. "Guess I was reminiscing a bit."

She handed him his coffee, then settled into a chair with her own. Angel jumped in her lap, flipping her tail a few times before curling into a ball and purring. "Were you close to your father?"

Sean hesitated only a moment. "I lived with my mother and stepfather most of the time. I was closer to them. But my dad and I got along well enough."

"And Margaret? Did you get along with her?"

"For the most part. I seemed to pass her somewhat narrow criteria for acceptable behavior."

"Unlike her son."

"Maybe Ethan was just too much like her," Sean answered with a faint sigh. "Both stubborn as mules.

Both determined to have their own way. Both entirely too proud to allow them to give in."

"And how often did you end up in the middle?"

His smile was decidedly lopsided now. "A few times."

"Why didn't she leave her estate to you? You were her stepson. You're an attorney—which was apparently almost obsessively important to her. You said you got along well with her."

"Getting along with her doesn't mean I was close to her, or that I understood the way her mind worked. I can only assume that she knew I'm well set financially and that I never expected to be named her beneficiary. Somehow she must have decided that you were the more deserving recipient."

"And it all comes back to that," she muttered, unable to repress her frustration. "Why me? How did she know about me?"

"Perhaps your investigator will eventually discover the answer to that."

Brenda cocked her head to look at him more closely. "You sound as if you don't really approve of my hiring Tony D'Alessandro."

He shook his head. "From everything I know, D'Alessandro is a reputable investigator. I trust that he won't try to stretch this case out to increase his billable hours, or that he won't plant doubts and concerns in your mind to keep himself on your payroll."

Despite what he said, there was a slight lack of confidence in Sean's voice—just enough to make her suspect that he *did* worry about those things. Only then did it occur to her that she had never even considered that Tony might pad his hours somehow, or deliberately play on her insecurities. She had been more concerned that he wouldn't believe her, and that he would turn down her case. And now, of course, she had something new to fret about, in addition to everything else.

She suspected that had been Sean's intention.

"I don't mean to increase your anxiety," he said apologetically. "It's just that I know you aren't in the habit of thinking of yourself as a wealthy young woman. You have to be very careful now about the motives of newcomers in your life."

She nodded gravely. "I'll be careful."

"At least you can be certain of my motives," he assured her with a charming smile. "I have nothing to gain by wishing you ill. As long as you're the beneficiary of Margaret's trust, I have a job as trustee."

And yet, she couldn't help thinking, that position also gave him a great deal of access to Margaret's fortune. He wouldn't be the first trustee to discreetly pad his own pockets with money he had been entrusted to supervise. And Sean could blame no one but himself for planting that tiny seed of doubt in her mind, since he'd just warned her to beware of every newcomer in her life.

Setting his coffee cup on a marble coaster on a side table, Sean reached for his briefcase. "There are several things I need to discuss with you today. The first concerns Ethan's cousin, Leland Grassel, who is intent on causing trouble for you. He doesn't have a legal leg to stand on, but he does have a right to file a protest against the will, if he can talk someone into hearing his case."

"Great. Someone else with a reason to hate me," Brenda muttered beneath her breath.

"No one hates you, Brenda," Sean assured her kindly. "They aren't harboring great love for Margaret just now, but it wasn't your fault that she drew your name out of a hat—or however she selected you."

She doubted that many people believed that.

Sean spent the next ten minutes outlining what they could expect from Leland's challenge, and then another half hour going over other business. "Have you noticed any problems around the house that need tending to? Any repairs I should schedule?"

"Do you suppose it would be possible for me to have caller ID telephones installed? I'm surprised Margaret didn't request the service for herself."

Making a note on the pad on his knee, Sean shrugged. "Margaret never answered the telephone. She had Betty, the housekeeper, for that, and Betty knew who Margaret would talk to. Are you concerned about unwelcome calls?"

"I would just like to know who's calling," she answered evasively.

"All right. I'll take care of that. Anything else?"

"No, that's all for now. You've been very helpful, Sean."

Closing his pad, he smiled. "That's what I'm here for."

She saw him out, then locked the door behind him and reset the alarms. She should feel better to know she had such a pleasant, congenial man on her side, she mused. Yet she just felt a bit hollow after her conversation with him.

Blaming her mood on stress and lack of sleep, she turned toward the back of the house. Cleaning litter boxes and doing a few other housekeeping tasks would keep her busy for a little while, at least.

ETHAN DEBATED for a while before picking up the telephone Tuesday evening and dialing the number of his late mother's house. Funny how he still remembered the number so clearly, even though it had been years since he'd dialed it.

Even though he knew better, he half expected to hear Betty's voice on the other end of the line. Instead, Brenda answered, sounding oddly anxious. "Hello?"

"Brenda, it's Ethan Blacklock. Is everything okay?"

"Of course." If she was surprised that he had called, she didn't allow it to show in her voice. "Why wouldn't it be?"

"I don't know. You just sounded kind of tense when you answered."

"I didn't know who was calling. Sean's arranging for caller ID to be installed tomorrow."

"Why? Are you receiving disturbing calls? Leland's not harassing you, is he? I told him to leave you alone, but he's never been in the habit of listening to anything I say."

"No, your cousin hasn't contacted me personally, though I understand he's been calling Sean and generally causing trouble. I just don't like to be caught unprepared."

Ethan could understand that sentiment. "Let me know if he starts giving you problems. I'll see what I can do to make him back off."

"Thank you. Um—why did you call, Ethan?"

"Because of Leland, actually. He's been trying to convince me to join him in challenging the will, and I wouldn't put it past him to insinuate to you and Sean that he has my support. I just wanted to reiterate to you that I'm not cooperating with him in any way."

"That was thoughtful of you. But not really necessary. I believed you when you said you wouldn't help him."

He noted that she didn't reassure him that she believed *everything* he had told her, but he supposed he should settle for what confidence he could get.

"So Sean's been helpful to you?" he asked, having noticed how easily she dropped his stepbrother's name into the conversation.

"Oh, yes, very."

"He's a decent guy—for a lawyer."

She chuckled obligingly in response to his jest, then sobered again. "Ethan, I've been thinking about your grandmother's Bible. It must be in this house somewhere. I just can't believe your mother would have gotten rid of it."

"You have more faith in her than I do."

"It just doesn't make sense that she would have thrown out something like that. Do you have other family members that might have wanted it?"

"No. Dad had no close living relatives. Maybe a few distant cousins, but they never expressed any interest in their family history or keepsakes."

"Then it must be somewhere in this ginormous house."

"Ginormous?" he repeated with a smile.

"It's the only word to describe it."

Ethan had used a few other adjectives to describe the place in the past, but he supposed hers was as good as any. "If you happen to come across the Bible, give me a call, okay?"

"I would rather you'd come look for the book yourself. You know the house better than I do, so you'll know more places to look than the obvious spots you checked when you were here before. I can stay here with you while you look, or I can clear out and let you have privacy, if you prefer."

"I doubt that Sean would agree to that," Ethan said without rancor. "He has a responsibility to keep track of everything—and he takes his responsibilities very seriously. And I'm sure your brother would want to hover over me, too, since he doesn't trust me as far as he can throw me."

"Just tell me when you want to come, and I'll handle whatever arrangements I need to make."

"I would like to look one more time, actually. I can probably take some time off Thursday afternoon, if that's convenient for you."

"I don't have any plans at the moment, actually. I'm still trying to figure out what I'm going to do next. What time do you want to come Thursday?"

"Three o'clock?"

"Fine. So I'll see you on Thursday."

"Yeah. See you."

As he disconnected the call, Ethan couldn't help asking himself if he had jumped on her offer because of his eagerness to find the Bible—or to see Brenda again. If it were the latter, well, that could possibly be the dumbest mistake he had ever made.

CHAPTER SEVEN

"I JUST CAN'T GET OVER THIS place. It's so big." Linda Grayson, Brenda's older sister, had been saying words to that effect ever since she'd arrived twenty minutes earlier on Wednesday. Brenda had just given her a quick tour of the house, and Linda was still dazed by the size and number of rooms.

"It's ridiculously large for one person. A housekeeper lived here full-time when Margaret was alive, but she stayed in the suite that opens off the kitchen. Sean keeps offering to hire a housekeeper for me, but I'm just not ready for that. I've been cooking simple meals for myself and doing my own laundry and dusting, but I'll probably have to agree to having someone come in once a week or so to do the heavy cleaning. The place is just so large."

"A housekeeper." Linda sank into a chair in the media room, which Brenda had decided would be the least intimidating place for their visit. "I just can't believe you're living this way."

"It's weird, isn't it? I'm still having a little trouble believing it, myself."

"Are you...comfortable here? Do you feel at home?"

"I feel like I'm staying in a hotel or something. A

big, empty one. I keep thinking I'll go back to my duplex any day, back to the life I had before. But I know I can't, because the duplex is gone."

"I know. I'm so sorry about all your things, sweetie. I know you had some items that meant a lot to you."

Brenda nodded. She had spent plenty of time thinking about everything she'd lost in the fire. Having painful moments when she would suddenly remember something else that was gone, and grieving all over again. "I'm trying to put it behind me. Richard keeps reminding me that I'm lucky just to have survived, and that I should be grateful I had this place to come to."

"He's right, I suppose. But you're still entitled to feel bad about what you lost. Don't let him discount your feelings."

"No, I won't."

The gray cat, Toby, sniffed Linda's ankles, then stood on his back feet, front paws braced on her chair, to study her. Wrinkling her nose a little, Linda gave the cat a gentle push to discourage him from climbing into her lap. Linda had never shared her sister's fondness for felines.

"All of this so you can take care of these cats," she muttered, waving a hand to indicate the entire house. "It just doesn't make sense. How did she know you? Where did she get your name?"

"If you can find the answers to those questions, you'll be the first. I don't seem to be any closer to knowing now than I was the day I got the call about Margaret's will."

"I'm sorry I couldn't be here for you sooner."

"Don't apologize. You live almost two hours away. And I know it isn't easy for you to get away, with the kids to worry about and all."

"Still, I would have come the day after the fire if Nicky hadn't come down with strep throat. I hated to leave him with James's mother and risk her getting sick again, since she's just gotten over that bout with pneumonia."

"I understand. Really. Richard has been great to help me out when I needed him, and so have others. I'm doing okay. What about you and James?"

"We're fine. He's still working crazy hours, but we're chipping away at those old debts. Everything's looking much better."

Brenda shifted in her seat, trying to decide how to carefully word her next statement. "Look, Linda, if this probate thing goes through the way Sean seems to expect, I'm going to have access to quite a bit of disposable income. Much more than I need just for myself. Maybe I could help you and James out a little? Pay off a few of your bills or something?"

Linda's entire body stiffened. "I said we're doing fine. We don't need charity—especially from my little sister."

Brenda sighed, having half expected her very proud sister to react just this way. "It wouldn't be charity. Just sharing my unexpected good fortune with my family. You would do the same for me."

But she doubted Linda would see it that way. After all, Brenda was the one Linda and Richard had been in the habit of watching out for. This sudden reversal of circumstances was going to be a difficult adjustment for all of them.

"If you do get that money—and from what I understand, there's no real guarantee that you will—you're supposed to use it for your own needs," Linda argued.

"You should bank most of it for your retirement, so you'll be taken care of in your later years. Mrs. Jacobs intended it that way, and I think you should respect her wishes."

Brenda knew better than to continue the debate when her sister wore that particular stubborn expression. She would just have to figure out a way to help Linda and James without stepping on their overdeveloped pride. Maybe Richard would have some suggestions about how to go about that.

"So, anyway," Linda continued, deliberately changing the subject, "what about your summer job at the bank?"

"I called my boss and told him I needed some time off, and that I probably won't be back this summer. I hated to leave without proper notice, but when I told him about the fire, he was very understanding. He kept asking if there was anything he could do for me. I think he was actually considering taking up a collection among my coworkers to help me replace my things. I finally convinced him that I had plenty of insurance and that I wasn't dealing with any financial problems. I didn't want to get into this will thing, since I still haven't figured out a way to explain it."

"It was nice of him to be so concerned about you."

"I know. He's a nice guy."

"So you haven't told any of your friends about your inheritance?"

"Only Diane," Brenda admitted. "Like I said, I just don't know what to say. I called a couple of people after the fire to assure them that I'm all right and that I'll be back in touch soon. I sort of led them to believe that I'd be staying with family for a while. I only have a few really close friends, and they're going to be pretty freaked when they see me in this place."

"Freaked?"

Brenda chuckled. "A term I must have picked up from a new friend, Carly D'Alessandro. She's great and easy to be with right now because she's used to having money of her own. She's not a snob or anything—far from it, actually—but she's not overly impressed by this house or my potential income, either."

"She's the one who took you shopping for clothes?"

"Yes. She's several years younger than I am, but she's very easy to talk to. I enjoy spending time with her."

"If she helped you pick out that outfit, she has really good taste. It looks great on you."

"Thanks." Brenda glanced down at the flare-leg jeans and fluttery red print top that she probably wouldn't have chosen for herself. It was one of the outfits Carly had talked her into, and she was surprised at how good it looked on her.

Linda stayed for another hour, but then she was ready to leave, visibly impatient to get home to her family. Brenda saw her off with a pang, aware that this inheritance situation had placed a new awkwardness between herself and her sister.

Was this a sign of how things were going to be in the future? Would her friends be as uncomfortable with her new circumstances as Linda had been? Carly had warned her about new "friends" suddenly appearing to take advantage of her new wealth, but Brenda was more concerned about keeping her old friends.

She couldn't help remembering Ethan's comment

that the money had never made anyone happy. A shiver of what might have been premonition went down her spine as she double-checked the locks on the door.

BRENDA FIGURED it must be a sign of how restless she was becoming when she found herself counting down the minutes until three o'clock Thursday afternoon. She really needed to get out of the house, she told herself with a shake of her head. She hadn't been out since her shopping expedition on Monday.

Now that she'd quit her bank job, she really had nowhere she needed to be. She wasn't even going to the animal shelter where she was a regular volunteer, calling, instead, to let them know that she was dealing with a "family situation," and wasn't sure when she would be back.

She shouldn't let her anxieties turn her into a recluse, or she'd end up crazy as a loon, she thought with a sigh.

When the telephone rang at a quarter to three, she was afraid it might be Ethan, calling to cancel. She was dismayed by how disappointed she was by that possibility, but she told herself it was only because she had been looking forward to having someone to talk to besides the cats.

She didn't recognize the number on the caller ID, but she scribbled it down on the pad she kept by the telephone. "Hello?"

"Is this Brenda Prentiss?"

"Yes, I'm Brenda Prentiss."

"My name is Patty Ann Grassel. Margaret Jacobs was my aunt."

It took a moment, but Brenda finally placed the

name. "She was your husband's aunt, actually. You are Leland's wife, aren't you?"

"Well…yes." Patty Ann seemed a bit startled that Brenda knew that. "Leland and I have been married for six years. We were both very close to Aunt Margaret."

"I'm sorry for your loss," Brenda said politely. "It must have been quite a shock for you to lose her so unexpectedly."

"It was devastating," the other woman answered dramatically. "There's such a hole in our lives now."

A hole that her husband seemed to believe could be filled with Margaret's estate, Brenda thought cynically. And then she felt a bit guilty for being so uncharitable. "I'm very sorry," she said again. "Is there something I can do for you, Mrs. Grassel?"

"As a matter of fact, there is. Before she passed away, Margaret promised us a few things as tokens of her gratitude for the care we gave to her in her last years. She died before final arrangements could be made."

"A few things?" Brenda repeated blankly.

"Yes. Her jewelry—family heirlooms, really. She wanted me to have it all. And because she knew how much Leland loves art, she promised him all the paintings in her collection. They used to get such pleasure out of looking at them together."

"I'm not sure why you're telling me these things, Mrs. Grassel. Did she list these bequests in her will?"

"I just told you," Patty Ann said with a newly sharp edge to her voice, "she died before she could take care of the formalities. Her death was so sudden, so unexpected. She had no way of knowing that she didn't have plenty of time to follow through on her promises."

"So you've called me because...?"

Her voice oozing charm again, Patty Ann replied, "I wanted to ask for your assistance, Brenda. I'm sure you've lost people who were important to you. Perhaps you lost some sentimental reminders of them in that terrible fire. Surely you can understand that Leland and I would treasure our little tokens to remind us of the aunt we loved so dearly."

Little tokens. An interesting way to describe a fortune in jewelry and art. "I think you had better discuss this with Sean."

"Sean won't do anything to help us," Patty Ann snapped. "He was always jealous of the relationship Leland had with Margaret, and he knew she wouldn't leave him anything because he wasn't really family. He won't even listen to us now."

"So what do you want me to do? Talk to Sean on your behalf?"

"Actually, I hoped you would turn out to be a sympathetic, good-hearted person who would want Aunt Margaret's wishes to be respected. Don't you think that would be the right thing to do?"

"If you're asking me to slip you things out of the estate without Sean's permission, then I'm going to have to refuse. I'm not allowed to take anything out of the house without discussing it with Sean first."

"But I told you." Patty Ann's voice had become shrill. "Aunt Margaret *promised* us those things. We were her family. You were a stranger to her. It isn't fair for you to have those things that mean nothing to you."

"I'm sorry. I can't help you, Mrs. Grassel. I really think you should talk to Sean."

"I should have known. You want everything for

yourself. Somehow you weaseled yourself into Aunt Margaret's will, and now you want it all."

"Please don't call here again." Brenda tried to keep her voice steady to hide the fact that she was shaken by the fury in the other woman's voice. "There's really nothing I can do to help you."

She hung up the phone while the other woman was still sputtering.

HER HANDS WERE STILL SHAKING when the doorbell rang. She took a moment to compose herself before she opened the door.

Apparently, she didn't do as good a job as she had hoped.

"Now what?" Ethan asked, studying her expression with narrowed eyes as he entered the house.

"I just had a call from your cousin's wife." She closed the door behind him. "It wasn't particularly pleasant."

"No conversation with Patty Ann is particularly pleasant. What did she want from you?"

"Just a few 'token items' of your mother's—all her jewelry and her art collection."

Ethan shook his head in disgust. "The woman's got nerve, I'll give her that. I hope you told her to get lost."

"I told her she should talk to Sean. She didn't like that. She said Sean is against them. She wanted me to just give her the things she wanted without discussing it with Sean. I told her I couldn't do that."

"Damn straight. You could get yourself in a truck-load of trouble pulling something like that without authorization."

"I'm aware of that. I would never do anything outside the terms of the trust."

"Don't let her upset you, Brenda. If she becomes a problem, just tell Sean. He'll take care of it for you."

"Yes, I will." She pushed a strand of hair behind her ear, suddenly self-conscious. It seemed like every time she saw Ethan, she was experiencing some crisis. She wondered if he would even believe that her life until this point had been relatively uneventful. "Would you like something to drink before you start your search?"

"No, thanks. I'm good. Where's your brother? I was sure he'd be here to protect you from me."

"Richard's tied up with work this afternoon. I told him you were coming by, and I told Sean. Neither of them are opposed to you looking for something that legally belongs to you. Sean had intended to be here to greet you and discuss some things with you, but he called a half hour or so ago and said that something came up at the office and he couldn't get away. He said to tell you hello."

She was letting him know, obviously, that others knew she had expected him today. She was just being cautious, of course. It wasn't that she didn't feel safe enough with Ethan, especially since Sean had assured her that he would be perfectly comfortable about her being alone with his stepbrother.

Richard hadn't been quite as confident. He had offered to reschedule his appointments so he could be here with her, but she'd reassured him that Sean would be here. She hadn't called him when Sean had canceled, because she had known he would have dropped everything to come "protect" her from Ethan.

Maybe she was as naive as her brother seemed to think, but she really had no fear of Ethan.

"I guess we'd better get with it, then. I'm sure Sean would want you to supervise my search."

As a matter of fact, Sean had asked her to keep an eye on him—just as a formality, he'd assured her. "I'll stay out of your way."

Ethan gave her a slightly crooked smile. "Actually, I'd enjoy the company. There are some memories in this house I would just as soon not face alone."

Though he spoke lightly, she didn't think he was joking.

They decided to start in the media room, a place he had neglected to search fully before, since it seemed unlikely the Bible would be stored there. "She redid this room since I was here last," he commented, opening a cabinet full of music CDs. "Upgraded the electronics, added the big plasma screen."

"I would guess that she spent a lot of time in this room, watching movies and enjoying her cats. That's just judging from appearances, of course—the collection of films and CDs, the cat play area, the stocked fridge."

"I'd heard she didn't get out much during the past few years. She gave up most of her charity board positions, usually after a falling-out with other people on the boards."

"I can see the attraction of staying in here," Brenda admitted, kneeling to stroke the four cats tangled around her feet. "It feels so warm and safe."

He shot her a look from another cabinet he'd been searching. "You're too young to talk that way. Have you gotten out of this place since you moved in?"

She concentrated on rubbing Missy's chin. "Not much. Of course, it's only been a few days."

Closing a third cabinet, he took a step closer to her. "Brenda, are you afraid to go out?"

"No, of course not," she said a bit too quickly. "I went shopping with a friend on Monday." And she'd been just a bit jumpy during that entire outing, wondering if she were being watched, hoping Carly wasn't in any danger just for being with her. But she saw no need to mention that now; already he seemed to think of her as a scared-of-her-shadow type.

"You shouldn't let a couple of disturbing events drive you into hiding."

"A couple of disturbing events?" she repeated, straightening slowly, wounded pride making her chin rise. "Someone tried to run over me. It's possible that someone burned down my house. Someone keeps making creepy calls that have me half-afraid to answer the telephone. I'm being accused of somehow conning my way into your mother's will, and of being greedy and selfish for not looting Margaret's estate on behalf of her nephew and his wife. All of this in less than two weeks after my quiet life was drastically changed by the death of a total stranger. Is it any wonder that I feel like hiding for a few days?"

Ethan had listened very carefully to her tirade, but he commented on only one item. "You're getting 'creepy' telephone calls?"

She'd been goaded into saying more than she had intended, but she nodded slowly. "Lots of them. Whoever it is just breathes into the phone most of the time."

"Most of the time? Has the caller said anything?"

"Only once, after I moved in here. It was only a whisper, and I couldn't hear the words."

"You couldn't make out anything?"

She twisted her fingers in front of her, but a slight hint of defiance was still in her voice when she answered, willing him to believe her. "No. As I said, it was just a whisper. I was nervous, and I couldn't hear clearly."

"Was it a man's voice or a woman's?"

"I don't know. I couldn't tell."

"Who have you told about the calls?"

"Tony D'Alessandro, the private investigator. And you."

He waited a moment, then asked in disbelief, "No one else?"

"No. There wasn't any proof, and I was afraid I already sounded paranoid about everything else. My brother would just get more nervous."

"Brenda, if you're receiving threatening calls, you should report them to the proper authorities."

"But that's the thing—they haven't been threatening calls. Just breathing and a few whispered words I couldn't understand."

"Yeah, but—"

"Look, I got caller ID, okay? I'm writing down the number of everyone who calls here, even your cousin Patty Ann."

He nodded. "It's your decision, of course."

"Exactly." So many decisions had been made for her during the past couple of weeks, it felt good to assert herself for a change.

He closed another cabinet. "The Bible's not in here."

"I didn't think it would be. Where should we look next?"

She followed him to the living room. He had already searched in there once, the last time, but he said he might as well be thorough this time. There was always the possibility he had overlooked something before.

She noticed that he didn't pause, as Sean had, to look at the two old family portraits displayed in that room. He actually seemed to go out of his way not to look at them. Interesting. Were these some of the painful old memories he hadn't wanted to face alone?

"Tell me about your landscaping business," she said, both as an attempt to distract him and because she was genuinely interested. "Do you own the business yourself?"

"Yeah. I worked for a couple other landscapers before I broke off on my own three years ago."

"What's your business called?"

"I came up with something really fresh and original. Blacklock's Landscape Design."

She laughed, as he had intended. She wasn't surprised that he'd eschewed cutesy or artsy names and opted for simplicity, instead. "Do you have a specialty?"

"Paying bills. I'm not real choosy about the jobs I take as long as I get compensated for them."

She watched him run a hand across the top of a tall curio cabinet filled with delicate china pieces. His hand came away empty. "Have you always liked landscaping?"

"Since I was a kid. I like being outside. I like watching things grow. I like the variety of colors and textures of plants and other landscaping materials. I like doing water features and outdoor kitchens and even playground areas."

"You enjoy your job," she summarized, a little surprised by the detail he had given to his answer. "I think that's great."

He looked suddenly self-conscious. "Yeah. Sorry I got carried away. I guess this house puts me back in the old habit of trying to defend what I've chosen and why."

"Your mother just couldn't accept it?"

He shook his head. "Maybe if I'd decided to be a brain surgeon, she could have eventually gotten over her disappointment that I didn't go to law school. Maybe. But a 'gardener'? No way."

"Well, I think landscape design is a very interesting career. I have to admit I don't know much about it, since I've spent the past few years in dorms and apartments, but I love flowers. Especially roses—they're my favorite."

"Yeah?" He dusted his hands on his jeans and headed for the next room with her—and two cats—close behind him. "I noticed Mother's gardens look like crap. Her roses used to be prizewinning, but they appear to be struggling now. She's really neglected the grounds since I left, maybe in a weird attempt to get back at me."

"I haven't really looked that closely at the grounds, other than to notice that the grass was recently cut and everything looked neat and trim. The backyard looks a bit neglected, I'll admit. I thought there would be a pool or a patio, or something."

"Mother didn't care for swimming, so she saw no reason for a pool, even when I begged for one as a kid. She said if I wanted to swim, or play tennis or golf, I could always go to the country club. She paid little attention to the backyard, because it couldn't be seen from the street. It was always kept neat and land-scaped, but it was never utilized the way it could have been."

"I assume Sean's been arranging for lawn care since your mother died."

"Minimal lawn care," he qualified.

They had moved into what Brenda had come to think of as the music room. A glossy black baby grand piano was the focal point of the room, along with a glittering crystal chandelier hanging above it. Stiff, not particularly comfortable-looking settees and chairs surrounded the piano in a very formal arrangement.

Ethan all but shuddered when he glanced at that piano. "I spent way too many hours in this room."

"Piano lessons?"

"Ten years of them," he confirmed grimly. "From the most humorless, rigid teacher you could possibly imagine. I was given no choice of any of the music I played. I was expected to practice a full hour a day, no matter what else I had planned, and then I had to perform for visitors whenever my mother 'requested' it."

Brenda looked at the piano again and pictured young Ethan sitting miserably on the bench, sur-rounded by stuffy guests in these formal seats. She almost shuddered, as well. "I suppose you hate playing piano now."

He grunted. "You would think so, wouldn't you?"

"You don't?" she asked, surprised.

"Nah. I don't play very often, but when I do, it's strictly jazz and pop—two genres that were taboo to my piano teacher."

As if to illustrate his words, he played a quick riff on the keys with his right hand. Just those few notes were enough to convince her that she would love to hear him play an entire piece. But he turned away and opened an intricately carved, Asian-style music cabinet, riffling through the piles of sheet music in a continuation of his search.

In an effort to assist him, Brenda opened the piano bench. It was empty, except for one sheet of music that appeared to be handwritten on staff paper. There was no title or signature on the piece. "I wonder what this is."

He glanced up from the shallow drawer he'd opened in an inlaid console table. He frowned when he saw what she held. He recognized it immediately. "It's a piece I wrote for a composition assignment. The only time I tried my hand at writing music. My teacher hated it and declared that I had absolutely no talent for composing."

"But your mother kept it. It must have been important to her."

He turned back to the drawer. "She probably forgot it was there, or she'd have tossed it."

Shaking her head, Brenda looked at the music again. Unable to resist, she played the first line with her right hand, mentally adding the bass notes to give a good idea of what the piece sounded like. "I think your piano teacher was full of bull," she said. "This is actually quite good. I'd love to hear it with a guitar accompaniment."

"I wrote it with that in mind," he said, somewhat quizzically. "You play, too?"

"Piano lessons for eight years with a teacher I liked

very much. Richard taught me to play guitar. I taught
myself hammer dulcimer when I inherited one from my
father's sister, who played folk music in cool, smoky
coffee clubs—until she died of lung cancer." She sighed
wistfully, reminding herself of her promise not to cry
again. "The dulcimer was one of the things I lost in the
fire."

"I'm sorry."

She replaced the music carefully in the bench and
closed the lid. "Thank you. Any luck?"

"No. It's not in here." He turned toward the door,
apparently anxious to get out of the room—and away
from painful old memories.

THEY SEARCHED the dining room, the kitchen and even
Betty's rooms, which were empty of everything except
the furniture. No Bible.

It was time to move upstairs, to the master
bedroom suite. Ethan wasn't looking forward to that
part of the search.

He'd looked in his mother's room last time, of
course, but only quickly, since he hadn't expected to
find the old Bible there. Now he conducted a more
thorough search, going through drawers of lingerie and
sweaters, and rummaging through the huge walk-in
closet still filled with his mother's clothing and accessories. He kept his emotions firmly banked during that
process, trusting that Brenda wasn't able to read
anything in his expression.

"Are you sure you wouldn't like something to
drink? I could make coffee or something and leave you
to do this in private."

He knew she was trying to be thoughtful, but he

shook his head. "I'd rather you would stay," he said, opening the front of a large, upright, wooden chest. Jewelry, both real and expensive costume, filled the numerous little drawers and hooks. His mother had never worn much jewelry at a time, but she'd had an eye for sparkly collectibles. And to think Patty Ann had expected Brenda to just hand all of this over to her with no questions asked.

"Make sure I don't slip anything into my pockets."

Brenda sighed audibly. "Would you stop that? I know you aren't going to pocket the jewelry."

"Just don't want to give Patty Ann any more ammunition against you." He closed the chest and moved toward the writing desk.

There wasn't much to be found in Margaret's desk. Some monogrammed notepaper. Stamps. A couple of her preferred fountain pens. An appointment calendar. Flipping through it, he noted that there were very few entries, a big difference from years past when all her days and most of her evenings had been filled with social and charitable activities.

He closed the drawer and moved toward the nightstand. He found a Bible in the drawer there, but it wasn't his grandmother's. This was a much newer release—a large-print edition. Obviously Margaret's own, though she hadn't been much of a churchgoer. It had always rather annoyed her that the various congregations wouldn't let her be in charge.

Some reading glasses, a box of tissues and a tin of cherry-flavored throat lozenges were the only other items in the nightstand. He heaved a breath and turned toward Brenda. "It's not in here."

"Then we'll keep looking," she said, waving toward the sitting room.

He wondered why Brenda was being so helpful. Still the guilt thing about inheriting his mother's estate? Seemed like she'd have at least some concern about him having ulterior motives in being here. Some fear of being alone with the man who stood to inherit if something happened to her.

Yet she had welcomed him without visible qualms, quietly assisting him in his hunt. The woman seemed to have no sense of self-preservation.

Or maybe she really was just as nice as she seemed, which was a relatively new concept for him. Yeah, sure, he knew some nice people; they just rarely had any connection to his mother. But since Brenda claimed not to have known his mother, he supposed she wasn't the exception to the rule, after all.

Pushing a black cat out of his way, he knelt to open a low cabinet that held a stereo system and some classical music CDs. Margaret had listened to music when she'd sat in here reading her morning paper and sipping the hot tea Betty had brought her every morning. The cat crowded back in front of him, poking its nose into the cabinet as if joining in the exploration.

Sighing, Ethan scooped the cat up and handed it to Brenda. "Maybe you should teach this guy the old lesson about cats and curiosity."

She smiled and rubbed her cheek against the cat's fuzzy head. "He knows you won't hurt him. Cats are very intuitive about people."

"Uh-huh." He tried to keep his tone dry and detached, but there was a gruff edge to it that disturbed him. He turned resolutely back to the cabinet, trying not to think about how good she looked standing there snuggling that cat, her blond hair and fair skin an intriguing contrast to the cat's thick, black fur.

CHAPTER EIGHT

A STAID WHITE SEDAN was right behind Carly's little red sports car when she turned into the driveway of the house she thought of as Brenda's. Everyone else still seemed to refer to it as "Margaret's house," but to Carly, this was where her new friend Brenda lived.

It hadn't been necessary for her to come today, but she had volunteered to bring the latest report from her dad. He had pointed out that he'd discovered nothing that he couldn't discuss with Brenda over the phone, but she had held firm to her opinion that Brenda should have everything in writing. Pretending she was offering only as a courtesy to him, Carly said she might as well drop off the report.

Tony hadn't been fooled for a minute, of course. He had known full well that Carly wanted to get out of the office on another nice afternoon, and that she enjoyed spending time with Brenda. He'd handed her the report, telling her in resignation to go. But as she'd left, he'd added a warning for her to be careful, proving that he wasn't taking Brenda's safety concerns lightly.

Carly wasn't worried about the sedan that had followed her onto the estate. She had recognized the driver in her rearview mirror.

Flipping her dark hair over her shoulder, she slid out

of her car, then smoothed her short khaki skirt over her thighs. Her red T-shirt fit snugly just to the low waist of the skirt, revealing an occasional glimpse of abdomen when she moved. Her legs were bare except for red thong sandals studded with tiny, glittering red stones.

Satisfied that she looked her best, she slid her sunglasses onto the top of her head and sent Richard Prentiss a smile as he approached her.

He looked delectable with his dark blond hair tousled in the breeze, revealing the high temples that she found rather sexy. He wore a white shirt, a gray suit and a muted-patterned tie, and somehow the boring clothes looked great on him. In the bright sunlight, his eyes looked almost sapphire blue.

The man was just hot, she decided as she had the last time she'd seen him. "Hello, Richard. Nice to see you again."

"You, too, Carly. How are you?"

"Fine, thank you. You look really good today. New haircut?"

He reached up self-consciously to smooth his hair. "Well, yeah. I went to someone new. Uh, so, you're here to see Brenda?"

She was amused that her casual compliment seemed to have flustered him. "Yes, I am. I see we're not the only visitors."

She nodded toward the black extended-cab pickup truck parked nearby. Stenciled lettering on the sides advertised Blacklock Landscape Design.

Richard scowled. "Margaret's son was supposed to come by today to search for a family heirloom. I thought he'd be gone by now." He looked around and frowned even more deeply. "I don't see Sean's car. He's supposed to be here, too. Surely Brenda's not alone in there with that guy."

"Let's go find out." Tucking the manila envelope under her arm, Carly latched on to Richard's sleeve and turned toward the house, pretty much towing him along with her.

Brenda opened the door to them. She didn't seem surprised to see either of them, though maybe a bit startled that they had arrived at the same time. "Come in," she said, stepping back.

"The latest report from Dad," Carly announced, handing Brenda the envelope. "It doesn't say much, just a list of leads he's pursued that didn't actually go anywhere."

"Did he tell you that, or did you read the report?"

Carly widened her eyes and pressed a hand to her chest. "Surely you aren't accusing me of snooping?"

"Oh no, of course not," Brenda replied with mock gravity, her blue eyes twinkling. Carly was struck again by the resemblance between Brenda and Richard.

"Where's Sean?" Richard demanded, looking around as if expecting to see Sean lurking behind the staircase.

"Sean had to cancel at the last minute. He had a work crisis."

Carly could tell that Brenda had deliberately spoken lightly, as if it were no big deal at all that she'd been here alone with Ethan Blacklock. Even Carly knew that wasn't going to fly—and she was right.

"Why didn't you call me?" Richard demanded. "You know I'd have made arrangements to be here, myself."

"And risk losing a client? Don't be ridiculous, Richard."

"Better than leaving you here alone with that guy."

"Damn, you got here too soon," Ethan drawled from the top of the stairway. "I was just about to conk her over the head and steal the silver."

Obviously, he'd heard Richard fussing about Brenda being alone with him, and he had taken offense. Carly studied the man who seemed to be the most logical suspect if someone was trying to hurt Brenda. She remembered that odd something she'd heard in Brenda's voice when she'd mentioned Ethan. A hint of fascination that had set off Carly's internal alarms. Now, seeing him, she could sort of understand.

Ethan wasn't polished or male-model handsome, the way her father and brother were—or even like Richard, who was entirely too attractive for Carly's peace of mind. Ethan reminded Carly a bit more of her uncle Jared, a weathered, work-toughened man who wasn't a stranger to manual labor and spent most of his life outside. Not a man who'd be happy behind a desk, she'd bet. Or answering to anyone else.

She knew she was making a snap judgment based on a first impression and the few things Brenda had said about him, but then she was pretty good at that sort of thing. Even her dad said so.

"Forget the silver," she told him. "Go for the jewelry. Much easier to pocket and then to fence. Higher returns for the least effort."

Ethan's scowl changed to an expression of slight confusion. Richard turned to Carly with a what-the-hell? look.

"I like to think I'm the practical sort," she told him primly.

Brenda laughed. "Carly D'Alessandro, this is Ethan Blacklock."

He came down the stairs to shake her hand. He gave her the usual male once-over, then almost immediately turned his attention back to Brenda. Rather a novel occurrence for Carly, but definitely one more note to add to her list of interesting observations.

"So what were you doing when we interrupted?" she asked.

"We're looking for Ethan's grandmother's Bible," Brenda replied. "Remember I told you that we couldn't find it last time he was here? We've been doing a more thorough search this time. We just got started upstairs."

"There's no need for me to take up any more of your time," Ethan told Brenda stiffly. "You have things to do here. I'll clear out of your way. If it ever turns up—"

"There's no need for you to go," Brenda insisted. "I'm sure we'll find it here someplace, if we look thoroughly enough."

"We'll help you," Carly volunteered cheerily, looping her arm through Richard's. "Won't we, guys? Four pairs of eyes are better than two."

"Oh, but—" Richard sputtered.

"That's not—" Ethan growled.

Brenda cut them both off. "I think that's an *excellent* idea."

Much better than going back to the office, Carly thought smugly. Searching for a lost heirloom could even be considered work related, for that matter.

Maybe not her personal job, but certainly the sort of thing the agency did on a regular basis. "I know I'd want to do everything I could to find something like that from *my* grandmother," she said. "Sentimental heirlooms are so much more valuable than practical things, aren't they?"

While both men were still trying to find excuses to get out of this impromptu treasure hunt, Brenda and Carly swept them up the stairs without giving either of them another chance to refuse.

WATCHING CARLY WITH THE MEN was a revelation to Brenda. She'd been around women who were relaxed with men, women who were skilled at flirting, women who were comfortable with their own beauty and sensuality. But Carly wasn't quite like any of those other women. While all those things seemed to be true about her, Carly still managed to come across as natural and genuine.

From what she had come to know of her, Brenda would not have described Carly as vain or shallow or scheming or manipulative. She was just…fun. Comfortable with herself. Honestly interested in other people.

Even Ethan seemed to loosen up a little with Carly around, though he wasn't as obviously taken with her as Richard was. Ethan smiled a little more in response to Carly. Richard walked into walls.

She was sure Richard was just harmlessly crushing on pretty, young Carly. He would know, of course, that nothing was likely to develop between the two of them. She could hardly imagine a less likely pairing.

Except, perhaps, herself and Margaret Jacobs's disinherited son.

She found herself alone with Ethan again in the last of the five bedrooms—the one in which she had been sleeping—when Carly decided they all needed cold drinks and towed Richard with her to fetch some. Ethan made a show of wiping his brow. "She's a bundle of energy, isn't she? Exhausting."

It was so disarming when he loosened up enough to tease. It made her feel as though she was getting a glimpse of the "other" Ethan, the one who schmoozed with clients, joked with his crew, hung out with his poker-playing friends. She wanted to believe that he wasn't always as angry and defensive as he had been during their early meetings—and with just cause, she had to admit. But now, when he was smiling, she found him entirely too intriguing.

Ethan glanced around the impersonally formal bedroom. "Mother redecorated in here, too."

"Did she?" Brenda looked at the traditional furnishings and accessories, the staid green-and-gold color scheme, the faded rug that was probably a frighteningly expensive antique, but just looked sort of… old.

"Yeah. Same furniture, but everything else that was mine has been replaced."

"This was your room?"

"Yeah. I pretty well cleared it out when I left, so unless she stashed the Bible in here since, it's probably not in here."

"I haven't been through every inch of the room, of course, but the closets and drawers were empty when I put my things away."

He nodded. "I'll take your word for it. We'll just move on."

She wrinkled her nose. "You know Carly won't let you get away with that. She'll insist that you look beneath the mattress and behind the furniture and under the rugs, just like she did in all the other rooms."

He heaved a sigh. "True. Carly is nothing if not thorough."

"Talking about me?" Glossy, dark hair swaying behind her, Carly swept into the room, handing Brenda one of the two canned drinks she'd brought. Richard tossed the other to Ethan, who caught it with a curt nod of thanks.

"I just said that there's probably no need to toss this room, since Brenda's been staying in it for several days without finding anything," Ethan explained.

Carly turned to Brenda. "I bet you've never looked under the bed."

Brenda sent a glance toward Ethan, who acknowledged her silent I-told-you-so with a smile in return. Left a bit flustered by that unexpectedly intimate exchange, Brenda cleared her throat quickly before answering Carly. "No, actually, I've never looked under the bed."

Lacking coasters on the polished walnut bedroom furniture, Carly set her soda can on the counter in the attached private bath and dusted off her hands in a symbolic readiness to get back to work. "You guys should pull that heavy dresser away from the wall so we can look behind it. If I were going to hide a package, I'd duct tape it to the back of something big and heavy like that."

"Carly, the Bible hasn't been hidden. Just misplaced," Ethan explained patiently. "There would have been no reason for Mother to hide it. It's more likely she stuffed it somewhere out of her way and we just haven't stumbled across it yet."

Carly waved off his words, obviously not satisfied with such a mundane explanation. "I'll look under the bed," she said, dropping to her knees and pulling bed skirts out of her way. "You men move the dresser."

Wearing almost identically resigned expressions, Ethan and Richard moved obediently to follow Carly's instructions.

THEY TOOK ONE LOOK at the huge, crowded-to-the-rafters attic and groaned in almost perfect unison.

"I'd forgotten how much stuff was up here," Ethan admitted ruefully. "It's been years since I've seen this."

"Didn't your mother ever get rid of anything?" Richard asked, looking at the piles in disbelief.

"Only my grandmother's Bible, apparently."

Carly shook her head. "I thought *my* family collected a lot of junk. At least Mom gathers up a bunch of stuff for charity every couple of years."

"It's going to take hours to go through all this," Brenda murmured, daunted by the number of boxes, trunks and other potential hiding places.

"Yes, it would." Ethan sounded as though he had reached a sudden decision. "It's almost six now. Time to call it a day."

"But the Bible's probably up here somewhere," Carly protested, looking fully prepared to dive in.

"*Somewhere* being the operative word," Ethan replied. "Really, Carly. I appreciate your help, but it's just too late in the day to start a job this massive."

Carly nodded reluctantly. "I suppose you're right. So when are we going to tackle it?"

"We?"

"Well, yeah. It's certainly too big a job for just one person. Or even for two, for that matter. The four of us should be able to go through everything in a few hours."

Richard looked a little startled to be volunteered for another search party, but Brenda noticed he didn't seem averse to the idea. It wasn't hard to figure out why, she thought dryly.

Ethan, too, seemed surprised by how avidly Carly had thrown herself into his quest. "You know, it's really not that big a deal. It's just an old family heirloom, not particularly valuable. Not life-and-death important...."

"It's important to *you*," Carly said, giving Ethan a look that was both very young and deeply perceptive all at the same time. "All of us can understand that. Can't we, Richard?"

The suddenness with which she had turned her attention to him had Richard stammering a bit when he said, "Uh, yeah, sure. We understand."

"Great. So, does anyone have plans for Saturday?"

Richard answered first. "I've got a couple of meetings Saturday, but I should be finished by around two."

"I, uh, need to work a while Saturday morning, but I suppose I could take the afternoon off," Ethan said.

"I have no plans for Saturday," Brenda murmured, then decided it would be just too pathetic to add that she had no other plans for the foreseeable future, either.

Carly clapped her hands in front of her. "Great. So, we'll meet here at, say, three o'clock? And, Ethan, we're going to find your Granny's Bible."

Looking just a little dazed, Ethan cleared his throat. "Um—thanks. That would be…great."

Brenda saw everyone to the door a few minutes later. She didn't expect to find Sean Jacobs standing on the other side when she opened the door for them. His finger hovering over the doorbell, Sean looked startled when the door opened before he could press the button. He looked even more surprised when he saw the group assembled in the foyer.

"Something going on?" he asked, his gaze focused on Ethan.

"We were helping Ethan look for his grandmother's Bible," Brenda explained. "We still haven't found it."

Sean nodded to Richard, then looked curiously at Carly.

Brenda made the introductions, simply referring to the other woman as her friend, Carly D'Alessandro. Sean probably recognized the surname, but he made no comment.

"It's nice to meet you, Sean. You're as cute as Brenda said you were." Turning a mischievous smile in Brenda's direction, Carly patted Ethan's arm and Richard's cheek. "See you guys Saturday."

She hurried then to her car, leaving everyone blinking after her.

"She seems, um, nice," Sean said lamely.

Ethan, for some reason, was glaring at Brenda. "I've got to go," he said abruptly. "See you, Sean."

Nodding to Brenda and Richard, he left without an explanation of his suddenly surly mood.

"I was just about to head home, myself," Richard said, then looked from Sean to Brenda. "Unless there's some reason I need to stay?"

"Not on my behalf," Brenda told him, pushing aside her embarrassment at Carly's parting quip about Sean being "cute."

"I'm only staying a minute, myself," Sean said, showing no further reaction to Carly's teasing. "I just stopped by to drop off a check for household expenses. I figured we'd handle it this way until I can make arrangements to have the funds transferred directly into your bank account."

"That was thoughtful of you, but you didn't have to come out of your way on my behalf. I could have stopped by your office."

Sean smiled warmly at her. "It was no trouble at all. Practically on my way home. Is there anything else I can do for you while I'm here?"

"No, thank you. I'm fine."

"You're sure?"

"Positive. Thank you, Sean."

Richard glanced at his watch. "I have to clear out. I'm meeting with a client in half an hour. Sean, it was good to see you again. Brenda, I'll talk to you tomorrow."

She responded to his quick hug, then waved as he drove away, leaving her and Sean standing in the foyer. "Would you like to come in for a while?" she asked, motioning toward the parlor.

"No, thanks. To be honest, I worked through lunch and I'm ravenous. I'm on my way to find dinner. Hey, would you like to join me for a meal somewhere? We could talk about the remaining decisions we have to make."

She hesitated for several long beats, then gave him a strained smile. "Thanks, but I'd better pass this time.

I'm tired and grubby from searching almost every room of this house today. I think I'd just like to crash tonight."

He didn't seem to take the rejection personally. His pleasant expression didn't change when he nodded and moved toward the door. "I'll leave you to it, then. Give me a call on my cell if you need anything."

"I will. Bye, Sean."

She closed the door behind him, set the locks, then activated the alarm system. Only after she had done all of that and was on her way to take a shower did she attempt to analyze why she hadn't accepted Sean's invitation. She should have at least been tempted. She hadn't been out in a while, it would be nice to eat a meal prepared by someone else, for a change, and Sean would certainly be a pleasant dinner companion. And yet she'd found herself mentally scrambling for excuses before he'd even finished asking her.

Was it spending time with Sean she'd been trying to avoid? Or simply leaving the house? Either way, she needed to get over her qualms and get back to living a normal life.

SHE WAS SLEEPING SOUNDLY when the telephone rang again that night. Too groggy to think clearly, she reached out in the darkness to snatch up the phone without checking the caller ID. "Wha—?"

The breathing was so angry, so malevolent this time that she could almost feel heat radiating out of the handset. Acting entirely on instinct, she slammed the phone back into the cradle without even trying to learn the caller's identity.

Only then did she wake up enough and calm down

enough to turn on the lamp and check the caller ID readout. She was more resigned than surprised to see that the number had been blocked. Had she been halfway coherent when the phone rang, she never would have answered it.

Glancing at the bedside clock, she saw that it was just after 1:00 a.m. She snapped off the lamp and lay back down, staring at the ceiling. Even though she knew it was probably a futile effort, she closed her eyes and tried to go back to sleep.

AT JUST AFTER FIVE O'CLOCK Friday afternoon, Carly entered the small reception room of Richard Prentiss's insurance office and immediately started making plans for redecorating. Talk about boring! The most she could say about the room was that it was furnished. Chairs. Tables. Lamps. Generic framed prints hung in uninspired groupings on off-white walls. Vinyl blinds on the windows, for crying out loud.

She shook her head. "Pitiful."

A heavyset woman in her late thirties with thick glasses and a cheery smile looked up from one of two reception desks. The other desk was cluttered with papers, indicating that someone usually sat there, but the chair was empty now. "Good afternoon. May I help you?"

She had seen Richard's white sedan parked outside, so she knew he was in. There was no one waiting in the reception area, but she supposed he could be with a client. "I just thought I'd see if Mr. Prentiss has any spare time. I'd like to talk to him about, um, life insurance."

"Life insurance?" The woman, whose nameplate

identified her as Robin Smith, looked at Carly rather skeptically. "May I have your name?"

"It's Carly. Carly D'Alessandro."

"Just a moment, please. I'll see if he's available." She stood and waved Carly toward a seat, then disappeared with a slight waddle down a short hallway that led to the back of the office space.

Carly didn't sit, but drifted around the reception area mentally rearranging the furniture and adding colors and textures. It wouldn't take a lot of money, she mused. Just a little flair for shopping and arranging.

Give her three hundred dollars and she could make this place impress; give her a thousand and she'd wow every potential client who dropped in, she mused, wondering how Richard would react if she made that proposition to him.

"Carly?" Wearing another one of his too-cute insurance-salesman suits, Richard came down the hallway with a quizzical smile, Robin Smith padding along behind him.

She smiled back at him. "Hello, Richard."

"Robin said you want to talk to me about insurance?"

She kept her expression innocent. "Why else would I be here?"

"Good question." Looking just a bit wary, he motioned back toward his office. "Come on back."

"It's after five," she commented, glancing at her watch. "Were you about to leave for the day?"

"I have to stay a little longer to catch up on some paperwork. Robin, you need to leave, don't you?"

She nodded. "I do if I'm going to be on time for Jo-Jo's ball game."

"Then get going. Cheer on the team for me, too."

"I'll do that." Grinning, she snatched an overnight-bag-size purse out from under her desk and headed for the door, moving much more quickly now.

Richard led Carly into his office and she almost sighed when she saw that his decorating scheme—early bland—carried over into this room. High ceilings, big windows, beautiful woodwork. The place had possibilities, but it really needed some work. Twelve hundred dollars, maybe fifteen, she mused. Tops. "Have you ever considered hiring a decorator?"

"Robin handled the furniture selection and decorating. I think she did a pretty good job."

"It all looks okay," she said, letting her lack of enthusiasm show in her voice. "Just kind of dull. You know how Brenda's place looks like it was decorated by someone's grandmother?"

"Yeah?"

"This could have been done by your aunt. All very proper and balanced and perfectly matched. And very dull."

Richard planted his hands on his hips and looked at her in bemusement. "Do you always say exactly what you're thinking?"

"I try not to deliberately hurt anyone's feelings, and I can keep a sworn secret until my dying day. Other than that, why shouldn't I be honest?"

"So what makes you think you didn't just hurt my feelings?"

"Did I?"

He had the grace to look a little sheepish. "No."

"There you go, then."

Hesitating only a moment, he motioned toward one

of the two straight-back chairs that sat posed stiffly in front of his oversize desk. "Have a seat, and then you can tell me why you're here. Is it about Brenda?"

She sank into the chair, wriggling a little in a futile attempt to get comfortable. "I was in the neighborhood and I thought I'd drop in. Dad sent me to pick up a digital camera he had repaired at the electronics shop in the next block. Since Brenda mentioned where your office is, I thought I'd say hi."

Richard propped a hip on the corner of his desk. "Well, now that you're here, is there anything you would like to discuss other than my boring decor?"

"I could help you with that, you know," she said seriously. "Presenting the right appearance is very important to a business. Potential clients who are impressed with your good taste and creative flair will naturally be more inclined to want you as their insurance agent."

"Will they, now?"

"Definitely. That's been my dad's philosophy ever since he opened his first little one-man investigation agency. Now he and my uncles—my mom's brothers—have a big, fancy security agency, and their offices are beautifully decorated."

"You're pretty close to your father, aren't you?"

She shrugged. "Well, sure. I mean, he makes me crazy sometimes, but he's pretty cool, for a dad."

"My dad was pretty cool, too. He was an accountant who played guitar in a country band on weekends."

"Brenda told me you lost both your parents young. That must have been hard for all of you."

"Yeah, it was rough. It helped some that the three of us were pretty close."

"I can tell Brenda thinks the world of you."

His smile crooked up on one side. "I think she would tell you that I make her crazy sometimes, but I'm pretty cool, for a brother."

She beamed at him, amused by the way he had quoted her. "I think you're pretty cool, too—for an insurance guy."

She would bet he hated the way his light skin flushed so easily. Just a slight hint of pink, but enough to be fascinatingly revealing. Compliments rattled him. But she wasn't sure whether he reacted that way to all compliments, or just the ones from her.

She had found herself thinking a great deal about Richard Prentiss lately. She wasn't sure exactly what it was about him that intrigued her so. But when a guy she'd been sort of hoping would ask her out—a twenty-four-year-old grad student with a poet's eyes and an athlete's body—had called to ask her for a Friday-night date, she'd heard herself making excuses. She'd told him she had other plans, even though she hadn't. And now here she was, sitting in Richard's office. Wondering if she had the nerve to do something about her attraction to him.

Because she wasn't yet ready to test her courage, she veered the conversation back to a topic important to them both. "I'm a little worried about Brenda."

His expression turned instantly grave. "What, specifically, are you worried about? Has your father learned something?"

"No, it's nothing like that," she said quickly, holding up a hand to reassure him.

"So why are you worried about her?"

"Is it characteristic of your sister to spend so much time alone, cooped up inside a house?"

"No, it isn't," Richard admitted. "Brenda's not exactly a party girl, but she goes out. She stays busy with a part-time summer job in a bank and volunteering in a local animal shelter. She has a couple of close friends from the school where she teaches—both of whom are also working summer jobs, but they usually try to get together once a week or so. I know she's talked to them by telephone since the fire, just to tell them what happened, but she hasn't seen any of them."

"That's what I thought. She hasn't been out of that house since our shopping trip Monday afternoon, has she?"

"Not as far as I know."

"That's not good."

"No…" Richard agreed, but so slowly that she read something more into his answer.

"You think it *is* good that she's staying inside the house?"

"Well, you've got to admit the place is secure. If someone is after her, she's safe in Margaret's house."

"She can't hide in there forever. She's young and pretty and fun. She should get out and have a good time, put some of this stuff out of her mind for a while."

Richard nodded. "You're right, of course. She should get out. I'll suggest it to her."

Carly sighed. What a guy thing to say. "I'll talk to her. Maybe I can coerce her into going out to a club or something next weekend. You want to go with us?"

"You'd want *me* to go?"

She smiled at him. "Sure. Why not? It'll be fun."

"I'm not much of a 'clubber,'" he admitted. "I don't drink, and I'm a lousy dancer."

She laughed, liking him even more for his self-deprecation. "I don't drink, either—by law, as well as by choice. But I love to dance. Maybe I can give you some pointers."

He looked visibly taken aback. "You aren't old enough to drink?"

She was used to that response, of course. "I will be very soon. But I'm sort of a control freak, and I like to always have a clear head. I'm not messing around with any substance, legal or otherwise, that might make me do something I'd regret later."

"You never do anything you regret later? I wish I could say the same."

"I didn't say I never make mistakes. But when I do, I prefer to have nothing or no one to blame but myself."

He didn't immediately respond, so she decided to get the conversation back on topic. "So, what do you say? Want to go out with a couple of hot women soon?"

He broke into a reluctant smile. "I've got to admit that's not the sort of proposition I hear very often."

She looked at him through her lashes. "I find that hard to believe."

She just loved that very faint wash of color that let her know when her efforts at flirting with him scored a direct hit.

Looking a little flustered, he pushed himself off the desk and stood beside it, his hands in his pockets. "First, of course, we'll have to convince Brenda to go out."

"Leave that to me," Carly said confidently. "I've got a talent for persuasion."

For some reason, he looked almost terrified by that comment.

She patted his arm, resisting the impulse to let her hand linger. "Don't worry, Richard. This is going to be fun."

He didn't look at all reassured.

CHAPTER NINE

BRENDA MADE HERSELF leave the house Saturday morning. Thanks to Carly's enthusiastic arrangements, she was expecting visitors that afternoon. As official hostess here, at least for now, she should provide refreshments for her guests, and she needed a few other things, too.

Though it wasn't the closest supermarket to Margaret's house, she drove several miles out of the way to shop where she usually did. Even these small connections to her simple, former life helped her retain her tenuous grip on normalcy.

For the past week it had felt as if the Brenda she'd been was slowly slipping away. A new home. New friends. New financial circumstances. It felt good to take hold of a familiar blue-handled shopping cart with a familiar squeaky wheel and wander down the aisles of her supermarket.

She bought pretty much her usual grocery items, by long-standing habit comparing prices and keeping a sharp eye out for sales. She was selecting a couple of apples in the produce section when she heard someone say her name. Glancing up, she felt her face freeze for a moment. "Diane."

Her closest friend from the school where they

taught, Diane Jackson O'Brien stood only a few feet away, looking startled to see her. A newlywed of less than four months, petite, red-haired Diane was a bundle of energy, a student's favorite among the first-grade teachers. She and Brenda had attended the same university, becoming friends there, and had applied to many of the same schools. They'd been delighted to be hired by the same one.

"I'm surprised to see you here," Diane said. "I thought you were staying with your sister since the fire. Have you found another apartment?"

"I, uh—" She sighed. "I really need to talk to you, Di. Are you buying any frozen foods that won't keep in your car for an hour or so?"

"No. I just came in to pick up a few things. What's going on, Brenda? I've been so worried about you since the fire."

"I know. And I realize I've been shutting you out. Let's pay for these things and then have coffee at that coffee shop next door. I'll tell you exactly where I've been living since the fire—if you can believe it."

Eyeing her curiously, Diane nodded. "You've certainly got me intrigued. You make it all sound so mysterious."

Brenda bit her lip. Diane had no idea just how strange her friend's life had become in the past two weeks.

A short while later, Diane's expression had gone from intrigued to dumbfounded. "You're living in a mansion?"

"I don't know if you'd call it a mansion, exactly. But it's big. You know that neighborhood. All the houses are big."

"Yeah, I know it. Never thought I'd know anyone who actually lived there."

"Never thought I would actually *be* living there," Brenda admitted.

"Did you ever figure out why you were named in the will?"

"Not a clue. I've even hired a private investigator to try to find a connection—*any* connection—between me and Margaret Jacobs. So far he's found nothing."

"A private investigator," Diane repeated. "Like, you know, one of those guys on TV?"

"Well, not exactly. He's very clean-cut and professional. More of a desk-and-computer jockey than a TV cloak-and-dagger type."

"But he hasn't found anything?"

"Not so far. Of course, I only hired him nine days ago. And he does have other clients."

"So, are you going to quit teaching?"

"Why would I quit teaching?"

Diane waved her hands, almost knocking over her foam coffee cup. "Well, you know. You'll have more money than you need. A great house to live in. A chance to travel, like you've always wanted to do. You're really going to show up five days a week for nine solid months if you don't have to?"

"I like my job," Brenda protested. "You know that."

"Two words. Cooper Owens."

Brenda shuddered—a purely instinctive reaction that occurred whenever she heard that particular name. "Okay, he was pretty awful. Not quite as bad as his harridan of a mother."

"They made your life a living hell last school year."

"Very close. But there were so many more perfectly delightful children in my class. I loved that part."

"Hey, I like teaching, too. But if I suddenly had all

the money I needed, didn't have to worry about paying bills or the mortgage, would I still commit to being in the classroom every day? Wiping snotty noses and settling squabbles and stopping one kid from eating crayons while trying to challenge another who's light-years ahead of the rest of the class intellectually? I don't know, Brenda. That would be a hard call."

Obviously, Diane was assuming that a change in finances meant that Brenda would change, as well. Would her other coworkers all look at her differently now?

She thought of the way the staff had treated another teacher, a woman who came in three days a week to work with gifted and talented students. Gloria Burroughs was married to a neurosurgeon and lived in an exclusive gated community—though not quite as exclusive as the neighborhood where Brenda was currently living. Gloria wore lots of diamonds and prominently labeled designer clothing, drove an expensive car and liked to talk about how she didn't need to work, but did so because she wanted to "give back to the community." Jealousy had certainly been a part of the reason the other teachers, eking out a living on their notoriously meager salaries, had never really liked Gloria.

This, Brenda thought with a sigh, was why she had been dreading telling her old friends exactly how big her inheritance had been.

"Are you going to have a party or something in your new home? Give us all the grand tour?"

Brenda hesitated. "I should probably wait before I do any entertaining. After all, the will is still in probate, so the house isn't even officially mine to use yet." Not to mention that she was still going through spells of trying to decide whether she should decline the inheritance and turn it back over to Ethan, despite what he said about not wanting it.

And wouldn't Diane and the others think she had lost her mind if she even admitted that she had considered turning down a fortune?

"Uh-oh." Diane's expression held a mixture of mischief and dismay.

"What?"

"You thought it was hard getting rid of Ross Lambert before. Wait'll he finds out you're rich now."

Brenda groaned. Ross Lambert was a guy she had dated a few times before Christmas. She blamed her lapse of judgment on the festive season, and her wistful longing to have someone special to share the holidays with. Diane had been blissfully making wedding plans at the time, and it seemed as though all her friends were paired off, making her unusually vulnerable when Ross had asked her out.

Ross had seemed nice enough at first, but it hadn't been long before she'd realized that he was the clingy and demanding type. Perfectly charming one moment, sullen and possessive in the next—and that after only three dates. She'd broken it off very quickly, but he hadn't been one to take her rejection gracefully.

She had almost reached the point of swallowing her pride and asking for big brother's assistance when Ross had finally accepted defeat. Even then, he'd continued to call and try to talk her into going out with him again at least once a month during the six months that had passed since she'd sent him away. It had been five weeks since she'd last heard from him, and she'd hoped he had finally gotten the message once and for all that she wasn't interested in him.

"Don't even talk about him," she ordered, shaking a finger at Diane. "It isn't funny—and I have enough to worry about now."

Diane blew a breath out her nose. "Wish I had those kinds of worries—too much money and too many options."

Brenda had finally told her friend that she had an appointment that afternoon, and cut their visit short, promising to stay in touch. She had no doubt that Diane would be on the telephone even before she left the coffee shop parking lot, spreading the word about Brenda's fancy new digs.

Worrying about how her inheritance would change her relationships with her old friends *and* her siblings, Brenda made the drive back to Margaret's house in somber silence. She didn't even turn on the radio, which was totally unlike her, since she usually liked listening to music while driving.

Pulling into the driveway, she used the garage door opener Sean had provided for her and parked her rather battered little economy car in the bay next to the gleaming Mercedes. As she climbed out of the driver's seat, she couldn't help thinking how out of place her car looked sitting there. She tried not to dwell on the obvious analogies between her car and herself.

ETHAN WAS THE FIRST to arrive that afternoon. Brenda let him in with a smile. "Both Carly and Richard have called to tell me they're running late," she said. "They should be here soon."

He almost regretted being the punctual type. It was

awkward enough being with Brenda when the others were around. Being alone with her even for a few minutes just didn't seem like a wise idea at all.

Especially when she looked so good.

She'd dressed for the job they planned to tackle today in jeans, sneakers and a snug-fitting, lime-green V-neck T-shirt. Her fair hair was twisted up and clipped, baring her slender neck. A few tendrils had escaped to brush her cheek, making his fingers itch to do the same.

"I made cookies," she said, motioning to a tray arranged on the coffee table. "Lemon bars. And there's freshly brewed coffee in the carafe. I figured we could use a jolt of caffeine and sugar before we get started."

"Sounds good." He helped himself to a cup of coffee, then plucked a lemon bar from the dish. "*Is* good," he pronounced after taking a bite.

She smiled, displaying a shallow dimple that held his attention for a moment before he made himself look back at his coffee mug. He tried to think of something to say. "So, what have you been doing to entertain yourself?"

Brenda shrugged a bit sheepishly. "I went to the supermarket this morning."

"Wow. How did you handle all that excitement?"

She gave him a chiding look. "At least I got out."

"Are you really so nervous about leaving here?"

"No, of course not," she said airily. And then she added a bit more gravely, "Maybe a little. You have to admit it feels…well, safe here."

He looked around the room and shrugged. "For you, maybe. For me, it feels more like a cage than a sanctuary. I never found anything out there as discouraging as what I dealt with in here."

"You really don't want this house?"

"How many times do I have to say it before you believe it? I couldn't wait to get out of this house."

She bit her lip, and he wondered if she was still trying to decide if he meant what he said.

"Have you had any more disturbing incidents?" He was aware of the inadequacy of his choice of words, but he wasn't sure how else to ask if anyone had tried to kill her in the past couple of days.

It was obvious that she knew what he meant, despite his awkwardness. "No. No phone calls. No speeding vehicles. No more fires. No more mysterious inheritances."

"Downright dull, huh?"

She smiled again. "Quite. Thank goodness."

His gaze lingered on her mouth long enough that she must have noticed. She cleared her throat and glanced away from him.

It hit him like a blow then, a realization he had been trying to avoid since the first time he'd met Brenda Prentiss. He wanted her.

He couldn't have her—at least, he shouldn't have her—but that didn't stop him from wanting. From imagining. From wishing he had met her when she was still a money-challenged schoolteacher who had never heard of Margaret Jacobs.

Even had he met her then, chances were slim anything permanent might have developed between them. He was still gun-shy when it came to emotional ties. As soon as a woman started showing signs of getting clingy—or worse, possessive—he was gone. But had his mother's money and her brother's suspicions not lay between them, they might have had a great time. While it lasted.

"Anyway," she said quickly, maybe sensing the direction his thoughts were taking, "I've almost convinced myself I've been overreacting. Letting my imagination get away from me."

"Those things really happened, Brenda. You didn't imagine them."

"I know they happened. But maybe I jumped to the wrong conclusion. Cars speed recklessly down the street where I lived all the time. We've always said it was a wonder no one was run down. And the duplex fire did start in my kitchen, somewhere around the stove. The fire investigator sounded convinced that I left a burner on, a tea towel too close. Because I was so distracted that evening, I have to admit it's possible he was right."

"And the phone calls? Can you explain those away as coincidence?"

"Someone has been harassing me with phone calls," she admitted. "But even if someone is angry enough with me to call and breathe at me, there's no reason to think I'm in any real danger from the caller."

"Do you have any theories about the caller's identity?"

"It could be Patty Ann. She made it clear that she's furious that I was named in Margaret's will, and that she and her husband should have inherited everything."

He nodded thoughtfully. "It wouldn't surprise me in the least if Patty Ann resorted to behavior like that. She always has been the silly, vindictive type."

"But not dangerous?"

"Not as far as I know," he admitted. And then he asked, "Is there any chance the phone calls aren't related to the inheritance? Is there someone with a grudge against you from your previous life? A disgruntled student, maybe? An ex-boyfriend?"

"Tony asked me those things, too. I reminded him that I teach second grade. The students are a little young to carry out a telephone harassment campaign, though I gave Tony the names of some parents who weren't particularly fond of me because I expected their kids to follow basic classroom rules. As for ex-boyfriends, there was one guy who wasn't happy with me for breaking up with him, but it seems unlike him to call without saying anything. He's one of those guys who thinks if he talks fast enough and long enough, he can convince anyone to do what he wants. My problem when he called in the past wasn't that he wouldn't talk to me, but that he wouldn't shut up."

Ethan wondered how long she had dated the jerk. How close they had been. Why she had dumped him—and how the guy would react to finding out he'd let a very wealthy woman slip through his fingers.

"The point is," she went on, apparently uncomfortable talking about her personal life, "that I've decided I've let my imagination run away with me. The close encounter with the truck was probably coincidental, and the fire was related to the inheritance only because my own distraction probably contributed to it. A series of phone calls is annoying, but hardly a sign that anyone is trying to kill me. I would like for Tony to do a little more digging into the mysterious connection between me and your mother, but I'm not going to let paranoia get the best of me."

"Good for you." Yet while he admired the renewed spark of spirit in her eyes, he found himself wanting to warn her not to be too complacent. Yes, it was possible that her two near misses had been coincidental, but it was also conceivable, however unlikely, that they had been deliberate acts.

"After all," she added with a too-bright smile, "you're the only one with a motive to kill me. And we both know you're no killer. Right?"

He still couldn't figure out how she could seem so confident about that, considering that she barely knew him. And that most people would say he really was the only one with a motive to harm her.

The doorbell rang before he could confirm her statement that he was no killer. Brenda jumped a little, then laughed self-consciously as she drew her gaze away from Ethan's. "I'll answer the door," she said, then hurried out of the room before he could say anything else.

THOUGH SHE TRIED to be discreet about it, Brenda watched Ethan closely while they searched the attic.

Carly and Richard had arrived within a couple of minutes of each other. After they'd each had a cookie and a few sips of coffee, they'd headed straight up to the attic. The way Carly had acted, one would have thought they were digging for precious gems, but her enthusiasm seemed to put Ethan at ease. Richard, of course, looked at Carly as if everything she said was simply brilliant.

She felt a bit petty for checking to see if Ethan was as taken with Carly as Richard was. And a bit foolish for being relieved that he didn't seem to be.

Of course, Ethan wasn't exactly walking into walls over *her*, either. But there were moments when he seemed to watch her with an intensity she could almost feel. She didn't think she was imagining that he was interested in her—but she wasn't quite sure why. Was it because of the mystery of her inheritance or was it more personal?

They went through box after box of boring household records—receipts, payroll and expense ledgers, maintenance records and warranties. Apparently, Margaret had never thrown away a scrap of official-looking paper.

There were trunks of vintage clothing, which both Carly and Brenda would have lingered over had Richard and Ethan not hurried them along. Photo albums. Holiday decorations. Furniture—mostly chairs and occasional tables. Boxes of awards and recognition plaques from professional and charitable organizations. Margaret's. Both of her husbands'. Even a few of her father's. Some academic awards from Ethan's school years, all the way through college.

"I won quite a few sports trophies and medals during the years, but she didn't see any reason to keep those," he commented. "I took a few of the important ones with me when I left, but I guess she got rid of the rest."

Carly gave Ethan a look of such melting sympathy that he might as well have just announced that he had lost his last friend. Ethan cleared his throat and bent to open a little antique cabinet that Brenda thought was much cuter than anything currently displayed in the house. She could tell that he was embarrassed that anyone might feel sorry for him because of his estrangement with his mother. Few people enjoyed being the object of pity, and she would bet Ethan disliked it more than most.

Carly had found another trunk that intrigued her. "What are these?" she asked, opening the metal container.

Ethan moved closer to look. Frowning, he lifted a leather binder from the trunk and opened it. "Damn," he said. "I'd forgotten about these."

Brenda looked around in response to his tone. "What is it?"

"My dad's coin collection. He used to let me look at it when I was a kid."

As curious as the others, Richard glanced over Carly's shoulder, then made a strangled sound as Ethan turned pages in the binder. "That's a 1910 Saint-Gaudens double eagle twenty-dollar gold coin. And there's a 1912. And a 1928. And, oh man, a 1908 D five-dollar Indian head gold coin. That one alone could sell for a couple of thousand dollars. We're talking major collection value here, guys. Serious money."

Ethan frowned, opening another binder and touching one of the cases displayed inside it. "His coin collection was one of the few subjects he got passionate about. Most of what he said went over my head at the time, but I remember enjoying his attention and I liked looking at the shiny gold coins."

"These 'shiny gold coins' are worth thousands of dollars," Richard murmured. "Well into six figures, I would guess."

"And your mother just stuck this in the attic?" Brenda asked in disbelief.

Ethan shrugged, but his voice was strained when he said, "She thought it was a silly hobby. She resented the time he spent on the collection when she thought he should be doing something more prestigious or productive. He didn't talk to her about it, so maybe she honestly had no idea of the value of the collection. She must have stashed this trunk up here right after Dad died more than twenty years ago, and never thought about it again."

"Your mother was more than a little eccentric, wasn't she, Ethan?"

Ethan merely nodded in response to Richard's rhetorical question.

"Maybe she was saving the collection for you," Brenda suggested. "She probably intended to give it to you someday."

"Yeah, maybe." But he didn't sound convinced.

"Anyway, it's yours now," Brenda said matter-of-factly. "Be sure and take the trunk with you when you leave today."

"Just like that, huh?"

Aware of Carly and Richard watching them, Brenda nodded. "Your mother left you everything that belonged to your father. This collection obviously fits that description. She must have wanted you to have it."

"It's worth a great deal of money. You shouldn't be so blasé about turning it over to me."

"It's yours. And say all you want about the monetary value, we all know the collection means more to you than that. It was your father's, and you have memories of sharing it with him. Why do you always have to pretend none of this matters to you?"

"Let's just say I'm accustomed to hiding my feelings in this house."

"Take the trunk, Ethan," she said more gently. "Richard and Carly are witnesses that you're taking only what was left to you in your mother's will, if that matters to anyone."

He nodded and closed the trunk. "All right. Fine. I'll take it."

"You might want to consider putting it in a safe," Richard, ever the professional, advised. "And you'll want to have the collection professionally appraised and listed in a separate rider on your insurance policy."

Carly laughed. "Dude. I *know* you aren't trying to sell him a policy before he even gets the coins home."

Even with all the other emotions swirling around her, Brenda was amused by how easily Carly could make Richard blush.

Her amusement faded quickly when Richard turned to her with a stern look in his eyes and said, "You know, Brenda, I'm kind of hungry. Why don't you and I go down and make some sandwiches or something for everyone while Ethan and Carly keep searching up here?"

CHAPTER TEN

"DO YOU REALLY THINK that was a good idea?"

Even though Brenda knew exactly what Richard referred to, she bought herself a little time by asking, "Was what a good idea?"

"Just handing that coin collection over to Ethan. That's a very valuable collection. Maybe you should have discussed it with Sean first."

"The will specifically stated that Ethan was entitled to anything that was his father's personal property. I can't see how anyone would argue that this collection wouldn't fit that criteria."

"Why didn't he mention the collection when he named the things he wanted?"

"I suppose he forgot about it, or assumed, as he said, that Margaret had disposed of it. Evidently, Margaret stashed the trunk in the attic after her first husband died, when Ethan was just a little boy. He hasn't seen it since."

"So we just happened to stumble on to what some people would consider a fortune in gold coins. A collection Ethan will take with him when he leaves."

"Yes," Brenda said, slicing a large knife through a ham-and-Swiss sandwich. "That's exactly what occurred."

"You have to admit that Ethan has suddenly gotten nicer to everyone—especially you—since you became so eager to hand things over to him. You even enlisted Carly and me to help him look for things."

"I didn't exactly enlist anyone. Carly volunteered—herself *and* you. As for Ethan, maybe he's being nicer because we've stopped accusing him—to his face, at least—of nefarious deeds. I don't find his behavior at all suspicious."

"You wouldn't," he muttered.

She looked up from the tray of sandwiches she had just set on the breakfast nook table, next to a basket of vegetable chips and a bowl of yogurt-based dip. "What's that supposed to mean?"

"C'mon, Bren, it's obvious you have a soft spot for the guy. I don't know if it's because you think he's attractive, or if you still feel guilty about inheriting his mother's estate, but you've practically bent over backward to accommodate him."

She felt temper warm her face. "Just because I'm trying to act decently toward a man who got shafted by his own mother, that doesn't mean I have any ulterior motives."

"Actually, you just made my point by saying he was 'shafted.' You don't know what really went on between Margaret and Ethan. Yeah, he makes her sound like an unreasonable tyrant of a woman, but we've only heard his side. You haven't talked to any of her friends or someone who knew more about what went on between them."

She had to concede that Ethan's was the only side she'd heard, but she thought that in itself was revealing. None of Margaret's friends, if there had been any, had come forward to talk to Brenda or tell her what, if anything, they knew about why Brenda had been named in the will, rather than Ethan.

"It isn't as if I've handed him the keys to the house," she said, hearing her own defensiveness. "I just want him to have the things he's entitled to in the will. As for the rest of it, I'm still processing everything, trying to make some decisions."

A cat rubbed against her ankles and meowed plaintively. Brenda glanced automatically at the shamelessly begging white cat. "Forget it, Fluffy. You've already been fed. You can have your usual kitty treat at bedtime."

"You're bargaining with the cats now?" Richard eyed her quizzically. "Better be careful, sis. You start hiding yourself away in this place, talking to the cats, and you're going to end up…well, peculiar."

"Carry these tea glasses over to the table, will you? Wasn't that why you came downstairs with me? To 'help' me?" Yet even when he had volunteered his assistance, she'd known she was in for another brotherly lecture.

She glanced at her watch. It was almost five-thirty. They had been searching the attic for over two hours without finding the Bible. Richard must have really believed she needed a warning, or he never would have left Carly alone up there with Ethan.

So what was it he thought was so important to warn her about? Was it just his disapproval of her giving Ethan valuable items from the estate? Or was he more concerned about her reasons for doing so? Richard had always been too perceptive where she was concerned. Did he sense that she was becoming a bit too fascinated by Ethan Blacklock?

And did he honestly think she needed to be warned that getting too involved with Ethan was not a good idea?

"ETHAN, LOOK!" Carly sounded excited, but he had learned not to expect much from that, since just about everything she found excited her. "It's a box of old books."

Okay, that had potential. He moved to examine her latest find.

Maybe it was because he still remembered the look Richard had given him as he and Brenda had left the attic that Ethan stood a couple of feet away from Carly. It had been very apparent that Richard hadn't liked leaving Ethan alone with Carly. Ethan could have told him he didn't have to worry about that. As much as he liked Carly—and he could certainly appreciate that she was a strikingly beautiful young woman—he just wasn't drawn to her in that way. Unlike Richard, obviously.

Of course, he doubted that Richard would be any happier to learn that Ethan definitely *was* drawn to Brenda in that way.

He watched as Carly pulled books out of the box and stacked them on the floor beside her. Children's books, mostly. Some classics. A couple of old dictionaries and other reference books. Even a few old textbooks. Nothing that looked particularly valuable. No family Bible.

Discouraged, Carly piled the books back into the box. "I'm beginning to think it's not up here at all."

"I think you're right. We've looked through almost everything."

"I was so sure it would be here. Some P.I. I make, huh?"

Her disgusted tone made him smile a little. "Is that what you want to do?"

"Well, no. But you'd think I'd have learned something useful after growing up in the business."

"Carly, you've been very helpful," he assured her. "You were the one who helped us make such a methodical search of the house. Looking under mattresses and behind furniture and in other cubbyholes Brenda and I never would have thought about. If Mother had hidden the book anywhere in the house, I'm sure you'd have found it."

"You're just trying to make me feel better," she said with a pout.

"True. Is it working?"

"Yes. Don't stop."

He chuckled and reached out a hand to help her to her feet. "I wouldn't want you to get a swelled head."

"Impossible. Perfect people don't get swollen heads," she said with a toss of her ebony hair.

Ethan laughed.

Richard caught them that way, laughing and still holding hands.

If looks could kill, Ethan thought, dropping Carly's hand and moving a safe distance away from her.

"Food's ready," Richard announced abruptly, then turned and stalked toward the stairs.

Following Carly out of the attic, Ethan decided that she looked rather pleased by Richard's snit.

That situation could certainly get sticky, he thought, but it was hardly any of his business. He supposed he could see why Richard would be drawn to Carly. She

was certainly pretty, and had a fun, contagiously enthusiastic personality to match. But she also had a P.I.
for a father, still even lived at home with her folks. Was
Richard really interested in seeing someone who
probably still had to be in by curfew?

That wouldn't have been Ethan's choice. He preferred women who were a bit more independent.
Already established in their own lives and careers so
they wouldn't get too dependent on him.

He sure didn't want to risk getting involved with
someone who would expect too much from him, or try
to change him or control him. He'd been there, with a
woman who hadn't been satisfied unless she'd been
trying to modify the way he dressed and talked, or
trying to convince him that he liked the same things
she did and had no use for his former friends or
hobbies. He'd been deeply infatuated with Christie
for a time, even lived with her for a few weeks. But
then he'd suddenly woken up to the realization that
he'd gotten involved with a woman entirely too much
like his mother.

That had been two years ago, his first and last
attempt at a serious relationship. Since then, he'd stuck
to casual, no-strings liaisons that made it easy for
either of them to walk away when things started to get
awkward. He couldn't see having an encounter like
that with pretty young Carly D'Alessandro—or with
Brenda Prentiss, for that matter.

He would bet Brenda was the type who would
expect at least a few strings from an intimate relationship. And if she didn't, she came equipped with an
overprotective big brother who would certainly look
out for what he considered to be her best interests.

Even discounting all the other uncomfortable reasons why he could never get involved with Brenda, the bossy older brother was an insurmountable barrier.

THEY SAT AROUND THE TABLE in the breakfast nook, eating sandwiches and chatting. At least, Carly and Brenda chatted. Richard was too busy glowering at Ethan, who was content to just watch the others while he ate.

"So how many cousins do you have?" Brenda asked, continuing a conversation about Carly's large, extended family.

"Dozens," Carly replied with a wrinkle of her nose. "Dad has two brothers and a few dozen cousins of his own. Big Italian-American clan who try to get together at least once a year for a formal reunion and several other times during the year for slightly smaller celebrations. My mother is one of seven siblings. Once they all found each other, they grew so close that they spend as much time as possible together."

"Once they found each other?" Brenda repeated curiously.

"That's an interesting story," Carly said, then took a bite of her sandwich.

Brenda exchanged a wry look with Ethan, both silently acknowledging Carly's pleasure in being the center of attention. "Well?" Brenda urged. "We're waiting to hear it."

Carly sipped her tea. "My mother was raised as the adopted, only child of Alicia Trent and Harrison Trent III. You know, Trent Enterprises?"

Everyone at the table knew the name. Ethan noted that Richard looked particularly taken aback by

Carly's family connections. The Trent fortune made his own mother's estate look practically penny-ante—which partially explained why Carly had been so blasé about Brenda's inheritance.

"Anyway," Carly continued, "after my mother's mother died, Mom found out for the first time that she had six biological siblings. She was stunned, but she wanted to find them. She hired my dad, who had a much smaller operation then, to track them down. While he was looking for them, he and Mom fell in love and got married."

Brenda was obviously enthralled by the story. "They found all of them?"

"Eventually. The siblings had been scattered after they were orphaned when Mom was two. Her oldest brother, my uncle Jared, was eleven, and the youngest child, my aunt Lindsay, was just a baby. Dad and his associates tracked everyone down and reunited them. Well, all but one brother, Miles, who died when he was a teenager, several years before Mom started the search. However, Miles left behind a daughter, Brynn, and now she's a part of the family, too. Part of both families, actually, since she married a D'Alessandro, my dad's younger brother, Joe. All of the Walker siblings—that was Mom's birth name—anyway, they've all married and had children and some of those children are married and parents, themselves, now, so it's one huge, close family."

"I can't imagine suddenly finding out as an adult that she had a whole family she never even knew about," Brenda said.

Carly nodded. "Mom said it took her a while to get used to the idea, but she bonded really quickly with them when they came together. Of course, most of the others remembered each other as children, since they were a little older when they were separated. Not Lindsay, though. She was adopted into a family before she was a year old, and she's really close to them. She lives the farthest away from the rest of the family and she hasn't been quite as involved in their lives as the others, but she's still very much part of the clan. Of course, I've known them all since I was born, so I can't imagine them not being together."

She looked at Brenda then. "Maybe because of Mom's history, Dad's first suspicion when he started your investigation was that maybe *you* had been adopted. He thought there might be a biological connection between you and Margaret Jacobs that you didn't know about."

Ethan felt the words hit him directly in the gut. It hadn't even occurred to him that he and Brenda could be related—and the very possibility made him sort of queasy. He did *not* want to be this strongly attracted to someone who could be a member of his own family!

But Richard was shaking his head. "That's crazy. I'm old enough to remember when my mother was pregnant with Brenda. I went with Dad to bring Mom and Brenda home from the hospital. Brenda looks just like my sister and my mother—and me, for that matter. Everyone always tells us we look alike."

"You do," Carly agreed. "Very much alike. And Dad found out very quickly that Brenda wasn't adopted. So, he started looking into familial connections between Margaret and your parents, but he hasn't found anything there, either. He's looking into their pasts now, seeing if maybe they knew each other as kids or went to school together—anything that would explain Margaret choosing their youngest child as her beneficiary. So far, he's found no connections at all."

Trying to look completely casual about the conversation, Ethan scooped some dip onto a funny-colored chip and stuffed it into his mouth.

"Growing up an only child is what made Mom want to have more kids of her own," Carly rattled on. "There are four of us—Jason, then me, then Katie and Justin, who's fourteen. How about you, Ethan? Did you ever wish you had brothers and sisters?"

He swallowed the chip. "Yes," he said simply, remembering the loneliness he'd felt until he'd gotten old enough to surround himself with friends and sports team members.

"Were you and Sean close?" Carly asked.

"We got along okay, but I wouldn't call us close. Sean spent most of his time with his mother and stepfather. His dad was a workaholic who wasn't home much, and my mother was hardly the maternal type, so Sean only visited occasionally. We both liked video games, so that's what we usually did when he was here. I had all the early game consoles."

"Richard has the latest video games *now*," Brenda murmured with a teasing look at her brother. "He's a fanatic."

Ethan shrugged. "Isn't everyone?"

Carly started another lively conversation, this time about favorite video games. She even managed to draw Richard into this discussion, since he couldn't remain unresponsive to her overtures. They finished the simple meal pleasantly enough, despite the undercurrents of emotion they all pretended to ignore. They cleaned up together, and then Carly turned to Ethan.

"I'm really sorry we didn't find your grandmother's Bible," she said.

He nodded. "Thanks. I guess Mother got rid of it, after all."

"Are you sure there isn't a safe in the house somewhere? Or a safe-deposit box in a bank where she might have stored the Bible?"

"If there were a secret safe in the house, we'd have found it by now," he said. "I'm sure Sean would know about any deposit boxes, but I can't imagine Mother would consider this item important enough to safeguard that carefully when she shoved a gold coin collection into the attic and forgot about it."

He was still amazed that they had found the collection in the attic. His mother had not been a careless or foolish woman. Even if she hadn't known the exact worth of the collection, she must have realized it was valuable. What had she been thinking to treat it so cavalierly? The truly prosaic and practical course would have been to sell it off after his father's death.

Brenda seemed to believe that Margaret had saved the coin collection for him. That Margaret had wanted him to have it with the rest of his father's things. That she'd even had the coins in mind when she had specified that he was to receive his father's personal possessions. But Brenda hadn't known Margaret—nor had she been around to hear the anger and bitterness of his final conversation with his mother. Had Margaret remembered the coins at that moment, she probably would have thrown them in a lake.

Yet, she had left him his father's things. And she had updated her will only eighteen months ago.

He supposed he would never understand what had gone through his mother's head. And it wasn't as if she could ever tell him now.

The telephone rang, and he noticed that Brenda's jaw tightened as she approached the kitchen extension. That subtle sign of nerves reminded him of the disturbing calls she'd been receiving. Was she anxious every time the phone rang now?

It annoyed him to think that someone was deliberately harassing her. If he found out that Leland or Patty Ann had something to do with this—well, he wouldn't do anything. None of his business, really, and he had vowed to stay out of it once he got his things. Still made him mad, though.

Brenda's expression cleared when she read the number on the caller ID screen. She was actually smiling when she answered.

Ethan's frown deepened when he realized that it was Sean who had put her in such a cheerful mood. She sure seemed to be getting chummy with old Sean. And Sean was certainly taking his responsibilities as trustee seriously, calling every day to see if Brenda was okay, and if there was anything she needed.

For some inexplicable reason, that annoyed him almost as much as the possibility that Leland was calling just to unnerve her.

CHAPTER ELEVEN

ETHAN DIDN'T LINGER LONG after they finished the
sandwiches. He was out the door only a few minutes
after Brenda finished speaking with Sean. After
thanking them for their help with searching for his
grandmother's Bible, he took his trunk full of gold
coins and left, giving Brenda one somber, inscrutable
look on his way out. A look that still made her shiver—
and wish she knew exactly what it had implied.

She wasn't sure why his mood had suddenly
changed. It was almost as if he'd been smiling one
moment and scowling the next, and as far as she knew,
nothing had occurred to trigger the switch.

She supposed he was disappointed about not finding
his grandmother's Bible. They'd all been so hopeful,
and so confident they would find it in the attic. Instead,
they'd found a fortune in old gold coins. She would
have thought that, at least, would make him leave
smiling.

But he'd said from the first time she'd met him that
he had no interest in the monetary value of anything
in this house. He seemed to take pride only in the
money he earned through his own efforts. Which, of
course, only made her feel more conflicted about her
sizable inheritance from a total stranger.

"Did you tell Sean about the coin collection?" Richard asked after Ethan left.

Brenda nodded. "I told him we stumbled across it while we were searching the attic. I explained that you realized the coins were quite valuable, and that Ethan took them with him when he left. I said that the three of us were witnesses that he simply took possession of one of his father's personal belongings, as permitted by his mother's will."

"How did Sean react?"

She cleared her throat, remembering the awkwardness of that part of her conversation with Sean. "He was, um, surprised that such a valuable collection was just sitting in a trunk in the attic. He hadn't known anything about it. He said maybe I should have waited to have the collection appraised and its ownership verified before I let Ethan take it, but he understood why I didn't. He knows how I feel about what Margaret did to her son."

"In other words, he didn't really approve of what you did, but he didn't chew you out about it because you'd already done it."

"Something like that," Brenda admitted. "But I'm not going to apologize for encouraging Ethan to take his own father's things. I would have no right to try to interfere."

"For what it's worth, I think you did the right thing," Carly told Brenda loyally. "I watched Ethan's face when he looked at those coins. Those weren't dollar signs in his eyes. They were memories of his dad."

"I saw the same thing," Brenda murmured.

Richard exhaled sharply and shook his head. "Or you could both be gullible enough to buy everything poor, disinherited Ethan Blacklock says."

"You are determined to believe the worst of Ethan, aren't you?" Brenda asked heatedly.

"I'm just trying to make you use some common sense. For God's sake, Brenda, look at everything that has happened to you in the past couple of weeks. You have to start being more careful. You can't just believe every hard-luck story someone tells you from now on."

"Don't treat me like an idiot. I'm not as naïve and gullible as you're trying to make me out to be."

"What's really bothering you, Brenda? The fact that I don't trust Ethan—or that my version of the coin collection's origins is as credible as his?"

Carly interceded before Brenda could say anything. "I'm sure Sean would have said something if he'd thought there was a problem. Don't second-guess what you did now that it's too late to do anything about it."

Richard nodded reluctantly. "Carly's right. There's no need to stew about it. Just be more cautious in the future. Maybe it won't even be an issue after this. There's really no reason to see Ethan again now, since we've pretty much given up on finding his grandmother's Bible."

"Don't you mean his alleged grandmother's alleged Bible?" Carly teased, making an obvious effort to lighten the mood.

Brenda found it difficult to force a smile. Her brother had just done a very efficient job of ruining her good mood. As difficult as it had been to hear him undermine Ethan's claim to the coin collection, it was even more depressing to realize that he was right about her having no reason to ever see Ethan again.

BRENDA WAS ON THE TELEPHONE with her sister Sunday afternoon when someone rang the doorbell. "It's probably Richard," she said with a sigh. "You wouldn't believe how he's been hovering the past week."

"He's in the habit of taking care of you," Linda said, sounding a bit defensive on her brother's behalf. "We both are. The fact that you've got all this money and this fancy house doesn't make us stop worrying about you."

Linda was still having trouble dealing with Brenda's change of circumstances, Brenda thought as she disconnected the call. She hoped this inheritance wouldn't prove to be a permanent sore spot between her and her sister.

She didn't recognize the man on her doorstep. He was around forty, heavyset, ruddy faced, his hair styled in an obvious comb-over. She should have checked his identity before she opened the door, she realized as she tried to block the opening with her body. Richard would really be annoyed if he knew how blithely she had just opened the door, assuming that he or Carly or Sean would be on the other side.

"Ms. Prentiss?"

"Yes?"

"You're younger than I expected." He smiled, a blandly pleasant expression that wasn't quite reflected in his somewhat squinty eyes. "I'm Leland Grassel."

"Margaret's nephew?" she asked, startled.

His expression turning somber, he nodded. "Yes. I can't tell you how much I miss her."

Richard's lecture about not believing every sob story she heard was still fresh in her mind. For some reason, it was easier to practice with this man than with Ethan. "I'm sorry for your loss," she said automatically, without moving out of the doorway. "Why are you here, Mr. Grassel?"

"I'd like to talk to you."

"I don't think that's a good idea. If you have something to say, you should probably speak to Sean. As I told your wife, I don't have the authority to change the terms of your aunt's will."

He grimaced. "Actually, I want to apologize on Patty Ann's behalf. She really shouldn't have tried to convince you to do something against your better judgment that way. She didn't tell me she had called until after the fact."

Brenda nodded noncommittally.

He seemed to realize only then that she wasn't going to invite him in. "Look, I know you've gotten chummy with my cousin Ethan during the past few days," he said, abandoning the overly friendly tone. "I think I should warn you that he isn't quite the nice guy that he pretends to be."

"Why would you feel the need to warn me about anything? I've been told that you were very angry about your aunt's will and that you're doing everything you can to have it overturned. That doesn't exactly predispose me to think of you as someone with my best interests at heart."

"You have every reason to doubt me. But you should be having those same doubts about Ethan. I understand he managed to talk you out of a very expensive coin collection."

She felt her eyes widen. "How did you hear about that?"

"You've been taken, Ms. Prentiss," he said without answering her question. "That collection belonged to my aunt's family before she ever married her first husband."

"I assume you have proof of that?"

"No, I don't," he replied with a regretful sigh. "But you have only Ethan's word that I'm wrong. Did *he* have proof that the collection was his father's?"

It was her turn to ignore the question. "What is it you want from me, Mr. Grassel?"

"There's really no need for us to fight this out in court. I don't know how you weaseled your way into my aunt's will, but I'm sure the courts will have questions about how an apparent stranger ended up inheriting so much when there are blood relatives who were overlooked. And there are plenty of witnesses to testify that my aunt and I had a good relationship and saw each other quite often during the past few years. You can be sure there will be plenty of questions about your past and your involvement in this will."

"If you expect that to bother me, then you're mistaken. There's nothing in my past I'm trying to hide."

"You play the innocent very well. But even if what you say is true, I'm sure you would prefer to avoid the inconveniences of extended legal battles. Not to mention the uncertainty of whether the court will eventually rule on your side. I can make those problems go away now—if you make it worth my while."

"And what would that take?" As if she had to ask.

"All I'm asking for is what should have been mine," he said in a tone that bordered perilously close to a whine. "Margaret was my aunt. Her money came from the law firm that was started by my grandfather. It isn't my fault that my parents threw their money away. I'm not asking for any more, really, than you've given Ethan. Just a portion of my family estate."

"You're asking me to split the money with you?"

"You can stay in the house," he agreed too quickly. "All I ask is part of the proceeds of the estate. Not only will I call off the lawsuit, but I'll put the word out that I support your inheritance, so that you can take a place in society without having people wonder if you pulled some sort of scam to get there."

"Are you an attorney, Mr. Grassel?"

His already florid face reddened. "No. I chose not to pursue that career."

"Neither did I. But I watch enough TV to know extortion when I hear it. And I have no intention of going along with it. You pursue as many lawsuits as you want, but don't contact me again."

She started to close the door in his face. He stopped her by planting one doughy hand against it.

"I don't know what makes you think you can trust Ethan and not me," he growled. "Unless Ethan's turned on that famous, fake charm of his. He's always been pretty good at convincing gullible women to fall for him. You've already given him a fortune in coins he didn't deserve. How much more are you going to let him talk you out of?"

She pushed against the door again. "Please go away before I call the police."

"I'm leaving. But ask yourself a few things after I'm gone, Ms. Prentiss. If Ethan's so wonderful, how come his mother was willing to cut her only son completely out of her life? And why would he suddenly become so chummy with the woman who inherited in his place, unless he hoped to get something out of it? Do you really think he simply forgot about a valuable coin collection, until you just happened to find it and then offered it to him because you felt so sorry for him? I bet he snapped it up quickly enough. He didn't let his so-called pride get in the way then, did he?"

She pushed again, and this time the door closed. She turned the locks quickly, but she was glumly aware that she'd been able to shut the door that time only because Leland had allowed her to do so.

ETHAN WAS WORKING on the plans for a new landscape design when someone knocked on his door late Sunday afternoon. Actually, it was more than a knock. Someone pounded on his door, completely ignoring the doorbell button.

Pushing himself away from the drawing board, he walked into the living room and glanced through the diamond-shaped window in the door. His eyebrows rose.

Opening the door, he asked, "Did you find the Bible?"

Dressed in a blue shirt that deepened the color of her eyes, and a short, floaty skirt that looked like something Carly might have picked out, Brenda shook her head in response to his question. "I need to ask you a question."

"You want to come in first?"

Biting her lip, she debated the invitation for a moment, then nodded and stepped past him. She spent several long moments studying his decor, which was obviously not at all what she had expected. "This is nice."

"Thanks." He knew she hadn't come to talk about his decorating tastes.

She drew a deep breath, and locked her fingers in front of her. It didn't take an expert on body language to interpret that she was nervous about what she was about to say.

He understood why when she blurted, "Did that coin collection really belong to your father?"

He might have been riled by the question had she not looked so damned worried. There was more to this than simple doubts, he decided. Something had spooked her, and even though he should have gone on the defensive, he found himself wanting to reassure her, instead. Which made him curse himself for a fool even as he said flatly, "Yes."

She waited a moment, but when he didn't elaborate, she spoke again. "Is there any way you can prove that?"

"No."

She sighed in exasperation. "I wish you wouldn't respond to everything with monosyllables."

He shrugged. "I answered your questions."

"And I'm just supposed to believe you?"

His patience stretched only so far. "That's right. If you've got a problem with that, you can take the damn trunk back with you when you leave. It's in my office. I'll even carry it to your car for you."

She blinked. "Just like that?"

"I never asked you for the coin collection," he reminded her gruffly. "It means something to me only because of the associated memories of my dad. It seemed to fit the guidelines of the will, so I took it when you offered it to me. If you've changed your mind—or if someone has changed it for you—fine. I told you from the start that I wasn't going to fight for a damn thing in that house."

"You know, I never asked for any of this, either," she snapped back. "I never wanted to be in the awkward position of giving you permission to take your own father's things, or being responsible for a house full of cats and valuable collectibles that people hate me for having, or having to fight your stupid cousin and his stupid wife or…"

Ethan thought he understood now. "Has Leland been bothering you again?" he broke in to ask.

She nodded. "He came to the house. He said the coin collection didn't belong to your father and that you conned me out of it. He tried to coerce me into paying him off so he would stop causing me trouble."

"That's extortion."

"Which is exactly what I told him. He seemed to think that because I've helped you find the things your mother left you in her will, I would be willing to let him help himself to whatever he wanted, as well. When he realized that I had no intention of doing so, he became furious."

"Leland is an idiot. Flunked out of law school the first semester after Mother bought his way in, and hasn't been worth a flip since. But how he thought he could get away with this crap…" He shook his head in disgust.

"He flunked out of law school?" That seemed to amuse her for a moment. "He told me he chose to pursue another career."

"Trust me. It wasn't his choice. Did he frighten you?"

"No," she said, a little too quickly. "Not really. He just made me mad."

"And he made you start doubting me again."

She looked down at the floor. "No."

"Brenda…"

She sighed. "Maybe a little," she muttered, barely loudly enough for him to hear. "Between him and Richard and Sean…"

"Sean's been warning you against me, too?" That rather surprised him. He and Sean weren't exactly bosom buddies, but he'd thought his stepbrother trusted him for the most part.

"No," she assured him, and this time her tone was more believable, "he just said I have to be careful about everyone. He told me it might have been better if I had waited for his okay before I gave you the coin collection, but he didn't seem at all upset with me for turning it over."

"You're young and pretty and you have access to a great deal of money now. There are going to be people who will try to take advantage of that. Richard and Sean are right to warn you to be careful."

"You're being nice to me again," she said, eyeing him with an expression he couldn't quite decipher.

"Don't read too much into that. There are plenty of people who would tell you that I'm not a particularly nice guy."

She moistened her lips. "Leland tried to warn me that you…"

Her embarrassed expression gave the rest of the warning away. "Leland suggested I might try to romance you out of your inheritance?"

She blushed. "He didn't say it in quite those words, but that was the basic idea, I suppose."

Some impulse made him reach out to stroke his fingertips along her reddened cheek. "Would it work if I tried?"

Her blush deepened. He could almost feel the heat against his own skin.

Her hair was impossibly soft when he brushed his hand through it. Like spun silk. "Funny thing is," he murmured, watching the light catch in the golden strands, "Leland has it backward. The inheritance is the main reason I'm *not* trying to romance you."

She looked up at him through her lashes. "Does that mean if it weren't for your mother's will…?"

"I never would have met you," he said regretfully. "But if I had, and there was no connection at all to my mother, yeah. It's entirely probable that I would have asked you out for drinks—or something."

She thought about that a moment, then smiled a little. "It's entirely probable that I might have accepted."

His heart gave a hard thump that must have knocked a little sense back into him. He dropped his hand and stepped back to a safe distance, speaking more brusquely. "All hypothetical, of course. The will is definitely an issue. There's nothing between us, and there never will be."

She merely looked at him.

He cleared his throat. "I said I won't fight you for anything, but I'm not getting into the middle of all this, either. I don't know why Mother chose you as her beneficiary, but that's for you and Sean to figure out. I think you're in for a lot of headaches and possible heartaches because of the will, but you should try to enjoy it. And if you want the coin collection back—"

"I don't," she cut in flatly.

He nodded. "Okay. Fine. So, if I were giving advice, which I'm not, I would tell you to have Sean call Leland and tell him to stay the hell away from you or you'll slap a restraining order on him. And you might have your big brother threaten to pound him while you're at it. Leland's a big enough coward that even Richard could intimidate him."

"*Even* Richard?" Brenda smiled a little. "That's sort of harsh, isn't it?"

"The guy sells insurance."

She laughed, which was exactly what he'd hoped to hear. Things had been getting just a bit too intense between them for his peace of mind. "The guy has a black belt in tae kwon do."

"You're joking."

"No. He taught martial arts classes to help put himself through college."

"Okay, had I known that, maybe I'd have been a little nicer to him."

Her smile faded. "This is all very awkward, Ethan."

His own amusement evaporated. "Us, you mean? Because that's not really an issue, since we aren't—"

"That's not what I meant," she interrupted quickly. "I was referring to the entire situation. I wonder if I shouldn't just walk away from it all."

"That's your decision, of course," he said, making sure that neither his tone nor his expression revealed his thoughts. "But you should think hard about that. The trust is set up to take care of you for the rest of your life. I'm sure your brother and sister would advise you to take advantage of your good fortune."

She made a rather helpless gesture with one hand.

"But I didn't earn the money. I didn't save for it, or enter a contest, or even buy a lottery ticket. It's just suddenly in my life. And I don't feel like I deserve it."

Ethan was coming to the conclusion that there was no one who deserved it more. Sure as hell not Leland. Nor himself, for that matter. "Take the money," he said wearily. "I've got my business, a small trust fund and a gold coin collection that would bring in quite a tidy sum if I ever need to sell it. If you're worried about me for any reason, don't be, okay? And do you really want Leland and Patty Ann to get their hands on my mother's things?"

She hesitated. "Margaret was his aunt. And apparently he spent time with her during the past few years."

"And I didn't," he growled. "I get it. But Leland's a vulture, Brenda. He started circling when I moved out of the picture, hoping to cash in on my mother's death. And now he's circling you. That soft heart of yours is exposed, and you'd damned well better protect it."

"I'm not quite as soft a touch as you seem to think," she said, lifting her chin in a defiant gesture that he found downright irresistible.

"You're pretty tough, huh?"

"When I have to be."

"Don't think anyone can get past your defenses?"

She was beginning to look wary, but she kept her voice firm when she answered, "Not if I don't want them to."

"Hmm." It must have been the reckless streak that had led him to walk away from guaranteed success and into an uncertain future that compelled him to reach out and tug her into his arms and press his mouth to hers. Even though he knew it wasn't a good idea.

And maybe Brenda had a reckless, adventurous side of her own, because instead of pushing him away, she clutched his shirt and kissed him back. As though she had wanted this as badly as he did.

Almost as suddenly as the kiss had started, it was over. Staring at her from a safe distance, Ethan pushed a hand slowly through his hair. "Well. I guess that proved something."

She spoke a bit hoarsely. "What?"

"Your defenses aren't quite as good as you thought."

Something flashed in her eyes. Might have been hurt or it could have been temper. Maybe a combination of the two. Her voice was much steadier when she spoke again. "I think we learned one other thing."

He watched as she crossed the room and reached for the doorknob. "What's that?"

She opened the door and looked over her shoulder. "You really aren't a particularly nice guy."

She was gone before he could come up with a witty response. The door slammed hard behind her.

SEAN CALLED MONDAY MORNING to invite Brenda to dinner that evening to discuss trust business. This time, she accepted. She even went out that afternoon and bought a dress for the occasion, using her own new credit card. She selected a dress in a bold red, because it looked like something Carly would wear. Or some other woman who wasn't afraid of her own shadow.

She was tired of being intimidated. Tired of being afraid to go out of the house. Tired of jumping every time the telephone rang. Tired of being pushed around and patronized and protected.

She was a woman who knew her own mind. A woman who could make her own decisions, and fight her own battles. A woman who could kiss a man and leave his eyes glazed.

Ethan might have pretended their kiss was no big deal. But she had looked directly into his eyes when he'd backed away. She had seen very clearly that he hadn't been nearly as unaffected as he'd pretended to be.

Which had only made her angrier when he'd tried to brush the kiss off as an object lesson, of sorts, to prove his point that she wasn't shrewd enough to protect herself.

She wasn't sure what had brought that kiss to her mind now, as she finished getting ready for dinner with Sean. Perhaps it was because it hadn't been far out of her thoughts since she had slammed out of his house.

She hoped the memory of that kiss was bothering him as much as it was her.

Although Sean had offered to pick her up, she had arranged to meet him at the restaurant instead. She wanted this meeting to be friendly, all while keeping some boundaries. It was bad enough that she and Ethan had already crossed a line that would make things very awkward between them from now on.

Sean greeted her with a smile and a warm handshake that might have lasted just a bit longer than necessary. "It's good to see you, Brenda. You look very nice."

"Thank you." Pulling her hand from his, she allowed him to help her into her chair.

As he took his seat on the other side of the table, it

occurred to her again what an attractive man he was. A few weeks earlier, she'd have found it exciting to dine at a fancy restaurant with a handsome attorney. But after everything else that had happened during the past couple of weeks, this dinner meeting seemed almost routine.

They made polite small talk while their meals were prepared and delivered to them. Only then did Sean turn the conversation to the reason for the meeting. "How are things going at the house?"

"Fine. The cleaning crew you hired was very efficient. It only took them a couple of hours to scrub the place from top to bottom. The cats are still recovering from the invasion of the vacuum cleaners, but I managed to pacify them all with kitty treats before I left."

"You really don't mind taking care of all those cats?"

"Not at all," she assured him. "They keep me company and give me something useful to do. Each one has a distinct personality and I've enjoyed getting to know them."

His mouth quirked into a slightly crooked smile that she couldn't help but return. "I'm afraid I'm not much of a cat person. They all seem alike to me. Rather mysterious."

She chuckled. "That's exactly what they want you to think. They like to keep humans guessing about them. They think it gives them the upper hand."

He sipped his wine, then set his glass down. "I do have some good news for you."

"I always like hearing good news."

"I'm pretty sure I've talked Leland out of contesting the will. I don't think he'll be bothering you again."

Brenda set down her fork, her heart giving a hard thump. "How did you do that?"

He shrugged, looking rather proud of himself, though he kept his tone casual. "I pointed out how much it was going to cost him to pursue a lawsuit. I reminded him that his chances of actually winning were very slim. And then I told him that he's lucky you aren't pressing charges against him for attempted extortion."

Brenda had told Sean every detail of Leland's demands the day before—though she hadn't mentioned her ensuing visit with Ethan. "What did he say?"

"He blustered, as usual. Said we couldn't prove anything. I agreed, but then I said we could certainly add to his court costs. Not to mention that we could make this fight very ugly, and very public. He backed off pretty quickly."

"I can't imagine it was quite that easy," she said, remembering Leland's angry persistence.

"I know how to handle Leland," Sean assured her. "He's greedy but basically lazy. Fighting you— fighting *us*—was starting to sound like too much trouble with too much risk involved. So, he'll take the money Margaret left him and he'll go away."

She grimaced. "It's just hard to believe he'll give up that easily. Both he and Patty Ann are so furious about the will. I don't think either of them will graciously accept defeat."

He reached out to pat her hand. "You've made it clear that you aren't going to cooperate with them, and I've let them know that I support you completely. There's no reason for them to harm you, since Ethan, not Leland, would be next in line to inherit. So you just let me worry about them from now on, okay?"

She reached for her wineglass to dislodge his hand from hers, hoping she had been subtle about it. "I have to admit, I have mixed feelings about this. Fighting Leland over the estate of his own aunt, I mean, when I didn't even know the woman."

"I'm sure Leland and his wife tried to convince you that they had a warm and loving relationship with Margaret, but that isn't exactly true. She couldn't stand Patty Ann and she made no pretense otherwise. She tolerated Leland because he was her nephew—and because her money kept him at her beck and call. He would jump through burning hoops at the snap of her fingers, and she liked that. But she didn't particularly like him, nor did she trust him."

Brenda sighed and shook her head. "This was one dysfunctional family."

"Tell me about it." He seemed more amused than offended by her remark.

"And what makes it even more awkward is that I'm getting all this money from a woman I don't think I would have liked very much had I met her."

It was Sean's turn to sigh. "Margaret was a...difficult woman. Stubborn and dictatorial and critical and demanding. She could be pleasant enough if things were going her way. I got along well with her because I rarely challenged her, and I believe the same was true of my father and her first husband. Ethan couldn't seem to resist butting heads with her. For as long as I knew them, they were locked in a power struggle, and neither one seemed able to pull out of it."

"That sounds so sad."

"I suppose it was. By the time they just gave up and went their own ways, there was really no relationship left to salvage. I've got to admit I never understood either of them very well."

"I thought you and Ethan got along well enough."

He shrugged again. "It was sort of the same situation I had with Margaret. Ethan and I got along because there was never any reason for us to clash. But as far as really knowing him—well, I can't say that I do."

"Do you trust him?"

"In what way?"

She used her fork to toy with a bit of fish on her plate. "Well...the coin collection, for example. He said it belonged to his father. He said its value to him was more sentimental than monetary. Do you believe him?"

"I have no reason not to believe him," Sean hedged. "And if it comes down to Ethan's word or Leland's, I would rather believe Ethan."

Brenda set down her fork. "So would I."

"However," Sean added, "I still think you should use caution, even with Ethan. As much as I would like to trust him, the truth is that I've seen him very rarely during the past ten years."

She would have felt better if Sean had given a more heartfelt endorsement of the man who had kissed her and left her head spinning.

"I have nothing but respect for Ethan," he added, as if sensing her disappointment with his reservations. "He's accomplished quite a bit on his own, when he could have coasted into a successful and profitable law career. With his intelligence and connections, Ethan wouldn't have had to put much effort into it, and he knew it."

"Ethan was a good student?"

"Scored off the charts on standardized tests. He graduated in the top of his college class without trying very hard, and his LSAT scores beat mine—and mine were quite good. Ethan's got the brains, but not the ambition. At least, not the kind his mother wanted from him."

"He seems to take pride in his landscape design business."

"Yes, he does. Even though he admitted to me that he needs to put a little more effort into it if he wants to grow larger than a one-man operation. For now, he seems to be content to just get by—pay his bills, meet his payroll, have a little extra money for fishing trips and other weekend entertainment."

"If that's what makes him happy…"

"It does seem to be all he wants for now. In which case…well…"

"What?" she asked, frowning at his tone.

Sean made a wry face. "It had to occur to Ethan that the estate would help him keep up the lifestyle he seems to enjoy so much. You know, working when he wants to, but still having the freedom to do the things he enjoys on his days off. Or if he wanted to expand his company into a bigger operation, he could have used the infusion of money. I guess it would be hard for most people to understand that money really means so little to a guy who grew up having pretty much everything he wanted."

"So you're saying you *don't* believe him? About not wanting the estate, I mean?"

"No, I didn't say that." His voice was just a bit too hearty. "It's just that I understand why your brother is so suspicious of Ethan. And why Leland suspects him of trying to get close to you in order to get his hands on the money."

"Leland told you that?"

Sean nodded. "It's his new pet theory. Leland is so obsessed with the money that he can't imagine other people wouldn't do anything to get their hands on it. He doesn't understand that you've been helping Ethan simply because you've got a good heart, and not for any other reason. Leland would find it impossible to believe you've even considered giving the inheritance back because you aren't sure you deserve it."

She didn't quite know what to say to that.

"You're a good person, Brenda. I don't know how Margaret knew about you, but she knew somehow that you were the right person to care for her estate. She didn't want it to go to Leland—and not to Ethan, either, unless for some reason you were unable to inherit. Stop trying to second-guess her and enjoy your good fortune. And let me worry about the details, okay? It's literally my job to take care of you."

As much as she prided herself in being self-sufficient, she had to admit that it felt good to know that Sean was there to help her through this strange and difficult transition. He had already done so much for her—not the least dealing with Leland on her behalf.

She needed to trust someone now. And because Sean seemed to be the only one with nothing to gain, he was the most likely choice.

CHAPTER TWELVE

THE TELEPHONE RANG not long after Brenda returned home from her dinner with Sean. She half expected the caller to be Richard. She was surprised when it was Ethan, especially considering the way they had parted the day before.

"Did you call to hassle me about how easily you can break through my defenses?" she asked him, taking the offensive.

"No. But I'm not apologizing for that, either."

"Then why *did* you call?" she asked, vaguely annoyed.

"I just wanted to let you know that Leland won't be bothering you again. I had a talk with him this morning, and I told him to leave you alone. I think I got through to him."

That surprised her. "I thought you said you weren't getting involved."

"I'm not involved," he said too quickly. "All I did was make a call. I owed you that much for the help you've given me."

"Nice of you," she murmured. "But as it happens, I already knew he'd decided not to challenge the will. Sean told me."

"Oh. I wasn't aware that Sean had talked to Leland."

"Yes. He and I had a dinner meeting to discuss estate business. He told me then that he had talked to Leland."

"You had dinner with Sean?"

"A dinner meeting," she corrected him. "He told me he'd convinced Leland to drop the challenge."

"*He* convinced him, huh? I bet he talked to Leland after I did."

"Leland's capitulation was probably the result of his conversations with both of you," she said diplomatically. "With both of you opposing him, it probably just seemed like too much effort with too little guarantee to pursue it any further."

"Yeah. Right. That, and the fact that I threatened to break his nose."

She sighed. "As impressed as I am by your muscle flexing, I really don't need you to threaten Leland— or anyone else—for me. I have an attorney, and I want everything handled legally and ethically."

"When you say you have an attorney, are you referring to Sean?"

"Of course. As trustee, his job is to look out for my interests."

"I'm sure that's what he's told you, but it isn't exactly accurate. His job is to administer the trust, itself. He's supposed to keep the estate healthy and profitable and to ensure that you receive no more or no less than what is authorized under the terms of the will. He will actually have quite a bit of influence in your life."

"Surely you aren't warning me against Sean now?"

"Keep in mind that Sean was once a part of this messed-up family, himself. I'm not saying he has an agenda of his own, but I don't really know him well enough to say for certain that he doesn't."

Remembering that Sean had used similarly vague language to warn her not to completely trust Ethan, she frowned. "So being named in your mother's will means there's no one I can trust completely, and I have to constantly be on guard against opportunists and fortune hunters."

"That pretty well sums it up."

"It sounds like a very cynical—and lonely—way to live."

"I would say that's entirely your decision."

"You're right," she agreed. "It is. And I've decided that I need to have people I can trust. My brother and sister. A few close friends. Tony and Carly D'Alessandro. Sean. And—for the most part—you."

There was a rather lengthy pause before Ethan repeated, "For the most part?"

"As long as you're not trying to teach me object lessons," she qualified.

"You're referring to the kiss?"

"Yes."

He chuckled, a deep, masculine sound that slid seductively through the phone lines and wrapped itself around her. "That wasn't an object lesson."

"So why did you kiss me?"

"Maybe I'll just let you figure that one out for yourself," he murmured.

"Ethan—"

"See you around, Brenda," he said and hung up.

She slammed the receiver home. Was the man *trying* to guarantee her another sleepless night? Because she had a feeling she would be thinking about his cryptic comment for a long time.

Just the memory of their kiss pushed all thoughts

of her dinner with Sean out of her mind. And she couldn't help wondering if that had been Ethan's intention.

IT WASN'T THE RING of a telephone that woke Brenda at three-forty-five the next morning. It was the sound of shattering glass, followed by the shrill screech of the alarm system.

Her heart hammering in her chest, she leapt out of bed, her bare feet hitting the floor with a thud. Memories of the duplex fire swirled nightmarishly in her head, leaving her confused about what she should do. Should she hide? Leave the room to see what had set off the alarm? Call the police?

The telephone rang, and she snatched up the receiver. "Hello?"

To her relief, the caller identified herself as a representative of the security alarm company. "Has your alarm system been activated?"

"Yes," Brenda gasped. "I was sleeping. I heard glass break downstairs, and then the alarms went off." They were still wailing, loud enough that she was having trouble hearing the dispatcher, who informed her that the police had been summoned and that Brenda was to lock the bedroom door and remain there until the officers arrived.

Brenda was the only person in the house when the police arrived, though they did find a large rock had been hurled through one of the windows into the living room. Shards of glass lay scattered across the antique rug, and a stately lamp had been knocked over, its china base broken. As far as the two responding officers could tell, no one had tried to enter the house.

Having been summoned by Brenda, Richard arrived just as the officers completed their search of the premises and had begun questioning Brenda. He was as disgusted as she was when one of the officers said that either the rock had been thrown by someone with a personal grudge against Brenda or as a random act of vandalism. Or maybe someone who'd been attempting to rob the place and had been scared off by the alarms.

"I think we could have figured those possibilities out for ourselves," he grumbled after the officers left. They had taken the rock with them as evidence, even though they could all see that it had been cleaned to a shiny state, with no visible fingerprints anywhere on it, leading them to suspect that the person who'd thrown it had worn gloves. The officers hadn't been particularly optimistic that they would learn the identify of the perpetrator.

"They're starting to have questions about me," Brenda said, voicing a realization that had occurred to her while she was being questioned. She pulled her new, short, red satin bathrobe more tightly over her summer pajama set, feeling a chill go through her, even though the kitchen where they sat over cups of coffee was quite warm. "This incident, on top of the fire last week, just seems too bizarre to them. They're wondering if I'm mixed up in something suspicious."

"The police sure haven't been much help," Richard concurred, pushing a hand through his tousled hair as he glared into his coffee cup.

"They haven't had much to go on, really. There's still no proof the fire was deliberately set, and with this incident happening in the middle of the night, I'm sure there were no witnesses, though they said they'd ask around tomorrow."

"I think it's time your private investigator starts earning whatever it is you're paying him. You should call him."

"Now? Richard, it's four-thirty in the morning."

"Yes, and someone just threw a rock through your window. You hired the guy to find out who's been harassing you. As far as I can see, he hasn't accomplished anything worthwhile to this point. Get him over here to see for himself what you're dealing with."

"But I—"

"You call him or I will. Damn it, I want some answers, Brenda, before you get hurt."

She persuaded him to wait until five. She wanted to take a shower first and get dressed. She felt too vulnerable in her pajamas and bathrobe.

Richard agreed reluctantly. He borrowed a razor from her and headed for one of the other bathrooms to shower and freshen up as much as possible considering he'd thrown on a T-shirt and a pair of faded jeans and sneakers with no socks when she'd called him. She suggested that he should go home and change if he wanted, but he refused to leave her alone just then. She didn't want him to see that she was relieved that he was staying for a while longer.

Brenda took her time showering and dressing in jeans and a yellow knit top. And then she lingered even longer over her hair and makeup. She suspected that Richard was pacing the floor in impatience, but she wasn't quite ready to face the day. Besides which, she figured Tony would appreciate a few extra minutes of sleep before Richard insisted on summoning him.

She set down her hairbrush and studied her reflection. She was pleased to note that she looked more angry than afraid, more defiant than cowed.

It was almost five-thirty when she rejoined Richard. He had brewed a fresh pot of coffee and heated some cinnamon rolls he'd found in the freezer, so the kitchen smelled great. Surprisingly enough, she was hungry.

It seemed quieter than usual in the kitchen without the cats rolling around and begging for treats. She had closed them in the media room, where they had a play area, toys, water bowls and litter boxes, after the police arrived, since all four curious kitties had wanted to help with the investigation. Because of the sharp glass still scattered in the living room, she had decided to leave them there until after the carpet had been vacuumed.

She lifted an eyebrow in surprise when she saw how many cinnamon rolls Richard had baked. She was hungry, but not *that* hungry. "Uh, Richard?"

The doorbell chimed through the house. "That will be your P.I.," Richard remarked. "I'll get the door."

"You called him?" she asked in exasperation. So much for all her delaying tactics.

"His card was lying by the phone. You took so long in the shower that I figured I might as well go ahead and call him." He left the room before she could reprimand him for his presumption.

Muttering beneath her breath, she pulled coffee cups and plates from a cupboard and set them on the table, along with napkins, utensils, cream and sugar. She was trying to decide if she had forgotten anything when she heard voices approaching the kitchen. Recognizing one of those voices, she quickly set out another cup and plate.

"That coffee smells good. Better put out another cup, though," Carly advised as she entered. "I called Ethan. He's on his way."

Brenda had been wondering how Carly could possibly look so fresh and coordinated at this early hour in the morning, but those last words stopped her cold. "You called Ethan? Why?"

Carly shrugged. "I figured he would end up being a suspect again. And I knew he would want to be notified."

Her father looked apologetically at Brenda. "She took it upon herself to do that. I told her she'd over-stepped her bounds, and you might not appreciate it."

Unrepentant, Carly moved next to Brenda. "Brenda and Richard and Ethan and I have all become friends during the past week. We worked well together looking for the family Bible—even though we didn't find it. Maybe we can work together to figure out who's got it in for Brenda."

"I feel compelled to point out that you aren't actually an investigator on this case," Tony said with a shake of his head. "You wouldn't be here now if you hadn't answered the phone and finagled an invitation from Richard."

Brenda shot a look at her brother, who wouldn't look back at her. So, he had known Carly was coming, and he hadn't mentioned it. This thing he had for Carly was really getting out of control.

Carly turned big, puppy dog eyes on Brenda. "When I heard what happened, I had to come check on you. Are you okay? That must have been a terrifying experience for you."

And Carly hadn't wanted to miss one minute of the excitement, Brenda thought cynically. Because she liked Carly, and couldn't really fault her for being eager and curious, she merely smiled and said, "I'm fine. But thanks for asking."

The doorbell announced Ethan's arrival. "Everyone help yourself to coffee and cinnamon rolls," she said, moving toward the door. "I'll let him in."

She wanted a chance to talk to him briefly in private, to assure him that she'd had nothing to do with summoning him. Carly hadn't known, of course, about the interactions between Brenda and Ethan since they had all parted Saturday, or how awkward it was that she'd brought Ethan here this morning.

He looked sleepy and disheveled when she opened the door, like a man who had been pulled abruptly out of his bed. His hair was rumpled, he hadn't shaved, and he wore a slightly wrinkled blue plaid cotton shirt unbuttoned over a solid blue T-shirt and faded jeans. One look at him made her mouth go dry.

She thought maybe he'd read her mind when he reached out for her. Instead, his hands fell on her shoulders and he looked intently into her face. "Are you all right?"

"I'm fine, Ethan," she assured him, disarmed by his show of concern. "Carly shouldn't have called you at this hour. I don't know what she was thinking."

"She was thinking I'd want to be called, and she was right. She was a little vague about what happened. Someone tried to break into the house?"

Brenda wondered if Carly had deliberately been that "vague" and misleading. "No one tried to break in," she said. "At least, we don't think so. Someone threw a rock through a window in the living room. It made a mess and set off the security alarms, but I was never in any danger."

She felt some of the tension leave his fingers. "I saw the broken window. You said it was a rock?"

"Yes. A fairly large one. Polished, and the person who threw it probably wore gloves, so there were no fingerprints. The police took it, anyway, for evidence."

She showed him the living room, with the broken glass and lamp. He studied the scene, then turned back to her, his eyes not quite as grim as they had been when he'd arrived. "It doesn't look as though anyone tried to get in."

"No. It was just a rock. A message, I guess." She crossed her arms and rubbed her forearms against a sudden chill. She knew the coolness was more emotional than actual; even this early in the morning, the air that wafted in through the broken window was quite warm.

She should have known her slight show of nerves wouldn't escape Ethan's sharp eyes. He reached out again, this time resting only one hand on her shoulder. "You were frightened."

"Startled," she corrected with a lift of her chin. "I was sound asleep when the alarms went off. Fortunately, the security company called almost immediately, so I knew the police were on their way."

"It's okay to admit that you were scared, you know."

She shrugged, and his hand fell to his side. "I handled it."

"So who do you think threw it?" he asked, watching her through narrowed eyes.

"Why don't we join the others before we get into that? They're waiting for us in the kitchen."

"The others." He looked as if he'd forgotten they weren't alone in the house. "Um, yeah. Okay."

She started to turn away, but then paused to look up at him. "Ethan?"

"Yeah?"

The words seemed to leap out of her mouth. "Were you really worried about me?"

He hesitated a moment as if surprised by the question. And then he muttered, "Yeah. I was. Damn it."

She didn't know whether to be more amused or unnerved by his grudging admission. Choosing the coward's retreat, she turned and led the way toward the kitchen and the relative safety of a crowd.

ETHAN REACHED two rapid conclusions during his conversation with the others who had gathered around the kitchen table for coffee and cinnamon rolls. Richard didn't seem to even suspect Ethan of throwing the rock through the living room window. And Tony D'Alessandro was not at all pleased with the developing rapport between Richard and Carly.

"So, what are you going to do to find out who threw that rock?" Richard asked Tony, his slightly aggressive tone perhaps giving an indication that he sensed the private investigator's wariness of him.

"What makes you think I wasn't the one?" Ethan asked Richard before Tony had a chance to speak.

Richard took a sip of his coffee before asking in return, "What makes you think I don't suspect you?"

"You'd have me pinned against a wall by now if you did. It's what I would do if I thought someone was terrorizing my kid sister—if I had one. And Brenda mentioned your black belt."

Carly looked at Richard with widened eyes. "You have a black belt?"

"It's a way to stay in shape." Richard gave a self-deprecating shrug.

Carly beamed at him as if he had just demonstrated mystical powers, and Tony's frown deepened.

Ethan studied the older man thoughtfully. Still slim and fit, his dark hair only lightly frosted with gray, Tony would be an effective deterrent to any nervous young man with designs on his daughter. Funny thing was, even knowing how young Carly was, Ethan couldn't imagine her being interested in twenty-year-old boys. She just seemed like the type to be drawn to older, more settled, more experienced men—as she obviously was drawn to Richard. To the understandable dismay of her overprotective papa.

Tony abruptly pulled the conversation away from Richard. "So if Ethan didn't throw the rock, who did?"

"Leland," Brenda muttered, wrapping her hands around her warm coffee cup as if she were fighting off another chill.

"The angry cousin," Tony said, proving he recognized the name. "Leland Grassel."

Brenda nodded. "Or his wife. Patty Ann."

Tony turned to Ethan. "Does it sound like something your cousin or his wife would do?"

"Frankly? No." Ethan shook his head. "I just can't see it. Lawsuits, yes. Harassing phone calls, maybe. But throwing rocks through windows? I doubt it."

"Why?"

"It's hard to explain, exactly. It just doesn't seem like their style. Is there any chance this could have been kids? Just random vandalism? Because I can't see anything to be gained by Leland, or anyone else, from throwing a rock through Brenda's window."

"Unless you see the rock throwing and the phone calls as part of a deliberate campaign of intimidation," Tony replied. "It all started almost as soon as she was named beneficiary of the will, and it hasn't really let up since."

"For what purpose?"

"To frighten her into giving up the inheritance."

"But what good would that do? If Brenda declines the inheritance, it all reverts to me. And since I'm not the one behind any of this, your theory doesn't add up."

"Unless," Carly said thoughtfully, "someone plans to knock you off after they scare Brenda away."

Her wording made his mouth twitch, and reminded him of her stated fondness for mystery novels.

Tony gave his daughter a look, then glanced at Ethan again. "Even if Carly's improbable scenario were true, that would still bring it back to your cousin, who's next in line to inherit after you."

Ethan smiled wryly. "You really think Leland has been making disturbing phone calls at all hours to Brenda, burned down her home and threw a rock through her window, all in the hope that she would disappear so he could somehow kill me and end up with the estate?"

Brenda shuddered. "Don't say that as if it were a big joke. It isn't funny."

He was sure she would have been that appalled no matter whose murder they had been discussing. He shouldn't take the horrified look in her eyes personally, no matter how tempting it was to do so.

"It does seem a little improbable," Richard commented.

"I think we're overreacting to what happened here," Brenda said firmly. "It was a rock, thrown through a window in the middle of the night. There was almost no chance that it would hurt anyone. The police officers seemed to think it was either random mischief or just a petty message, and I tend to agree with them."

"A petty message from whom?" Tony asked.

She glanced at Ethan. "I still think it's Leland. He was furious with me for not cooperating with him. And then both Ethan and Sean ordered him to leave me alone. They made it clear they would try to block his efforts to get rid of me. Sean said Leland has given up on contesting the will, so Leland has to be fuming about that. Maybe the rock was just a parting shot. A way to express just how frustrated he is that nothing worked out the way he wanted it to."

"That makes sense," Richard conceded.

"It doesn't mean he's finished," Carly added. "For all we know, he could dial the phone or toss a rock through another window anytime he starts feeling sorry for himself again."

"Not after I have a talk with him, he won't," Richard growled—and Ethan noted that, just for a moment, the guy looked like someone with a black belt.

"Maybe you should let me handle that part," Tony cautioned. "I'll have a talk with Mr. Grassel as your sister's representative. I'll ask some questions about his whereabouts at the time the rock was thrown, make some noises about looking at his telephone records, let him know we're on to him. I'll leave him with the warning that he'll be the first person we come to anytime something unnerving happens to Brenda— whether it's a phone call or a rock or anything else that upsets her."

"Dad's good at that sort of thing," Carly assured Brenda. "He does stuff like that all the time, and it almost always works."

"I just want an end to all of this," Brenda said, looking at Tony. "I don't want to jump every time the phone rings, or wake up to the sound of sirens again."

"I'm sure my talk with Grassel will solve some of those problems," Tony assured her.

"And if that doesn't do it, *I'll* take care of it," Richard said.

Ethan gazed into his coffee cup, figuring he might as well keep his own misgivings to himself. No one seemed to have much faith in his doubts that Leland had thrown that rock, so he might as well save his breath. None of his business, anyway, he reminded himself.

But he wasn't so sure Brenda should start celebrating the end of her problems just yet.

CLAIMING A HEAVY SCHEDULE, Tony was the first to leave. Carly had brought her own car, so she stayed, saying rather transparently that she wanted to help Brenda clean the mess in the living room.

It was no shock that Richard didn't take off, especially since Carly was still there, but Brenda was a little surprised when Ethan seemed inclined to linger awhile. He and Richard helped to gather all the larger pieces of glass so that Brenda could sweep up the rest with a hand vacuum, making sure no sharp slivers were left behind.

Examining the broken lamp, Carly shook her head. "This is a goner. No big loss. I know it was expensive, but it's really ugly."

Richard dropped another wedge of glass into a metal trash can with a noisy clang. "As tactful as ever."

Carly laughed. "Brenda knows this place needs redecorating. And I don't think Ethan's going to take offense at the criticism of his mother's taste."

"You've got that right," he murmured, dumping a handful of glass into the can. "I told her once that her style should be called Early Mausoleum."

Brenda raised her eyebrows. "That must have annoyed her."

He grinned, making him look younger—and making her heart skip a few beats. "Why do you think I said it?"

To her disappointment, his smile faded very quickly, to be replaced by a fleeting expression that might have been regret. He turned away before she could be sure, but she wondered if it had occurred to him that there would be no more quarrels with his mother. No chance to put the old animosities behind them.

On an impulse, she rested a hand on his arm. Just for a moment—but long enough to let him know that she was sorry his relationship with his mother had ended so sadly. He looked down at her with an intensity that made her heart stutter again, and then he gave her a very faint, and very personal, smile.

It was at that very moment that she knew she was as far gone as the ugly lamp. And she was more anxious just then than when the security alarms had awakened her so jarringly.

Richard suddenly let out a mild curse, and Brenda looked quickly away from Ethan. Her cheeks were warm, and her heart had started beating again, although at roughly twice its usual rate. At first she thought her brother's displeasure had something to do with her and Ethan, but then she saw the blood on his hand.

She gasped. "Richard, you're bleeding. How bad is it?"

Carly immediately abandoned the lamp. "You've cut yourself?"

Richard held up his uninjured hand in a calming gesture. "It's just a shallow cut. Trust me, it isn't serious."

"It's bleeding a lot." Carly's face blanched dramatically.

"You sit down," Ethan said, pointing to her. "C'mon, Richard, I know where Mother kept the first aid kit. I'll stick a bandage on that for you."

Brenda stayed with Carly when the guys left the room. "Do you need to put your head down? You've gone awfully pale."

"No, I'm okay. I just don't do blood very well. He was really dripping, wasn't he?"

"It really was a minor cut," Brenda assured her. "If I thought he needed stitches or anything, I would be dragging him to a doctor, myself."

"I know." Carly drew a breath and pushed her hair away from her face, which was slowly regaining color.

"I'm getting better. I used to keel over every time I saw the first drop of blood. Mom says I'd better get over it before I have kids, especially if they're anything like my youngest brother, Justin."

"I understand it's easier to handle when you have to," Brenda said with a smile. "My sister was always the squeamish type, too, but now she has two utterly fearless kids, and she's learned to deal with just about anything. She's told me she stays calm, cool and collected during every crisis, then falls apart when everything settles down."

"I bet Richard makes a really cool uncle," Carly said with a sigh.

"He's okay, I guess. He doesn't see the kids much, since he's usually pretty busy with his job. Uh, Carly—"

Before Brenda could say more, Richard and Ethan came back in, Richard sporting a small adhesive bandage on his right hand. "No more blood," he told Carly, holding up his hand to prove it.

"That's a relief." She smiled and stood, looking good-naturedly sheepish. "It looks like Ethan did a good job of patching you up."

"I stuck a bandage on it," Ethan replied with a shrug. "It wasn't exactly brain surgery."

Carly giggled. "Our hero."

It was all Brenda could do not to laugh when Ethan's cheeks darkened. Carly didn't usually have much trouble making Richard blush, but this was the first time she had gotten to Ethan.

"We need to get this window fixed," Richard said, sounding a bit grumpy all of a sudden.

"I'll call Sean," Brenda said, then grimaced.

"Maybe I should have already called him. He might be annoyed when he finds out he was the last to be notified."

"He'll get over it," Ethan muttered, and now *he* sounded cross, for some reason.

Richard glanced at his watch. "I have a midmorning meeting. Maybe I should call and reschedule—"

"You'll do no such thing." Brenda planted her hands on her hips and gave him a stern look. "Go to your meeting, Richard. I can handle everything here. I don't need you to stay and hold my hand."

"I have to go to work, too," Carly said reluctantly. "Unless you need me for anything, Brenda?"

She knew Carly would love nothing more than to have an excuse not to go to work that day, but she had to be honest. "I really don't. I'm fine. I'm sure Sean will send somebody right away to repair the window, and we've pretty much taken care of everything else."

Carly sighed. "I guess I'd better go, then. I'll walk out with you, Richard."

Richard looked at Ethan, who glanced at Brenda before saying, "I've got a job site to check on later today, but I'll stay long enough to make sure someone's coming to fix the window. If Sean doesn't know anyone, I have a few contacts in the business."

Perhaps Richard would have lingered awhile, since Ethan was staying, but Carly practically towed him out of the house. Both promised to call Brenda later, Carly adding, "You have *got* to get out of this house. Let's make plans to do something, okay?"

"Sure. That sounds like fun."

She could hear Carly chattering to Richard all the

way out of the house, which made the silence between
her and Ethan even more noticeable when she turned
nervously back to face him.

CHAPTER THIRTEEN

"I WANTED TO TALK to you alone," Ethan said as soon as the others were gone.

"Yes, I got that impression."

Leaving the living room with its broken window, they moved to the media room, where they were greeted noisily by the indignant cats. Ethan motioned for her to sit down, and she settled on one end of the big sofa, joined there immediately by Angel, who curled familiarly in her lap. She expected Ethan to choose a nearby chair. Instead, he sat on the couch beside her.

"What is it?" she asked, concerned by his somber expression. Her hand, which had been absently stroking Angel's head, stilled in sudden dread.

"I don't want to worry you, especially since your brother and the D'Alessandros seem to have reassured you this morning—"

"But?"

"But I still don't think Leland threw that rock. And I doubt very much that it was Patty Ann."

She hadn't realized just how much the others had put her at ease until her stomach clenched in response to Ethan's words. "You kept trying to tell us that earlier."

He nodded. "No one wanted to hear me. Leland does make a logical suspect. There's no one else who makes sense—other than me."

"And no one believes you did it."

He shrugged. "They're keeping an open mind about me, anyway."

"But, Ethan, if it's not Leland, then who?"

"We keep assuming it has something to do with the will. I can't help wondering if we might be following the wrong trail. I know I've asked you before, but are you *sure* there's no one from your own life with a grudge against you? An acquaintance who's jealous of your new circumstances? Or maybe that guy you dated?"

"I haven't heard from him in months. And I really don't think any of my friends or acquaintances would be involved. For one thing, very few of them know about my new circumstances."

"We're missing something," he muttered, shaking his head. "There's more going on here than we're seeing on the surface. I just wish I knew what it is."

"Maybe it isn't as complicated as you're trying to make it. Maybe this time it really is the obvious answer. Leland and Patty Ann have made no secret of their anger and their bitterness toward me. Making harassing phone calls, or throwing rocks—neither of those actions would be inconceivable from people who are willing to resort to bribery and extortion, would they?"

"I guess not," he conceded reluctantly. "And I'm hardly an expert on my cousin or his wife. It just doesn't feel right."

"Maybe you just don't want to believe it of them," she suggested. "He is your cousin, after all."

Ethan snorted. "Trust me, I have no illusions about him. To be honest, I wish I were confident that he was the one behind all of this. Then I'd think maybe it was over."

"But you don't think it's Leland," she said, comprehension creeping into her and leaving her feeling a little sick. "So you don't think it's over. You think something else is going to happen."

He reached out to cover her hand with his. "I'm not saying anything else *will* happen. I just don't want you to get too confident."

"I should stay afraid, you mean."

"I didn't say that, either. Just keep your guard up."

"I don't like this," she said with a sigh. "I was never afraid before Sean contacted me to tell me about the will."

"You never had this much money before. It's a trade-off."

"You didn't think it was all worth it," she reminded him. "You walked away."

"I walked away from my mother," he corrected her. "The money—well, that wasn't so bad."

She looked down at their hands, and then back up at his face. "So, why aren't you trying to talk me out of it?"

"So far I've gotten a gold coin collection from you."

He wasn't smiling when he said it, but she smiled a little anyway, sensing that he was testing to see how she would react. "Have you sold it yet?"

"It's not for sale."

"Then that's sort of defeating the purpose, isn't it?"

His mouth quirked then, just a little. "Forget the money. Maybe I have another reason for wanting to keep you here."

He was still holding her hand, a fact she was intensely aware of. Her voice was just a little hoarse when she asked, "What's that?"

Before he could answer, a sturdy white body launched itself from the floor and landed on the couch between them. Fluffy, jealous of Angel, meowed and butted against their joined hands, shamelessly begging to be stroked. A moment later, the black cat jumped up to join him, and then the gray, all of them demanding attention, climbing over each other in competition.

Typically, Ethan's reaction to the jarring intrusion was a curse, while Brenda couldn't help laughing.

She would have thought the rather dangerous moment of intimacy between them would be broken, the tension released by the absurdity of the interruption. So, she was taken completely by surprise when Ethan reached over the cats, caught her by the shoulders, and smothered her laughter with his mouth.

Their one, brief kiss had been more prickly than passionate. Too fleeting to give her much chance to resist—or to respond.

With this kiss, he took his time. And while the thought of resisting did enter her mind, it evaporated almost immediately.

Her hands, which had been full of cat, settled on his shoulders, then crept around to the back of his neck. He needed a haircut, but his thick, soft hair certainly felt good when she closed her fingers around it.

Sweeping cats out of the way with a gesture that was impatient but still careful enough to satisfy her, he tugged her more fully into his arms. She tilted her head and let her lips part, a tacit invitation he accepted immediately.

THIS HAD BEEN BUILDING, Brenda realized dazedly, since the first time they'd met. Since she'd looked into his eyes and seen so much more than she had expected.

Each time they'd been together since, there had been...something between them. An awareness. An attraction. A connection.

Whatever she might call it, it was real. And it had only intensified with every encounter.

He kissed as skillfully as she had fantasized that he would—and she *had* fantasized, she acknowledged now, closing her eyes in order to concentrate more fully on sensation. And what sensations they were.

His lips were firm, and yet soft at the same time. His mouth was warm, deliciously damp, his tongue rough, yet gentle.

He lifted his head, and she thought it was over. She braced herself for a quick retraction or a defensive comment. Instead, he shifted his head to a new angle and kissed her again, as if his hunger had not yet been sated. Since hers wasn't either—not by a long shot—she nestled closer to him and opened her mouth beneath his again.

She didn't know how much time passed before he slowly, oh so reluctantly, lifted his head again. Her eyelids were heavy, but she forced them upward to gaze wonderingly into his face. His eyes were still very dark, his lips slightly parted to allow ragged breaths to pass between them.

Gazing into his face, she thought of how familiar he had become to her in such a short time. Not quite a month, and yet she already felt as though she knew him so well.

She was aware that her brother would groan to hear that, would remind her that she really didn't know Ethan at all. He would probably accuse her of trying to turn Ethan into the man she wanted him to be, rather than facing the reality that he could be very different, indeed.

Or was that her own deeply buried common sense whispering a warning to her not to trust too much, too fast? Not to believe too deeply in breathtaking kisses and concerned gestures that could very well prove to be false. Not to risk being hurt by giving her heart to someone who wasn't what he appeared to be.

"If you make one sarcastic comment now," she said before he could speak, "I'll strangle you."

He looked momentarily surprised by her threat, and then amused. "Fortunately for my windpipe, I wasn't going to make a sarcastic comment."

"Good." She gathered a disgruntled Angel into her arms and rested her chin on the soft little head, needing a warm body to cling to. "And don't make any snide remarks about proving that I need to work on my defenses, either."

He sighed and pushed a hand through his hair. "Trust me, I can't do that. Not when my own defenses are damned near nonexistent where you're concerned."

She couldn't help but be a little pleased by that. "So you're admitting that the reason you kissed me this time is…?"

"Because I've been wanting to kiss you again ever since the last time. Because I've been spending way too much time thinking about doing a hell of a lot more than kissing you. Yeah, I'll admit it. But that still doesn't make it a good idea."

She peered at him over the head of the calico. "Why, exactly, is it a bad idea?"

He looked at her as though he couldn't believe she'd had to ask. "You want a list?"

After giving it a moment's thought, she nodded. "I think I do."

Ethan shook his head, but cooperated. "First, there's the fact that you took what some people would consider my rightful place in my mother's will."

"Do you resent me for that?"

"No, of course not. I've told you that plenty of times."

"That doesn't seem like such a big deal, then."

"Are you kidding? You know very well that just about everyone else would assume I was trying to get my hands on the money."

"I've never really cared about what everyone else assumes. And it didn't seem to be the money you were trying to get your hands on a few minutes ago."

"That's true," he said, giving her an all-encompassing glance that warmed her cheeks—along with a few other parts. "But when you consider reason two, it makes it even more awkward."

"Reason two?"

"All the things that have happened to you since you became the beneficiary. If someone really is waging a campaign against you, I'm still the one everyone's going to point to."

"Since I've already made it clear that *I* don't suspect you, this argument falls under the same heading of me not caring what other people think."

Faint lines of strain became visible at the corners of his mouth. "Reason three—I'm not looking for a relationship right now."

"Neither am I. I didn't realize we were discussing a relationship. I thought we were just talking about being attracted to each other—for now—and wanting to see where it leads."

He blinked a couple of times, then scowled. "Where that sort of thing usually leads, for me, is into bed," he said bluntly.

She wondered if he was testing her again. Without hesitation, she replied, "That's certainly an option."

Her frankness caught him off guard, but he recovered quickly. "After that, it almost always turns into an awkward, sticky situation in which some woman takes me on as her personal remodeling project and tries to give me an 'extreme makeover.' From the way I comb my hair to the way I walk and talk and cut my meat. Choosing my clothes and my friends and my hobbies and my…"

As if suddenly aware that he'd gone off on a rant, he stopped, looking a bit sheepish.

With one eyebrow raised sardonically, Brenda murmured, "Dude. You've been in some suck relationships."

That made him laugh. "And *you* have been spending too much time with Carly."

She smiled wistfully at him. "You really should laugh more often."

"Which brings us to reason four," he said, his amusement gone. "Maybe you aren't afraid of me—but you scare the hell out of me."

"Of all your reasons," she said, setting the cat aside, "I believe I like that one best."

"It was supposed to be a reason we *shouldn't*—" Ethan began. She cut him off by wrapping her arms around his neck and pressing her mouth against his.

"THIS IS A *REALLY* BAD IDEA." Ethan's voice was muffled against her throat, his hands busy.

Lying beneath him on the bed in the room that had once been his, Brenda tugged at his T-shirt, having already disposed of his overshirt. "So you keep saying. Duck your head, okay?"

He ducked and the T-shirt slid off. She tossed it recklessly aside.

Her shirt followed, landing in a crumpled heap on top of his. He went to work on the fastening of her flesh-colored bra. "Your brother would kill me."

"My brother," she replied, fumbling at the waistband of his jeans, "needs to worry about his own love life. Lift up."

He did, even as he muttered, "Sean would tell you this is—damn, that feels good—this is probably a mistake."

"Sean is responsible for the estate, not my personal life." She ran her hands across his chest and shoulders, savoring the muscles bunched beneath his tanned skin. She was very close to purring like one of the cats.

Ethan's hand hovered just above her right breast. "Maybe we should—"

"Ethan?"

His eyes lifted to hers. "Yeah?"

She arched into his palm. "Shut up."

His fingers closed spasmodically around her. "Right."

Tugging his head down to hers, she made sure his mouth was too busy for him to bring up any more reasons why they shouldn't be doing exactly what they both wanted to do.

LACK OF SLEEP, combined with all the events of that morning, took their toll, and Brenda fell asleep in Ethan's arms. She woke alone. Somehow she knew that Ethan was no longer in the house.

Her hair was tangled around her face, and her body felt deliciously damp and sore and heavy. She lifted her face from the pillow and peered blearily at the clock.

It was still quite early in the day, not long after she'd have awakened on an average Tuesday morning. Not that she'd had many average days lately, she thought, wincing a little as she rolled out of the bed and reached for the red satin robe.

Ethan had left a note on the nightstand, scribbled on a sheet of paper torn from a spiral notebook. She didn't know where he'd found the paper. It took her a moment to decipher the message on it. Ethan's handwriting was terrible, but she was so far gone she found even that endearing.

"I'll call you later," he had written. "Don't forget to call Sean and have the window repaired."

He hadn't signed the note, nor had he added a more personal message. Ethan wasn't the type to write flowery compliments, she mused. Nor had he murmured any to her earlier. But the passion and tenderness with which he had made love to her, the heat and hunger in his kisses, the honest appreciation in his caresses—those gestures had conveyed a great deal to her.

She only hoped she hadn't read too much into them.

She took a quick shower, then redid her hair and makeup. She paused with a cosmetic brush in her hand, staring at her reflection. Her cheeks were rosy enough without enhancement. Her eyes were almost a feverish shade of blue, and her lips were still dark and just slightly swollen. There was certainly no need to add much color.

She set her brush down and pulled on her clothes. She was reminded, for some reason, that she owned nothing that had belonged to her previous life. The life she was beginning to think of as Before Margaret.

Only the day before she had felt as though the Brenda she had once been was slowly slipping away. She certainly was like a stranger to herself today. Wearing a stranger's clothes. Sleeping in a stranger's bed—and not alone.

Making love to a man she had known less than a month was not something the old, sensible Brenda would have done. But that sheltered young woman had not had her life threatened, her home burned down, her whole world tilted on its axis.

That woman had never met Ethan Blacklock.

She would like to think this morning had been the result of a new sophistication on her part. That she had acted on impulse, letting herself be carried away by attraction—a way to relieve the stress of the past few weeks by indulging in a morning of mutual pleasure with a fascinating, appealing and talented lover. The sort of thing a woman of the world indulged in without regrets or expectations. The kind of woman who could share her body without losing her heart.

Yet there was still enough of the old Brenda left to warn her it wouldn't be that easy for her. Maybe there were no regrets, exactly, but there were definitely second thoughts. She certainly had no expectations, which didn't mean she wouldn't indulge in a few secret yearnings.

As for her heart? She hadn't lost it, she assured herself. And then she sighed heavily as she added that she knew exactly where it was. Ethan had taken it with him when he'd left, as surely as he'd taken the gold coins the last time he went away.

THOUGH THERE WASN'T anything he needed in particular, Ethan found himself stopping by the nursery Tuesday afternoon after spending most of the day at the job site. Granted, he'd been so distracted there that one of his crew had asked him if he was coming down with something. He'd denied it, though a nagging voice in his head had asked him if he'd been sure he'd told the truth. He was afraid he *was* coming down with something; he just didn't want to admit what it was, even to himself.

Raine smiled when she saw him, and the warm affection in her expression answered his own question about why he had come. Raine was as close as he had left to real family, and he needed a little familial support just then.

"Ethan." She reached up with a work-callused hand to briefly touch his jaw. "You look tired."

He tugged affectionately at her brown-and-gray braid. "Now what kind of greeting is that? You're supposed to tell me how good I look."

"You're too handsome for your own good, and you know it," she retorted.

Her words made him smile. He wasn't handsome, never had been. Sean had been the pretty boy in the family. Yet Raine had always carried on about how good-looking he was. Funny thing was, he had no doubt that she believed it. Love really was visually challenged.

"What can I do for you today?" she asked, glancing around to make sure the few other customers were already being attended to.

"Actually, I have some business for you."

She looked intrigued. "It's always nice to have more business. What is it?"

"You know how you used to go over every week or so and tend to Mother's rose gardens?"

She nodded, her expression going somber. "She had gardeners to do the mowing and the edging and weeding and all the other yard work, but I was the only one she trusted to feed and prune her roses. She paid me very generously for my time—and we always had a nice visit while I was there. At least, we did until we had our, um, final disagreement over you."

With a sigh, she continued, "After that, it was always strictly business between us. She gave me messages through the housekeeper and she stopped coming out to visit or inviting me inside when I made my rounds, as I called them. We'd see each other occasionally, and we were cordial enough, but it was never the same between us. And then, just over a year ago, she sent a message that my services were no longer needed."

"I'm sorry I came between you," Ethan said regretfully. "I know Mother enjoyed your friendship."

"And I enjoyed hers, but I still say you had every right to do what you wanted to do with your life, even if Margaret and I might have preferred that you go to law school and the guaranteed success you would have found there. I thought she had finally accepted your choice, as I did, until that last battle three years ago when you started your own business. I guess that was when she realized that you were never going to change your mind."

"Yeah. Until then, she thought it was just a phase I was going through. But starting my own business, putting my name on it and everything, that seemed like a slap in the face to her. I can still hear her yelling at me to get out of her house, that she had never wanted a gardener for a son, and she was sorry she had ended up with one."

Raine's eyes filled with tears.

Instantly regretting his bitter, pain-laced words, Ethan wrapped an arm around her shoulders. "Don't look like that, Raine. You know I've been happy with my business. I'm not at all sorry that I struck out on my own, even though I'll admit I wish Mother could have accepted it so we could have had some sort of relationship these past few years. If I had listened to the two of you and gone to law school, I'd have been a miserable man the past ten years. You wouldn't have wanted that, would you?"

She gave him a watery smile. "You know I wouldn't. I've always wanted the best for you."

"I know. Now let's quit talking about the past and get back to business, shall we? How'd you like another lucrative side job?"

"Doing what?" she asked, wiping her eyes with the back of one hand.

"Taking care of the roses again. They look terrible."

Her now-dry brown eyes widened dramatically. "The roses? Your mother's roses?"

"Yeah. I got a good look at them yesterday, and they're in really bad shape. They need pruning and thinning and feeding and spraying. Some of them probably need to be pulled up and others replanted. I'll have to clear it with Sean, but I know he'll approve it, since he said he wants the place well maintained."

"I don't understand. Are you moving back into the house? Did that woman—I forget her name—did she turn down the inheritance?"

He shook his head. "Brenda's been living in the house since her own apartment burned down. I told her the roses look like crap, but she said she doesn't know much about roses. I figured hiring you again would be advantageous for both of you."

Turning to stare at him in bewilderment, Raine asked, "You've been talking to her?"

"Yeah." Because Raine knew him so well, he tried to keep his voice ultracasual. "We've seen each other a few times. She's been helping me look for something that belonged to my dad, something important to me, but we haven't been able to find it. She's actually a very nice person. I think you'll like her, if you'll give her a chance."

She frowned. "It doesn't matter how nice she is, I still don't think she should be living in your family home, helping herself to your mother's things. I don't know what she did to convince Margaret to put her in your place, but it's just not right."

"C'mon, Raine, did you ever know Mother to allow herself to be convinced to do anything she didn't want to do? According to Brenda, she never even met my mother. She has no idea how she ended up in the will."

"And you believe that?"

"I have no reason not to," he replied. "From everything I can tell, Brenda's as honest as they come. I know you're rabidly loyal when it comes to me, Raine, and I appreciate it—but don't let that prejudice you against Brenda. Give yourself a chance to meet her before you decide you don't like her, okay?"

She hesitated a moment, her expression still harder than he was used to seeing, but then she softened. "If that's what you want me to do."

It was kind of nice to have someone that ready to fight battles for him. To be on his side, no matter what.

"I'll talk to Sean and get back to you about when you should start with the roses, okay? And then you'll want to talk to Brenda and make arrangements with her, as well."

She nodded, her smile a bit stiff. "All right. You know I can always use the extra income. Thanks for thinking of me, Ethan."

"Hey, that's what friends are for, right? Besides, you've referred my business plenty of times. I owe you."

"I've always been willing to help you in any way I could, Ethan."

He wondered what she would say if she knew exactly how friendly he had become with Brenda Prentiss. Raine was already prepared to dislike Brenda. If she found out what had happened between them yesterday, she would probably label Brenda both as a probable gold-digger and a potential heartbreaker.

He was pretty sure she would be wrong on the first count. As to the second, he hoped he had enough sense not to let this thing between him and Brenda come to that.

CHAPTER FOURTEEN

CARLY'S HANDS WERE FULL of bags when she stood in front of Brenda's door Tuesday evening. She looked at the doorbell button with a frown, wondering how she was going to manage it without dropping everything. She was just about to resort to kicking the door when it opened.

She recognized the man who stood looking at her in surprise from the other side. "Sean, isn't it? Brenda's trustee?"

"Yes," he confirmed. "It's nice to see you again, Miss D'Alessandro."

"Carly," she reminded him.

Brenda, who had been standing behind Sean, stepped forward. "Hi, Carly. Wow, that smells good."

Carly had called to inform Brenda that she was bringing take-out, figuring after the eventful day Brenda had endured, she wouldn't be in the mood to cook. Brenda had seemed grateful for the gesture, and genuinely pleased that Carly was coming by. Something in her voice, however, made Carly wonder if anything else had happened after she and Richard had left that morning.

"You said you like Chinese," she reminded Brenda. "I've brought enough for a small army."

"You're welcome to join us for a bite before you leave, Sean," Brenda offered politely, taking Carly's hint.

He smiled, but shook his head. "I would love to, but I have an appointment this evening."

He took Brenda's hand in his and smiled down at her. "If you need anything else, you call me, okay? Don't wait so long to call next time. I don't care if it's the middle of the night, I'm available if you need me."

"That's very kind of you, but I hope there won't be any more middle-of-the-night calls to anyone," Brenda replied. "Goodbye, Sean. Thank you for taking care of everything so efficiently today."

"My pleasure. Ladies." Giving them a humor-ously old-fashioned bow, he left them alone with their food.

"I think he has a thing for you," Carly said, follow-ing Brenda to the kitchen.

Brenda sighed loudly. "I might be flattered by that, except that you seem to think everyone has a thing for me."

"Not everyone. Just Sean. And, well, Ethan."

Brenda kept her back turned to Carly as she pulled dishes out of a cabinet, but her voice sounded a little funny when she said, "Don't be ridiculous."

Because Carly had her suspicions about the way Brenda felt about Ethan, she let that subject drop—for the moment. "So, how are you?" she asked as they took their seats at the table. "Did you manage to get any rest today?"

"A little," Brenda replied, piling steaming food onto her plate. "This looks great, Carly. It was very nice of you to offer to bring it by."

"I figured you could use some food. And some company."

"You were right on both counts."

"The front window looks good. I couldn't even tell that it had been broken."

"Mmm-hmm. The team Sean sent to repair it was very efficient. They had it done by three o'clock this afternoon."

Carly stabbed a fork into a pile of noodles. "Guess you're glad you've got Sean to turn to during all of this."

Brenda sent her a suspicious look, but since Carly kept her expression deliberately innocent, Brenda merely nodded and said, "Yes, he's very helpful."

"Dad said for me to tell you he talked to Leland Grassel today. Leland denied having anything to do with the thrown rock. Apparently, he was very indignant about the accusation and ordered my father out of his office. Leland said he's told everyone he isn't fighting you any longer, and he won't change his mind if everyone will just leave him alone."

"Did your father believe him?"

Carly shrugged. "He said there's really no proof either way without witnesses. Still, he said if Leland did throw the rock, maybe he'll be less likely to do anything like that again if he thinks you're on to him."

Brenda looked disappointed, but resigned. "I suppose I knew it was unlikely we'd find proof that Leland was the one who threw it. Still—"

"Still, it would have been nice to know for sure," Carly finished for her.

"Exactly."

"Ethan didn't seem to think it was Leland, did he?"

Brenda's voice took on that odd note again, the one that seemed to appear whenever Ethan's name was mentioned. "No, he didn't. But he didn't have any better suggestions, either."

"Is Richard coming over tonight?" Strangely enough, Carly heard something in her own voice that made her think of the way Brenda had sounded when she talked about Ethan.

Brenda shook her head. "He had plans for the evening. I convinced him not to change them."

"Plans? Like a date, you mean?" She'd tried to speak casually, but wasn't sure she had entirely succeeded.

"No, I think it was business. Some sort of professional networking thing."

"Oh." Carly bit into an egg roll in an effort to mask her intense relief, then nearly gasped when the hot filling scalded her tongue. "Ouch. Careful, the egg rolls are still steaming."

"I'll keep that in mind, thanks." After a momentary pause, Brenda said, "Maybe I should be the one pointing out that you seem to have a thing for my brother."

"It's true," Carly admitted with a sigh, giving up any attempt at subterfuge. "I can't help it. He's just so cute. And so concerned about you and serious about taking care of you. Every time he gets that funny little pucker between his eyes, I just melt, you know?"

"Way too much information. He's my brother, Carly."

"Okay, sorry. But I still think he's hot."

Brenda waved a hand in front of her face as if she'd suddenly been struck blind. Carly giggled.

They finished their dinners, then cleaned up together. Afterward, they moved into the living room so that Carly could see the repaired window up close.

"You're right," she agreed. "They did a really good job. It looks great. I assume the security strips will be replaced soon?"

"Tomorrow."

"Good. This really could be a great house with a little redecorating," Carly said, stroking the gray cat she'd carried into the room with her. "Have you had any of your old friends over since you moved in?"

"No. I haven't felt comfortable with that yet."

Carly shrugged. "I'll admit this house isn't what I would call comfortable, but it could be. And there's plenty of room to entertain."

"That isn't what I meant. I just…well, I don't feel at home here yet. I don't feel right about entertaining here. And with everything that's been going on…" She let her voice trail off.

"That makes sense. But if you want to have one or two of your close friends over, I can't imagine that anyone would object. You're living here now, Brenda. Sean seems perfectly comfortable with it, Ethan has no objections, even Richard's starting to get used to it. I really think you should just let yourself enjoy it. Tell Sean you want to get rid of some of this fussy stuff and bring in some things that reflect your own personality. Unless you just really don't like living here?"

"I don't mind living here, for the most part. It's just so big and so empty, sometimes."

"Do you get scared?"

"Not usually. I mean, it's a nice neighborhood, and I have the cats for company and the security system for safety. I have to confess the rock through the window shook me up, though."

"Do you ever think about…her?"

"Her?" Brenda looked confused for a moment, then asked, "You mean Margaret?"

"Well, yeah. I mean. She…you know…"

"She died here. I don't believe in ghosts, Carly."

"Neither do I," Carly assured her quickly, wondering if she'd have been as brave about staying here alone. "I just wondered if you ever think about her."

"Of course. She's the reason I'm here, after all. I spend a lot of time thinking about her, and wondering why she chose me."

Carly wandered over to the side table on which the family photographs were displayed. She had noticed them before, of course, and had studied them surreptitiously, but now she gazed openly at them. "They don't look very happy, do they?"

"No. They don't. Of course, those posed, family portrait things often are stiff and uncomfortable looking."

Carly thought of the photographs covering every surface in her home. Posed, candid, formal, casual…in all of them, her family looked happy. Loving. Studying the people with whom Ethan had spent his childhood, Carly realized that she had been taking her own special family for granted for much too long.

"No wonder Ethan has issues," she murmured.

"Issues?" Brenda repeated.

"Like you have to ask what I mean."

Brenda sighed. "No. I don't have to ask. Let's go to the media room, okay? This one's too stuffy."

"Great light in here," Carly murmured as they

moved toward the door. "Nice, high ceilings. Beautiful molding. We could make this room perfectly comfortable, even keeping it more formal than the media room or the music room."

She realized only after she'd spoken that she had said "we." If Brenda noticed, it didn't seem to bother her. "Maybe I will think about redecorating—once things settle down."

It was the first time Carly had heard her refer to the future. She was very pleased to hear it now.

Now if only she could find out what was going on between Brenda and Ethan....

THE DOORBELL RANG late Thursday afternoon, and Brenda had to get up off the floor to answer it. She'd been playing with the cats, and she brushed multicolored hairs off her clothes as she walked to the front door.

She looked through the viewer and paused before opening the door. She needed just a moment to compose herself, to make sure her face was inscrutable and her voice was steady. "So you decided to show up again, did you?"

Ethan eyed her without smiling, his hair looking as though he might have run his hand through it a couple of times while he'd waited for her to answer the door. Was it possible that he was also trying to hide an attack of nerves? "I should have called."

She crossed her arms. "I haven't been waiting by the phone."

"I didn't think you would be. Are you going to invite me in?"

She stepped out of the doorway. "Of course."

He moved into the entryway and kicked the door

closed behind him. "Let's just get something straight. Everything I said about why we shouldn't get together? Still stands."

"I agree."

Maybe he'd been braced for an argument. He hesitated a moment, then nodded. "We had an itch. We scratched it. End of story."

If he was being deliberately blunt in an effort to shake her, he was going to find out that she was tougher than she'd given him reason to believe. "That explanation works for me."

Maybe he'd wanted her to argue with him. His frown deepened, and he looked at her suspiciously. "So that's it?"

She shrugged. "If you want it to be."

"What do *you* want?" he challenged her.

No way was he going to draw her into that. "I want seafood," she said, dropping her arms to her side. "Shrimp, crab legs, scallops. For some reason, I've been thinking about seafood all day."

Now it was his turn to try to hide his surprise. "I could go for some seafood."

She nodded. "I'll get my purse. You're driving."

He didn't protest.

Without asking for her input, he chose a moderately priced chain seafood restaurant. She had no complaints, since she and her friends ate there often. Their casual jeans outfits fit right in with the family-style atmosphere, and the food was always good, so he had made a sensible selection.

He helped her down out of his tall pickup truck, then kept a hand on her back as they made their way into the restaurant lobby. She was intensely aware of his touch, and something about the way he looked at her when he opened the door for her made her suspect that he was just as conscious of that point of contact between them. Nor did he seem to be in any hurry to put any distance between them, despite what he'd said earlier.

The lobby was crowded, as always, and the harried hostess took Ethan's name, then gave them a plastic disk that would vibrate and flash lights when their table was ready. They waited in the nautically themed bar, where Brenda sipped a pink drink in a cutesy glass. It didn't surprise her when Ethan ordered a beer.

The bar was too loud for them to carry on a real conversation, especially with a baseball game playing on the corner TV, so they simply talked as best they could about the merits of the game. Ethan seemed surprised that Brenda liked baseball; she admitted to preferring football, but she watched baseball enough to keep up. They didn't have to wait long until they were summoned to their table.

It was quieter in the dining room, especially in the cozy corner booth in which they were seated. They placed their orders, and were quickly served salads and cheese biscuits. Only then did Ethan ask, "So, what have you been up to since Tuesday?"

She speared a cherry tomato with her salad fork. "The window was repaired and the security system checked out. Sean came by Tuesday evening to make sure everything was okay, and then Carly and I had Chinese food and watched a movie on DVD. Yesterday I went back to the animal shelter where I volunteer and spent a few hours helping out."

It had felt good to reconnect with her old routine

and with the animals she loved. None of her fellow volunteers knew about her inheritance, and she had kept it that way for now.

Ethan hadn't been asking for a step-by-step account of her days, but she wanted him to know that she truly hadn't been sitting in the house waiting for him to call or come by. The fact that he hadn't been far out of her thoughts since he'd left Tuesday morning was something he did not need to know.

"No more problems?" he asked.

She shook her head. "Not so far. Everything's been very quiet. Carly asked me if I thought the house was haunted."

His mouth twitched. "By my mother? Doubtful. If Mother went to the trouble of haunting anyone, it would be me."

"I never know what Carly's going to say or do next. That's why I enjoy her company, I guess."

"Yes, well, try not to let her talk you into an exorcism. Trust me, it would take more than that to get rid of Mother if she didn't want to leave."

Some people might have thought he was speaking rather callously of a woman who'd been dead less than a month. Knowing his convoluted feelings about his mother, Brenda wasn't surprised that he chose to hide them behind sardonic remarks.

"So, tell me more about your landscaping business," she said, changing the subject after their dinners were served. "How many people work for you? How many jobs are you working on now?"

He answered briefly, but she asked more questions until finally he told her quite a bit about his company. She watched his face when he let himself be swept away with his enthusiasm for the business he'd started and built up with nothing more than hard work and determination. He was so proud of what he'd accomplished, she thought. So much more than he would have been had he chosen to drift into the life that had been predetermined for him, the career path that had been cleared by nothing more than an accident of birth.

How could anyone who knew him not understand that about him? How could anyone who loved him not admire that self-sufficient side of him?

He had just finished describing an intricate water garden his crew was constructing when he seemed to realize how long he'd been talking about himself. He stopped abruptly. "I didn't mean to get carried away."

"I like hearing about your business," she assured him. "I would love to see the site you were just describing to me. It sounds beautiful. I've always wanted a water garden, with a waterfall and goldfish."

"So have one put in. That backyard could sure use some kind of landscaping other than those boringly arranged plants Mother kept back there. There's plenty of room for a waterfall, a pool, a patio with a grill and a dining area. Maybe even a spa."

She studied him more closely. "You've given this some thought."

He nodded. "That underutilized backyard always bugged me. I practiced doing landscape designs by laying out plans for that one on a lot of occasions."

Her expression must have revealed something of what she was thinking. He sighed. "No, I'm not sitting around wishing I had the house. I like my house, Brenda. It has a small yard, but that's because I don't have a lot of time to take care of my own place. You know how that goes."

"Like the plumber whose own pipes are always clogged."

"Exactly. If I wanted a bigger place, I'd have one. I have all I need, or want, for now."

She made a face. "I know the feeling. I feel ridiculous rattling around by myself in that big, five-bedroom house."

With a shrug, he said, "It would be tough to take care of four cats in a smaller place."

"Was that your mother's excuse?"

"No, Mother was just pretentious."

She smiled, then turned her attention back to her dinner. "This is really good. Exactly what I wanted tonight."

Nodding, he swallowed a grilled scallop before saying, "Anyway, back to the lawn. I talked to Sean today and recommended someone to salvage the rose beds. If you have no objections, he said I should have her call you."

"Her?" Brenda repeated casually.

"Raine Scott. She's the one who put in the rose gardens and tended them for years. She was a friend of my mother's when I was growing up, and she was actually the one who got me interested in landscaping in the first place."

"Really?" Her good mood restored, she reached for her water glass. "I'll look forward to meeting her."

"You'll like her. She's great. Just…well, give her a little time to warm up to you before you make up your mind about her, okay?"

Brenda set the glass back down. "Is she shy? Or just the type who's slow to get to know people?"

"Neither, actually. But she is an extremely loyal friend, and she considers me sort of a surrogate son."

"Oh." As comprehension sank in, she set down her fork. "She doesn't like me because I took your place in your mother's will."

"She doesn't know you, Brenda. True, her first reaction was to be suspicious and resentful of you, but she's cool. She'll come around when she understands that you had nothing to do with the situation we're all in. I told her she would like you when she meets you, and she trusts my judgment."

Brenda wasn't significantly reassured. "All of your friends must hate me."

"They don't hate you." But the way he shifted in his chair made her suspect he was glossing the truth. "Besides, what do you care what my friends think?"

She nodded slowly. "You're right, of course." It wasn't as if she would ever meet them, after all.

Her appetite gone now, she pushed away her mostly emptied plate and took a sip of water to try to wash down the lump in her throat.

Ethan set his fork on his empty plate. "Do you want any dessert?"

"No, I'm full. But feel free to have something, yourself."

He shook his head and motioned for the server to bring the check.

Brenda reached for her purse. "This was my idea. It's my treat."

She could tell he was prepared to argue, maybe to give her a defensive speech about how he could afford a couple of meals. "I'm spending your mother's money," she reminded him. "So just hush about it, okay?"

He smiled. "Yes, ma'am."

She was a little surprised by his surrender, but disarmed enough by his smile that she couldn't manage to sound smug when she said, "That's settled, then."

HE DROVE HER BACK to the house—she still couldn't quite think of it as "home"—and then he walked her to the front door.

"I'll have Raine call you," he said, glancing at the struggling rose gardens.

Though she wasn't exactly looking forward to speaking with someone predisposed to dislike her, Brenda nodded. "I'd hate to see all these beautiful roses lost. And heaven knows I don't know what to do for them."

She opened the door. "Do you want to come in? I could make coffee. And I have some ice cream, since you didn't have dessert at the restaurant."

He hesitated, then asked, "What kind of ice cream?"

"English toffee."

"Sounds good. Maybe just a scoop."

Leading him inside, Brenda headed straight for the kitchen. She had to pause to acknowledge the cats who had rushed out to greet them. Kneeling, she patted heads and rubbed exposed bellies. "Okay, settle down, guys. You can all have a treat when we have our ice cream."

"You really don't mind living with all these cats?"

She smiled at the expression on Ethan's face. "Now

you sound like Sean. As I told him—no, I don't mind. I like the cats. All four of them. It's funny how they're so different, personality-wise."

He grunted, as if skeptical of that claim.

Pulling ice cream dishes from a cupboard, Brenda shook her head. "Didn't both of you grow up around cats?"

"If you mean because of Mother, you've forgotten a couple of things. Sean didn't live here most of the time—and Mother didn't share."

Brenda looked up from scooping the ice cream. "She wouldn't let you play with her cats?"

"She was afraid I might hurt them," he answered, his face expressionless. "You know how rough and clumsy boys can be."

She set his ice cream in front of him. "Sometimes it's very difficult for me to hold my tongue about your mother."

"I was just telling you why I don't care for cats," he muttered. "But I'm through complaining about my childhood. It's not like I had it all that bad. I grew up with plenty of money in a nice neighborhood. I was never physically abused. I made some good friends, had some fun in a variety of sports, went to good schools. Then when I decided to strike out on my own, I had my grandfather's trust fund for a cushion and lucked into some excellent apprenticeship programs before I started my own, so-far-successful business. I'd say that makes me a pretty lucky guy, on the whole. Wouldn't you?"

"When you put it that way, I guess you are," she agreed, but she still felt sorry for his lack of loving familial support. She wondered if any amount of professional success could ever completely make up for the pain his difficult mother had caused him.

"So, what about *your* childhood?" he asked, turning the conversation around. "Was it happy?"

"Very. We didn't have a lot of money, but we were a close family. My parents loved music, so all of us learned to play instruments. We would play and sing in the evenings, and go for picnics on the weekends— totally cornball, I guess."

"It sounds nice."

"It was." She dipped into her ice cream, looking down to hide her expression. "It was just too short. I lost my dad, and then my mom by the time I was twenty-three. I wasn't ready to let go of them yet."

"I'm sorry, Brenda. I've done so much griping about my past that we've barely mentioned yours. I haven't even told you how sorry I am that you lost everything in that fire."

She forced a smile, not wanting to let the mood turn maudlin. "I didn't blame you for being a little prickly about that. After all, you were practically accused of setting it."

"More than 'practically,'" he retorted. "Your P.I. roused me out of bed the next day and demanded to know where I had been all night. And then your brother nearly went postal on me when he opened the door and saw me standing there. You were the only one who didn't look at me as though I were a mad arsonist."

"I just couldn't see you sneaking into my kitchen and starting a fire," she admitted. "You're just not the sneaking-around type."

"You're right," he agreed gravely. "If I were going

to start a fire, I'd do it right out in the open where everyone could see me."

She laughed. "That's not really what I meant, but you get the general idea."

His gaze seemed to linger on her mouth long enough to make her a bit self-conscious. She rose to rinse out her dish and set it in the dishwasher. "How about that coffee?"

"No, thanks." She hadn't realized he'd also risen until he spoke. "I guess I'd better be going."

She turned, only to find him standing directly behind her. Moistening her lips, she looked up at him. "Yes, I suppose…"

He was looking at her mouth again. "You suppose what?" he prompted when her voice faded.

"Hmm?" How could he still smell so fresh and good this late in the day? He must have stopped by his place after work to shower before coming here. For some reason, she found that rather touching.

"Damn it, Brenda. Stop doing that."

She blinked, and tried to clear her suddenly clouded mind. "Stop doing what?"

"Stop looking so darned good."

That made her smile, albeit tremulously. "I'm not sure whether to thank you or to apologize."

"I think you'd better hit me, instead."

"Why would I want to— Oh." The last word was muffled by his mouth after he jerked her unceremoniously into his arms.

He was definitely not the flowery phrases type, she had just enough brain power left to think. But, oh, could this man kiss.

She stood on tiptoes and wrapped her arms around

his neck. His mouth tasted like ice cream, and his tongue was deliciously cold when it swept across her lips and dipped inside.

Their mouths warmed rapidly, as did the rest of them. Brenda could almost feel her blood heat. Her heart was beating so fast and so hard that she was sure Ethan could feel it, too. After all, she was pressed so closely against him that there were no mysteries left between them.

She certainly knew exactly how *he* was feeling at that moment.

He shifted, and she was suddenly pressed back against the refrigerator. Ethan's hands were splayed on either side of her, trapping her between his arms. He kissed her until her knees weakened and she had to cling to him to stay on her feet. And then he kissed her again.

Eventually, they had to breathe. He lifted his head just far enough to allow them both a few ragged gulps of air.

"What about—" Brenda had to clear her throat, and even then she sounded choked when she continued, "What about your four reasons why we shouldn't get involved?"

He rested his forehead against hers. "Every single one of them still applies. Including the last one. Especially the last one."

The last reason had been that she scared him. She didn't want to argue with him, but she really didn't think it was fear that was making him tremble just then.

Because they were plastered all over each other, and Ethan was still very prominently aroused—as she was, for that matter—she had to ask, "So, what do we do now?"

"We start using our heads," he murmured against her cheek. "Keeping our distance."

She couldn't help noticing that his hand had slipped beneath the hem of her blouse even as he spoke. She swallowed hard in response to the feel of skin against skin. "And, um, when are we going to start?"

"We really should start—" His hand slid upward and closed over her breast. "Tomorrow," he said hoarsely. "We'll start tomorrow."

"Sounds like a plan," she murmured, and pressed her mouth to his again.

THIS TIME SHE ROUSED when he tried to leave the bed, probably because she was lying on his left arm, her head on his shoulder. She didn't know what time it was, but it was still completely dark in the room.

"Where are you going?" she asked groggily.

He stilled in his efforts to extricate himself. "I was just—uh—"

Leaving, she thought, mentally completing the sentence. Trying to slip out before the inevitable confrontation with the glaring reality of daylight.

"Uh-uh," she said, tightening her grip on him. "Not this time."

"But—"

She slid her smooth, bare leg up higher on his hair-roughened one. Her breasts brushed his chest when she leaned over him, her mouth hovering a mere breath above his. "It's not tomorrow yet."

His body reacting with impressive speed, he slid

his hands down her back to her hips. "Good point," he whispered against her lips, and shifted her more fully on top of him.

ON AN IMPULSE, Carly drove to Brenda's house rather than straight to the office early Friday morning. She thought maybe she'd beg a cup of coffee, check to make sure Brenda was okay—and then maybe do a little more snooping about Brenda's sexy brother, she added with an unabashed grin.

Maybe she would be a little late to work, but she wasn't overly concerned about that. Her dad would frown, but he wouldn't fire her. Unfortunately.

Her father had a soft spot for Brenda. An almost fatherly interest in the young woman who had found herself in such a perplexing situation. It bothered him that he hadn't been able to accomplish much on Brenda's behalf. Carly would bet that he had yet to bill Brenda a dime.

He'd given up on not talking to Carly about the case, since Brenda had been so inclusive of her. He had admitted his frustration to her about finding absolutely no connections between Brenda and Margaret Jacobs.

Carly had no ideas to suggest, but she had told her father that if the answers were out there, he would be the one to find them. He had thanked her for her faith in him, but for one of the few times in her life, she had seen self-doubt in her father's eyes.

Maybe it was that as much as anything that had her turning on the street where Brenda now lived. Perhaps if she and Brenda put their heads together and brainstormed, they could come up with a few new leads for Tony to pursue.

She braked in front of Brenda's house and lifted her eyebrows in surprise at the sight of the pickup truck parked in the circular drive. The lettering on the doors identified it as belonging to Ethan, not that she had needed the confirmation. And the morning dew still glistening on the windshield let her know the truck had been there quite a while. All night?

"Oh, man," she murmured aloud. "Richard would freak."

She turned her car around and headed in the other direction, passing another big, dark pickup on her way out of the neighborhood.

She would definitely be calling Brenda later.

CHAPTER FIFTEEN

THE SUN WAS STREAMING through the windows when Brenda woke again. She was rather surprised to find Ethan still there. He was awake, lying on his back with one arm beneath her and the other crooked behind his head, gazing at the ceiling as if he were reading something interesting there.

He didn't look at her, but somehow he knew she was awake. "I think I'm in trouble."

She considered his words for a moment, then asked, "Because you didn't leave?"

"Because I didn't *want* to leave," he corrected.

It seemed odd that his glum tone should make her so cheerful. She knew better than to let him see it. "Maybe you'd like some breakfast before you go?"

"Sure. Why not?"

The resignation in his tone reminded her so much of the gloomy donkey in the *Winnie the Pooh* stories that she just had to laugh.

That made him turn his head to look at her. "Something amuses you?"

"You sounded as though I just offered you your last meal."

He was quiet for a moment, and she wondered if he

was annoyed by her teasing. But then the corners of his mouth twitched. "Sorry."

"So, what would you rather have? Eggs or waffles?"

"Whatever you're in the mood to make."

"Waffles, then." She started to roll to reach for her robe, but he tightened his arm around her to stop her.

She looked at him curiously. "Is there something else you want to say?"

"Just this," he said and tugged her head to his.

The kiss was long and thorough. Her head was spinning by the time he released her. She blinked at him, unable to form coherent words.

"I just thought we should start the morning over," he said, then reached for his clothes.

Brenda's hand wasn't quite steady when she picked up her robe. One thing for certain, she wasn't laughing at him now.

BRENDA SHOWERED QUICKLY before cooking breakfast, donning a pair of khaki shorts and a red T-shirt, pulling her hair into a loose ponytail and leaving her feet bare. Ethan took his turn in the shower while she prepared the meal, appearing just as she finished. He wore the same jeans and unbuttoned cotton shirt over a T-shirt that he'd worn the evening before, but he still managed to look fresh, and so appealing that her mouth went dry at the sight of him. She hoped she was able to conceal that reaction as she poured him a cup of coffee and set a plate of waffles and sliced strawberries in front of him.

They turned on the small television set tucked into the kitchen while they ate so Ethan could check the weather report. There was a chance of rain that afternoon, and he said he had to leave right after breakfast to make sure something was finished at one of his sites before the rain began.

Brenda didn't try to detain him, nor did she make any effort to start a serious discussion with him. They ate with a minimum of conversation, and that was mostly about the headlines on the morning news.

Afterward, she walked with him to the front door, cats weaving around their feet.

"So you've got my cell-phone number," he said, hesitating before opening the door. "Call it if you need anything, especially if anything else happens, okay?"

She nodded. "Thank you. I hope things go well for you at work today."

He put a hand on the doorknob, but he didn't open the door yet. "What are *you* going to do today?"

"I—" she lifted one shoulder in a slight shrug "—I don't know yet."

"Don't let anyone send you into hiding," he advised gruffly. "Just be careful if you go out."

"I won't hide. Not anymore," she assured him. "But I will be careful."

"Good." He opened the door then. "Guess I'd better shove off."

She wanted to ask if she would hear from him again—and when. She wanted to know how he felt about the night they'd spent together, and what he'd meant by his cryptic remarks that morning. But all she said was, "Okay. See you."

He touched her cheek in a gesture so sweet and so gentle that it brought a lump to her throat. "See you," he said. Something about his tone made the simple words a promise.

He left without saying anything else. He didn't even kiss her goodbye. But the look he gave her as he walked out was every bit as effective.

ETHAN HAD LEFT HIS PHONE in the glove box of his truck when he and Brenda went into the restaurant the evening before. Because he had been…distracted afterward, he hadn't thought to take it back out.

After arriving at the job site Friday morning, he checked messages before getting out of his truck. There were several, but only one that he returned.

"Hey, Sean, it's Ethan. You called?"

"Yeah. I tried to reach you at home last night, and then tried your cell when I kept getting your machine."

"I was…busy last night. What do you need?"

"I just wanted you to know I've prepared a release for the coin collection. I'm going to send you a couple of copies. You should sign one and return it for my files, okay?"

Sean was a stickler for covering every base. "Yeah, sure. Send it on."

"Everything okay with you?"

"Fine. How about you?"

"Good. I had a nice dinner with Brenda earlier this week. It seemed like she was becoming more comfortable with her new circumstances. Of course, that was before this latest incident."

Ethan wondered if Sean was fishing for something. If so, he wasn't taking the bait. "Yeah," he said noncommittally.

"I spoke with Leland again yesterday, to give him an idea of how soon after probate that he can expect to receive his inheritance. Now that he's dropping his contest of the will, of course. I sort of casually mentioned the rock throwing incident, and he went off on a rampage. Said the P.I. had been to see him, and had pretty much accused him of the crime."

"He claimed innocence, of course."

"Yes, of course. Fairly convincingly."

"So you don't think he had anything to do with it?"

"I really can't see Leland throwing a rock through Brenda's window. Whether he hired someone to do it for him, I couldn't say. But there is, of course, the possibility that he had nothing at all to do with it."

Which was a possibility that had been nagging at Ethan ever since Carly had called him. "So, if not Leland, then who?"

After a rather lengthy pause, Sean replied, "Someone who resents Brenda being in that house, I suppose. Who doesn't think she has a right to Margaret's estate."

Ethan scowled. "Look, if you're even implying that I could be connected to any of this—"

"I didn't say that," Sean said quickly. But he didn't deny it, either.

"I'm getting fed up with trying to defend myself every time something happens around Brenda."

"Leland said pretty much the same thing."

Ethan muttered a curse.

"I'm not accusing you of anything, Ethan. I don't know who's been bothering Brenda. I'm not even saying I can't sympathize with whoever it is. I mean, she really *did* just luck into a pretty good deal here, without doing anything to earn it, as far as we know."

Ethan found that comment confusing. He'd thought Sean had been supporting Brenda fully during the past few weeks.

Was Sean now saying that he had resentments against her, himself? Was he actually hinting that someone was justified in harassing Brenda? Or was he trying to play sympathizer in an attempt to ascertain for himself whether Ethan was harboring resentments he hadn't admitted to?

"But it's not my place to judge her," Sean added quickly, "or to second-guess your mother's decisions. My job is simply to administer the estate to the best of my ability, and that's what I intend to do."

"Brenda's as much an innocent bystander in all of this as the rest of us are. She didn't ask to be named in the will, and she certainly didn't ask for anything that's happened to her since."

"Sounds as though you've got a soft spot for the pretty heiress," Sean murmured, and now his tone was just short of mockery.

"First you accuse me of having a vendetta against her, and now of having a thing for her? Make up your mind, Sean."

"The thing is, I wouldn't really blame you either way. She's…well, she's intriguing."

"I've got to go. Send me the forms. I'll sign them and get them back to you. Goodbye, Sean."

He punched the button to disconnect the call. And then he shoved the phone roughly into its belt holder, and threw open the door to his truck.

"WHAT ARE YOU GOING TO DO TODAY?"

Ethan's question echoed in Brenda's mind for a long time after he left for his busy day. She had to get active again, she thought with a frown. Visiting the animal shelter yesterday had been a good start, but now she had to figure out what to do with the rest of her life.

She had spent the past three weeks drifting. Confused and afraid, pretty much paralyzed when it came to making plans for her future.

Now she had some important decisions to make. And as much as she valued her siblings' advice, these were decisions she was going to have to make on her own.

As she so often did when she was debating a problem, she went for a long drive, tuning her radio in to a favorite station and letting the music swirl around her in the car. For some reason, she drove to her old neighborhood. Though the building clouds foretold the rain that was predicted, it was still a warm, pleasant day, and the children who weren't indoors playing video games were celebrating summer vacation on Rollerblade skates and skateboards.

She had to drive carefully down her old street, which made her remember the recklessly driven truck that had almost run her down. Had it been only two weeks ago? It seemed like longer, somehow.

So much had happened since that day. Maybe she had needed to return here to remind herself that she was still the same person, she mused, pausing her car to gaze glumly at the burned-out shell of her former home.

A month ago, she had been living in that little duplex, counting pennies, working at the bank until school started again, spending time with her friends and her volunteer work. Like most of her single friends, she had hoped to meet a nice guy, fall in love, get married, have a family.

She had never expected to get wealthy on a teacher's salary, nor had money been one of her criteria for suitable dates. But that hadn't worried her much, since nearly everyone she knew had to live on a budget, squeaking by until paydays, saving carefully for emergencies and luxuries.

How could she have even dreamed then that only weeks later, she would be living in a big, fancy house, with enough money to provide her every need and involved with a man she barely knew?

In a way, she had a chance to go back to her simpler life of before. Her apartment and her former possessions were gone, but they could be replaced. She could give up the inheritance, go back to the bank for what was left of the summer, report to her classroom in the fall. Keep looking for a man with a lot less baggage and fewer complications than Ethan. She could stop looking over her shoulder and wondering who was trying to harm her—or romance her—for her money. Because she wouldn't have any.

And yet…

She was starting to rather like the house. Not the way it was decorated, of course. But she liked the floor plan, the kitchen and the media room with its cat playground and comfy sectional sofa. When she looked out at the backyard, she could see Ethan's vision for it, with the patio and tables and pool.

And the money was seductive, as well, she had to admit as she put her car into gear and drove slowly away from the burned duplex. It wasn't that she wanted to go on a big shopping spree. She still had no particular interest in designer clothes or flashy jewelry. She just wasn't a "bling-bling" kind of person. But it would be so nice not to have to worry about paying her bills, affording health insurance or taking an occasional vacation. Being able to do a few things for other people—like her sister, if she could ever convince Linda to accept help.

And then there was Ethan. Even with all the complications connected to him, she wasn't sure she was prepared to walk away from him. Every time they parted, she wondered if she would ever see him again, and every time he came back, she had to ask herself why he had. And yet…there was something about him that she found irresistible.

She wouldn't go so far as to say she had fallen in love with him. But she wouldn't say she hadn't, either. Either way, she knew she was in danger of having her heart broken. Yet even with that possibility looming over her, she knew she wouldn't turn him away the next time he came to her.

She drove past the bank where she had planned to spend the summer working. She had enjoyed the work, for the most part, and had made some friends there, but if she was strictly honest with herself, she would have to admit she had no burning desire to return.

Teaching was a different story. She really did like her job—Cooper Owens and his like, notwithstanding. She had spent five years in college preparing for this career, and she wasn't ready to call it quits just yet. One way or another, she would perform her job and maintain her friendships with the rest of the staff. She wouldn't let the money change her, or get in the way of her relationships with other people.

Which meant that she had finally decided not to refuse the inheritance. She still didn't know why she'd been chosen. She still didn't know who resented her selection badly enough to harass her. She still had some feelings of guilt about taking the money she had done nothing to earn. But she couldn't go back to the life she'd had before. And she might as well admit that she didn't really want to.

Because she wasn't prepared to give up everything about her old life, she had to find a way to somehow blend the two. She had been avoiding her old friends; it was time to let them back in.

She turned the car back toward the house she was trying to think of as home. She had some phone calls to make.

NO ONE HAD EVER ACCUSED Carly of being shy. Nor at all timid about going after something she wanted. At ten o'clock Friday morning, she took a break from computer entries to dial Richard's office number.

"Hi, Robin, it's Carly D'Alessandro," she said a moment later. "I met you last Friday, remember? You were leaving for your son's baseball game. Did his team win?"

"I remember meeting you. And, yes, Jo-Jo's team won. Thanks for asking."

"Great. So, is Richard available?"

"Hold on a minute. I'll see if he can take your call."

She wasn't kept holding for long.

"Carly? Hi, what's up?"

Just the sound of his voice made a little shiver run through her. She thoroughly enjoyed it. "Remember what we talked about when I came to your office?"

"Redecorating?"

"Oh, right. That, too. Have you given any more thought to my suggestions?"

"As a matter of fact, I have. Can you do anything for less than a thousand? Because that's about all I can spare for a decorating budget just now."

She tried to rein in her excitement and speak matter-of-factly. "Absolutely, I can do it for under a thousand. You'd really let me?"

"Sure. You made some good points about present-ing a polished and professional front to potential clients. So why don't you work up a plan and I'll look it over and approve it, and then you can have at it."

"I'll start working on it this weekend. But that isn't why I called."

"You asked if I remember what we talked about when you were here."

"Yes. We said we needed to take Brenda out for some fun. We said maybe this weekend. So, it's the weekend. How about tonight? Or tomorrow night, if that would be more convenient for you and Brenda."

"Um, what did you have in mind?"

At least he sounded open to suggestions. "Dinner, maybe. Then someplace where we can listen to some music. You and Brenda can have drinks, if you want, and I can have a fancy coffee. I love those."

He hesitated a few moments, and she held her breath. She released it when he said, "Brenda might enjoy that."

Okay, so maybe she would have preferred a little more enthusiasm from him, but at least he wasn't re-jecting the suggestion. "I think it would do her a world of good," she said cheerfully. "How about tomorrow night, just to give everyone time to make plans?"

"Okay. My schedule for this weekend is flexible."

"Then I'll call Brenda and clear it with her. One of us will get back to you with the time and other details."

"That will be fine."

Satisfied, she decided to push her luck a little. "Maybe we could invite Ethan?"

There was a definite pause this time, and Carly could almost feel the telephone receiver go a few degrees cooler in her hand. "Why would we want to do that?"

"Well, let's face it, Ethan's been through a lot in the past few weeks, himself. He lost his mother, he was disinherited, he can't find the family Bible that means so much to him, he's been accused of all sorts of terrible things. He could probably stand to have a little fun, too."

"Maybe he has other people he'd rather have fun with. What makes you think he'd want to spent any more time with the three of us? Brenda's the woman who replaced him in his mother's will, I'm the guy who accused him of most of those terrible things and your father has been trying to find proof that he did them."

"Or didn't do them," she corrected him. "And Ethan doesn't seem to blame us for any of those things. I think we all get along very well."

"So you really want him to come, huh?" Richard sounded cross now. "Are you starting to get a thing for this guy? I doubt that your father would approve."

Carly hoped her grin wasn't as obvious as his jealousy. "I think you know that Ethan hardly looks twice at me when Brenda's around."

He didn't like that, either. "Surely Brenda knows better than to get involved in a tangle like that."

"I wouldn't bet on it. And, by the way, I think you also know that Ethan isn't the guy I have a thing for."

"Uh—"

Once again, she had rendered him speechless. And she was delighted. She decided to make her escape while she had the advantage. "I'll call Brenda. She can decide whether she wants to invite Ethan. Talk to you later, Richard."

She was still smiling when she hung up. Her smile

faded when she looked up and saw Peck Verady lounging in the doorway, sulking.

"You could've told me you have a boyfriend, instead of leading me on the way you've been doing," he muttered.

This time, she was the one who was stunned almost to speechlessness. "I have *not*— I don't— Would you stop lurking around eavesdropping on me?"

"So who is this Richard guy, anyway?"

"Peck, didn't I ask you to get those figures for me?"

Tony's quiet question had the effect of making Peck jump as though he'd just been cattle-prodded. "I was just getting around to that. Uh, sir."

"Why don't you get to it *now?*"

Peck scurried off. Tony took his place in the doorway, leaning against the jamb with his arms crossed over his chest. "About this Richard guy…"

BRENDA HAD JUST HUNG UP the telephone after talking to Diane when the phone rang again. She picked up the receiver. "Hello?"

"Hi, Bren, it's Carly. How's it going?"

She smiled. "Everything's fine. How about you?"

"Good. Do you have any plans for the weekend?"

"I've invited a couple of my teacher friends over for dinner tonight."

"Hey, that's great. It will feel more like home to you once you've entertained your old friends there."

"That was my intention," she admitted.

"But you're free tomorrow evening?"

"Yes. Why?"

"Richard and I have a great idea."

Eyebrows rising, Brenda murmured, "You and Richard?"

"Mmm-hmm. We spoke on the phone this morning and we thought it would be fun for us all to go out this weekend."

Though she was intensely curious about why Carly and Richard were making weekend plans together, Brenda asked, "What did you have in mind?"

"We thought maybe we'd go out to dinner and then to a club or something for music and maybe some dancing."

"You talked my brother into going to a club? Even considering dancing?" Brenda shook her head in amazement.

"How do you know it wasn't his idea?"

Brenda let her silence speak for itself.

"Okay, it was my idea," Carly admitted. "But he agreed."

"Maybe you would prefer I claim other plans for tomorrow night?" Brenda teased. "Then it would be just you and Richard."

Typically, Carly laughed without any indication of self-consciousness. "No, I want you to go, too. It will be fun for all of us to go this time. And maybe Richard will get a little more comfortable with the idea of asking me out if we spend a little more time together."

"You seriously still want to go out with him?"

"I haven't really made any secret of that with you, have I?"

"Well, no. I just wasn't sure you were serious."

"Oh, yeah. I still think he's hot. And I like him. But I think he's got some hang-up about the age difference between us."

"I'm sure he's aware of that," Brenda agreed. "Fourteen years is a pretty big gap, Carly. Especially since you aren't even twenty-one yet."

"I just can't see that it makes any difference at all," Carly argued stubbornly. "You'd go out with a nice forty-year-old guy, wouldn't you? That would be the same gap."

But there was more to Richard's hesitation than an age difference, Brenda suspected. The fact that Carly was still a college student living with her parents while he was a divorced man who'd been on his own since Carly was in preschool had to have occurred to him.

It wasn't so much the age gap, but the experience gap that probably gave Richard pause.

As much as Brenda liked Carly, she couldn't help worrying a little about this development. Richard was the one who stood to get hurt if Carly managed to get through his defenses and then moved on, as she was very likely to do.

He had already been hurt badly once, by the ex-wife who had found someone more "exciting." Brenda understood exactly why Richard was extremely wary of his attraction to another young woman who was still in the process of deciding who she was and what she wanted in her life.

"What do you think about asking Ethan to join us?" Carly asked, abruptly changing the subject.

Just hearing Ethan's name reminded Brenda that she was in no position to pass judgments on anyone else's love life. "Um, why?" she asked, blatantly stalling.

"I just thought it might be fun to have him along. He's a pretty cool guy when he's not being defensive or grumpy."

Brenda wondered how Ethan would feel at hearing himself described that way. Coming from Carly, it would probably amuse him. "It's your party. You should invite whoever you like."

"Nice way to put all the responsibility on me," Carly retorted, a smile in her voice. "But I don't mind calling Ethan and inviting him, as long as you have no objections."

"I have none, though I'm not sure he'll accept. But, um, did you mention this idea to Richard? Inviting Ethan along, I mean."

"Sure, I told him."

"And what did he say?"

"He was delighted with the idea."

Brenda laughed. "Yeah. I'll bet."

They talked a few more minutes, and then agreed to meet at Brenda's at six the next evening for their outing. Carly volunteered to call Richard and Ethan with the details. She seemed very pleased with herself when she disconnected.

Brenda, on the other hand, worried that Carly's seemingly simple outing could become very complicated, indeed.

BRENDA MADE ONE MORE phone call before her guests arrived for the evening. She called her sister.

Once again, Linda sounded just a bit stilted when she spoke. They had never had trouble talking before, in spite of the physical distance between them. Even when Linda and James had been going through such a difficult time with the collapse of their business and their son's illness, Linda had always had a special warmth in her voice for her younger sister. Brenda wasn't at all happy with the way things were between them now.

She asked first about her nephews, the one topic always guaranteed to put Linda in a good mood. It worked again this time, as long as they kept the conversation centered around the children. The minute it turned to Brenda's life, Linda stiffened up again.

Brenda told her about the casual dinner party she was throwing that evening.

"You've invited people to that house?" Linda fretted. "Are you sure that's okay?"

"Yes, it's okay. Why wouldn't it be? This is where I live now."

"Well...it isn't exactly your house. The will is still in probate, isn't it?"

"Yes, it is, but since Leland Grassel dropped his challenge, Sean assures me that probate is just a formality."

"I see."

Was that just a hint of disapproval in Linda's voice? Maybe even disappointment?

"You've decided not to refuse the inheritance, then?"

Brenda stroked the head of the gray cat sitting in her lap. "You know how hard I've thought about this. I debated every side of the argument with myself—and with Richard, for that matter. I don't know why Margaret wanted me to inherit her estate, but she must have had a reason. I think it's my responsibility now to make sure I use the money wisely and ethically."

She fought the urge to add that she wanted to share her good fortune with her family. She was afraid Linda would take offense at that again. She had never had to be so careful about what she said to her sister before, and she didn't like guarding her words now.

She was determined not to let this money come between her and her family.

"Well, I'm happy for you, Brenda. I really am. Just be careful, okay? Living in that neighborhood, with that kind of money—you're sort of out of your league, you know? Let Richard know everything that's going on with you, and listen to what he tells you, okay?"

Linda was talking to her as she would to a child. A few weeks ago, Brenda might have reacted to that with irritation, since it was one of her pet peeves with her siblings. This time, she merely counted to ten, then said meekly, "Yes, I will."

"Good."

There was a rather awkward pause, and then Brenda said, "I guess I'd better get ready for my guests. I'll talk to you later, okay?"

She hung up with a rather hollow feeling, and the hope that her stilted conversation with Linda wasn't an omen of how her evening with her friends would go.

CHAPTER SIXTEEN

BRENDA HAD INVITED three people to her spur-of-the-moment dinner party. Diane, of course, and two other teachers from the school—Amber Short and Melissa Barnes.

Amber was thirty, divorced, a heavyset brunette with an infectious laugh and a sharp, clever tongue. Twenty-five-year-old Melissa had light brown hair, perpetually surprised-looking brown eyes, and a tiny diamond on her left hand that signified her engagement to an ebullient youth minister. The four of them had spent a lot of time together during the past school year.

She had been prepared for their stunned reaction to her new home, of course. She had braced herself for a barrage of curious questions about how she had received the inheritance and what it would mean for her future. She had even halfway expected a little awkwardness at first about her change of financial status.

She hadn't expected that awkwardness to last all evening.

"It's this house," Diane commiserated after the other two left not long after dessert. Diane had stayed to help Brenda clear the kitchen, during which Brenda had confided her disappointment with their other friends' stilted behavior. "It's so stuffy and formal, it's hard to relax. We're not used to places like this. Amber lives in a mobile home, Melissa's still living with her mom, and Alex and I are living in that tiny little apartment. This is just overwhelming, you know?"

"I know it seems that way at first," Brenda argued, "but what about the media room? That's certainly comfortable, and it's where I took everyone after dinner. But they still couldn't seem to be comfortable."

"Brenda, it's a *media room*." Diane drawled the syllables out to emphasize them. "Since when do any of us have media rooms?"

Growing impatient, Brenda shook her head. "This is silly. It's not as if this is a mansion, exactly. We have other friends with nice homes. Amber might live in a trailer park now—a pretty nice trailer park, actually—but that's because she's planning to move to Houston next summer and she didn't want to commit to high rent or a mortgage. And Melissa's living with her mom to save money for her wedding."

"You're right, of course. It isn't just the house," Diane admitted as she wiped her hands on a paper towel and tossed it in the compactor. "It's this whole situation. Inheriting a fortune from a stranger? Moving into a big house still furnished with someone else's things and decorated with someone else's old family portraits? And there's something about you that's different."

"Different in what way?" Brenda demanded.

"I don't know, exactly. It's not that you were being boastful or anything. None of us thought that. It was more the opposite—you were practically apologizing for your windfall. But it's like you weren't telling us everything, even though you kept saying you wanted us to know what was going on with you."

Brenda had always been able to trust Diane to speak her mind. And she *had* asked Diane to help her understand why Amber and Melissa had acted so oddly during the evening, so she shouldn't complain that Diane was being so bluntly candid.

The problem was that Diane was right about Brenda holding out on them, and maybe the others had sensed it, as well. Brenda had told them a little about her life since the inheritance and the fire, but she had withheld the more unsettling incidents. The phone calls, the speeding truck, the rock and the confrontations with Margaret's nephew. She hadn't wanted to worry her friends, but maybe she had come across as more secretive than protective.

Nor had she told them about Ethan, other than to say that she had met Margaret's son and that he hadn't given her any problems about the will. She didn't doubt that her expression and her voice changed when she spoke of him. It was impossible for her to even think about Ethan without a significant change in her blood pressure.

"Okay, you're right," she confessed to Diane. "There are some things I haven't told you."

Motioning for Diane to sit at the kitchen table, Brenda took another chair and let the words spill out. She told her friend about everything—except the deepening relationship with Ethan, a secret she wasn't ready to share with *anyone* just yet.

"I had no idea you were going through all that," Diane gasped. "The police have no clues about who's been harassing you?"

Brenda shook her head. "No. We don't even know for certain that the same person has been responsible for everything. But I think the rock might have been a parting shot. Nothing has happened since—not even a creepy phone call. It probably was Leland, and maybe he's given up now that I've made it clear I'm not going to be scared away."

"What about the P.I. you hired? Hasn't he found out anything?"

Remembering Tony's apologetic frustration the last time she had spoken with him, Brenda answered regretfully, "No. I told him there was no need to go on with his investigation. I'm pretty sure Leland was the one causing the trouble, but he left no proof anywhere. And Tony was unable to find any connection between me and Margaret Jacobs. All his inquiries led to dead ends. He even talked to her old friends and her longtime housekeeper, but none of them had ever heard of me or my parents. I'm beginning to wonder if I'll ever know why she chose me."

Diane glanced at the four cats rolling around on the kitchen floor. "It's gotta have something to do with the cats, right? I mean, that seems to be the only thing you and Margaret have in common."

"It certainly seems to be. But I haven't ruled out the possibility that she knew my parents somehow."

"If that were the case, why just you? Why not your brother and sister?"

They had discussed all this before, with the others, but Brenda didn't blame Diane for asking the same questions over and over. After all, she'd been doing the same thing for the past three weeks. "I don't know."

Diane glanced at her watch. "I really should go. Are you sure you'll be okay here by yourself?"

"Of course. I'm not afraid of being here. This house has an amazing security system. It worked perfectly when the rock was thrown. And," she added with a smile, "I have my guard cats."

Diane watched as Fluffy made a lunge at Toby, missed, and went skidding across the stone floor. "Oh, yes, I can see where they would terrify any potential intruder."

They both laughed, and then Brenda walked Diane to the front door.

"I'm planning to redecorate," she said, motioning around them. "Make the place reflect my own personality more. Sean said it's okay if I do."

"That would certainly help," Diane agreed. "Don't worry, Brenda. I'm sure everyone will get used to the changes and start treating you like yourself again. Eventually."

"I hope you're right." Brenda opened the door and stepped out into the warm evening air with her friend. Since it wasn't yet nine o'clock, it wasn't completely dark, though the sky was turning a deep purple. The scent of roses wafted around them, and they could hear the musical sound of the spotlighted fountain that was the centerpiece of the front lawn.

"It is a nice place," Diane conceded, pausing for a moment to admire. "I can see why you've decided to stay."

Brenda had just opened her mouth to reply when a dark pickup truck turned into the driveway. She caught her breath in momentary alarm, then released it slowly when she saw the letters painted on the side of the door.

"Who is that?" Diane asked curiously, hesitating on the top step.

Brenda watched as Ethan climbed out of the truck and moved toward them with his easy, very masculine grace. "That's Ethan Blacklock."

"That's Ethan? Well, that explains a few more things," Diane murmured cryptically.

Brenda didn't have a chance to respond before Ethan reached them.

"Ethan Blacklock, this is my friend, Diane O'Brien."

He nodded courteously to the redhead. "I hope I'm not interrupting anything."

"Actually, I was just leaving. Thanks for dinner, Brenda. I'll call you soon, okay?"

"'Bye, Diane. Drive carefully."

With one last, inquisitive glance at Ethan, Diane climbed into her little car and drove away.

Brenda looked up at Ethan. "I wasn't expecting you tonight."

"I can go if you want me to."

She stepped backward into the house. "I don't want you to go."

He followed her inside, kicking the door closed behind him.

MOONLIGHT FILTERED IN through the bedroom window, creating lazily shifting shadows in the corners of the room. The door was closed, so the cats were all downstairs, and it was very quiet in the house.

Brenda lay with her cheek on Ethan's shoulder, a position that was becoming very familiar to her. It made her feel as though she had known him for a very long time. She didn't even want to think about how short their acquaintance had been in reality.

Neither of them had spoken in a while—for her part, at least, because she hadn't been able to. She was just now recovering enough breath to form intelligible words.

Actually, they'd hardly spoken at all since Ethan arrived. He had closed the door behind him, reached out for her—and somehow they had ended up in her bed, their lovemaking so frantic it might have been weeks rather than hours since they had last been together. By the time they were sated, she hadn't been able to form a coherent thought, much less speak. Judging from the way Ethan's breath had been heaving from his chest, and his heart had raced beneath her cheek, he'd been in much the same condition.

Now that enough time had passed to restore a semblance of control, she said, "I'm glad you're here."

Tightening his arm around her, he made a grunting sound that she interpreted to mean that he was glad to be here. A typically male response to her words, she thought with a misty smile.

His chest was only lightly dusted with curling hair. She scraped her fingertips gently through it, enjoying the way his muscles contracted reflexively beneath his skin. "How was your day?"

"Okay," he said without much enthusiasm.

She propped her chin on her hand to look at him in the watery light. "Problems?"

"Nothing major. How about your day?"

"It was all right. I had a few friends over for dinner. Diane, and two other teachers from our school."

"Didn't it go well?"

"It was nice to see them. I've missed my friends."

"But?"

"But it was different," she confessed with a sigh. "They treated me oddly. Not badly, just oddly. As though a different house and a little more money make me a different person."

"I think you were warned that might happen."

"Yes. You all told me things would change with my old friends, and that I had to be careful of the motives of new friends. I just didn't want to believe it."

"If it makes you feel any better, my friends are acting kind of weird lately, too."

"Your friends? Why?"

"They can't understand why I'm okay with you being named in Mother's will. They don't know why I'm not fighting you, and they sure don't understand why I don't resent you. I mentioned to one of my friends that I'd been by here a couple of times, looking for the Bible with your assistance, and he thought it was really odd."

"I haven't even told anyone you and I have spent any time alone together," she admitted. "I can't imagine what they would say."

"I can," he said, sounding grim.

"Carly likes you. And apparently, Richard has no problem with you joining us tomorrow. Er, Carly did call you, didn't she?"

"She called."

"Did you agree to join us for the evening?"

"Does anyone ever say no to Carly?"

"Probably not very often," she said, amused by his wry tone.

"Which is probably why Richard isn't saying much about me coming along. I think he'd take a nosedive off a tall building if Carly asked him to."

"You're probably right. He does seem to be taken with her, doesn't he?"

"Mmm."

Taking that as an affirmative, she dropped her head back onto his shoulder. There were other things she would have liked to discuss with him. Her concerns about her future with her friends. Her distress over the new chasm between her and her sister. Her worry about Richard ending up heartbroken over Carly.

And then there was their own relationship. What was going on here? What expectations, if any, did he have for them? Was this just a fling for him or did he have feelings for her?

Because she didn't know if he was interested in her personal problems—especially those concerning the inheritance—and because she wasn't sure she wanted to hear the answers to her questions, she remained silent.

After a moment, Ethan asked, "What did you serve for dinner?"

"A vegetarian lasagna with salad and bread. Cheesecake for dessert."

"I had a bologna sandwich. On stale bread."

Amused again, she said, "I have leftovers."

"Leftovers?"

The way he said it made her think so vividly of an eager puppy perking its ears in response to an intriguing sound, that she burst out laughing. "I'll heat some up for you."

"That would be great."

She wasn't hungry, so she sipped a cup of herbal tea while Ethan ate with the enthusiasm of a man who'd been on the verge of starvation. "This," he said, swallowing a large bite of lasagna, "is really good."

"Thanks. My sister gave me the recipe. Linda's a fabulous cook."

"She hasn't been around much, has she?"

"She's very busy. She lives two hours away, and she works full-time and has a husband and two young children. We talk by phone when we can, but I don't get to see her as often as I would like."

"Are you close?"

Brenda was aware that she hesitated a little too long before she replied. "Yes, we're very close."

He looked up from his plate with one eyebrow lifted.

"We are close," she said again. "But all of this is taking a toll on us, too. Things have…changed, and Linda isn't sure how to handle it."

Ethan chewed thoughtfully, then swallowed before saying, "You and your brother don't seem to be having any problems."

"Things haven't changed as much between Richard and me," she said with a slight shrug. "He thought I had to be guided and protected before, and now he's even more convinced of that. If anything, he's become even more active in my life. Before, he was so focused on getting his new business off the ground that sometimes several weeks would go by when we wouldn't see each other."

"Judging from the past couple of weeks, that's hard to imagine."

"I know. I love my brother, but he can be a little… overassertive sometimes."

Ethan discreetly let that pass without comment. "You're lucky you have family," was all he said, reminding her poignantly of how alone he was.

She sipped her tea in an attempt to soothe the lump in her throat, then nodded toward Ethan's almost-empty plate. "Would you like some dessert?"

"You said you have cheesecake?"

"Yes. With strawberries to go on top, if you like."

"I like."

She had noticed before that Ethan had a sweet tooth. She cut him a generous slice of cheesecake, then scooped fresh, sliced strawberries over the top before setting the plate in front of him.

"Thanks. It looks good."

She refilled his glass of ice water, which was all he had wanted for a beverage, then took her seat at the table again. "Your friend Raine called today to set up an appointment to look at the roses."

"Yeah? How'd it go?"

"She was very pleasant. A little reserved, maybe, but entirely polite."

He nodded in satisfaction. "I told you you'd like her."

"Well, I don't like her or dislike her," Brenda felt compelled to point out. "I haven't actually met her yet."

"You'll like her."

"You're probably right. Like I said, she sounded nice enough. She's coming Monday to look at the roses."

"She'll have a cow when she sees what shape they're in."

Brenda wrinkled her nose. "They're really not that bad."

"Trust me. Raine will think they are," he said, and dug into his cheesecake.

Cupping her mug of now-cool tea between her hands, Brenda wondered how he would react to her next announcement. "I'm thinking about doing some redecorating here in the house."

"You should," Ethan said with a shrug. "Do whatever you want to it. Man, this is good cheesecake."

"You, uh, really don't mind if I change some things?"

"Why would I?" he asked, looking genuinely confused.

"Well, this was your home."

"I haven't lived in this house in more than ten years. Quite a few things have been changed since I was here—and I didn't like it then. Paint the place pink and purple, for all I care."

"I'm not going to go that far," she said with a smile. "But I would like to bring in some brighter colors."

"Yeah, that would be better." He swallowed the last of the cheesecake, then pushed away his plate and downed the rest of his water.

While Brenda had slipped into a purple tank top and plaid pajama bottoms for their kitchen raid, Ethan had thrown on his jeans and T-shirt, leaving his feet bare. His hair was still rumpled, and he needed a shave.

Sometimes when she looked at him, it was all she could do not to melt into a graceless puddle on the floor. Unfortunately, she wasn't very good at hiding her thoughts. Especially from Ethan, it seemed.

He glanced across the table at her, went still for a moment, then stood and held out his hand.

Rising slowly, Brenda gestured toward the table. "The dishes…"

"I'll do them," he said, his voice suddenly gravelly. "Later."

Forgetting the dishes, she went into his arms.

ETHAN STAYED for breakfast again the next morning, though he was obviously antsy about hanging around too long. Brenda was a bit saddened by the fact that he was still hung up on keeping their relationship secret, but she supposed it really was too soon to go public.

It was too soon for a lot of things, actually, but that was another issue.

"You go ahead and take your shower," she urged him, donning her tank top and pajama bottoms again. "I'll have breakfast ready when you're out."

"Sounds good. Thanks." Catching up with her at the foot of the bed, he kissed her lingeringly. "I'll have to make breakfast for you sometime," he murmured off-handedly when he released her and moved toward the bathroom. "I make killer omelets."

He closed the bathroom door behind him, and Brenda released a long, schoolgirl-with-a-crush sigh. Just the sound of it echoing in her own ears made her frown at her giddiness and all the dangerous things it implied. This was getting way out of hand, she warned herself. Especially since she still had no clue what Ethan was thinking when it came to their future.

The cats were all meowing for breakfast and attention when she entered the kitchen. She gave each one a rub and a greeting, then filled their food and water bowls. Leaving the cats eating and pushing each other out of the way, she crossed the room and opened the refrigerator.

She couldn't help wondering how many more breakfasts she and Ethan would share together. But since that question fell into the range of speculation about the future that she'd been trying to avoid, she put it out of her mind and concentrated on assembling the ingredients for a hearty breakfast of scrambled eggs, bacon, toast and sliced cantaloupe.

She had just finished slicing the cantaloupe and was reaching for the bacon and a skillet when the telephone rang. She reached for the kitchen extension. "Hello?"

"Brenda, hello. It's Sean. I hope I'm not disturbing you too early on a Saturday morning."

She smiled. "Good morning, Sean. And, no, it isn't too early."

"How are you? No more unpleasant incidents?"

Something about the way he said it trivialized her problems so much that she almost bristled, but then she reminded herself that Sean always spoke that way. After all, he was an attorney. "No, I'm fine."

"Glad to hear it. Listen, the reason I called—and I know it's last minute, so feel free to refuse—someone gave me tickets to a touring production of *Chicago* this evening, and I wondered if you would like to go with me."

Brenda was so surprised by the invitation that it took her a moment to respond. "I'm sorry, Sean, but I already have plans for the evening."

"Hey, that's cool. I said it was last minute. I'm glad you're getting out."

"I'm trying to get back into a more normal routine."

"Good for you." To prove he had no hard feelings, he continued in a chatty tone, "So you haven't heard any more from Leland or Patty Ann?"

"Not a word. I guess they've finally given up."

"Let's hope so. And Ethan?" he asked casually. "Have you spoken to him lately?"

"Once or twice," Brenda answered, equally nonchalant.

"Did you ever find his family Bible?"

"No," she said sadly. "I guess we've given up on that, too. There just doesn't seem to be anywhere else to look."

"I'm sorry to hear that. Ethan must be disappointed. You, um, haven't turned any more items over to him, have you?"

"No, I haven't," she answered, stung. "Ethan isn't trolling for handouts, Sean. Nor am I trying to slip him anything he isn't entitled to. You've been notified about everything he's taken."

"Hey, listen, Brenda, I wasn't trying to imply that you've done anything wrong. I'm sorry if it came across that way. As for Ethan, well, I'm sure he isn't being friendly to you just to try to get something more out of the estate."

He said the right words, but something about his tone implied just the opposite. Brenda wondered if she was reading too much into the conversation. She was admittedly overly sensitive when it came to Ethan. And maybe she had some tiny, secret, reluctant questions about Ethan's motives, herself. After all, he wasn't exactly being forthcoming with his feelings about her. And he did seem pretty intent on keeping their…affair, for lack of a better word, secret.

"Yes, you did make it sound that way."

"Again, I'm sorry. I guess I get carried away with my responsibilities at times. And well, I worry about you. You haven't had a lot of practice with people trying to take advantage of you for your money, and I worry that your generous nature will lead you into trouble. I'm not saying Ethan's the type to take advantage of your inexperience, of course. I'm simply reminding you that you have to question everyone at first."

"Thank you, but I really don't need to be reminded of that again," she said coolly. "I think I've gotten the message."

"Okay. I'll try to stop being so overprotective. I'll talk to you again soon, okay? And in the meantime, call me if you need anything at all."

"Yes, I will. Thank you."

She hung up, then simply stood there for a long moment with one hand still on the receiver. She hated that Sean's words had dimmed her good mood, but she promised herself she wouldn't let his unfounded warnings undermine her budding relationship with Ethan—whatever that entailed.

She didn't believe a word Sean had implied, of course. She was sure Ethan didn't have any ulterior motives in being with her. Was it inconceivable that he found her attractive and desirable and interesting?

Swallowing hard, she turned—only to freeze when she saw Ethan standing in the doorway, looking at her with an expression that reminded her of the first time she had seen him. His face was hard, his eyes angry and defensive.

"How long have you been standing there?"

"Long enough to know that Sean's accusing me of pocketing the silver again."

"Ethan, he didn't—"

"And long enough to hear the doubt in your voice when you told him you trust me."

"I *do* trust you," she insisted, but even she heard the uncertainty that time. It wasn't that she honestly believed he was pocketing the silver, as he called it. But did she trust him not to break her heart at the end of this whirlwind affair they had found themselves involved in? That was a different story.

"I've known all along that this was a bad idea," Ethan said, pushing a hand through his still-damp hair. "It's just too complicated."

He turned toward the doorway. "I think I'll skip breakfast and head on out to work."

"Ethan, wait." She hurried after him, skidding to a stop only a few steps away from him. He paused, but he didn't turn back to look at her. "Don't let Sean's implications ruin everything."

"It isn't just Sean," he said roughly. "It's what everyone will think. If I can't get the money one way, I'll try to get it another way. Right?"

"Since when do you care what anyone else thinks?"

He started to respond, then stopped and shook his head. "I have to go. I'm sorry. I'll talk to you later, okay?"

She wasn't going to beg him to stay, or to talk to her. She wasn't going to plead with him to reassure her about his feelings for her, especially since he'd never bothered to express any. And she certainly didn't want to know that it had been nothing more than great sex for him, even if she had tried telling herself that she could be content with that.

Now she knew she had been lying to herself. It seemed that she had been hoping for more, after all. A great deal more, perhaps.

No matter what some people thought, she really hadn't changed at all. She was still the generally optimistic, slightly old-fashioned, hopelessly romantic woman she had been a month earlier, before she'd ever heard of Margaret Jacobs.

Maybe Sean—and Richard and Linda and Carly and Tony—had had reason to worry that she was too naive and trusting to protect herself.

"What about tonight?" was all she asked.

"Maybe I'd better pass on tonight. It was bound to get awkward, anyway."

"Ethan—"

He looked at her then, his expression so conflicted that her heart twisted in instinctive sympathy for him. "I've got to go," he said.

She nodded mutely and moved out of his way.

CHAPTER SEVENTEEN

BRENDA COULDN'T STAY IN after Ethan left. She knew she would just sit there brooding, moping pathetically over him, wondering if she would ever see him again. Reliving every kiss, every touch, every ragged cry of pleasure. Replaying all the warnings and fighting the doubts in her heart.

Too many hours of that would be guaranteed to send her over the edge.

She changed the sheets on the bed, her actions mechanical, her mind deliberately blank. And then she took a long, hot shower and dressed in a bright red shirt and a short denim skirt with sandals in preparation for the heat of the late-June day. She spent a bit of extra time on her makeup to hide the trace of tears that had leaked out during her shower, and the purple smudges that had developed beneath her eyes since Ethan had left.

She called Carly before she left the house. "We're still on for tonight, right? Six o'clock?"

"You bet. I'm looking forward to it. Everyone's meeting at your house, and then we'll—"

"Ethan won't be joining us," Brenda blurted.

"What? Why? He told me yesterday he—"

"Yes, well, he's changed his mind."

Carly asked quietly, "What happened, Brenda?"

"He just—"

"Brenda, before you answer I think you should know I'm aware that something's been going on between you and Ethan. I, um, saw his truck outside your house early one morning this week."

"Oh."

"I mean, maybe I misinterpreted what I saw?"

"No," Brenda said with a sigh. "You didn't misinterpret it. Ethan and I— Well, we…"

"That's what I thought. The sparks between you two have been pretty intense all along, you know? Richard's even noticed, I think, though he hasn't wanted to admit it. So what's gone wrong?"

"We had a…a disagreement, I guess. You see, Sean called and he…well, it's too long to get into over the phone."

"Ethan and Sean, huh? I saw this coming."

"What do you mean?"

"Well, obviously they're both attracted to you. It's a competition thing."

Grimacing, Brenda shook her head. "No, it isn't like that at all. It's—look, why don't you come a little early this evening and I'll tell you about it? But, I don't want Richard to hear about any of this just yet, okay?"

"Are you kidding? Didn't I tell you I know all about bossy older brothers? Trust me, anything you tell me is strictly confidential."

"Thanks." It would feel good to talk about it with another woman, Brenda decided. She had a feeling Carly would actually have some useful input. "I'll see you then."

"I'll be there at five. We'll have an hour of girl talk before Richard arrives."

"Okay. See you then."

Brenda hung up and went looking for her purse. If Carly was coming over for girl talk, they needed something to bond over. Since Carly was too young for wine, they could have tea, and maybe some crunchy raw vegetables and yogurt dip or something.

Maybe she would buy a new dress to wear that evening, she thought, unplugging her new cell phone from its charger and slipping it into her purse. She'd buy something in a bright color, to lift her spirits. Maybe she'd run into her favorite bookstore, find a new release from one of her favorite authors. It would give her something to do when she was home alone later, rather than think about Ethan—as if even the most enthralling work of fiction could accomplish that.

Her last stop would be the grocery store for cat food and the things she needed for that evening. With that plan in mind, she headed out, determined to enjoy her day despite the rotten way it had started.

Avoiding the empty house, she spent quite a long time on her outing. She wiled away much of what remained of the morning in a bookstore, had lunch in a nearby deli, then scoured stores for just the right new dress for dinner that evening. She settled on a filmy turquoise sundress that flattered her figure and made her wish Ethan could see her in it, a thought that irritated her again.

She then stopped by the grocery store, picking up quite a few things, more than she had intended to buy.

She actually wasted so much time that she worried about not being ready by the time Carly arrived.

It was a few minutes after three when she parked her little car in the garage next to the unused Mercedes. That gave her just over forty-five minutes to prepare her appetizers and then change for dinner in time to greet Carly. She would have to hurry.

As she walked to the back of the car to remove the shopping bags from her trunk, she realized that she had forgotten to lower the garage door. Sunlight and fresh air poured into the tidy interior of the garage. She made a mental note to close the door on her way into the house.

Her back to the open doorway, she reached into the trunk of her car for the first bag.

Something hit her on the back of the head, hard enough to make lights explode in front of her eyes and cause her knees to buckle. Before she could recover from that first blow, she was hit again.

She was tumbling face-first into her trunk when she lost consciousness.

ETHAN WAS IN HIS TRUCK when his cell phone rang at five-twenty. Keeping one hand on the steering wheel and his eyes on the road, he lifted the phone to his ear with his other hand. "Hello?"

"Ethan? It's Carly."

He grimaced. He supposed he should have expected this call. Carly must have found out he wasn't planning to join her party. "Listen, Carly—"

She broke in before he could finish. "Have you heard from Brenda?"

Startled, he replied, "Not since this morning. Why?"

"I don't know where she is." There was just a hint of fear in Carly's voice. "She was supposed to be here at the house, but she's not answering the door. I've tried calling her new cell-phone number, but she doesn't answer."

"I thought you weren't meeting until six."

"She and I had decided to get together early. I told her I'd be here at five. I've been ringing the doorbell for the past twenty minutes. I can hear the cats meowing inside, but there's no sign of Brenda."

"Have you called her brother?"

"Yes. He hasn't heard from her, either. He's on his way over. He said he'd be here in fifteen minutes."

"I'll be there in five," Ethan said in sudden decision, a cold sense of premonition gripping him.

He tossed the phone aside and turned the truck at the next intersection. He was closer to a ten-minute drive away from the house, if he followed the traffic laws, but he fully intended to be there in five.

Carly stood at the front door when Ethan arrived seven minutes after disconnecting the call. Wringing her hands, she moved forward to meet him. "Still nothing. I'm getting really worried, Ethan. It doesn't seem like Brenda not to be here when she said she would be."

Ethan placed a hand on the back of his neck, squeezing to relieve the tension. "No, it doesn't seem like her," he agreed. "Maybe we should call the—"

A white sedan pulled into the driveway. "That's Richard's car," Carly said. "Maybe he's heard from her since I talked to him."

But Richard's face was grim when he climbed out

of the car and joined them. "I've called her cell phone a half dozen times. No answer. I even called her friend Diane, but she hasn't heard from her since she left here last night."

"Maybe she went out to run some errands," Carly said, trying to sound hopeful. "Maybe she lost track of time."

Ethan's stomach was slowly tying itself into knots. "Is that like her?" he demanded of Richard, though he suspected he already knew the answer. "To lose track of time when she's expecting company?"

"No." Richard looked worried sick, himself. "No, she wouldn't do that."

Ethan nodded, having expected that answer. "Maybe we should call the police."

"The police won't do anything about a missing adult for at least twenty-four hours," Carly responded, her face just a shade paler than it had been a moment before. "I think we should call my dad."

Richard selected a key on his keychain. "Let's search the house first. Maybe she's in the shower. Or maybe she fell asleep."

Or maybe she'd simply fallen, Ethan thought, remembering how his mother had died in that house less than a month earlier. His eyes met Richard's, and he had the feeling that Richard was remembering the same thing. "You have a key?" he asked unnecessarily.

Richard inserted it into the lock. "Yes."

"And the security codes?"

"I know them. Brenda wanted to make sure I could get in if necessary."

"Does Sean know about this?"

Richard shrugged. "I don't know. I didn't ask her if she'd told him. Brenda has a key to my place, too, for what it's worth."

Ethan followed Richard and Carly into the house, which was quiet and empty except for the three cats who ran to greet them. They were followed more slowly by the calico, who seemed poised to run in response to the first quick movement.

Ethan's reaction to seeing the cats was mixed. He still couldn't see cats without remembering his mother's strange bond with them. And yet, now he also remembered how Brenda had looked stroking and snuggling them.

Carly was already kneeling to pet them, as if reassuring them when she was the one who seemed to be in need of reassurance. "They seem excited to see us. I wonder how long Brenda's been gone?"

Reacting to the edge of panic in Carly's voice, Richard rested a soothing hand on her shoulder. "We'll find her, Carly," he said. "I'm sure she's fine."

She straightened and leaned against his arm, giving him a look that made Ethan glance away uncomfortably.

They searched every room of the house. Brenda wasn't in any of them.

"Surely if she'd been caught in traffic or had a flat tire or something like that she would have called one of us," Richard said, pacing the media room. "She would know we were worried. You said you were supposed to meet her at five, Carly?"

Carly nodded. "She wanted to talk."

She looked at Ethan then. "She said you and she had quarreled. I think she was kind of upset about it," she said with just a touch of aggressiveness. "Maybe that's why she's late. Maybe she's somewhere thinking about your argument and she forgot to look at her watch."

Richard rounded on Ethan. "What the hell were you and my sister arguing about?"

"It was a personal matter," Ethan snapped back. "I can't imagine that it would have anything to do with her taking off like this."

At least, he hoped it had nothing to do with it, he added to himself. Brenda had seemed more angry than distressed when he'd left. More defiant than distraught. "Maybe Sean's heard from her. I know he called her this morning."

"I want to know what the hell is going on," Richard said, his voice rising to a near shout in his frustration.

"So do I!" Ethan snapped back.

"I think I'd better call my dad," Carly said, digging her cell phone out of her bag. "Do you know Brenda's license plate number, Richard?"

"Would she be in her car or the Mercedes?" Ethan asked, remembering that Sean had made the bigger car available to her.

"I assume she's in hers," Richard replied coolly. "She said she wouldn't be comfortable driving your mother's car."

"Maybe we'd better make sure." Ethan headed for the garage, the one place they hadn't checked. With the others right behind him, he opened the door that led from the kitchen into the garage.

He froze when he saw the two vehicles parked side by side. He heard Carly gasp and Richard utter a startled curse.

"Where the hell is she?" Richard grated.

"She must be in the house *somewhere*," Carly said desperately, turning back toward the kitchen. "Maybe she's in the attic. Neither of you looked in the attic, did you?"

"Wait." Ethan had caught sight of something on the garage floor, behind Brenda's car. He hurried toward it, kneeling to scoop it out from beneath the car. He held it out to show the others.

Carly's face lost what little color had been left in it. "That's Brenda's purse. I helped her pick it out."

Both Ethan and Richard looked automatically at the closed trunk of the vehicle, and then at each other. Ethan figured he must look as sick as Richard did, both of them frozen with dread.

"Where is she?" Carly whispered tearfully, jerking them both out of their momentary paralysis.

Ethan dropped the purse and jerked open the driver's door of the sedan, relieved to find it unlocked. A trunk release was built into the side of the driver's seat. He yanked on it hard enough to almost break it off.

"She's here!" Richard shouted when the trunk popped open.

Carly gave a strangled cry. Ethan set her out of his way as he rushed back to the trunk.

Brenda lay curled in the cramped space, her denim skirt tangled around her thighs, her legs bent uncomfortably in front of her. Her hands and feet were strapped together with silver duct tape, and when Richard pushed her hair out of her face with an unsteady hand, they saw that another strip of the tape covered her mouth. There was blood in her fair hair, and on the gray carpet beneath her head. Her eyes were open, but glazed, and for a moment, Ethan thought the worst.

But then she blinked, and his heart started to beat again.

Together, he and Richard lifted her out of the trunk and laid her on the floor between the two vehicles. Carly hovered behind them, giving directions and warning them to be careful. She called for an ambulance while Richard and Ethan knelt beside Brenda, working together to free her from the duct tape.

She moaned when Ethan pulled the tape painstakingly from her mouth while Richard freed her hands. The sound was dry and raspy, and just a bit panicky.

"It's okay, honey," he said, brushing her hair away from her colorless cheeks, then cupping her face between his hands. "You're going to be fine."

Richard cradled her hands between his. "I'm here, sis. Carly's called for an ambulance, so someone will be here real soon to make sure you're okay."

She moistened her lips, then grimaced at what must have been the taste of tape residue. "Could I have… water?" she croaked.

"Better not, until after the medics have checked you out," Ethan replied. "You don't want to risk nausea at this point."

"I'll get a damp cloth and wash your face," Carly offered, eager to do something to help. "I'll be right back," she called over her shoulder as she dashed toward the door into the house.

He didn't want to let her go even for a moment, but Ethan left Brenda with Richard while he moved to open the garage door for the ambulance crew. He thought he heard the faintest whine of a siren in the distance, very gradually growing louder.

"Brenda," he said, kneeling beside her again,

relieved to see that her eyes were slowly clearing. "Did you see who did this to you?"

She started to shake her head, but stopped the movement with a groan. "No," she said from between her teeth. "I didn't— I don't remember…"

"We'll find whoever did this," Richard vowed, his voice tight with fury. "One way or another, someone's going to pay for this."

Ethan wasn't reassured that Richard looked directly at him as he made the angry promise.

CHAPTER EIGHTEEN

TIME SEEMED TO PASS in a haze of noise and pain and confusion. People poked at her, asked her questions, took her temperature and her pulse and her blood pressure, shone lights into her bleary eyes. She was given shots and then had her head bandaged with adhesive strips to hold the wounds closed and swaddled in gauze to keep everything in place.

Richard hovered around her, holding her hand and barking orders at the medical staff until someone ushered him firmly away. She didn't know what had become of Ethan and Carly, though she could still hear Ethan's voice echoing inside her head.

He had sounded so upset when he'd croaked her name. She remembered him brushing back her hair, calling her "honey." She remembered how safe she had felt then after being alone in the dark for so long.

She didn't remember much else.

The doctors assured her that it wasn't unusual for her not to be able to recall the attack itself. Maybe the details would come back to her, they said. Or maybe they wouldn't.

Because she had a concussion, the doctor wanted to keep her overnight for observation. Brenda protested, "I would rather go home."

"Brenda." Richard, who had been allowed to return once her wounds had been tended, stepped closer to the side of the emergency room bed and rested his hand on hers, carefully avoiding the IV needle taped to the back of her hand. "You have a concussion. You need to be monitored tonight, just to make sure you're okay."

"You can stay with me," she said pleadingly. "I don't want to stay here, Richard. Please."

"I'm sorry, but I think you should listen to the doctor. If everything goes well tonight, we'll get you out of here tomorrow morning, okay?"

Fretfully, she moved her head on the pillow, wincing when discomfort shot through her stiff neck. The wound, itself, was still deadened, but she suspected it wouldn't be long before the feeling returned with a vengeance. She subsided with a disgruntled mutter. "What about the cats?"

"Don't worry about the cats. They'll be fine."

She was moved by gurney into a room for the night. A double room, though the other bed was empty. It was the first time she'd been in a hospital room since her mother's death. She shuddered at the memory of those long, terrible weeks.

For some reason, she couldn't look at the empty bed on the other side of the room. She focused on the friendly nurse who was helping her get settled into her own bed for the night.

Richard stepped outside again while Brenda was being transferred into the bed. He told her that he would call Linda and assure her that there was no need to leave her children and make the two-hour drive to the hospital tonight. Richard came back in a few minutes later with visitors—Carly and Tony.

Tony expressed his concern for her, then gently asked if she could give him any details of the attack. She told him the same thing she had told the police officers who had asked her earlier. She remembered nothing between leaving the grocery store and waking in the trunk of her car, bound and gagged, hurting and terrified. She didn't know how much time had passed before she'd heard voices in the garage, and then the trunk was opened.

She also very clearly remembered Ethan touching her face with trembling hands, but that was a detail she saw no need to include for anyone else. It was a memory she suspected would replay repeatedly in her own mind.

Everyone was quiet when she finished speaking, looking at her sympathetically. The bustling noises of a busy hospital wing wafted in through the partially opened door, along with the various smells that took her back to those weeks she had spent sitting by her mother's side. She shivered with a sudden chill.

Carly sat on the bed at Brenda's side, lightly touching her arm as if seeking reassurance that Brenda really was okay. Richard took the visitor's chair beside the bed, while Tony chose to stand. The gravity with which they all watched her made her self-conscious. "Where's Ethan?"

The others exchanged glances, but it was Carly who answered, her voice just a bit indignant. "He's been taken in for questioning."

"What?" Brenda lifted her head, then groaned when pain shot from her nape to the middle of her back.

Richard started to rise, but Carly waved him back into his chair as she helped Brenda lie back down on the pillow. "I'm so sorry, Brenda. I think it's my fault that he's in trouble."

"It isn't your fault," Richard said impatiently.

She gave him a look that simmered with annoyance—the first time Brenda had seen Carly look at Richard with anything other than fascination. "There was no need for you to tell the police that Brenda and Ethan had quarreled," she said, then looked apologetically back at Brenda.

"When you disappeared, I sort of panicked. I mentioned that you and Ethan had argued, because I wondered if maybe that had something to do with you taking off. I didn't think Ethan had anything to do with it," she added pointedly. "I thought you might be upset and needed some time to be alone. And I thought maybe Richard would know where you would go to do that."

Brenda glared at her brother. "What did you say to the police?"

"Look, they asked me what's been going on with you, and who might have a motive to harm you. I answered honestly. We've all agreed that Ethan's the only one with anything to gain if you're out of the picture. That already came up when the police were investigating whoever threw the rock through your window. Add that to the fact that you'd quarreled earlier and he wouldn't tell me what it was about, and the police were naturally interested in talking to him."

Brenda remembered the interviews with the police after the rock incident. They hadn't known quite what to make of her tale of a mysterious inheritance and a series of vaguely menacing phone calls. Learning that the only person who stood to gain in the event of her death was an invited guest on that day had also confused them.

She had no doubt that they would be interested in him again. "Our argument was none of your business."

"Yeah, that's what he said. But I think finding you bleeding in the trunk of your car made it my business."

"I don't. Besides, what about Leland Grassel? Isn't he just as much a suspect as Ethan? Leland and I quarreled, too, if you'll remember."

Tony cleared his throat. "There's a little more to the police interest in Ethan than the quarrel," he murmured. "I just talked to one of my friends in the department. While you were being treated, they were asking if any of the neighbors had seen anything. One of them reported seeing a black truck speeding away from your place at just after three this afternoon. Whoever made the report didn't get a good look at the truck or the license plate, just saw a dark blur that was noticeable because of the speed at which it was traveling."

"Ethan drives a dark pickup," Richard pointed out with a deepening frown.

Unable to argue with that, Brenda bit her lip for a moment, then remembered something. "His name is written all over the side. Surely someone would have seen that."

"As I told you," Tony said, "the witness didn't get a good look at the truck. She said all she saw was the back of the bed, and she didn't get a look at the plates because she didn't realize there was any reason to study it that closely."

"Yes, but still. A lot of people drive dark pickups in Dallas."

Tony nodded. "I'm not disputing that. But it does bear considering."

"Wasn't Ethan at work?" Carly asked her father. "Surely that could be verified."

"His crew said he arrived late and left early today. They hadn't seen him since a little after two." Tony looked almost contrite as he shared that further bit of news. "Leland Grassel was at his office all afternoon. A coworker has verified seeing him there at around three o'clock."

Which gave Leland a pretty solid alibi—and Ethan none.

"I don't care what anyone saw," Brenda said stubbornly, her fingers clenching on the bedsheets. "I still can't believe Ethan had anything to do with this."

"I don't believe it of him, either," Carly said loyally, though her eyes were troubled. "I'm sure the police will find some evidence to clear him."

"You know it's unlikely the police will find anything at the scene," Tony said. "They can't really go by fingerprints, because both Ethan and Richard touched everything there while they were rescuing Brenda. The car, the duct tape, the garage door. Unless the police find someone else's print, and that one belongs to someone with prints on file somewhere, there really were no clues except for the eyewitness who saw the dark truck."

Which meant that Ethan was in real trouble, Brenda realized with a sick, sinking feeling. "They can't prove that he did it, either. Right?" she asked Tony.

He shrugged. "Circumstantial evidence can be pretty strong, if there's enough of it."

"Tony, I need you to find out who did this to me. Help Ethan clear his name."

Tony hesitated. "And if I find evidence that he *is* the one who attacked you?"

"You won't."

She watched as Richard, Tony and Carly exchanged worried looks. And then she closed her eyes and pictured Ethan's face as he made love to her with so much passion and tenderness that she'd thought she would simply melt with it. She'd seen anger in him when he spoke of his mother, but she had never felt anything other than completely safe with him. She refused to believe she had been that wrong about him.

Despite the evidence to the contrary, she simply couldn't believe it. And she prayed she wasn't being a gullible, romantic idiot who had fallen for one of the oldest cons in the book.

Richard was looking at her somberly when she opened her eyes again. "I've got to admit I didn't really think Ethan would resort to something like this, but after hearing what Tony just told us, I'm wondering if I was wrong. We have to consider the possibility, Brenda."

She shook her aching head. "There's no way I believe that Ethan knocked me out and stuffed me in the trunk of my car, only to come back later and pretend to look for me. Why would he do something like that? If he was really trying to get me out of the way, wouldn't he have killed me while he had the chance instead of just hitting me and tying me up?"

"I agree, Richard," Carly said. "Ethan was shaking like a leaf when he helped you take her out of the car—just as we all were. He's the one who insisted I call an ambulance and then the police."

"All things he would have done if he wanted to lead

us down the wrong trail," Richard retorted. "He's the one who led us to the garage in the first place. He had no way of knowing she would still be breathing when we opened that trunk. If we'd waited much longer, she might not have been."

Carly gasped in response to his bluntness.

It was at that moment that Ethan walked into the room, looking at Richard with a scowl that proved he'd heard every word Richard had just said.

ETHAN HAD KNOWN he should stay away from the hospital after leaving the police station, but it seemed his truck had driven there almost of its own accord. He simply had to know if Brenda was all right. The sight of her lying pale and motionless in the trunk of her car still haunted him.

Hearing Richard Prentiss accuse him of attempted murder made him wish he had listened to his instincts and gone straight home.

"Ethan!" Catching sight of him, Brenda held out a hand. The way it shook broke his heart.

Ignoring her brother, he moved to the side of the bed opposite the one on which Carly sat and caught her hand in his. "How are you?"

"I'm okay," she said impatiently—and obviously untruthfully. "What happened to you? Did the police believe you when you told them you had nothing to do with this?"

Her faith in him touched him more than he wanted the others to see. He kept his voice steady when he replied, "They didn't have enough evidence to charge me with anything. Yet. They still consider me a 'person of interest.'"

"Tony's going to help you prove your innocence," she assured him. "I just asked him to do so."

Ethan frowned. "I don't need you hiring anyone to clear my name. I can take care of myself."

"Or maybe you don't want Tony looking too closely into your movements today," Richard charged.

Carly sighed loudly. "Richard."

He glanced at her without apology. "Someone has to say it. Who else has a motive? No one ever tried to hurt my sister before all this inheritance stuff came up. And now the one person with the most to gain keeps hanging around, maybe looking for opportunities to get rid of the one thing that stands between him and his mother's money."

"The only thing that stood between me and my mother's money was me," Ethan argued flatly. "I could have gotten myself written back into her will anytime I wanted. All I had to do was go along with everything she ordered me to do. If I really wanted the money bad enough to kill for it now, don't you think I'd have been willing to grovel for it then?"

"Maybe she died before—"

"Richard, stop it," Brenda said, still clinging to Ethan's hand. She pressed her other hand to her temple as if to stop the pounding there. "Ethan wasn't the one who attacked me."

Tony seemed to make an effort to drag his attention away from Carly and Richard. He searched Brenda's face. "You sound so certain of that."

"I am."

Ethan wondered if she had spoken a little too firmly. Who exactly was she trying to convince? Everyone else—or herself?

Tony, for one, wasn't convinced, though he still seemed to be keeping an open mind. "Are you remembering anything about the attack? Did you see your attacker? Enough, at least, to tell that it wasn't Ethan?"

With an apologetic look at Ethan, Brenda answered reluctantly, "I don't remember seeing anyone, but I know it wasn't Ethan. And don't ask me how. I just know."

Richard shook his head. "That's hardly reassuring, Brenda. If you didn't see who hit you, then you can't rule anyone out."

"Ethan is not a stupid man. He's aware that every time something happens to me everyone looks at him. He's also aware that if he were locked up for hurting me, he wouldn't get a penny of the money. Even worse, it would all go to the cousin he can't stand. Right, Ethan?"

He nodded slowly, giving her a slight smile. "That's all true, of course. Including the part about me not being stupid."

She smiled weakly at him in return, then glanced at Tony. "So you need to look at people outside this room when you're searching for culprits."

"I'll look at everyone," he assured her. "And if it makes you feel any better, I haven't reached any conclusions about anyone."

She nodded gratefully, then rubbed her head again. "I'm sorry, but I'm really tired."

"You should get some sleep. We'll talk tomorrow." Tony stood, nodding toward his daughter. "Let's go, Carly, so Brenda can rest."

Richard rose. "I'll walk you out. I'll be back in a few minutes, Bren. Are you coming, Ethan?"

Though he knew Richard wouldn't like it, Ethan stood his ground. "I'll sit with Brenda until you get back."

Richard froze, looking prepared to order Ethan out of the room. Carly sighed and tugged at his arm. "C'mon, Richard, how stupid would the guy really have to be to try anything when we all know he's right here?"

EVEN IN HER PAIN, Brenda couldn't help but be just a little amused by her brother's sheepish expression. Carly really had a knack for putting Richard in his place when he started getting a little too bossy.

Richard left the room without another word to Ethan.

"You know the reason he's walking out with them is so he can tell Tony not to accept your vouching for me quite so easily," Ethan muttered, pulling up the chair Richard had been using earlier so that he could sit very close to Brenda's side.

"I know. But Tony is more objective than Richard. He won't accept the easy explanation, the way everyone else seems to be doing."

"Are you really okay?" Ethan asked, his voice gentling. "You look pretty rough."

"Just a dull headache starting," she admitted, moving her head a little against the pillow. "It could have been a lot worse."

He stood and walked to the sink on one wall. He dampened a thin white washcloth that was lying there, then folded it and laid it gently on her forehead. "How does that feel?"

"Good," she said with a sigh. "Thank you."

"I've had a few concussions in my time."

"A few?"

"Yeah. I went through a phase of participating in extreme sports when I was a teenager. Just to annoy my mother, of course."

Her eyes closed, Brenda smiled. "What kind of extreme sports?"

"Motocross, mostly. Skateboarding. Rodeo. You name it. If I thought my mother would hate it, I tried it."

She opened her eyes to look at him. He was back in the chair, very close to her, his eyes resting on her face in concern. "Are you still doing those things?"

He chuckled. "As you pointed out earlier, I'm not a stupid man. The last concussion was enough to convince me to find some new hobbies. I pretty much stick to running, fishing and poker these days."

"Glad to hear it. Concussions aren't exactly fun."

"No, they aren't." He paused a moment, then said, "Thank you for sticking up for me with your brother. I don't know if you really have that much confidence in my credibility or if Richard was just annoying you, but I appreciated what you said, anyway."

"Ethan." She put a hand on the cloth to hold it in place when she turned her head to look at him more squarely. "I do not believe you hit me on the head and stuffed me into my car. I don't know who did, but I know it wasn't you."

She wondered why his frown only deepened in response to her words. She would have thought he would be at least a bit reassured by her trust in him. Instead, he shook his head. "The thing is, you shouldn't know that. I did have the opportunity, and the motive. You have nothing but my word that I had nothing to do with it."

She smiled, her earlier doubts beginning to evaporate—wisely or not—in response to the sincerity in his expression. "That's all I need."

He leaned forward, his elbows on his knees, his hands clasped inches from her shoulder. "As relieved as I am, it worries me that you're so trusting. Someone really did attack you today. You could have been killed. Until we find out who did this, you're going to have to be suspicious of everyone."

"Even you?"

His mouth crooked up just a little at one corner. "Maybe you shouldn't carry it quite that far."

"Trust me. I won't."

Touching her cheek, he murmured, "I was a real jerk to you this morning."

"Yeah. You were."

He smiled briefly, then added, "But I wasn't wrong. It is complicated for us. Even more so now that the police—and your brother—think I tried to put you out of commission."

"It's complicated," she agreed. "But I'm not ready for it to be over."

He lifted her hand to his mouth and brushed his lips over her knuckles. "Neither am I. But I'm not sure we have much choice about that."

As if to illustrate his words, Richard came back into the room then. "I'm back," he said needlessly to Ethan. "I'll be sleeping in that chair tonight, just to make sure my sister remains safe. You can leave now."

Releasing Brenda's hand with a slight squeeze, Ethan stood. "I'm going. Brenda, have someone call if you need me. I'll check on you tomorrow, okay?"

She waited until he had reached the doorway before speaking. "Ethan?"

Looking back over his shoulder, he asked, "Yeah?"

"I make my own decisions."

After only a momentary hesitation, he nodded and then walked out of the room.

SOMETIME DURING THE NIGHT, Brenda woke, hurting and disoriented. Her rest had been fitful because of her strange surroundings and regular visits by night nurses.

It wasn't a nurse that had disturbed her sleep this time. She had awakened with a start, so perhaps she'd been dreaming, though she couldn't remember any details.

She forced her heavy eyelids open and looked at the recliner where Richard was sitting guard, despite her arguments that it wasn't necessary for him to do so. There was enough light in the room for her to see that he had his head back and his hands crossed on his stomach. He appeared to be asleep. She wouldn't disturb him, she decided.

Turning her head in search of a more comfortable position, she frowned when she saw a figure lying in the other bed. Someone had been brought into the room in the middle of night? Without her even rousing? How strange.

At that moment, the woman in the other bed turned her head to look at Brenda. Brenda gasped, recognizing the shadowy face from photographs and a large oil painting.

Margaret Jacobs was lying in the other bed, gazing at her with glittering, rather feverish-looking eyes.

"Brenda?" Richard had roused instantly in response to the sound she made, and now he stood over her, one hand on her arm. "Are you okay?"

She looked up at him, her heartbeat hammering in her throat. "That woman," she whispered. "She looks like—"

"What woman?" he asked, frowning in confusion. "Who are you talking about?"

She turned her head again.

The other bed was empty, the sheets and blanket neatly spread, undisturbed.

"Brenda?" Richard prodded after several long moments of silence. "What's wrong?"

She couldn't tear her gaze away from the other bed. "I…guess I was dreaming."

"Are you in pain?"

"A little."

"I'll call the nurse."

"All right."

The vision had been so clear, so real. *Had* she been dreaming, or had the bump on her head left her this addled? Or was there something more behind the eerie vision than a simple hallucination?

AFTER BEING HOME for just over an hour on Sunday, Brenda was already growing tired of being treated like an invalid. She half lay reclined on the couch in the media room. Though she kept trying to get up and move around, every time she started to rise, someone urged her back down.

"Do you need anything, honey? Are you thirsty? Is there anything I can get for you?"

One cat in her lap and one beside her, Brenda shook her head in response to her sister's offer. She had to make an effort not to wince with the movement. All it would take was one sign of discomfort to have Linda freaking out again, trying to push pain pills down Brenda's throat. "No, thanks. I'm okay. Really. Why don't you sit down for a while?"

It was just the two of them for the moment, Richard having left to pick up fried chicken for three.

"I don't know if I *can* sit," Linda replied, though she perched on the edge of a chair. "Every time I sit still for very long, I think of how close we came to losing you. Pacing and fussing keeps me too busy to think about what happened here yesterday."

"Let it go, sis. I'm okay. The police are tracking down clues, and Tony's on the case. I'm going to take extra precautions for a while. I'm living in a near fortress here. You can stop worrying so much about me."

Linda looked pointedly at the bandages still wrapped around Brenda's head.

"I'll be fine," Brenda repeated more firmly.

But Linda would not be consoled. "I've had a bad feeling about all of this from the beginning. Nothing about this entire situation makes sense. You getting the house and that money, someone attacking you because of it. I don't like it, Brenda."

"I know you don't."

"And it doesn't have anything to do with jealousy." There was enough defensiveness in Linda's tone for Brenda to suspect that someone had accused her of that ignoble emotion. Richard, probably. "I would be thrilled with your good fortune if it weren't under such suspicious circumstances. And if your life wasn't in danger because of it."

"I have never believed your concern had anything to do with jealousy," Brenda assured her with absolutely honesty. Stung pride, perhaps, but not jealousy.

The faint lines of stress around Linda's blue eyes and full mouth eased a little. "Good."

The doorbell rang, and Linda jumped. "Who do you think that is?"

"I won't know until I answer it, will I?" Setting Angel aside, Brenda started to rise, but Linda shook her head.

"No, don't get up."

"It's probably Carly." Or Ethan, Brenda thought with a quickening pulse. She hadn't heard from him yet that day.

"I'll get it. You stay right there."

Sighing, Brenda sat back as Linda left the room.

She returned a few moments later with Sean Jacobs following behind her. Holding a beautiful bouquet of cut flowers, he moved swiftly toward the couch, his handsome face creased with concern.

"Brenda, I'm so sorry about what happened to you. I was shocked when I heard about it. How are you?"

Swinging her feet to the floor, she sat up straighter, ignoring a slight wave of dizziness. "I'm fine, thank you, Sean. Just a lump on the head. You've met my sister, Linda?"

"We introduced ourselves when she let me in." He sent Linda one of his charming smiles. "You two look so much alike you could almost be twins. I can see that beauty runs in the family."

Brenda was tempted to roll her eyes, but Linda looked pleased by the cheesy remark. "You said you're Brenda's attorney?"

"Sean's the trustee of Margaret's will," Brenda corrected. "He takes care of the estate and disburses my payments from it."

"Oh. Can I get you anything, Mr. Jacobs? I made fresh coffee a little while ago."

"Please call me Sean. And no, thank you. I'm only staying a few minutes."

"Then let me put those flowers in water. I'm sure you and Brenda have business to discuss."

"The flowers are beautiful, Sean," Brenda said as her sister carried them out of the room. "Thank you."

"You're welcome. So, let's talk about what happened to you. I understand you don't remember any details?"

She wondered who he had been talking to. "No."

Leaning slightly forward in his chair, he kept his eyes focused intently on her face. "You didn't see anything? You have no idea who attacked you?"

"None," she replied, wondering why he seemed so intense about it. Was he among those who suspected his stepbrother? "But I know it wasn't Ethan."

"How do you know that?" he asked, looking worried.

She gave him the same answer she had given everyone else the day before. "I just know."

Sean was no more reassured than the others had been. "I think you should be careful, Brenda. God knows I don't want to think Ethan would do something like this, but you have to admit—"

"No," she cut in flatly. "I don't. It wasn't Ethan."

If she was wrong, then she was an idiot who deserved whatever she got. But she wasn't wrong.

As he had said, Sean didn't stay long. Making her promise to call him if she needed anything, he left with one last warning to her to use extra caution until her attacker was behind bars.

Carrying the vase of beautifully arranged flowers, Linda came back into the room soon after Sean had left. She set the vase on a table where Brenda could see it, then took her seat again. "Sean seemed very nice."

"He's been very helpful to me. As busy as I'm sure he is with his other clients, he has always made time for me."

"He's very good-looking. Is he single?"

"Yes, but don't start matchmaking again," Brenda ordered in fond exasperation. "I'm not interested in Sean."

"No," Linda muttered crossly. "Apparently you're much too interested in the only man who has any motive to harm you."

"Richard needs to keep his mouth shut," Brenda grumbled.

"Richard," her brother said as he entered the room just in time to overhear, "is going to do his damnedest to look after you, despite your refusal to cooperate. If that includes enlisting Linda to help me convince you to listen to reason when it comes to Ethan Blacklock, then that's what I'll do."

"He does have a point, Brenda," Linda murmured.

Brenda sighed. "I am not going to discuss this again right now. I'm hungry. Did you bring the chicken, Richard?"

"It's in the kitchen," he said with a sigh, disgruntled by her refusal to listen to his warnings about Ethan.

"I'll bring you a plate, Brenda."

Brenda held up a hand to stop her sister from rushing to the kitchen. "I'd rather eat at the kitchen table."

"The doctor said you should take it easy today," Linda insisted. "Just lie back and I'll bring a plate to you here."

While she knew her sister needed to feel useful today, Brenda was getting very close to outright rebellion. A look from Richard was all that kept her from jumping up and marching to the kitchen, anyway. Well, that and the knowledge that she was entirely likely to fall flat on her face if she tried to move that quickly.

"Who sent the flowers?" Richard asked after Linda left the room.

"Sean brought them by."

"He must not have stayed very long."

"No, it was a very brief visit."

"What did he have to say?"

"He just wanted to tell me to call him if I need anything. It was very thoughtful of him."

"Did he say anything about Ethan?"

"Not in particular," Brenda replied without a qualm. After all, Sean had said he didn't want to believe Ethan had anything to do with the attack on her. She saw no need to tell her brother that Sean hadn't exactly rushed to Ethan's defense, either.

ETHAN LOOKED GLUMLY at the white sedan parked in Brenda's driveway, knowing it belonged to her brother. He didn't recognize the red minivan, but his guess would be that it belonged to her sister. He didn't expect either of her siblings to welcome him with open arms, but he hadn't been able to stay away.

He hadn't slept much the night before. Every time he had closed his eyes, he'd seen Brenda lying so pale and still in the trunk of her car, or bandaged and shaken in the hospital bed. He knew now that there was no longer any use in pretending to himself that his feelings for her were shallow or fleeting. Though he was reluctant to put a label on it, he couldn't dismiss the way he felt. And he needed to see her today. He'd held out until late afternoon, but he couldn't wait any longer.

Wearing a scowl, Richard answered the door. "I guess I was halfway expecting you," he muttered.

"You should have been. How is she?"

Richard shrugged. "Sore. Shaky. Stubborn."

The last almost made Ethan smile. Because he knew Richard hadn't been joking—especially not with him—he contained his brief amusement. "I'd like to see her."

"And you think I'm just going to lead you to her?"

Ethan looked Richard directly in the eyes and spoke quietly. "Brenda pointed out yesterday that I'm not a stupid man. We both know that you aren't, either. Do you really think I'm the one who attacked your sister?"

Richard hesitated a long time. Ethan waited with held breath while the other man made his decision. He released the breath in a long exhale when Richard finally shook his head. "As much as I try to convince myself that it's the only answer that makes sense, something about it just doesn't compute for me. I wrestled with it most of the night, and I just can't picture you doing something so vicious and so cowardly. Not to Brenda."

"It wasn't me, Richard."

"Damn it." Richard's shoulders sagged just a little, as if he'd just let a large chip fall from them. "I guess

I believe you. But if I find out I'm wrong, I swear I'll track you down."

"You aren't wrong."

Richard started to move out of the doorway, and then he paused. "This doesn't mean I trust you with my sister," he seemed compelled to add. "I know there's something going on between the two of you, and I don't like it."

"I can't say I really blame you," Ethan replied candidly.

"I want you to promise me you won't hurt her. In any way."

Ethan shoved his hands into the pockets of his jeans and continued to look Richard in the eyes. "It would make us both feel a hell of a lot better if I could promise that."

He half expected Richard to close the door in his face then. Instead Richard made a sound that might have been resignation and turned without another word to lead the way to the media room.

Even Ethan noticed the way Brenda's face lit up when she saw him enter the room. He didn't blame Richard for looking so disgusted, but as for himself— well, it felt good to have her look at him that way. Entirely too good, he thought, remembering Richard's concern that Brenda was going to get hurt one way or another because of her relationship with Ethan. And once again he wished he could promise Richard or Brenda—or himself—that it would never happen.

She looked a little pale, but significantly better than she had the last time he had seen her. Her eyes were much brighter, though there were still faint shadows beneath them. Her hair had been washed and arranged to hide the bandages at the back of her head. She wore a little makeup—probably in an attempt to make her look somewhat less pale.

"You look a lot better," he told her.

"I feel a lot better. Ethan, this is my sister, Linda Grayson. Linda, this is Ethan Blacklock."

Under any other circumstances, he might have found the look Linda gave him mildly amusing. Had he been introduced as the neighborhood Peeping Tom, he doubted that she would have looked at him with any less animosity and suspicion. Yet deeply ingrained manners made her say, "It's nice to meet you, Mr. Blacklock."

"It's Ethan. And before you ask, no, I didn't hit your sister on the head."

"I believe him," Richard announced, though he looked rather glum about it. "The guy's a pain in the ass, but I don't think he'd stoop this low. As he said, himself, if he'd wanted the estate that badly, he'd have made amends with his mother when she threatened to disown him. He had the chance to fight the will in court—and, considering that Brenda's claim was tenuous, at best—he might well have been successful, but he chose not to follow that course."

"And that's what convinced you that he didn't do it?" Brenda asked, looking pleased.

"Actually, it was something Carly said that I couldn't get out of my mind," Richard admitted.

Though Ethan wasn't surprised that Carly had been the one with the most influence over Richard, he had to ask, "What did she say?"

"It was something about the way you looked when we found Brenda in her car," Richard answered vaguely. "The point is, I'm taking a big leap here and saying I mostly believe that you didn't do it. So what we have to do is figure out who did attack her."

Ethan hadn't missed the qualifier in Richard's statement of belief in him, but he thought he'd better settle for what trust he could get from Brenda's brother. He scooped a cat from the couch and sat on the opposite end from her. "What has Tony found out?"

"Nothing more than the police, I'm afraid," Brenda replied. "He did verify that Leland really was at his office Saturday afternoon."

Not particularly surprised by that information, Ethan nodded. "I didn't really think it was Leland, anyway. My cousin is all bluster and little action. He's both lazy and cowardly. It took guts to attempt something like this in broad daylight in a residential neighborhood, and I just can't see Leland pulling it off."

"So where does that leave us?" Richard asked in frustration.

Ethan grunted. "Your guess is as good as mine."

"What if Brenda gives up the inheritance?" Linda asked, still avoiding Ethan's eyes. "Would she be safe then? I mean, she can certainly get by without all of this if it means that she would no longer be in danger."

Ethan was the one who responded. "The biggest flaw in that logic comes back to the fact that I'm the only one who stands to profit if she walks away. But I'm not the one who's been giving her trouble. So there's a chance that declining the estate wouldn't make her any safer. Just the opposite, maybe. At least here she has a good security system and all of us to watch out for her."

Linda looked at him then, and he was struck by how

strongly she resembled Brenda. For that reason alone, it pleased him that she seemed to make up her mind to trust him—at least to the same extent that Richard did. "Can I get you something to drink, Ethan? There's fresh coffee in the kitchen. And I made a chocolate cake while Brenda was resting after lunch."

Brenda chuckled in response to his expression. "My sister and I both tend to cook when we're stressed," she murmured. "We got it from our mother."

Richard grinned briefly. "Dad always complained that he gained ten pounds every time Mother was worried about something. The more troubled she was, the more she baked. Sometimes the kitchen would be full of cakes and pies and cookies and brownies."

"Which never went to waste as long as you were around," Linda said.

Richard sighed wistfully. "Man, I can still almost taste her black forest cake. And her pastries. Both you girls are good cooks, but neither of you has ever quite mastered her pastry dough."

Both sisters solemnly agreed with his assessment of their mother's baking skill. They reminisced for another minute or two while Ethan looked on, feeling very much the outsider in this strikingly similar-looking family with their shared memories of an obviously happy home life.

And then Linda shook her head and returned abruptly to the present. "I'm sorry, Ethan, we've gotten distracted. I offered you coffee and cake?"

"I would like that, thank you."

"I'll bring some for everyone."

Richard jumped to his feet. "Let me help you, Linda. You can't carry it all alone."

Unable to resist a moment longer, Ethan leaned closer to cup Brenda's cheek in his hand. Her skin felt cool. Soft. So very tempting. "Are you really okay?" he asked, searching her eyes. "You aren't in any pain?"

She smiled and tilted her head to nestle her cheek more snugly into his palm. "I'm fine. Still a little sore, but mostly just ready to get off this couch. Linda and Richard have hardly let me lift a finger today."

"They love you."

"I know." She said it with such simple confidence that he wondered if she had any idea what a precious gift that really was. The comforting knowledge that her family loved her and would be there for her, no matter what.

Because he didn't want to think about such things just then, especially not in this house where he'd spent his own less-than-rosy childhood, he focused on something much more pleasant. He leaned closer to brush his lips against hers.

He'd meant for the kiss to be quick. Just a furtive taste while her siblings were in another room. He should have known he wouldn't be content with that. One kiss led to another, longer one. And then her arms were around his neck and his were locked behind her back and he was kissing her with all the emotions that had been locked inside him since Carly had called him to tell him that Brenda was missing.

He wouldn't have been able to bear it if he had lost her after parting with her so angrily that morning.

"Damn it!"

The angry interjection from behind them brought him abruptly to his senses. He released Brenda almost too quickly, turning to face Richard with his defenses already in place.

He was prepared to be thrown out on his ear, but Richard merely scowled and placed the tray he was carrying on the coffee table. "At least try not to do that when I'm around to see it," he muttered.

Brenda's giggle was just a bit breathless. Since Ethan was still trying to remember how to breathe himself, that didn't surprise him.

CHAPTER NINETEEN

FOR A WOMAN with a concussion and a nameless enemy who had locked her in the trunk of a car, Brenda was astonishingly happy. Ethan was back, looking at her with emotions in his eyes that made her pulse race giddily through her veins. And Richard seemed to have accepted Ethan's innocence and the fact that Brenda was old enough to make her own choices.

Even her recently strained relationship with Linda seemed to be back on their old terms, though Brenda didn't doubt that it would cause problems if she were to offer Linda money again.

They sat in the media room, eating cake and drinking coffee while the cats rolled and played on the floor around them. Richard and Linda still weren't exactly comfortable with Ethan among them, but they seemed to be slowly relaxing, and Brenda knew better than to rush things.

"Look at those silly cats," Linda noted, laughing as Missy took a flying leap at Fluffy, sending them both tumbling into Toby. "Are they always this high-spirited?"

Brenda smiled. "You know cats. They sleep seventeen hours a day and play the other seven."

"More trouble than they're worth," Ethan grumbled.

Brenda looked at him with a lifted eyebrow. His attitude toward cats—these cats, in particular—could prove to be a problem.

"I'm going to have to see about changing your attitude about my feline friends," she teased him.

For some reason, he frowned rather than smiled. "I don't need anyone changing my attitude," he muttered, barely loudly enough for her to hear.

Remembering his mention of former girlfriends who had seen him as a makeover project, she sighed heavily. She'd known all along that she was getting involved with a man who had heavy baggage, but she didn't like being compared to his past lovers. He should work on his own sense of humor.

Before she could respond, Linda asked, "What's that cat got in its mouth? The calico, I mean."

Looking around to see for herself, Brenda noticed Angel backing out from beneath the couch, where the quietest kitty had been hiding from the others' roughhousing. What appeared to be a torn scrap of white paper was gripped between Angel's sharp little teeth.

"Angel, what is that? Give it here."

She leaned down to snag the slightly damp paper, which must have been trapped beneath the large couch. It was damp and a little dusty, but she could see that it had been ripped on all four sides. Some typed words remained on the page, just fragments of sentences. She scanned them, then went very still.

"Brenda?" Ethan must have been watching her closely. "What is it?"

Mutely, she looked up at him, and then handed him the scrap of paper. She didn't need to look over his shoulder as he read the words. She had them memorized.

Only a part of a sentence remained on the torn page, but there was enough for Brenda to know that they were momentous. She could see the impact the words made on Ethan as he read them.

> "…and I bitterly regret giving my child up for adoption. I should never…"

TONY LOOKED at the scrap of paper and then at the somber faces surrounding him, waiting for him to tell them what the words meant. He shook his head. "I have no idea."

Brenda exhaled slowly, only then realizing that she had been holding her breath. She didn't know what had made her think that Tony would be able to shed some light on the cryptic message on the paper Angel had unearthed.

She looked at Ethan, who had said very little since they'd found the paper. His earlier good mood gone, his face and eyes had gone hard, hiding whatever emotions he was feeling now.

He was watching Tony now with intense concentration. "Is there a possibility that my mother gave a child away for adoption?"

"There's a possibility," Tony admitted. "I found nothing like that in my background check of her, but a woman with her money and her legal connections would have known how to make certain records disappear."

"So it's possible that Ethan has a brother or sister

out there somewhere?" Carly asked in wonder, waving a hand vaguely toward the windows to indicate the outside world. "Just like Mom and her brothers and sisters who were all separated as children?"

Brenda knew that Ethan had already considered the possibility, but hearing the words aloud still visibly affected him. Though perhaps she was the only one who noticed, since his only reaction was the jerk of a muscle in his cheek.

"Let's not get ahead of ourselves here," Tony warned. "We don't even know that Margaret typed these words. It could have been a letter she received from someone else. A friend who was confiding her feelings to Margaret, for example."

But Carly, for one, didn't seem convinced of that. "From everything we've heard of Margaret, she wasn't exactly an ideal confidante."

"Hardly," Ethan muttered.

"I think there's more to it than that," Carly continued. "I think there's a possibility that she had another child and gave it away, for some reason. Maybe it was her first child, born when she was young and unmarried. She would definitely want to hide something like that because of her social status, right? Maybe that first child found out the truth and is angry at being left out of the will."

"So you're saying that it's possible I have a murderous older sibling?" Ethan asked her crossly. "Sorry if that doesn't exactly make me jump with joy."

"You have to admit there could be something to Carly's theory," Richard said, earning himself a glowing look from Carly.

Looking at the smile Richard gave Carly in return,

Brenda thought she'd finally figured out why her brother was being so unexpectedly accepting of her relationship with Ethan. Richard was well aware that he was caught up in a situation that was almost as problematic as hers. That he had fallen hard for someone who was just as unlikely a match as Ethan was for her.

She no longer had any doubts that Richard had very strong feelings for Carly. He was so obviously in love with her, though as far as Brenda knew, he still hadn't made the first move to do anything about it. Maybe he never intended to do so, though she wasn't sure Carly would let him get away with that. Because she had her own problems to worry about now, she looked to Tony again. "Even if Carly's speculations were true, how would that involve me? Why would she name me in the will? Because I really can't believe that I…"

"You aren't the child that Margaret gave away," Tony assured her when her voice faded. "There is no doubt that you are the biological offspring of Tom and Caroline Prentiss. Trust me, that was the first thing I checked."

She couldn't look at Ethan just then. "So how do we find out if she did give a child away? And is there any other avenue we can explore to find out my connection to Margaret?"

"Starting today," Tony told her grimly, "this case is my top priority. I promise I'll do everything I can to find your answers, Brenda."

"Thank you." She knew that he had taken her seriously before and had done a great deal of research on her behalf. But she also knew that there hadn't been an urgency to the case before.

After all, who would really complain about being

left a fortune from a stranger? The speeding truck incident had been seemingly random, apparently unconnected. The phone calls had been annoying, but not really threatening, and very likely explained by pointing to Ethan's angry cousin. The rock through her window had been a bit more disturbing, but had put her in no danger—and once again, it had been too easy to blame that on Leland.

This latest attack was something none of them could shrug off. She knew exactly how close she had come to dying then. There had been moments while she'd lain bound and bleeding in that trunk that she had been convinced she would not survive. Had Ethan and Richard not found her when they did…

She shuddered.

Now all the clues they found had to be taken seriously. And this letter was definitely a clue. Tony wouldn't brush it off.

ETHAN COULDN'T STAY in that house any longer. Every time he looked at Brenda with her brother and sister and Carly with her father, he was vividly reminded of his own family. Of the mother who had pretty much thrown him out of her life. And now there was a possibility that she had once given away another child.

"I've got to go for a while," he told Brenda, drawing her aside while the others talked. "Call if you need me, okay?"

She searched his face, apparently seeing too much there. "Don't you want to talk about this? You and I could go into another room to talk in private, if you want."

He shook his head. "I've got to get out of here," he admitted. "Just for a few hours."

"Then let me go with you," she said, clutching his arm. "You don't need to be alone right now."

He covered her hand with his for a moment, then resolutely removed it. "I'm used to being alone. I've gotten to where I like it that way."

Hurt flashed quickly through her eyes, and she stepped back. "If that's what you want."

He should have made a more compassionate excuse, he thought as he slipped out before the others noticed. He should have said something about how she needed to rest. He shouldn't have been so callous when she was only trying to help him.

But maybe it was better this way. Maybe she needed to know that he was pretty much a bastard. Selfish. Rebellious. Coldhearted. Weren't those all descriptions his own mother had used to describe him? Among others, of course.

Unlike the others, he had no family to turn to when he was feeling angry and confused. Instead, he went to the one place where he had always felt at home. He went to the nursery to see Raine.

BRENDA HAD INSISTED that her sister should head home to her children, promising to call Linda if they discovered anything else, no matter how minor. Linda had clearly been anxious to return to her family, but just as reluctant to leave her sister. Only Richard's assurance to her that he wouldn't let Brenda out of his sight for long convinced her to go.

Carly remained at the house after her father left. Tony was impatient to get started on new investigation angles on Brenda's behalf, but she told him she wanted to stay with Brenda. Having seen Brenda's expression after Ethan left so hastily, Carly thought she could use a friend now.

Brenda looked pale, she decided. And no wonder. She'd only been out of the hospital a few hours, and she'd been inundated with visitors ever since. Not to mention her complicated relationship with Ethan Blacklock.

"Okay, here's what's going to happen," she said, taking charge with her usual self-confidence. "Brenda, you're going to put your feet up on that couch and nap while Richard and I start dinner. After we eat, Richard's going to make himself scarce for a while so you and I can girl-talk about our love lives without your nosy older brother listening in. Anyone have any objections to that plan?"

"Well, actually—" Richard began.

Carly gave him a look.

"No," he concluded smoothly. "No objections."

"It sounds good to me," Brenda said, giving Carly a grateful look. "I could use a rest."

Leaving Brenda comfortably settled on the couch with a pillow, a soft chenille throw and two cats, Carly all but dragged Richard to the kitchen. "She's exhausted," she said, opening the refrigerator door to peer inside. "This is all getting to be too much for her."

"I agree. I'm glad you got her to agree to rest. But, uh, about that love life thing…"

She pulled a package of chicken breasts and a bunch of fresh broccoli out of the refrigerator and gave him a teasing look. "Worried that your name will come up?"

He must be getting somewhat used to her, she decided. He didn't even blush that time, though he looked a little flustered when he said, "No, of course not."

"Because it probably will," she said, laying the chicken on the counter and opening the pantry.

"In, um—what context?"

Setting a package of rice next to the chicken, she glanced at him as she opened the freezer. "I'll probably ask your sister for some advice."

"Advice about what?"

She turned then, hiding a sudden attack of nerves behind an impudent tone. "Maybe I'll ask her what it would take to get you to kiss me."

Richard went very still, his eyes so intense on her face that she felt her smile fade nervously. "Don't even joke about that."

Bracing her hands on the counter behind her, she kept her gaze steady on his. "What makes you think I'm joking?"

"Carly…"

"You might have noticed that I'm not particularly fragile, Richard. If you aren't interested, just tell me so. I won't get all upset, and it won't make any difference between us. We can still be friendly and relaxed when we're together."

"It isn't that I'm not interested," he said. "It's just that…"

Her heart beating a little faster, she dropped her hands and moved toward him. "I'm sure you have a whole list of reasons why you don't think we should pursue this any further, but I think you should know that I'm going to have a very powerful argument against every one of them. It would save us both a lot of time if you'd just keep it simple. Do you want to kiss me or not?"

"I've been wanting to kiss you pretty much since the first time I saw you," he said with a candor that brought a lump to her throat.

She stopped in front of him and tilted her face upward. "So why don't you?"

Smiling a bit weakly, he shrugged. "Maybe I'm afraid of your father."

Walking her fingers up his chest, she leaned closer. "I'll tell you a little secret about my father."

"What—" He had to stop to clear his throat. His hands settling on her hips, he tried again, "What secret?"

Going up on tiptoe, she spoke against his lips. "He doesn't have a black belt."

Richard started to laugh, but the sound was choked off when she pressed her mouth more firmly against his.

BRENDA WAS RATHER surprised to wake on the couch and realize that she had slept for quite a while. She hadn't really expected to sleep, but she supposed the events of the past couple of days had simply overcome her.

Swinging her feet to the floor, she noted that her head still ached a bit, but not as badly as before. She had really needed that time to herself, she decided, grateful to Carly for suggesting it.

"So you're awake." Carly smiled at her as she strolled into the room, her near-black eyes gleaming, her olive cheeks a little flushed. "Did you rest well?"

"Yes, I did. Thank you."

"How would you like to actually eat at a table this time? Think you can make it to the kitchen?"

"Definitely. I'm getting tired of this room." Brenda stood cautiously and was pleased when the room only made a revolution or two before steadying.

Pretending she wasn't hovering, Carly motioned toward the doorway. "You go ahead. I'll bring up the rear."

Probably to catch her if she fell, Brenda thought in resignation, but she moved obediently toward the door. "Where's Richard?"

"He just left. He said he had a few things to do at his place, because he hasn't been home since yesterday afternoon. He told me to tell you he'll be back later and he plans to spend the night here to keep an eye on you."

"What about dinner? Isn't Richard eating?"

"He already ate. You slept for quite a while, actually."

"Did I?" She wasn't wearing a watch, so she had no idea what time it was, though long shadows were slanting through the windows. "I guess I was more tired than I realized."

"Who could blame you? It's been a tough week."

She could say that again. Brenda looked at the food arranged buffet style on the kitchen island. "Wow. That looks good."

Carly laughed self-consciously. "I make three dishes. Chicken, broccoli and rice casserole is one of them. I was just lucky you had the ingredients."

Brenda was already filling a plate. "Have you eaten?"

"No. I waited for you."

They carried their dinners to the kitchen table and sat comfortably across from each other.

Brenda had just scooped the first bite of casserole into her mouth when Carly said, "Richard kissed me today."

Brenda nearly choked on her dinner. She swallowed hastily and reached for her tea glass.

"Sorry," Carly said, watching her. "I guess I should have given you a little more preparation for that."

Finally able to speak again, Brenda agreed, "Yeah. Maybe."

"Do you mind? About Richard and me, I mean."

"Why would I mind?"

"Well, you know. You hired my father. You weren't expecting me in the bargain."

"Actually, I think of meeting you as one of the nicest things that has happened to me lately," Brenda replied with absolute honesty.

Carly dimpled. "That was nice. Thank you. I feel the same way."

"But I still have to warn you to be a little careful," Brenda felt compelled to add. "Richard was burned badly by his marriage and divorce. He's still pretty gun-shy. I wouldn't want either of you to get hurt."

"I know. He told me a little about his divorce while he ate. It was really painful for him, wasn't it?"

"Very. I'm surprised he talked about it, actually. He rarely does."

"He said he thought I should know a little more about him before we go any further. Not that it made any difference to me, of course," Carly added. "I mean, I'd already figured out that he had been hurt. And I knew our age difference scared him. He's having a hard time getting his mind around dating a college student.

"And my huge family worries him, too, I think," she added. "The funny thing is, lately I've been having all these feelings of being smothered and crowded by parents and my siblings and my zillion aunts and uncles and cousins, but ever since I started hearing about Ethan's childhood, all I can think about is how lucky I've been to have such a big, loving, supportive family. And I think they're all going to be crazy about Richard once they meet him."

Which made it sound as though Carly already considered herself and Richard a couple, if she was planning his introduction to her family. Brenda thought it said quite a bit about how strong Richard's feelings were for Carly that she had somehow gotten past the defenses he'd been attempting to build against her since the first time he'd met her.

"So, anyway, now that I've shared with you, it's your turn. What did you and Ethan fight about yesterday? And the usual tell-me-to-butt-out-if-it's-none-of-my-business advice applies, by the way."

It seemed so long ago since Brenda and Ethan had parted so curtly. Hard to believe it was only the morning before. "He overheard me talking to Sean on the phone."

"Oh." Carly nodded as if that explained a lot. Pushing her long black hair behind her shoulder, she added, "He's jealous of Sean, huh?"

"No, it isn't like that. He thought Sean was warning me not to trust him too much, and it annoyed him."

"Yeah, I'm sure it did. But he's still jealous. Why else would he have gotten mad at you?"

"He wasn't mad at me, exactly. He said everyone would think the same as Sean implied. That he was playing up to me just to get his hands on the estate. I told him I didn't care what anyone thought, but he wouldn't listen. He just said he'd known from the start that it was a bad idea and that it would be better if we just forgot about it. And then, of course, I did get mad."

"Well, no wonder. That was a jerky thing to say *after* you and he…well, you know."

Though her cheeks felt a bit warm, Brenda nodded. "Yeah, I know."

"Men," Carly said in heartfelt irritation.

Brenda nodded again, even more vigorously this time.

"So Ethan was really freaked by the paper you found, wasn't he? Do you really think he has a brother or sister out there somewhere?"

"I don't know, but you're right. He was freaked." And he had done what he usually did when he was troubled by something. He had bolted, preferring to be alone rather than turning to her—or anyone else—for support.

She wondered if the scars Margaret had left on his heart would ever heal enough for him to let anyone else into it.

CHAPTER TWENTY

ETHAN WAS IN HIS OFFICE Sunday evening, trying to figure out how to work a requested ten viburnums into a landscape designed for no more than five when someone rang his doorbell. He glanced automatically at the clock on the wall, noting that it almost 9:00 p.m. Fairly late for a drop-in caller.

His first thought was that it might be Brenda. He hadn't spoken with her since he'd left the house earlier. He hoped she wasn't out at this hour in her condition because she was worried about him, or anything foolish like that.

He set down his pencil reluctantly. He wasn't in the mood for company. Not even Brenda's. Maybe especially not hers, since it was so much harder to push back the anger and the hurt when she was around to stir so many emotions in him.

He walked into the living room and opened the door just as the bell chimed again. He had not expected to see Richard Prentiss and Tony D'Alessandro on the other side, both looking very serious.

Lifting an eyebrow, he asked, "Have you come to haul me off to jail?"

"Is there any reason for us to do so?" Tony inquired, smiling very faintly.

"Not as far as I know. But that hasn't stopped anyone so far from trying to get me there."

"We need to talk to you," Tony said. "Do you mind if we come in?"

Ethan stepped out of the doorway and motioned them in.

Both men looked around with surprise and interest when they entered his living room, a reaction he had come to expect from first-time callers. Ethan didn't offer refreshments. He was impatient to hear whatever it was that Tony had to tell him. He could tell by the way they were acting that it was fairly major.

"I take it you've learned something new?" he asked Tony, waving them both toward chairs.

After being seated, Tony cleared his throat. "Yes, we have. I'm not sure how you're going to feel about it."

"Look, Ethan, this is sort of personal, family business for you," Richard said abruptly. "If you want me to wait outside, I will."

"From the way you're talking, I assume you already know what it is."

"Yes, I do. I happened to be at Tony's office, talking to him about, er, something else when one of his employees came in to announce what he'd found out. I asked to come along because I'd like to discuss with the two of you how this new information affects my sister. Carly's staying with Brenda for now."

Ethan shrugged. "You might as well stay. What's the new information I'm not going to like?"

Tony took over the conversation then. "After that scrap of letter turned up today, I went to my office and called in a couple of my best computer people. Young guys. Cocky, a little weird, kind of obnoxious, but they can hack—er, access just about any records that have ever been officially recorded. All completely legal, of course."

"Of course," Ethan murmured, straight-faced.

"While they were doing research, I got on the phone, calling Margaret's housekeeper and some of her old friends."

"I thought you'd already talked to all of them. No one knew anything."

"I wasn't asking the right questions," Tony replied, just a hint of chagrin in his voice as he admitted the mistake. "I asked about the past few years, trying to find out the connection between Margaret and Brenda. Failing in that, I looked for some link between Margaret and Brenda's parents. But I never asked anyone about your birth."

Ethan went very still. "What are you talking about?"

"How much did your mother tell you about your birth, Ethan?"

"Not much. She wasn't one to share fond reminiscences. Why?"

Tony and Richard exchanged a quick glance, and then Tony asked bluntly, "She never told you that you were adopted?"

MAYBE ETHAN HAD SIMPLY been hit with so many emotional blows during the past month that he'd gone rather numb. "No," he said flatly. "She didn't. Do you know that for a fact?"

Tony nodded. "I'm pretty sure. It was something about that scrap of paper that made me suspect the truth. The words that were written on it seemed entirely out of character from what I know of your mother. She didn't seem to be the type to agonize over past decisions, or pour her feelings out on paper."

"No, that wouldn't have been like her at all."

Adopted. If it were true, it would explain a great deal.

"That's what I thought. So I had my people do some digging into your mother's medical records. It turned out she had a partial hysterectomy at a very young age, in her early twenties, due to cancer. That was several years before you were born, of course. She would not have been able to bear a child. Three years ago, she had her ovaries removed when they, too, turned cancerous."

Ethan was as stunned by that as he was by the other news he'd been given. "Mother had cancer that recently? She never told me."

"She told no one, apparently. I suppose she saw it as a sign of weakness. She told everyone she was taking an extended cruise."

"I remember the cruise. She spent four weeks touring the Greek islands. It was not long after she returned that she and I had our last falling-out." Seeing Tony's expression, Ethan said more slowly, "She never went to Greece?"

"Not at that time," Tony replied quietly. "That was all a fabrication. She wouldn't even let Betty visit her in the hospital, though Betty, of course, nursed her through her recovery period afterward. The cancer was contained in the ovaries, and she refused to pursue precautionary chemotherapy afterward. Betty told me her recovery period was short and that she was back into her regular schedule within a few weeks with no one being the wiser."

Ethan pushed a slightly unsteady hand through his hair. "We'd been quarreling for so long by then that I suppose she didn't want me to see her in a weak position."

"When I mentioned the possibility that you had been adopted to Betty, her voice changed so dramatically that I realized I had stumbled on to something. I had to pull out all the charm I possess even to keep her on the line."

And that, Ethan thought, was considerable. "So she told you that I was adopted?"

"Let's just say she pretty much confirmed what I had already figured out on my own. She's very fond of you, Ethan. She regretted the division between you and your—between you and Margaret. And she was appalled to learn that you've gotten caught up in a situation that has everyone looking at you with suspicion. She vouched for your integrity, and insisted that you would never do anything to harm anyone."

While he appreciated the approbation, Ethan couldn't figure out why no one had told him the truth through all those years. His mother had never given a hint that he wasn't her biological son, even during their angriest and most venomous quarrels. "How could I have never known?"

"With her influence and money, not to mention her connections in the legal community, it wouldn't have been all that difficult for her to have the records buried. I suppose she considered not being able to carry a child another flaw she didn't want the world to see."

After listening in silence to that point, Richard

spoke to Ethan. "There was also her obsession with having you join the law firm. Perhaps she considered it her duty to provide another generation to keep the firm going."

Remembering how fiercely she had fought for that outcome, Ethan thought Richard was probably right.

After a moment's silent reflection, uninterrupted by the two men who sat quietly watching him, Ethan let out a long exhale. "This answers some questions for me, but I still don't understand what Brenda has to do with any of this. How did she end up in the will? And what would my being adopted have to do with someone trying to hurt her?"

"I'm still not sure about the first question. But the second one brings us back to the scrap of letter that turned up today. The resentful tone made me suspect it was written to Margaret by your biological mother. I wondered if she was unhappy with the way things had turned out between you and Margaret."

That brought Ethan's head up sharply again. "You know who my biological mother is?"

"Not exactly," Tony replied, pulling a sheet of paper out of his shirt pocket. "But Betty had developed a suspicion during the past couple of years. She was reluctant to say it directly, but she gave me a few hints."

He handed the paper to Ethan. "These are the notes I took when I talked to Betty. She thinks there's a chance that this could be your biological mother. She didn't want to say anything before because she considered her a friend and didn't want to cast suspicion on her without proof. But she said she knows for a fact that this woman and Margaret had some very heated—and quite recent—arguments about the way Margaret treated you during the past few years."

Ethan glanced at the neatly written notes of the conversation with Betty. His eyes locked on the name that seemed to jump out at him from the page. And suddenly he knew the truth.

He jumped to his feet. "We need to get to Brenda. Now."

BRENDA WAS BACK in the media room, this time accompanied by Carly as they curled on the couch eating popcorn and watching television. They had looked through Margaret's film collection, but the titles there had all seemed so heavy and depressing on a night when they needed mindless entertainment.

Carly looked at her watch during a commercial. "I wonder what's keeping Richard? He said he would try to be here by nine."

"He'll probably be here soon. Do you want anything else to drink?"

"Yeah. Sit tight, I'll get it." Carly crossed to the wet bar, then knelt to peer into the small refrigerator. "What do you want?"

"Are there any more of those diet root beers Richard stocked?"

"Several."

"I'll have one of those. He won't mind me getting into his stash tonight."

"He's a root beer fan, is he?" Carly asked, carrying the frosty can and a bottled water for herself back to the couch.

"He's addicted to the stuff."

"I'll keep that in mind," Carly murmured.

Brenda rolled her eyes.

They both looked around when they heard a sound from somewhere else in the house. "I should have known," Brenda said. "I swear Richard is part psychic. The minute I open one of his root beers, he catches me—"

But it was a woman who appeared suddenly in the doorway of the media room. Her long, braided brown hair was streaked with gray, and her lined, sun-weathered face was set in a hard expression. Her flowing, almost whimsical clothing made an odd contrast to the lethal looking weapon she held in her right hand.

The handgun was aimed directly at Brenda.

Brenda recovered from the initial shock before Carly did. Still, she barely recognized her own voice when she asked, "Who are you?"

"I'm Ethan's mother," the woman answered, taking another step into the room. "And you are harder to get rid of than a cockroach."

"YOU AREN'T ETHAN'S MOTHER," Carly accused the woman, lifting her chin to prove that she wasn't intimidated by the gun. "Ethan's mother is dead."

"His adoptive mother is dead," the woman replied coldly. "I know. I was here the night she died."

Brenda felt her eyes go wider, but she tried to remain calm. "I know your voice. We spoke on the phone, didn't we? You're Raine Scott."

Raine nodded curtly. "That's the name I've used for the past twenty some-odd years. It's the only name Ethan has ever known for me."

Holding her water in her left hand, Carly groped with her right for Brenda's free left hand. She clutched it in a grip that belied her steady tone. "When you say you were here the night Margaret died…?"

"I didn't kill her!" Raine said sharply, sensing an accusation in the unfinished question. Her loud, sharp tone startled the cats, who all dashed from the room. "The stupid woman fell while we were arguing about Ethan. Believe me, I didn't want her dead. Not before she put Ethan back in her will, where he rightfully belonged."

So many puzzle pieces fell into place with that one sentence. Brenda blinked at the import of it. "So you're the one," she whispered.

"All I was trying to do was scare you away," Raine said fiercely. "They told me you weren't sure you should accept the inheritance, and I just wanted to help you make up your mind. But you got greedy. You wouldn't go away."

"I offered the money to Ethan. He wouldn't accept it."

Raine nodded. "He's a proud man. Stubborn. Independent. I'm afraid he got that from me. But if you'd had any sense of ethics or fairness, you would have realized this estate should have been his. He was her son by law. He put up with her demands and her tyranny and her coldness all those years, only to end up with nothing. It wasn't fair."

"He didn't exactly end up with nothing," Carly said. "He has his business. And Brenda gave him a very expensive coin collection that belonged to his…that belonged to Margaret's first husband."

Raine didn't even seem to hear her. Her eyes were slightly unfocused when she murmured, "He was ten when I found him. So young and vulnerable. And his eyes were so guarded and lonely. I knew the first time I saw him that she hadn't been good to him. He had the social and financial advantages I had dreamed of for him, but he was still unhappy. So I became his friend. I became *her* friend, just so I could always be there when he needed me."

"He loves you, Raine," Brenda said, clinging to Carly's hand. The root beer was still in her right hand, but she was afraid to make any sudden moves to set it down. Instead, she tried reason. "He's told me about how much you mean to him."

"I love him, too," Raine said fiercely. "I told him I would take care of him."

"By killing Brenda? Did you really think that would work?"

Brenda wished Carly would stop challenging Raine that way.

"She shouldn't have been in the will," Raine almost spat. "She took my Ethan's place, and no one even knew who she was or how Margaret knew her."

Brenda gave Carly's hand a warning squeeze. "Didn't you realize that Ethan would be blamed if anything happened to me? He was the only one with anything to gain from my death. Everyone accused him of trying to hurt me. He was the prime suspect from the very beginning."

That only seemed to make Raine angrier. "He wouldn't have been blamed for an accident. If I'd hit you with the truck I borrowed from the nursery—or if you had died in that fire that started in your kitchen—there was nothing to pin either incident on Ethan. I made sure he had an alibi every time."

So they really had been attempts on her life, Brenda

thought with a sinking feeling. She would have liked to know how Raine broke into her kitchen to start the fire without leaving evidence behind, but it seemed more important to stay on topic for now. "Ethan didn't have an alibi for when you stuffed me into the trunk of my car. He was almost arrested for that. He's still under investigation. I know that isn't what you want."

"He was supposed to be at work!" The feverish glint in Raine's brown eyes let Brenda know she had touched on a sore point. "He told me he was going to work. I didn't know he'd left."

"And what about now?" Carly asked, picking up on Brenda's efforts to keep Raine talking about Ethan. "How do you know he won't be blamed if something happens to Brenda now?"

Raine tilted her chin in a smug gesture. "He has company. I drove by his house on the way here. Whoever it is will vouch for him. As far as anyone will know, someone broke into this house to rob the place."

"How did you get in here, Raine?" If only she could keep her talking, Brenda thought desperately.

"I have a key. I've had one for years. Just in case I needed it. I spent a lot of time here, you know. Margaret and Betty welcomed me when I came, until Margaret blamed me for influencing Ethan to go into landscape design. It wasn't that hard to pocket a key on one of those visits."

"Did Margaret ever know you were Ethan's real mother?" Carly asked, doing her part to stall.

"Yes, she knew," Raine answered bitterly. "I wrote her a letter eighteen months ago telling her the truth, and letting her know how sorry I was that I gave my child to a woman who so did not deserve him. She refused to believe me. And she told me that no one was going to force her to stop trying to make *her son* accept his responsibilities to the family name he carried."

Eighteen months ago, Brenda thought, stunned. Just about the time that Margaret had named her in the will. What did that mean?

"You aren't a killer, Raine," Carly said gently, still holding Brenda's hand tightly. "You didn't kill Margaret. And you didn't kill Brenda yesterday when you had the chance."

"I thought I *had* killed her," Raine said bitterly. "There was so much blood, and she never even moved while I was tying her up and putting her in the trunk. I thought she would be dead by the time anyone found her. I should have finished her off then, but you're right, of course. Killing doesn't come easily to me."

"Then let us go," Brenda urged. "You don't want to do this, Raine."

"I have to," Raine said simply, raising the gun again. "I'm doing it for Ethan."

Ethan's voice from behind her made her freeze. "Raine, *no!* Don't."

BRENDA FELT HER HEART STOP, and then start pounding again at double speed in response to hearing Ethan's voice. Turning her head to look at him, she saw the fear etched on the face she had grown to love. Fear for her, she realized.

Though she knew he was as intensely aware of her as she was him, he wasn't looking at her. His eyes were focused intently on Raine—the woman who claimed to be his mother.

Only then did Brenda notice Richard and Tony.

Both stood some distance behind Ethan, and both were poised to throw themselves forward at the first opportunity. Their faces were as tense as Ethan's, Tony concentrating on his daughter, Richard looking rather wildly from Carly to Brenda and back again.

"Don't do this, Raine," Ethan said again. "Put the gun down. Please."

Raine's hand trembled a little, but the gun remained pointed at Brenda. "She stole your money, Ethan. It isn't fair. You've been through so much. You deserve to be comfortable and secure. You deserve a nice home and a few luxuries. You *earned* them."

"I never wanted those things," he said gently. "The money was never important to me. All I ever wanted was for my mother to love me."

One solitary tear slid slowly down her cheek. "I'm so sorry I couldn't give you that. I was…sick…for a long time after you were born. I didn't know the people who took you would be so cold to you."

Brenda's eyes met her brother's. He looked at the soda can in her hand, and then back at her face, shifting his weight on his feet in a very subtle signal that he was prepared to act quickly.

"But you did give me that, Raine." Ethan's voice was so gentle that it brought a lump to Brenda's throat. Surely Raine couldn't be unaffected by it. "You were the one person I could count on to support me, no matter what."

"I tried. When I found you, and I realized how they treated you, I did my best to be your friend. The only way I could live with what I had done was to tell myself that at least you would never have to worry about money. You would be able to live well, to be accepted in society, to have security as you grew older. If you had only gone to law school, as Margaret wanted you to do. Or if you had just tried a little harder to get along with her. She would have changed her mind about the will had she lived a little longer. I know I could have convinced her, if I'd just had a little more time."

He risked one quick, encouraging glance at Brenda before looking at Raine again. "I know you've always wanted the best for me."

"I've always watched out for you, Ethan," she said. "Always. Just as I'm taking care of you now."

She lifted her other hand to grip the gun between them, spreading her feet in a resolute stance. The barrel was pointed straight at Brenda's head now, and her hands had stopped shaking. "Don't worry, Ethan. No one will blame you now. There are witnesses. Whatever price I have to pay, it will be worth it for me, as long as I know you'll be given what is rightfully yours."

"Raine, no!" Ethan stretched out a hand to her, and his was not at all steady. "You want me to be happy? Then don't do this. Don't hurt Brenda."

She frowned. "Why? She's nothing to us."

"She is to me."

Brenda sagged in relief again when Raine turned her head to look at Ethan in bewilderment. "But she hurt you. You came to me this morning because you were angry and hurt. You wouldn't tell me why, but I knew it was because of her."

"No, it wasn't that. It was something I'd learned about Margaret that upset me. Brenda hasn't done anything wrong. She's the one truly innocent party in all of this. If you hurt her, I would never forgive you. And I wouldn't touch a penny of the money, Raine. Do you hear me? Not a penny."

"But, Ethan…" For the first time, uncertainty was visible in her face. "Don't you understand? It's yours. It's all yours. It was meant to—"

Looking at her brother, Brenda threw the root beer can with all her strength against the wall nearest her. The carbonated beverage exploded. Immediately following suit, Carly threw her water bottle, causing even more noise and confusion. Brenda tugged at Carly's hand, and together they dived off the couch and onto the floor.

CHAPTER TWENTY-ONE

THE PAINFULLY LOUD CRACK of a gunshot, followed by the sound of breaking glass, made Brenda and Carly flinch. Carly made a sound that was part gasp, part scream. Brenda was too frightened to make any noise at all, not that it would have been heard over the pandemonium in the room.

She risked looking up. Tony had the gun now, holding it safely out of the way while Richard knelt by Raine, who lay sobbing on the floor while Ethan stood nearby. Brenda didn't know who had tackled Raine. But she had seen her brother move lightning fast before, and she would bet he had done so again when she had given him the opportunity.

Whoever had moved first, it was all over now. She stood shakily, pulling Carly with her. They clung to each other for a moment, and then moved toward the others.

Tony was on his cell phone, presumably calling the authorities. Richard rose to put both hands on Brenda's shoulders, searching her face intently. "Are you okay?"

Covering his hands with hers, she nodded. "I'm fine. Just shaken up."

He kissed her cheek. "Maybe you should sit back down. You look like you're going to fall over any second."

"No, really. I'm okay."

After a moment, he nodded and released her to turn to Carly. He hesitated an instant, and then held out his arms. She stepped into them, burrowing into his chest while he bent his sandy head over her darker one.

Watching them, Brenda swallowed, struck again by how strong the connection between them had become. She glanced quickly at Tony, who had disconnected his call and was now watching his daughter with an expression that held resignation, acceptance— and a lingering trace of paternal worry.

Only then did she look at Ethan. He gazed back at her with an expression that held too many emotions for her to identify the strongest. Raine lay at his feet, curled into a fetal ball, whimpering softly.

Brenda rested a hand on Ethan's arm, feeling the tension still gripping his muscles. "Thank you."

"You shouldn't be thanking me," he said, his voice rough. "It was because of me that you were almost killed."

"It was because of you that I wasn't," she corrected him.

His jaw worked, but all he said was, "Maybe you should be checked out by a doctor. This couldn't have been good for your concussion."

"I'm okay. I don't need to see a doctor." She glanced at the older woman who lay in such abject surrender on the carpeted floor. "Shouldn't you say something to her? She's so upset."

"*She's* upset?" He looked at her in disbelief. "She was going to kill you!"

"I know. But still—" She couldn't bear to look at Raine, so alone and so anguished. Dropping her voice, she said, "She's obviously ill, Ethan. And she loves you. In her mind, she did it all for you. You said yourself, that she had always been there for you when you were growing up. Maybe you should be there for her now."

"I don't know if I can. When I saw that gun pointed toward you…"

She gave him a tremulous smile. "I know. I saw it in your face. But I'm fine. And she needs you."

He gave her a dubious look, then glanced toward Raine. Still he didn't move.

Because she couldn't stand it any longer, Brenda knelt by the older woman, herself. "Raine," she said, gently laying a hand on the woman's shoulder. "Let me help you up. You can sit on the couch until someone comes to take you to get help."

Raine turned her face away.

Carly knelt at Raine's other side, gently taking hold of her arm. "Let us help you, Raine," she said, seconding Brenda's words. "You'll be more comfortable on the couch."

"It was all for Ethan," Raine whispered.

Brenda shivered a little because she recognized the breathy sound. Raine had been the one who had called her, so angry she could do nothing but breathe heavily into the other end of the line.

But pity made her push those dark emotions to the back of her mind, and say quietly, "We know, Raine. You love him."

Raine didn't even seem to hear. She wrapped her arms around herself and began to rock slightly, her eyes fixed and unfocused.

Brenda looked at Ethan, but he seemed almost as

distant then as Raine. He looked at her, and then at Raine.

And then he turned away.

EIGHT DAYS LATER, on the first Monday in July, Brenda sat alone in the media room, gazing somberly at the hole in the wall. Someone was coming the next day to repair it, and she would be glad when all traces of that nightmarish encounter with Raine were gone.

It seemed strange to know that it was all over now. She no longer jumped when the phone rang, nor looked over her shoulder when she stepped out of the house. Everyone had finally stopped hovering over her, watching her as if she might fall apart if they let down their guard. They had all accepted at last that she truly was fine.

The will was moving through probate with no further holdups, and Sean had assured her that all legal strings would be neatly tied up very quickly. Sean had been both surprised and relieved to learn the identity of her tormenter. He had admitted privately to Brenda that he had begun to believe it was Ethan. He hadn't wanted to accept it, he had added, but the evidence had been fairly strong, especially when the case against Leland had begun to fall apart.

Sean hadn't asked her to dinner or the theater or anything else again, so Brenda hoped he had gotten the message that she wanted to keep their relationship friendly but professional.

Raine had been admitted to a mental health facility where she was being extensively evaluated. Tony had expressed doubts that she would ever stand trial for any of the things she had done. She had suffered a complete breakdown after being led away from the house, he had informed Brenda. And it wasn't the first time. His research had uncovered the fact that she had been admitted to institutions on at least two occasions in her youth, including a two-year stint after she'd given birth to Ethan.

Apparently she had held herself together for the past twenty years by focusing on her job at the nursery and on her obsession with making sure that Ethan never lacked for anything. No one knew exactly how she had found him ten years after giving him up, but there was no longer any doubt that she was his biological mother.

Brenda hadn't seen Ethan since Raine had been taken away. She had tried to talk to him then, but he'd been emotionally closed to her. Telling her he had needed some time alone, he'd left with a promise to call after he'd come to terms with everything he had learned.

He hadn't called yet.

Missy, the little black cat, wound around her ankles, meowing for attention. Brenda scooped her up and snuggled her beneath her cheek. She had enjoyed the cats' company during the past week, just as she had appreciated the visits from her brother and the calls from her sister, and the support shown by Carly and Diane and her other friends. But there was still a hole in her life—in her heart—as raw and deep as the one in the wall in front of her. And she wondered if that one would ever be fully repaired.

Some people might be surprised to learn that after gaining so much during the past few weeks, she was more aware of her losses. The treasures from her past

that she'd lost in the fire Raine had set. And Ethan—
for whom she had fallen so fast, so hard and so thoroughly.

Love at first sight? She didn't know if it could be
called that, exactly, though Richard certainly seemed
to feel that way about Carly. But Brenda had known
within days that Ethan was the man with whom she
could spend the rest of her life, even knowing the challenges a relationship with him would entail.

If only Ethan had felt the same way…

On an impulse, she carried the contentedly dozing
cat up the stairs and into the master bedroom. She
hadn't stepped into this room since she had searched
it with Ethan, looking in vain for his family Bible. Now
she paused in front of the painted portrait, grimly
studying the face of the woman who had done so much
emotional damage to the boy she had adopted as her
son.

"Why couldn't you just love him?" she asked the
portrait aloud, her voice echoing a bit in the empty
room. The empty house. "Why couldn't you see how
lucky you were to have him?"

Maybe Margaret had fought her own demons.
Maybe she simply hadn't known how to offer love to
her son, other than to try to push him onto the path she
thought best for him. Maybe she had died wishing she
had done things much differently.

"I wish you had left something to tell us why you
made the decisions you did," she said to the painting.
"A diary, a journal, a letter. Something."

In response to Brenda's voice, Missy yawned and
stirred restlessly in her arms. Brenda set her down and
watched as the cat turned and ran out of the room, as

if eager to be somewhere else. With one last glance at the portrait, Brenda followed more slowly, turning out the light behind her.

Some impulse took her back to the media room. All four of the cats were in there now, playing with each other and climbing on the elaborate cat tower in their corner of the room. She watched them for a moment, a faint smile on her face that slowly began to fade.

This was the room where Margaret had spent the most time, here with her beloved cats. If she *were* going to leave any clues behind, this would be the most likely place for her to do so. But they had searched this room, she reminded herself. She and Ethan had looked through every cabinet, every drawer, every shelf. They had found nothing.

And then she remembered that they'd finished in here before Carly had arrived to impulsively join their hunt for the Bible. Carly, who had insisted they look in less obvious places, like under furniture and behind paintings on the wall. Brenda and Ethan had been looking for something misplaced, forgotten. Carly had insisted on searching for something that had been hidden.

Maybe Carly had been on to something. After all, Brenda and Ethan had missed finding the scrap of paper that had eventually led Tony to Raine.

She turned and looked at the massive sectional sofa from beneath which Angel had emerged with the paper. Feeling a bit foolish, she went down on her knees and reached under one end, slowly working her way down. Finding nothing. Almost giving up. Until…

Her fingers brushed something hard. Her heart beating a little faster, she closed her hand around it and pulled it out. It was a rather large, though shallow, box constructed of yellow cardboard. What some people might call a memory box, Brenda thought with a rush of excitement.

She sank to the couch, holding the unopened box in her lap. She was suddenly afraid to lift the lid. She wondered if she should call Ethan, and wait for him to arrive before she opened the box. But what if all they found inside were bills or household receipts or some other mundane and completely unhelpful contents? Ethan would likely think she had used the box as nothing more than a ploy to get him to come back.

Taking a deep breath, she lifted the lid.

ETHAN STOOD on the doorstep of his mother's—of Brenda's—house, he corrected himself. He was there in response to a voice mail message from Brenda.

"Ethan," she had said. "I need to see you. I've found something in the house that I know you'll want to see. Please call me when you get the chance."

Rather than calling, he had come by after work. So there he stood, in his grubby clothes and scuffed boots, still flushed from a day spent in the Texas July sun, trying to get up the nerve to ring the bell. Under his left arm, he held a large, rather heavy box—something he wanted Brenda to have before he told her goodbye for the last time.

It was ridiculous how nervous he was. For a man who claimed to be afraid of very little, it made no sense that one rather fragile-looking young woman could rouse so much apprehension in him. But hers was a deceptive fragility, he reminded himself, thinking of all she had suffered through at Raine's hands. She had survived all of that with her spirit intact, even finding the courage and compassion inside her to offer comfort to Raine while they had waited for the authorities to take the troubled older woman away.

When she had been able to reach out to Raine—his own biological mother—Ethan had been so filled with rage and betrayal that he couldn't follow suit. Just remembering the sight of Raine leveling that gun at Brenda had made him want to lash out, to get revenge. Had Raine been a man, he would have very likely expressed that wrath with his fists.

He'd known at that moment that Brenda deserved a hell of a lot better than him. She was simply too good for him, plain and simple. And he had decided then that he would never tell her how he felt about her, would never try to use her too-soft heart to tie her to him.

His temper had cooled somewhat in the past eight days, as he'd learned more details of Raine's troubled past, but nothing he had discovered made him any more confident that he was worthy of Brenda. Before, he'd thought his mother was a cold, manipulative wealth-obsessed woman. Now he knew that his real mother was a woman who had been in and out of mental institutions for years, who had never told anyone—if she even knew—who had fathered him.

What kind of legacy was that to offer a woman? Was that really the man she would want to be the father of her own children?

Maybe he would go see Raine someday, after he'd had a little time to heal from what she had put him through. But for now it was much too soon. For now, he had to let Brenda know that there could be no future for them. And then he was going to have to take some time to get over the pain that was going to cause him. He figured that might just take the rest of his life.

Hiding his turbulent emotions the best he could behind an expressionless face, he punched the doorbell button. Best to get this over with, as quickly and as painlessly—at least for Brenda—as possible.

She answered the door wearing a lime-green sleeveless dress and looking like the answer to a lonely man's prayer. Her blond hair was soft and loose around her pretty face, her blue eyes were clear and warm and her soft mouth was tilted into a smile. How could she look so welcoming after he had treated her so badly?

He had warned her from the first time he'd met her that she was too kindhearted for her own good.

"Come in," she said, then glanced at the box he carried as he moved past her. "What is that?"

"Something for you to open later." He set it on the foyer table, pushing an expensive antique vase out of the way, and then he turned back to Brenda. "You said you found something?"

She nodded. "It's in the kitchen. I just made a fresh pot of coffee. You can drink a cup while you look through the things I found."

He saw the yellow box on the table as soon as he entered the kitchen. "That's it?"

She nodded and moved toward the coffeemaker. Something about her posture told him that she wasn't quite as calm as she was pretending to be. Whatever she had found in that box must be important. His grandmother's family Bible, maybe? Only now it occurred to him that she hadn't been his grandmother. And it hadn't been his family history recorded in her Bible.

"Where did you find this?" he asked, motioning toward the box.

"It was under the couch in the media room, pushed way back so that I had to really stretch to reach it. It was one place we didn't think to look before. Angel finding the paper under there made me think to look for more."

Ethan found himself hesitating for a moment before lifting the lid off the box. He wasn't sure he even wanted to see what was in there now. He was still dealing with the revelations about who he really was, and how that changed the image he'd carried of himself.

"Open it, Ethan," Brenda urged, understanding in her tone. She set a cup of coffee on the table for him. "You'll find some answers in there."

"I haven't even figured out what questions to ask yet," he muttered.

"I know." She touched his arm briefly before moving to pour herself a cup of coffee.

Just that fleeting touch left his skin tingling, his pulse racing. This was going to be harder than he'd even expected, he thought grimly.

He opened the box.

The Bible was there, wrapped carefully in tissue paper. He touched the worn leather cover almost reverently, remembering the times when he and his father—damn it, the man he had known as his father—had sat together reading the names written on the pages inside. Howard Blacklock had known even then that Ethan wasn't his biological son, but he had given no hint of that knowledge as he and Ethan had discussed the Blacklock family history going back some six generations in that Bible.

Shaking his head, he looked at the other things in the box. Photographs, mostly. Many of them of him at different stages of his youth. Some were of Margaret's own childhood. He recognized her parents and her sister in them. Margaret, herself, looking serious and intense even as a teenager.

And, finally, there was a white envelope with a name written on the front in Margaret's recognizable script. The envelope was addressed to Brenda Prentiss.

He looked up at her in question.

"Read it," she urged him from the chair on the other side of the table where she had been quietly watching him.

The envelope had already been opened, proving that Brenda had read the contents. He slipped out two sheets of white paper folded together. Dated more than a year earlier, the letter had been typed and printed, probably on the computer in the media room. He scanned the first words.

Dear Brenda: I'm not sure you will remember meeting me, since I wasn't using my true name then, but perhaps these words will help you recall the brief time we spent together. I have never forgotten the kindness you showed to me at a time when no one else seemed to care.

The letter went on to describe the ten days Margaret had spent in the hospital three years ago for her cancer operation, which had been followed by a few complications that had kept her hospitalized longer than she had expected. There had been no private room available—even for her—for the first few days after her surgery, and she had been angry and embarrassed to have to share a room. Her pain and bitterness had caused her to lash out at the hospital staff, she admitted in the letter, and she had quickly become one of the least favorite patients on the ward.

Only Brenda, spending hours a day with her dying mother in the same room, had been patient and kind with Margaret, making sure she was comfortable, bringing her magazines and flowers when she brought the same for her mother, gently admonishing the increasingly impatient hospital staff to please try to be tolerant of a woman who was obviously alone and frightened. Brenda had even coaxed Margaret into conversation on a few occasions. She had told Margaret about her cat, Domino, and had made Margaret admit to being a cat fancier, herself.

Margaret had thought at the time that she wished her son could meet a nice girl like Brenda, though she had known better than to try to arrange an introduction. Ethan would have never given a woman his mother recommended a second look. He was much too rebellious against any gesture that he saw as his mother trying to control him.

I love my son, Brenda. But he has always seen me as his adversary, rather than his mentor. Had he only listened to me, he would be comfortably settled as a partner in my father's law firm, perhaps ready to start a family of his own with a lovely young woman like yourself. Instead, he works himself ragged trying to establish a business that faces competition from much larger, more established companies, spending ridiculously long hours at that backbreaking manual labor. He has been blessed with so much—intelligence, privilege, wealth, the finest education—and he has chosen to throw it all away.

It had been that resentment toward Ethan, coupled with her gratitude to Brenda, that had caused her to rather impulsively change her will eighteen months ago. Though Margaret didn't mention it in this letter, Ethan knew that was about the same time Raine had revealed the truth about her identity to Margaret, and had begun to quarrel so acrimoniously with Margaret about Ethan's future.

Margaret had secretly kept tabs on Brenda during the months after she left the hospital, and everything she learned had made her respect the young woman more, she wrote. She was a schoolteacher, which Margaret considered a suitable and genteel occupation for a young woman, and she volunteered at the animal shelter and seemed to live a rather quiet and responsible life—all admirable qualities to Margaret. Much more appropriate than the path her own son had chosen, she had added bitterly.

She had added that she would probably change her will back to the way it had been should Ethan suddenly develop some common sense and go to law school—in which case Brenda would never read these words—but she wanted everything spelled out in case anything happened to her prior to that time.

Not once in the letter did Margaret admit that Ethan was not her own biological son. Had it really been a matter of pride to her? Or had she really thought of him as her own son? Her own possession, he added dourly.

He supposed those were among the questions he would never have answered.

He tossed the letter on the table. "So now we know. You did meet her. You honestly didn't remember?"

Looking at him a bit anxiously, Brenda shook her head. "That was a horrible time for me. My mother was dying, and we both knew it. I thought it would kill me, too. She was all I could focus on during those terrible weeks."

"And yet you were kind to my mother."

A little frown developed between her eyebrows. "We couldn't afford a private room—and there weren't any available, anyway. It was an unusually hectic time for the hospital, during the peak of a flu outbreak that killed quite a few senior citizens and small children that year. I vaguely remember the woman who called herself Evelyn Smith, because it seemed so sad that she had no one to be with her during her illness. Not one visitor. Everyone thought she was horrible, but I thought she was just lonely and scared. She seemed so grateful when I spoke to her."

She shook her head then, obviously making an effort to repress her lingering sadness at the loss of her mother. "It was no wonder I didn't recognize Margaret in the portrait. She was so well-groomed and poised then. The woman in the hospital was pale and hollow eyed, with her hair all limp and messed up, the way people look when they're very ill. And as I said, I was focused much more intently on my mother than on the woman in the next bed. Mother had several roommates during those weeks. I can't really remember any of them all that well."

She paused with a bit of a wince, adding, "I think

I had a flash of memory when I was in the hospital after Raine attacked me. I thought I saw Margaret Jacobs in the other bed. I wish I had been collected enough then to try to make sense of that odd vision."

Had it been anyone else, Ethan might not have believed her story. Because it was Brenda, he accepted it completely. "Evelyn was my mother's middle name. Smith was her mother's maiden name. She was so paranoid about being seen in her vulnerability that she didn't tell anyone—especially me—that she was having surgery. Coupled with her obsession with me going to law school, and her bizarre decision to name you in her will, I'm beginning to think she was as crazy as Raine. Hell of a pair of moms I ended up with, wasn't it?"

"Ethan—"

But he didn't want her feeling sorry for him now. He was taking care of that well enough for himself. "Thank you for sharing this stuff with me, Brenda. As you said, it answered a few questions. Now we can put it all behind us. And by the way, I'll be returning the coin collection sometime this week. You'll need to make arrangements to have it safely stored."

"Why would you do that?" she asked, leaping to her feet when he rose abruptly.

"And don't tell me it's because Harold Blacklock wasn't your real father," she added before he could say those very words. "He legally adopted you. That makes you his son in every court in this country. He considered you his own son—as did Margaret, obviously. And he probably would have wanted you to have his coins, just as she must have, even when she was so unreasonably angry with you for living your own life."

The gleam in her eyes told him she wouldn't accept his decision, and that she would be willing to fight him on this for as long as it took to convince him. He decided to save them both some time. "Fine. I'll keep them. Thanks. But I'd better take off now. See you, Brenda."

She caught his arm, clinging to him with a force that rather surprised him. When she spoke, her voice was as angry as he'd ever heard it. "Damn it, I *knew* you would do this! Don't you dare try to tell me you don't care about me, Ethan Blacklock. I saw your face when Raine held that gun pointed at me. You can't lie to me about what I saw."

Even the memory made him shudder—and he doubted that she missed that, either. "It just wouldn't work, Brenda. You deserve better."

"Don't tell me what I deserve. And this exaggerated humility doesn't really suit you, Ethan. I suggest you drop it."

Stung, he looked around at her. "I am not—"

"You've had a difficult life," she said flatly. "You grew up rich, with a mother who didn't love you enough. And now you've found out you were adopted, and your real mother was unstable enough to try to kill me. I grew up without much money, and I lost the parents I adored entirely too early. I've spent the past month running through flames and dodging bullets and falling head over heels in love with a man who is so stubborn and so thickheaded and so damned prickly that it makes me want to scream sometimes. But you know what? Those are all just hard facts. We can sit around and brood about them for the rest of our lives, or we can get over it and let ourselves be happy from now on."

Maybe he had been afraid she would cry when he made it clear he was ending it between them. Or maybe he'd thought she would let him go with wounded dignity. He had not expected her to confront him by making him feel like a total fool.

"It isn't quite that easy, Brenda."

"Did I say it was going to be easy?" she asked irritably. "Did you even hear me hint that I care about that? I'm not a quitter, Ethan. And I'm not overly worried about facing challenges. I care about you. If you don't feel the same way about me, then have the courage to admit it. If you do feel the same way, then for God's sake, have the courage to stay and fight for me."

"Everyone will say—"

"I don't care what everyone will say, either!" she snapped. "If it's the money you're worried about, then stop it. I'll turn it all back over to you and let everyone think *I'm* the gold digger. Or we'll give it all away. Because we both know that the money isn't what really matters to either of us."

She seemed to have an answer to everything. "You really aren't worried about getting involved with a man who comes from such a mentally unstable heritage?"

"You aren't mentally unstable, Ethan. You're just about the sanest man I know. You had to be to survive Margaret and still turn out to be so strong and so proud and so resourceful."

"Don't start romanticizing me, Brenda," he muttered. "Trust me, I'm no hero. I—"

Her disbelieving laugh made warmth flood his cheeks. "Didn't you listen to the way I described you?" she demanded. "Did it sound like I think you're a perfect hero? I know your flaws, Ethan. And if you haven't seen mine clearly enough, then you will before long. We're both human—and I happen to think we're pretty amazing together."

She was the first person in his entire life who saw him exactly as he was, and seemed to have no interest in changing him. Even Raine had wanted things for him that he hadn't wanted for himself, proving that she hadn't really known him, after all.

Brenda knew him. And she had said she loved him, anyway. Unconditionally.

How was he supposed to resist that, when it was exactly what he'd been longing for since before he could even remember?

"You could do a hell of a lot better for yourself," he said, making one last attempt at nobility.

She cocked an eyebrow. "Are you trying to tell me what's best for me, Ethan? Because I don't like having people make decisions for me any more than you ever have."

Startled, he realized that he had been doing exactly that. How many times had he been told that others knew what he needed? What he should want? And how many times had he promised himself he would never do that to anyone else?

"This is really what you want?" he asked her, searching her face with his heart in his throat.

"This is what I want," she replied quietly, her own heart reflected in her eyes. "I love you, Ethan. Exactly the way you are. Please don't change a thing for me."

"You've already changed me," he said roughly, pulling her into his arms. "You've taught me that love shouldn't be a trap that tries to bind you and change you. It should set you free to be exactly who you are. You've set me free, Brenda. And I love you."

Her breath caught in what might have been a choked sob. "Ethan—"

He crushed her mouth beneath his.

HE EARNED HIMSELF a few extra points with her when she opened the gift he had brought her. Several long, contented hours had passed—most of that time spent in her bed—before he remembered it.

Leaving her lying tired and flushed against her pillows, he had pulled on his jeans and gone downstairs to retrieve the box, dodging cats along the way. "I guess I'm going to have to get used to you guys," he had muttered. "Looks like you're going to be part of my life for a long time."

They had meowed up at him, and he could have sworn at least a couple of them were laughing at him.

When the box lay open in front of her, Brenda looked up at him with tears cascading down her cheeks. "You knew you loved me when you bought this, didn't you? You had to have known then."

"I knew," he said gently, wiping her face with his thumb. "I was just too cowardly to admit it."

Looking back down at the hammer dulcimer he'd purchased for her only days after she had told him about the one she had lost in the fire, she drew a deep, unsteady breath. "Thank you. It's beautiful."

"I know it isn't the one that belonged to your aunt. But maybe you can make new memories with this one."

She set the instrument aside and opened her arms to him. "I intend to make a great many new memories," she murmured against his lips. "We both will."

Losing himself in her kiss, Ethan felt as though he
had finally found the treasure he had been searching
for all his life. He had found love.

* * * * *

Don't miss the next novel in Gina Wilkins's
exciting family saga,
THE ROAD TO REUNION,
available February 2006
from Silhouette Special Edition.

Everything you love about romance...
and more!

*Please turn the page for Signature
Select™ Bonus Features.*

WEALTH
BEYOND RICHES

BONUS
FEATURES
INSIDE

Author Interview:
A Conversation with
Gina Wilkins

How did you begin your writing career?

For almost as far back as I can remember, I
wanted to be a published writer. I was encouraged
in my love of books by my parents, and in my
enjoyment of Harlequin/Silhouette romances by
my mother, for whom books were a welcome
escape from the demands of a full-time secretarial
career and four active children. Almost from the
time I could hold a pencil, I entertained myself by
writing my own stories. I received a degree in
journalism, but my first love was always fiction—
especially romance. I had my share of rejection
letters during the learning process, but my own
stubbornness, my husband's never-wavering
encouragement and my wonderful agent's efforts
led to my first sale to Harlequin/Silhouette in
1986. I've been writing happily full-time ever
since, with more than seventy published books
behind me and a lot more stories "percolating."

Was there a particular person, place or thing that inspired this story?

Most of my ideas come from newspaper articles. My morning routine consists of drinking a diet cola, eating a brown sugar-and-cinnamon toaster pastry, and reading every page of the daily *Arkansas Democrat-Gazette.* I cut out articles that intrigue me, and file them away for future stories (I've been carrying a page from a 1985 newspaper for almost twenty years, and I use that page to illustrate to students how any article can be turned into a novel by asking a few what-if questions). There was no particular article that inspired WEALTH BEYOND RICHES, but I've always been fascinated by people who become instant millionaires through lotteries or luck or other unexpected sources. How would that wealth change the person's life? Her relationships with her family and friends? The way she thinks of herself? How would it affect any new relationships she makes after the windfall? And what if...? And so was born the premise for Brenda Prentiss's story of sudden wealth and slightly risky romance.

What's your writing routine?

My family would probably laugh to hear the word *routine* applied to anything I do. Other than my morning newspaper ritual, I have very few routines—which is why I was never particularly suited to a standard nine-to-five job. I tend to be a "binge-and-purge" writer, sometimes writing an hour a day, other times spending sixteen hours at the computer, until I find myself typing gibberish and have to rest. I do most of my writing in my head—in the shower, in the car, at the mall, at a coffee shop—so that by the time I actually sit down to write, the story is fairly well developed. I still prefer to write with a fine-tip rollerball pen in a wire-bound journal (I can spend hours choosing journals), always with music playing in the background—anything from country to pop to new age to alternative rock. When I type what I've written, I set my computer jukebox on random play, so that I might hear a Christmas carol followed by a twangy country number or a rock anthem or an instrumental classic or a Native American chant or a Celtic song ("The 1812" by Bond is playing as I write this. Next up, I think, is something by Tim McGraw). Music is an integral part of my creativity, and I indulge myself shamelessly in CDs and legal music downloads. It's not the most efficient routine, but it's the method that has worked best for me— and I'm a bit too superstitious to try to change anything now!

How do you research your stories?
I spend a lot of time on the Internet, of course, which has been a wonderful invention for writers! I have also been known to pick up the phone and

dial random strangers with questions. When I wrote about firefighters, I called a local fire department and pretty much asked the guy who answered what he was wearing (to his bemusement). When I wrote about a wedding dress designer, I called a well-known Arkansas-based designer, introduced myself and asked a dozen questions, all of which she answered patiently. When I needed to talk to a rodeo cowboy, I called a local Western store, said that I was a writer and that I was hoping to find someone who knew a lot about the rodeo circuit. The man who had answered the telephone simply drawled, "You're talking to him, ma'am. What can I do for you?" It's been my experience that most people love to talk about their areas of expertise, and I've enjoyed the contacts I've made doing research.

How do you develop your characters?
I've always said that my characters develop themselves. I honestly don't know how. It takes me a couple of chapters to really get to know the people in my stories, and often they surprise even me with the things they do or say in those first chapters. My husband says this is the same way I get to know real people—it takes me a little while to warm up to strangers, because I've always had a tendency toward shyness with new people. Characterization is absolutely the most important part of storytelling, as far as I'm

concerned. My favorite authors are those who make their characters come to life for me. It's the same way with movies and TV shows; even if the plot or story development is a bit weak, as long as I like the characters, I generally enjoy the ride.

If you don't mind, could you tell us a bit about your family?

I've been married since February 1977 to my college sweetheart, John, who can usually be found at his beloved wood lathe or in a duck blind. We have been blessed with three amazing offspring—Courtney, who is completing her doctoral studies in microbiology, Kerry, a medical student, and David, still in high school and considering a computer graphics career, though he says he's still open to suggestions. They received their science and math talents from their father, but they all have my twisted sense of humor (I'm not sure those are equal contributions, but it's definitely true).

When you're not writing, what are your favorite activities?

I love to read, of course, and I always have a stack of books waiting for me to find the time to enjoy them. I like to shop a bit too much for my thrifty husband's peace of mind, and I have a real passion for those decorating programs on the home and garden television channel. He and I both like antique stores and flea markets—I head for the glassware (I collect cut glass toothpick holders) while he beelines for the tools and old iron corn bread pans. I enjoy watching football games and NASCAR races with my daughters while the two guys in the family do other things (traditional gender roles have never particularly applied to us). But my very favorite thing to do is to spend quality time with my family. My kids and I are fiercely competitive game players (I love card games and have even been known to take on the younger generation at the video game console, where I am always soundly defeated). John tends to stay on the sidelines when we play games. For some reason, our version of take-no-prisoners Uno makes him nervous.

What are your favorite vacations? Where do you like to travel?
I must admit that I'm married to the ultimate homebody. He loves being at our home on ten acres in Arkansas (close enough to the shopping malls to satisfy me, but rural enough to give him breathing room). We don't travel much, but when we do, we like the mountains and the beach. We take a lot of weekend car trips to beautiful Arkansas destinations such as the Ozarks and Hot Springs National Park. Memphis and New Orleans are other favorite weekend retreats. We also spend a lot of time in Branson, Missouri,

where we enjoy attending the shows, admiring the crafts and shopping in the outlet malls. (Okay, the guys would just as soon skip that last part, but they indulge me.)

Do you have a favorite book or film?
I have way too many favorites to list them all. I particularly enjoy romantic suspense, perhaps because that's a different type of story than I usually write, so it feels like a break from work. Bullets flying, dashing heroes, gutsy heroines and a dash of comic relief win me over every time.

Any last words to your readers?
I would just like to thank the readers who have taken the time to let me know that they've enjoyed the stories I always dreamed of telling. I'll admit to being a bit technologically challenged, so I'm still catching up with the computer age, but the e-mails and snail mail notes that I receive are all precious to me. It thrills me to know that the Walker family has found a home in the hearts of so many fellow romance fans, as they have in my own heart.

Behind the Scenes— A History of the Walker Family

by Gina Wilkins

A LONG TIME AGO I found myself fascinated by feature stories about biological family members reunited after many years of separation. I played with several variations of that theme, but none of the stories I began seemed to work—until a character named Michelle Trent introduced herself to me one day.

Soon after the death of her adoptive mother, Michelle had learned that she had been separated as a toddler from six biological siblings. Michelle wanted to try to find her siblings, but she wasn't sure how to begin. That was when dashing private investigator Tony D'Alessandro slipped into my mind, clearing his throat to get my attention (and the lovely Michelle's, of course).

The original *Family Found* series (initially released under my pen name, Gina Ferris) became very special to me and to many of my readers. The Walker siblings had gone very different ways during the twenty-plus years they were apart, but the bonds between them grew strong as they were reunited one by one. The first five books led to other connected books as more members of their extended families—and a few of their friends—demanded their own stories.

Having lived with these characters for so long, I feel as if I know them as well as some of my real friends. I had to do some "creative adjustments" at times to make original dates and character ages fit into the new stories, but that's the fun of being a writer. We create our own worlds, and our own rules, though I have tried to stay as faithful as possible to the original stories. And because I still have a weakness for that dashing P.I., I thought it might be interesting to approach this newest Family Found connected story, WEALTH BEYOND RICHES, through Tony's agency, which allowed me the chance to get to know new characters while revisiting some of my favorites from past books.

For those of you who are new to the Walker and D'Alessandro families, perhaps you would like to know a bit more about their history. I have indicated corresponding book titles in parentheses.

Hank and Hazel Walker were an unhappily married, financially strapped couple from Texarkana, Texas. Hank was an alcoholic and Hazel chronically ill, and no one who knew them could understand why they stayed together—or why they continued to have children—seven in all—Jared, Layla, Miles, twins Joe and Ryan, Michelle, and Lindsay. Hank died when Hazel was pregnant with their seventh child. Hazel died eight months after Lindsay's birth. The children were separated—to the heartbreak of the older siblings—and sent in very different directions.

Twenty-four years later Michelle Trent learned about her siblings. She asked Tony D'Alessandro for assistance in finding them (FULL OF GRACE). During the course of his investigation, Michelle and Tony fell in love. They were married after a whirlwind courtship, and during the next few years had four children of their own—Jason, Carly, Katie and Justin.

Michelle was reunited first with Layla, married to Kevin Samples and the mother of three children, Dawne, Keith and Brittany (who found romance of her own in THE BORROWED RING, November 2005).

They were devastated to learn that one brother, Miles, had not survived to adulthood, having died when he was eighteen. What they didn't know then was that Miles had fathered a daughter, Brynn, born after his death. Brynn was united with her aunts and uncles several years later (HER VERY OWN FAMILY). She married Tony D'Alessandro's brother, Dr. Joe D'Alessandro, and they named their son Miles.

Jared Walker, single father to teenage son Shane, was tracked down by one of Tony's operatives, Cassie Browning (HARDWORKING MAN). Both Jared and Shane fell in love with the irrepressible redhead, and they became a family, which was completed by the birth of Jared and Cassie's daughter, Molly, a year later. (Molly is the heroine of her own book, THE ROAD TO REUNION, available from Special Edition in February 2006.) Shane later married Kelly Morrison (THAT FIRST SPECIAL KISS) and they have two daughters, Annie and Lucy.

Lindsay had been adopted by a family in Arkansas, and was involved in a romance with Dr. Nick Grant, a former foster son of her parents, when Tony located her (FAIR AND WISE). Staying close to both her families, she and Nick eventually married and had two children, Jenny and Clay.

Twins Joe and Ryan were the last of the siblings to rejoin the family, having run away from an unsatisfactory foster-home situation when they were only teenagers. (I can't tell you how many letters I received from readers who were concerned that I would leave the twins unfound—they should have known me better than that!) Joe and his wife, Lauren (whom he met when he served as her bodyguard in their book, FAR TO GO) have one son, Casey. Ryan married Michelle's longtime best friend, Taylor (LOVING AND

GIVING), and they have twin sons, Andrew and Aaron. Joe and Ryan became partners in Tony's investigation agency.

Thoroughly confused yet? I'm sure you wonder how I keep them all apart, but I really do know these people much too well. And being from a very large extended family, myself—with more siblings, in-laws, nieces and nephews, aunts, uncles and cousins than I could possibly count—I've always believed in the philosophy of "the more, the merrier." So it's entirely possible that some of these old friends will reappear in future books, along with the many new characters who are crowding my mind, waiting impatiently to introduce themselves and share their stories with me.

Author's Journal
by Gina Wilkins

I have never been intrigued by the study of
genealogy. I have no burning interest in family
trees—not in the lists of names and dates and
"begats" that make up most such lists, anyway.
To the despair of my relatives who are into such
details, I don't really care if I am distantly related
to Major General Big Shot from the Great War
Between the Whoevers. But tell me stories about
the individuals on that family tree, make those
stories come to life for me, and I'll listen happily
all day. In fact, I listen just as contentedly to old
family stories from strangers I meet in the beauty
shop or doctors' waiting rooms or in line at the
grocery store—and I seem to be the type that
people love to tell their stories to. Family tales
fascinate me, whether my own or those of
acquaintances or the many fictional families I
have come to know and love through years of
avid reading.

I believe my lifelong interest in being a writer came from my mother. She loved to read, and she shared that pleasure with me, but she also told me stories about her own childhood and her family's intriguing history. Dozens of stories, often illustrated by the boxes of old photographs she has collected and cherished during her lifetime, and told with such detail and humor that they never grew old for me.

The eldest of four sisters, Mother has become the family historian—keeper not of the names and dates and facts and statistics, but of the stories, the gossip, the trivia and scandals that make up a real family. She has worked for the same employer for more than fifty years, and she plays much the same role in her job—filing away the photos, remembering anecdotes about literally dozens of associates who have passed through her life. Any time anyone needs historical information about our family—or the company she works for—they come to Mother. She has rarely written any of these stories down (I wish she would), but she has repeated them so many times that I know most of them by heart, and I have tried to share them with my own children.

Perhaps I was influenced to write romance by the stories she told me of her grandparents, who met on a Mississippi riverboat early in the last century. Their Romeo-and-Juliet courtship resulted in my great-grandfather being disowned by his family because of his marriage and his subsequent religious conversion. I never met Great-Grandfather Sam, but I know that he was a charming and very funny man who once said he wanted to be buried in a Catholic cemetery because "the devil would never think to look for a Jew turned Baptist there." My mother repeated that joke to me, and helped bring to life the amusing grandfather she had adored.

I heard stories about my mother's parents, whose courtship was also problematic with their families. Both of her parents had passed away by the time I was in middle school, and it always fascinated me to think of my grandparents as young lovers defying their families to be together.

I heard about my mother's childhood— when she would take the train from Little Rock, Arkansas, to visit her mother's family in Nashville, Tennessee, being responsible for her younger twin sisters when she was barely old enough to look out for herself. She vividly described the early mornings when she went to work with her father, a milkman, and "bounced bottles" off the truck (her term for carrying the glass bottles of milk to the doorsteps of the customers). I heard about her reaction to the bombing of Pearl Harbor when she was only nine, and about the first time she saw a television (she predicted that it was a fad that would never last). I know that she sometimes felt overshadowed by her dark-eyed, dark-haired twin sisters, Joyce and Loyce, who gathered so much attention when the family went shopping. (Everyone said they looked just like the Dionne quintuplets, who were so often in the newspapers at that time.)

I know that my mother, valedictorian of her class, chose to defy her own family's wishes and marry instead of go to college, because she was always stubbornly determined to follow her own path. I've been told that my mother's high school ring is lost somewhere in the backyard of their old family home because her youngest sister decided to play pirate and bury a box of treasures. Neither the ring nor the other "treasures" her youngest sister gathered that day—including a nice pocket watch—were ever recovered. I know that youngest sister had two imaginary friends named Popeye and Didi. My aunt Gerry was ten and a half and the imaginary friends were long gone by the time I was born, but Mother brought them to life for me as clearly as she did the real relatives I never had the fortune to meet.

I heard about my grandfather's baby sister, who died when a porter forgot to lower a step and my grandfather's mother fell off a train and landed on her child. She was the same great-grandmother who stuffed cigarette butts into the posts of her old iron bed so that no one would know she'd been smoking—only to have her family find the evidence of those forbidden cigarettes after she died (something else that happened long before I was born). I've read the V-mail letters my great-uncle sent his mother during World War II, scraps of yellowed, red-white-and-blue-bordered paper my mother has guarded for so many years. I've even heard stories about my father's family—from my mother, since Daddy is still not much of a talker.

Having grown up hearing all those wonderful stories—and so many, many more—how could I not have developed a fondness for weaving my own tales of closely knit families? And how could I have wanted to write about anything other than romance?

I can only hope the happy endings my stories provide leave my readers with the same warm satisfaction my mother's stories always gave me.

SHOWCASING…

New York Times **bestselling author**

JOAN HOHL

HOME TO LOVE

**A classic story about two people
who finally discover great love.…**

"Ms. Hohl always creates a vibrant ambiance
to capture our fancy."
—*Romantic Times*

Coming in February.

Firefly Glen...
there's nowhere else quite like it.

National bestselling author

KATHLEEN O'BRIEN

FIREFLY GLEN

**Featuring the first two novels in
her acclaimed miniseries
FOUR SEASONS IN FIREFLY GLEN**

Two couples, each trying to avoid romance,
find exactly that in this small peaceful
town in the Adirondacks.

Available in February.

Watch for a new FIREFLY GLEN novel,
Quiet as the Grave—coming in March 2006!

**A breathtaking novel of
reunion and romance...**

THE
F RTUNES
OF TEXAS:
Reunion

Once a Rebel

by Sheri WhiteFeather

Returning home to Red Rock after many
years, psychologist Susan Fortune is reunited
with Ethan Eldridge, a man she hasn't gotten
over in seventeen years. When tragedy and grief
overtake the family, Susan leans on Ethan to
overcome her feelings—and soon realizes that
her life can't be complete without him.

Coming in February

Silhouette®
Where love comes alive™

$\mathcal{S}ignature\mathcal{S}elect$™

COMING NEXT MONTH

Signature Select Spotlight
THE PLEASURE TRIP by Joanne Rock
Working as a seamstress on a cruise ship called the *Venus*,
Rita Frazer hasn't been feeling very goddesslike lately. But when
the ship hosts a fashion show, Rita figures she has a chance at
being a designer until she finds *herself* on the runway, instead of
her designs. But Rita's found her muse....

Signature Select Collection
AND THE ENVELOPE, PLEASE...
by Barbara Bretton, Emilie Rose, Isabel Sharpe
Three couples find romance on the red carpet at the glamorous
Reel New York Awards—where the A-list rules and passion and
egos collide!

Signature Select Saga
DEAD WRONG by Janice Kay Johnson
Six years ago, prosecutor Will Patton's girlfriend stormed out on
him. That night, she was brutally raped and murdered. Wrapped
up in his own guilt and anger, Will developed a powerful thirst
for justice...and was determined that no criminal would ever walk
free again. Now he's returned to his hometown, but his return is
greeted by a gruesome discovery. In order to track down this serial
killer, Will teams up with detective Trina Giallombardo, only to
realize that if he falls for her, she'll be next....

Signature Select Miniseries
FIREFLY GLEN by Kathleen O'Brien
Featuring the first two novels in her acclaimed miniseries
Four Seasons in Firefly Glen. Two couples, each trying to avoid
romance, find exactly that in this small peaceful town in the
Adirondacks.

The Fortunes of Texas: Reunion Book #9
ONCE A REBEL by Sheri WhiteFeather
Returning home to Red Rock after many years, psychologist
Susan Fortune is reunited with Ethan Eldridge, a man she hasn't
gotten over in seventeen years. When tragedy and grief overtake
the family, Susan leans on Ethan to overcome her feelings—and
soon realizes that her life can't be complete without him.